Also By the Author

The Menmenet Series
The Two Kites
The Great Cat of R'a
The Bull of Mentju (forthcoming)

MURDER AT MOUNT VERNON

Robert J. Muller

A Founding Fathers Mystery

Poesys Associates

San Francisco

All rights reserved. Published in the United States of America by Poesys Associates, San Francisco.

www.poesys.com

ISBN: 978-1-939386-02-1 (print)
ISBN: 978-1-939386-03-8 (ebook)

LCCN: 2019918800
LC Record available at https://lccn.lco.gov/2019918800

Library of Congress Subject Headings:
Washington, George, 1732-1799 — Historical Fiction.
Detective and mystery stories, American — Historical Fiction.
Mount Vernon (Va. : Estate) — Historical Fiction.
Slavery — United States — Historical Fiction.

Illustrations by Mary L. Swanson
Cover Design by Brandi Doane McCann (eBook Cover Designs)

Published February 22, 2020
First Edition

To GW, the inspiration

Reflect, if you will: that man whom you call your slave was
born of the same seeds as you—enjoys the same sky—breathes,
lives, dies, just as you do. It is possible that you will see him a
free man, and equally possible that he will see you enslaved.
Seneca, Letters on Ethics 47:10

The players in this drama of frustration and indignity are not
commas or semicolons in a legislative thesis; they are people,
human beings, citizens of the United States of America.
Roy Wilkins, 1963 testimony to Congress

People are trapped in history and history is trapped in them.
James Baldwin, "Stranger in the Village", 1953

List of Characters
fictional characters marked with *

At Mount Vernon (the Mansion House and the Mansion House farm)

General George Washington	owner of Mount Vernon; hero of the Revolution
Martha Custis Washington	the General's wife
Major George Augustine Washington	the General's nephew and farm manager
Fanny Basset Washington	Major Washington's wife
Eleanor Parke Custis (Nellie)	Mrs. Washington's granddaughter
George Washington Parke Custis (Wash)	Mrs. Washington's grandson
David Humphreys	ex-aide to the General, friend, guest, biographer
Tobias Lear	private secretary to the General
John Fairfax	Mansion House farm manager
Frank Lee	enslaved butler, brother to Will Lee
Will Lee (Billy)	enslaved valet to the General, brother to Frank
Doll	enslaved elderly matriarch; former cook
Christopher Sheels	enslaved servant, future valet to the General
Hercules	enslaved cook
Thomas	white servant at the Mansion House
Edward	white servant at the Mansion House
Captain Winterbottom*	visitor to Mount Vernon, friend of Humphreys
Colonel Charles Thomson	secretary to the Continental Congress; election emissary

At Plantation Farm

Julius*	enslaved overseer of Dogue Run farm; murder victim
Morris	enslaved overseer of Dogue Run before (and after) Julius
Alice*	enslaved worker at Dogue Run, wife of Julius
Jack*	enslaved worker at Dogue Run
Israel*	enslaved worker at Dogue Run
Davy Gray	enslaved overseer at River Farm
Will	enslaved overseer at Muddy Hole Farm

At the Grist Mill

Joseph Davenport	miller in charge of the Grist Mill
Ben	enslaved miller
Tom*	enslaved cooper
Davy*	enslaved cooper

At Gunston Hall and Springfield Farm

George Mason	founding father, leader of antifederalist faction, neighbor of the General, Fairfax County magistrate
Sarah Brent Mason	Mason's second wife
George Thompson	Gunston Hall overseer
James	enslaved butler at Gunston Hall; father of Chancey
Lucy*	enslaved worker at Log Town
Chancey*	enslaved worker at Log Town; James's daughter
Nace	enslaved overseer at Occoquan farm (another Mason farm)
Martin Cockburn	Fairfax County magistrate, justice of the peace, neighbor and friend of Colonel Mason, antifederalist; resident at Springfield; "Ko-burn"
Cujo	Enslaved overseer at Springfield Farm

At Alexandria

Colonel Robert T. Hooe	merchant, Fairfax County Sheriff; pronounced "Hoe"
Mrs. Robert Hooe	Colonel Hooe's wife
John Williamson	clerk to Colonel Hooe
Dr. James Craik	the General's personal physician
Coachman*	coachman to Colonel Hooe
Colonel John Fitzgerald	merchant, head of Potomac Company, ex-aide to the General
William Hutchison*	preeminent slave-catcher in Alexandria
Lizzie Casey*	barmaid at the Spring Gardens tavern
Samuel Johnson*	seaman on a ship in the harbor
Dick Steptoe*	ex-soldier, vagrant on the wharves
John Augustus Brown*	mate on the brig Harriet
The Coroner	Official of Fairfax County who conducts inquests into unexplained deaths

Other Characters

General Benjamin Lincoln	Massachusetts general in the Revolution
Captain John Marshall	Richmond lawyer; future Chief Justice of the Supreme Court
General Henry Knox	friend of the General in New York, future Secretary of War
James Madison	friend of the General, representative from Virginia to the Congress
Colonel Alexander Hamilton	ex-aide to the General, financier in New York, future Treasury Secretary
Thomas Jefferson	Minister to France; former Governor of Virginia, future Secretary of State
Colonel Thomas Marshall	Kentucky politician; father of John Marshall
General James Wilkinson	Kentucky resident, conspirator at disunion
Lord Dorchester (Guy Carleton)	Governor-in-Chief of Canada
Colonel John Connolly	Tory; emissary of Lord Dorchester
Colonel Henry "Light Horse Harry" Lee	landowner in Kentucky; friend of the General
Davy Gray	enslaved overseer at River farm
Will	enslaved overseer at Muddy Hole farm
Caesar* and Gabriel*, Jessie*	enslaved workers at Muddy Hole and River farms (murder victims, wife of murder victim)

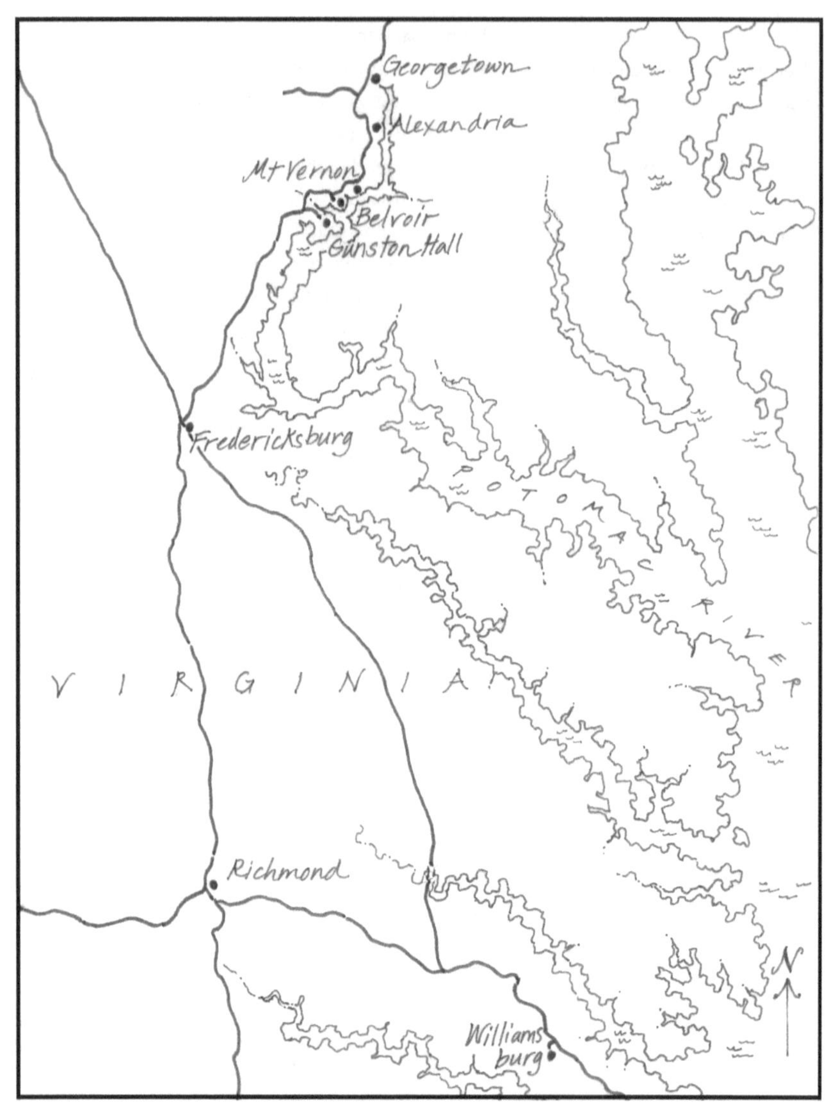

Virginia, 1789

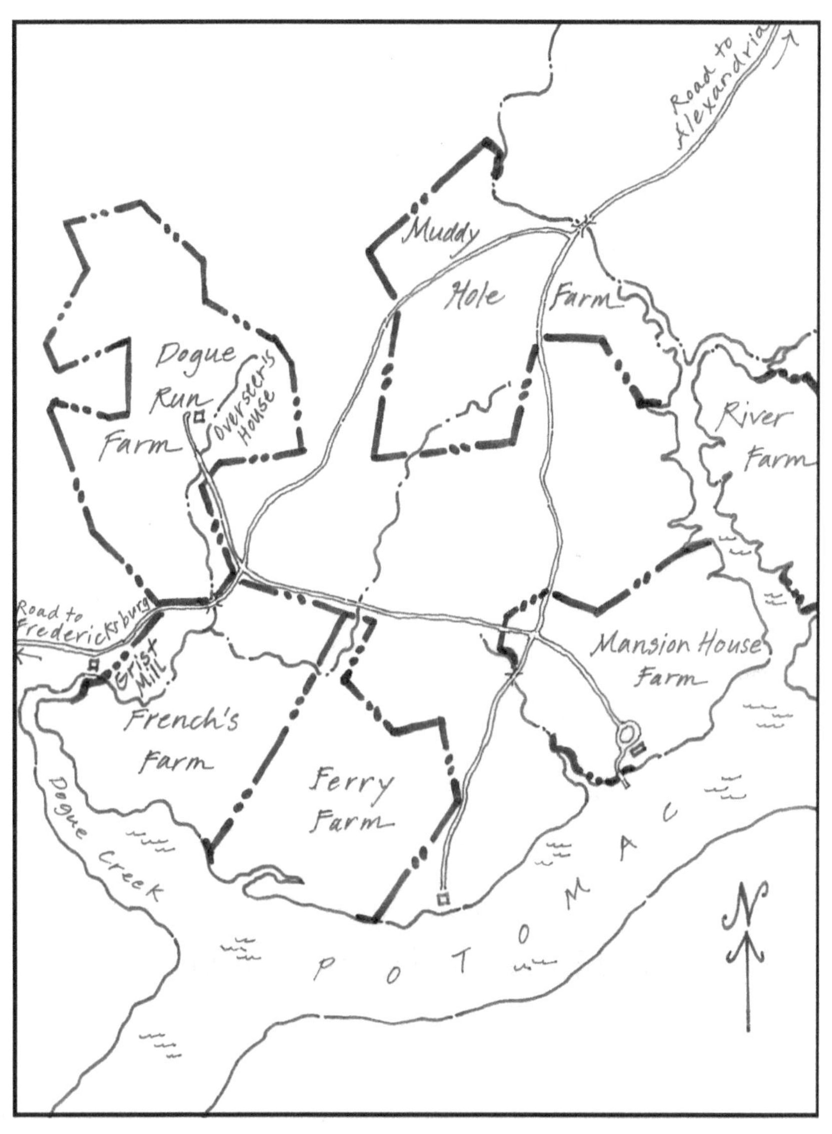

Mount Vernon Plantations

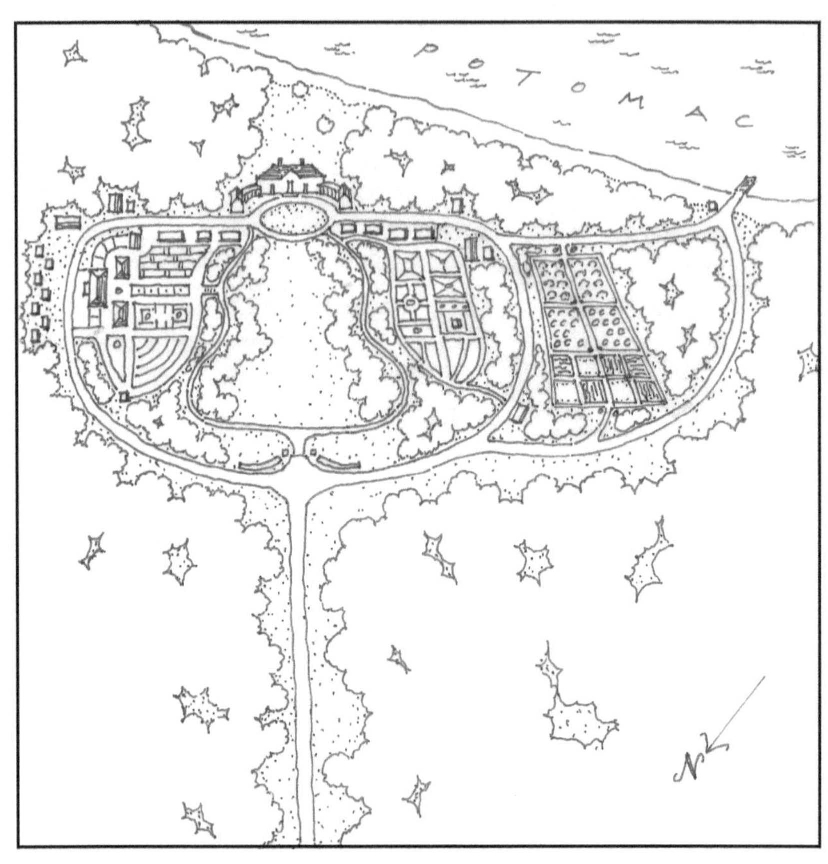

Mount Vernon
Mansion House Farm

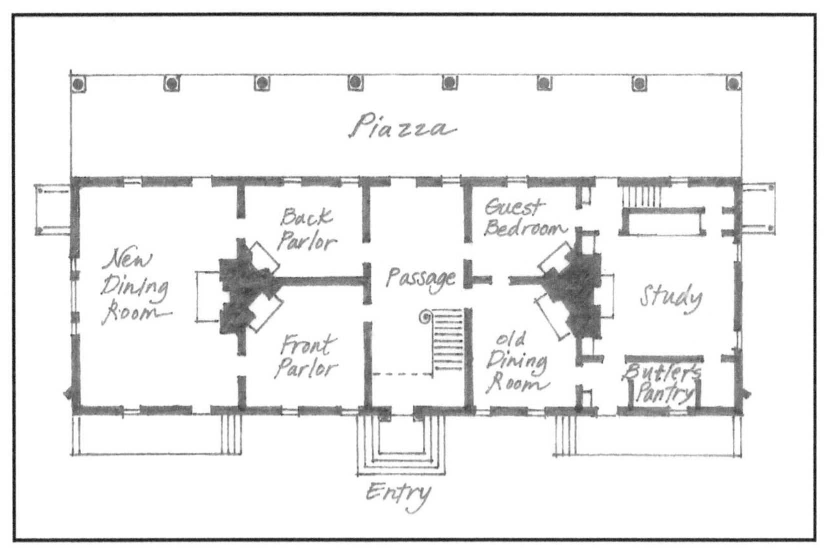

Mount Vernon
Mansion House Plan
Ground Floor

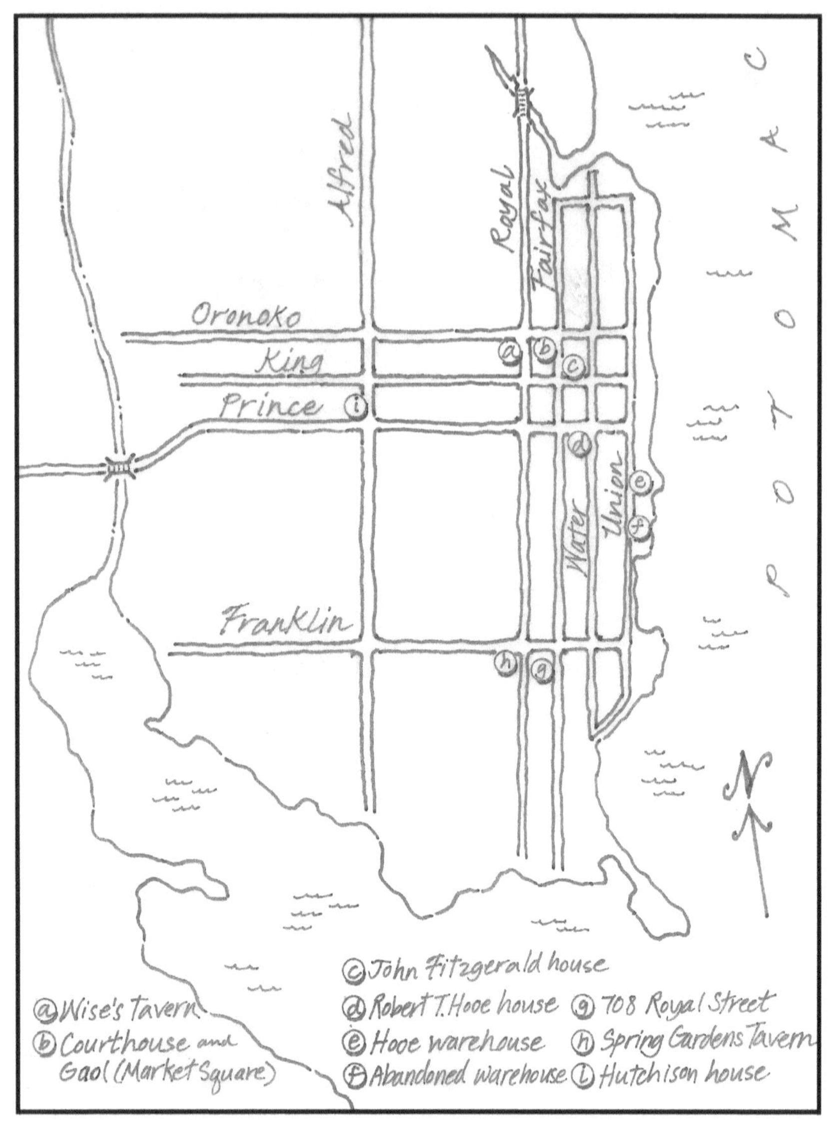

Alexandria, Virginia, 1789

Prolog

June 28th, 1778, early afternoon

The Commander-in-Chief, General George Washington, sat easily on his steed in the devilish midsummer heat on Perrine Hill near Monmouth, New Jersey. He watched the battle from above the carnage. General Knox's artillery pounded the massed British troops at the bottom of the hill beyond the hedgerow being defended by the Continentals. The General had spent most of the early afternoon positioning and rallying his troops on the hill and supervising the long cannonade.

Suddenly the cannon fire quieted for a moment, a cloud of smoke cleared, and the General saw a strange sight on a small hill to the side of the main battlefield. He saw his Negro valet, Billy Lee, mounted on his horse, with his telescope to his eye, looking down at the British lines. He was surrounded by the other generals' valets on horses. Billy had gathered them together in imitation of his master on the main hill.

Simultaneously, the British sighted the group. Clearly thinking this was a flanking brigade ready to attack, an enterprising British gunnery Lieutenant sighted and fired a cannon shot at the corps du valets, just as the General was pointing them out to his aides as a good joke.

The cannon shot passed through a tree right next to Billy Lee, taking several branches as it flew. The other horses started and reared, some galloping off down the hill to the rear. The General, mouth opening to shout, found himself moving on his horse toward his endangered slave. Billy never moved. He kept observing the British through his telescope. He shut the telescope with precise movements, replaced it in its case, took up his musket, and placed a ball presumably where he thought it would do the most good.

The General reigned up his horse and looked on in admiration. He exclaimed to his officers, pointing, "There, gentlemen, is true courage!" The General saluted his valet with his sword, but Billy took no notice; he was gathering his remaining troops to retreat in good order down the little hill. He disappeared from sight.

Resuming his outward stoic calm, the General privately reflected while the guns resumed their furious cannonade. He had often thought it a pity that Billy was not a servant but a slave. It occurred to him that, given his experiences in Massachusetts and New York and New Jersey, there was little reason to doubt that Negroes were soldiers as good as any, free or not. A deeper feeling emerged this day, a hollow feeling deep in his stomach: was there any reason not to make Billy Lee a free soldier instead of a slave? But there was: property, value, reputation, custom, interest, all were against it. The General dismissed this impossible desire for the nonce, knowing he would revisit it in time. But not just now.

The General looked again at that little hill. Colonel Rhea, the local man knowledgeable about the terrain, looked as well, then suggested the hill provided an excellent opportunity. The General sent Colonel Rhea to General Greene to order the repositioning of his troops and artillery to a flanking-fire position on the hill to fire on the British cannons and troops from a second direction. Finally, some hot work to be done after the long, cold winter at Valley Forge.

The General smiled.

1

SUNDAY, MARCH 1, 1789, MORNING

The black face, sightless, stared up at me, cold and dripping in the thin March light. I was on one knee in the mud next to the icy Potomac River, examining the damage to the head.

"Damn, Humphreys!"

I looked up sharply at the General. The General never swore. He stared down at the dripping and tangled and disheveled corpse, appalled and showing it, which was also something he seldom did.

Mr. John Fairfax came stumbling back to us, wiping his mouth with a handkerchief after relieving himself of his breakfast.

"It's Julius, isn't it? The overseer at Dogue Run." Mr. Fairfax's eyes were showing too much white.

"Yes." The General's tone was dry and clipped.

"He's dead." Mr. Fairfax, a young man with no experience of war, was clearly distressed by the decomposing body he had pulled out of the river that morning. The General and I had seen much worse in the War, of course, but to see this on a sunny, cold March morning at the Mount Vernon Landing was unsettling, to say the least.

The General recovered himself. He looked at me with exasperation in his gaze and compressed lips. I acknowledged Mr. Fairfax's statement of the obvious. "Yes, apparently. And not today." The puckering of the skin, the bloating of the belly, all indicated some time in the water, but the body looked altogether too much like a man to have been in the water more than a few days. I'd seen men pulled to

3

shore two or three days after a battle with that same appearance, defeated and decomposing quickly. We had not usually lingered long around their bodies; the onrushing corruption was rapid after they came out of the water. One never gets used to the smell. But the Potomac was still icy and cold, and that would have preserved the body.

I turned the head, looking at the crushed side of the man's skull. "Is it possible the man fell and hit his head? The damage here is severe."

The General asked, "Mr. Fairfax, exactly where did you find the body?"

"I saw it washed up on the bank of the river when I came down to fetch some tools left here yesterday." Mr. Fairfax looked very much as though he wished he had slept in that morning.

The General looked around at the wharf and the muddy shore. "There is nowhere to fall here that would cause such damage, Colonel." He used my formal title rather than my last name, telling me he had recovered himself completely from his initial shock.

"Could he have drifted here from somewhere else?" I asked.

"No; the main river currents don't run into shore. Mr. Fairfax, did you give Julius leave?"

Mr. Fairfax shook his head silently. Julius, as a slave, required a leave from his master to absent himself from his farm. Dogue Run Farm was a half-hour ride away from Mount Vernon proper, to the northwest.

"And I certainly did not. He did not float here from Dogue Run, as it is downriver. I conclude he is dead from a blow, delivered here by someone else, and he fell into the river and washed ashore after some time in the water here, perhaps under the wharf." The General looked around and saw the little crowd of Negroes that had gathered. The General instructed several of them to check the surrounding area for blood on stones or other possible weapons. After a short while, they returned with no result.

My mind filled with questions. "So if someone murdered him, they have carried off the weapon. Why Julius? Why here? Who would want to murder him? How was it accomplished? When was it done?"

"All very good questions, Colonel; and yet I am more concerned with the possible impact on the political situation I face."

I grimaced; the situation we had debated day in and out for six months: whether to accept the Presidency of the new United States if the electors chose him. As I was his former aide-de-camp, close friend, house-guest, and biographer, he felt I could give him good advice on the decision. I was not alone, however; everyone who spoke to him or wrote to him had an opinion, and it was the same: to accept. But he disagreed, unwilling to give up his "vine and fig tree." And now this murder to complicate things.

The General stood with his arms folded, looking out at the Potomac flowing by, icy chunks bobbing slowly along the shore, knocking up against the pilings of the wharf. Mr. Fairfax shifted from foot to foot in the cold.

After a short time, the General turned to me and asked, "Do you know Mr. Martin Cockburn, Colonel?"

"No, sir, I do not."

"Mr. Cockburn is the close friend and neighbor of Colonel George Mason of Mason's Neck, just down the river. I have cut Colonel Mason completely since he became so vocal in opposition to the ratification of the new Constitution. He has become the antifederalist leader of Fairfax County. Mr. Cockburn's plantation, Springfield, adjoins Colonel Mason's plantation, Gunston Hall. Mr Cockburn too is one of the leading antifederalists in the County. He is also the County magistrate who would investigate this murder."

"I see, sir—we can expect little sympathy from that quarter."

"Very little." The General continued to stare at the river. "I now have a choice to make, Colonel. I must choose whether to bury the man immediately in the Negro graveyard up the hill without further action, a convenient option, or to call in the authorities to investigate the murder."

I was appalled. "Your Excellency, you cannot possibly allow this murder to go unpunished."

"I can, as his owner, and given the political situation, I should. I should call it accidental death."

"It is monstrous!" As a longtime guest at Mount Vernon, I had seen slavery and its consequences in all sorts of different situations, but this one was new to me. I could not accept it.

The General grunted, then agreed. "It is indeed, sir. One of my people murdered, and such a choice to make because of politics. Monstrous indeed. I cannot say how much I resent this act against my property."

The General, whose calm demeanor never varied, stepped down to the river. He picked up a stone, turned it over in his hand, then drew back his arm and hurled it far out across the river. I was reminded of a tale he had told me one evening. When he was a young man, a friend challenged him to cast a stone to the far side of the Potomac. He cast the stone but failed to reach the other side, as the river is very wide. Now, the General's eyes narrowed against the cold breeze as he watched his stone splash far out among the chunks of ice and sink without a trace. Knowing the General as I did, I knew he felt as much for the man as for the property. I looked down at the mass of decaying flesh that had been a slave and shuddered with cold and distress.

Turning from the icy river, the General looked around. There was no work on the plantation of a Sunday, and the group of Negroes grew as word of the gruesome discovery spread. He pointed at one, then another of them. "You, Adam, and you, Ned, carry poor Julius up to the ice house. Get some fresh ice from the river and some straw to refresh the supply already there, and remove any stored items to the Mansion House cellar. Mr. Fairfax: do you ride over to Springfield plantation on Mason's Neck and inform Mr. Cockburn about the situation. Then Colonel Hooe, the Sheriff, in Alexandria. Please ask Mr. Lear to ride there and fetch him as well, or if he cannot, then one of the servants. Do you need detailed instructions?"

"No sir." Mr. Fairfax turned and ran up the path toward the stables.

As the two men gathered up the body, the General dismissed the others to their Sunday business.

As we walked up the hill toward the Mansion House, the General said, "Julius lived with the woman Alice at Dogue Run. I must go there to inform her of his death. Will you come, Colonel?"

"Certainly, Your Excellency. It cannot be a pleasant task for you to perform alone."

2

SUNDAY, MARCH 1, 1789, MID-MORNING

By the time I had donned my riding clothes, the General was already at the stables. He had given orders to the stable boy to saddle my horse along with his own. We mounted and rode out along the drive. The Dogue Run quarters were about two miles from the Mansion House down the Fredericksburg road.

The ride was easy, no more than a half hour at a walk. The General was pensive during the ride, saying little but for a single comment about a field we passed. He had plans to change the crop to try to improve the output of the field. He said nothing about Julius, his wife Alice, or Julius's death.

We rode up to the overseer's quarters at Dogue Run, which looked to be in dilapidations. The huts that formed the slave quarters were worse, but that was their normal state, unfortunately. This was the state of all the slave "quarters" on the plantation, aside from the family quarters building at the Mansion House farm. But the additional row of ramshackle cabins behind the new greenhouse was a constant reminder to me of the injustice of slavery. I had asked the General on several occasions whether it would be better to house his slaves as he did his servants, but as with other aspects of slavery, he demurred. He said that such housing was just the way of things in Virginia.

The General knocked on the door and said, "Alice? We must speak with you." The ramshackle door slowly opened, and a small, frightened woman looked out at us. Recognizing the General, she backed away into the house, and we entered.

The single room had two rustic chairs and a bench along with a single, very basic bed frame. The small fireplace had a few cooking implements scattered around it and a small store of food items nearby. There was no fire alight at the moment. Alice stood near the fireplace, wringing her hands with worry. The General removed his hat, walked over to her, and said, "Alice, I'm very sorry to tell you that we have found Julius's body in the river. He died sometime in the last few days."

Alice's face crumpled. "I knew, I knew. He didn't come home two nights gone. He just didn't come home."

The General asked, "Why did you not send for me right away?"

She looked away, then said, "Very sorry, sir. Julius was gone lots of nights, I didn't worry much about it. Until today. He's never been gone this long."

"Gone away many nights. Indeed. His job was to be here, supervising the people working on the farm. And away at night, many nights, without leave. Indeed." I sensed the General's anger from the austerity of his face. "But no matter now. Alice, we need to find out who killed Julius."

"Killed him?" Alice looked at the General without understanding. Her eyes lifted to his and she said, "You mean he didn't just drown hisself? You mean he got killed? Somebody killed him?"

"Yes, I am afraid that is so."

Her lips clamped as her eyes went again to the floor. She began to tremble.

"Alice, do you have any idea who might have done this to Julius?"

She shook her head, stepping back a little without looking at him. I couldn't help but feel sorry for her, but it was obvious that she was more afraid than grief-stricken.

I said, "Alice, please don't worry about being in trouble, I am sure your master does not intend any punishment. Will you tell us what you know so that we can find the person who did this?" Still no response.

The General glanced at me, then looked again at Alice and asked, "Why was Julius gone at night? Just night-walking to friends? Or was something else happening?"

She looked up at him speechlessly, shaking her head, lips clamped tight.

"You must tell us, Alice."

Alice took another step back, still shaking her head and looking down at the floor and trembling even more. I sensed the terror she felt was for a punishment visited upon her solely as a result of her husband's behavior. I touched the General's sleeve with a silent plea for compassion.

He again glanced at me impassively, but said, "Well. We can discuss that later. We will have to see what we can find out from the others here. But now, Alice: I must ask you to gather your things. I think it best for now that you go up to the Mansion House. I shall send over a new overseer later this afternoon who will live here now, and I fear you cannot stay. Please go to my wife and ask her to settle you in the quarters and give you work. We will talk with you again later, once you are settled. I am very sorry for your troubles."

Alice nodded without saying anything, still trembling, and turned to the short task of sorting out her few personal belongings and bundling them up in a piece of cloth. We stood by until she was ready to leave, then escorted her to the door. Alice set out along the road to the Mansion House, trudging slowly away to her fate.

"I cannot help but feel that something must be done for her, sir," I said, looking after her.

The General was surprised. "Something will be done, Colonel. Mrs. Washington is very good with her women at the house; she will settle Alice and all will be well. That is why I directed Alice to the house rather than just leaving her here in the quarters to work. Also, she will be near at hand when she is ready to answer our questions."

I realized that the General and I saw things differently. Where I saw a new widow devastated by tragedy and terrified by the prospect of punishment as a slave, he and his good wife saw only a servant that needed placement elsewhere, a normal process and fact of life on a plantation.

"Sir, I fear this change will simply compound her agony and terror, you must see that."

The General smiled slightly. "Rather too poetic, do not you think, Colonel? I suppose that is possible, but what alternative do I have? There must be an overseer by Monday morning's work time, and that overseer must have a house, and I cannot very well supply the house with a woman in it. Mrs. Washington will see to her settling in and will be kind toward her. She will not be punished, and she will at least lose her terror of that. Once she is settled, we will question her again about her husband and his habits."

I shook my head. "I fear I cannot be as sanguine, sir; you know my feelings on slavery. Forgive me, but I can see only evil coming from all this."

The General sighed and said, "Yes, Colonel, I understand. You wish me to free all my people as a moral duty." He looked around the shabby overseer's cabin. "The result would be disastrous for my family. Much of my wealth is in my people, and freeing them would destroy that wealth. As well, the 1782 Virginia Act mandates paying for the support of freed slaves who cannot support themselves, to avoid their becoming a draw on public funds. I cannot support such an expense for nearly a hundred people. It is far more important to me, at this moment, to get my farm functioning properly. My family depends on it. My livelihood depends on it. I am not secure from want. Even if I accept the call to the Presidency, I shall not take a salary, and everything thus depends on having a working farm to generate the income we need to live."

I could only reply, "I understand, Your Excellency."

The General stared out at his farm stoically and offered a further explanation. "Colonel, I lived too many years in my youth with the restrictions and limitations of relative poverty and a difficult family circumstance. I cannot allow myself to return to it, to retreat backward to a time of trial. I need my people to work the farm. I need competent overseers to ensure they do so to the utmost of their capacity. This is my duty as a plantation owner and as the head of a family. You will understand this more fully, Colonel, after you marry and start your own family."

We walked out into the cold day.

3

SUNDAY, MARCH 1, 1789, MID-MORNING

The Dogue run fields stretched out around us, punctuated by the little cabins that housed the slaves. The General said, "I visit these fields every few days, you know. I have often worked with Julius to determine the best use of the people here. Mr. Fairfax has reported no problems with the farm. I must now admit that we simply did not see what was in front of us."

I nodded and asked, "How do you wish to proceed, Your Excellency?"

He replied, "I think it incumbent upon myself to gather some information before I assign the new overseer. I had recommended to Mr. Fairfax earlier this year that he see to preparations for spring planting along with fencing work and drainage improvements. I will inspect the fields now to ascertain what the people here have done."

The General's people, so-called I suppose as an emollient term to use in place of the less salubrious "slave," were without doubt the best source of information about the farm. They did all the work, after all.

The General continued, "Perhaps while I ride out into the fields, Colonel, you could assist me by gathering information from the people here."

We walked over toward the quarters. The General called out his people from their Sunday rest, and the men and women gathered in the space in front of the overseer's house with their children. When it appeared that no more were to come, the General addressed them, just as he had so many times addressed his soldiers before battle. It was as cold today as it had been at Valley Forge, I'm sure. The huts of the slaves were not much better than the huts of the soldiers at that time, nor were the soldiers' clothes much better that winter than the rags of the people I was viewing. There was less snow on the ground now, though, and more fear.

The General spoke. "I must tell you all of a distressing event that has occurred at the Mansion House farm today. We have found Julius, your overseer here, dead in the river, near the Landing. We are convinced someone murdered him, but we do not know by whom. I will send over another overseer later today or tomorrow. In the meanwhile, anyone with any information about this dreadful thing must come forward with it." He looked over the faces turned toward him, but there was no movement at all: a frozen tableau on a frozen day.

"Come now. Someone must know something." There was an uncomfortable shifting of feet and clearing of throats, but no one said anything.

"Very well, then. This is Colonel Humphreys, who will select a few of you to question about events on the farm. I will leave you to it, then, Colonel."

The General mounted his horse and proceeded off to his tour of inspection of the farm. I set to work. I chose as I would choose soldiers for a raid, looking for the subtle signs in the men that would tell me they would do their duty. I did not ask for volunteers; the men before me did not appear anxious to distinguish themselves. No one would meet my eye. I reflected briefly that it was so much easier to deal with free men in a straightforward way, and again how much I wished the General would reconsider manumission.

I walked up and down the line of Negroes, debating with myself on each one's usefulness to my quest. I chose one sturdy, middle-aged man and one older boy and dismissed the others, mostly women and children, whom I felt would contribute little to my understanding of events.

"Come along, then; we'll go into the overseer's house to get in out of the cold." I guided them into the little house. The pair entered gingerly, stepping across the floor as though it were made of live coals. I realized they had never been inside before. I pulled together a rickety chair and the bench and sat myself in the chair, indicating the bench to the Negros.

"Well, now. What's your name?"

"Jack, sir, massa."

"Sir will do, Jack, thank you. And yours?"

"Israel, massa."

"All right, Israel. Just call me sir. And what do you two do on the farm?"

"Field labor, sir, whatever needs doin'," said Jack.

Israel nodded, then added, "Sometimes my mama has me workin' on things round here."

"And Julius is the one that tells you what to do every day?"

"Yessir."

"How was Julius as a man to work for? Was he fair?"

Jack said, "Just fine, sir, massa. No problems atall. Just fine."

"Israel?"

The boy nodded, "Yessir, just fine for me too."

"Is there anything amiss with the work in the fields?"

"Nosir, we all just do our work, just like Julius says." Jack stared at the floor.

"And after work? Much night walking?"

The pair looked at each other, then back down at the floor. Jack said, "Don't know about that, sir. We all keep our selfs to our selfs, you understand."

"Have any people run away to get away from Julius?"

Jack looked alarmed at this, eyes wide. "Nosir, nosir, nobody run off in a long while. Julius ain't give nobody no cause to run off." Israel, startled by the older man's vehemence, looked at him with round eyes.

"But Julius wasn't here every day, was he?"

"Nosir, just most times."

"And did you know where he was when absent?"

"Nosir, he never said nothin' to us about it." Israel nodded in agreement.

"Was there anyone here at all who had problems with Julius?"

"Nosir, not so's I know anything about it."

"Nobody who would do him harm?"

"Nosir." Jack was more confident in his opinion on intended harm.

"Was there any person here who was close friends with him, aside from Alice?"

"Not particular, sir." Jack paused a moment, looked at me, then added. "See, Julius was the boss, it kinda made it hard to like him much."

"Understandable. Now, I want you both to think back. Did you notice anything wrong or out of place over the last few weeks or days? With Julius or anyone else?"

Jack looked at me, pausing long, then said, "Week ago, sir, we had a scare, miller Ben and a couple of mill coopers come by and say they got stuff missing and do we know about it. Nobody knew nothing' here. Julius told 'em off, and they went away."

"Israel, Were you around for that?"

Israel smiled for the first time. "Yes indeed, sir. Julius was right put out *that* day. Words I didn't know. Know 'em now, sir, yes, sir." Jack shook his head in distress, whether at the swearing or the boy's obvious delight in it I did not know.

I asked, "Julius didn't have anything to tell the mill men?"

Israel replied, "Not about the missing stuff, just about themselves."

"And did they say what was missing?"

"No sir, they didn't get to it before Julius ran 'em off."

"Sounds like quite a to-do."

"Yessir!"

"Jack, did anyone tell you what stuff was missing?"

"They never got round to saying, massa. Sir." The man pressed his lips tight, not willing to say more. His eyes flicked to Israel, then back down at the floor.

"Do things go missing from the farm a good deal?"

Jack looked up at me with a blank expression, then looked back down and said slowly, "No sir, nothin' like that happens atall."

"So Julius never had to punish anyone for taking things from the fields?"

"Nosir, everything's just fine here."

"And he never punished you, Israel?"

"Nosir. Sometimes my mama give me what for, but that's different. Ain't never been whipped or nothing since I been working the fields, sir." Israel said this with pride.

"Indeed. I am sure your mother knows you well. But Julius went away sometimes?"

Israel looked apprehensively at Jack, who was shaking his head again. He stuttered, "Yessir, n-nosir, not very often, sir. S-sometimes."

Heavy going. It covered most of the possibilities, though. I knew the pair had the information I wanted. It was obvious that Jack wanted to tell me nothing and that Israel was willing but inhibited by his companion's example. The room seemed to me filled with a compressed and hidden dread that I could not break through. Perhaps no one in my position could pull out more information; but I had to try.

"Do you know what Julius would do when he went away?"

"He just would say he had business, sir, and to keep our arses working." I noticed Jack's hand trembled a little on his knee as he told me this.

"He didn't say what kind of business? Would he carry anything with him?"

"Nosir, nothing. He just walked down toward the creek, sir, or up the road."

"And when he came back, did he bring anything with him?"

Jack just stared at the floor and shook his head; Israel looked at Jack, then quickly down at the floor without saying anything more.

I was fairly sure this was all the information I was to get from them. "All right, you may go now. Thank you."

Jack was out of the door in a flash. Israel left the little room with less careful steps than he had entered with, not looking back. They carried what they knew with them. I was left knowing very little more than when I had started except that even innocuous questions can generate fear in men that had everything to fear. And that the Grist Mill people had a problem with Julius. I went out again into the yard.

The General had returned from his inspection and waited patiently, sitting on his mount. I joined him and reported on the interrogations I had conducted.

He said, "Indeed; Julius would leave the farm mysteriously, even though his place was here and without any leave. I must get Mr. Fairfax to ensure the next overseer is more diligent. From my inspection, it appears that even with Julius gone so often, the people have done their work. I found that there were fewer livestock than there should be; I will follow up on that with Mr. Lear. We should visit the Grist Mill, I think, before returning to the Mansion House."

4

SUNDAY, MARCH 1, 1789, EARLY AFTERNOON

The General explained the situation at the Grist Mill to me as we rode the mile or so down the road from Dogue Run. "Back when poor Roberts was there, I would not know from one week to the next whether we would get any casks of flour; a drinker, you know. Roberts knew his business, he had many years of experience with all kinds of mills, but drink was the ruin of him. Joseph Davenport, his successor, may not be the best miller I have ever employed, but he has produced flour and meal consistently and with care, and he does not drink to excess. The Negro miller Ben has been working at the mill for years as well."

The General had built his mill just before the War as he expanded his crops from tobacco to wheat and corn. The mill provided revenue from sale of the various grades of flour it produced, and it also produced the cornmeal that supplied Mount Vernon's people with their staple food, and the General with his hoecakes. The mill and its equipage were aging, and the General was considering ways and means of upgrading or renovating it to produce more flour for sale.

We approached the mill, which is situated along Dogue Run itself. The Run provides the water for the millpond that runs the wheel. The Run and its pond being frozen at this time of year, the mill was not in operation.

"Let us ride up to the house and see Mr. Davenport first, before we speak with his people," suggested the General. "I should have thought

Mr. Davenport would notify me immediately had there been problems at the mill."

We rode across the small bridge over the millstream, then rounded the big old mill building and rode up the path to the little house. The yard and its pen were alive with cows, geese, and pigs, who did not seem to mind the cold. Mrs. Davenport was working in the pen, feeding the geese. We tied our horses to a rail, then walked up to the house. The General knocked on the door. It was shortly opened by the miller, Joseph Davenport, whom I'd met several times during my stay at Mount Vernon. He was of middle age with graying brown hair, with stout arms and legs ready for work and an alert expression of face. He seemed surprised to see us.

"Gentlemen," he said. "I was not expecting a visit! Welcome, welcome. Come along in." He backed away from the door into the small house. The General removed his hat, as did I, and we entered, knocking the mud from our boots first. The miller pulled a couple of basic chairs from the wall, brushed them off, and we all sat facing one another.

"I suppose," said the miller, "that you've come to talk about the state of the mill. The stone and machinery are functioning, but barely, as you're aware, sir. Of course, the time of year ..." He waved a pudgy hand in the direction of the mill.

The General smiled briefly, then said, "I am sure everything is fine there, we will work out a plan for replacing the mill equipment soon. But, no, that is not why we came. Have you heard about Julius?"

"The overseer at Dogue Run? Has he finally run off?"

The General sat back in his chair. "Run off? I'll ask you to explain that, sir, if you please."

"Well, that Julius, he's the kind of Negro you have to watch. Nothing to complain about, just my doings with him ain't always been what I'd like."

"Indeed. I perceive you harbor ill feelings toward the man."

"Yes sir, that I do, that I do," said the miller. "I don't much care for back-talk from ones such as that."

"I hope your feelings do not get in the way of productive work at the mill?"

"Oh, no, sir, not atall, not atall. I work with 'em, but you can't ask me to like it much."

"And your last encounter with Julius, when was that?"

The miller thought for a moment. "Well, sir, not in a donkey's age, really. I made clear I hadn't any truck with him or his business awhile back, see? Told him to get off the place and back to where he belonged. Weeks ago, sir. And good riddance, far as I'm concerned."

"Indeed. I am sorry to inform you that Julius has been found murdered. We found his body earlier today down by the Landing at the Mansion House."

"Jesus save us." Davenport squeezed his eyes closed and opened them wide, giving his round face a comical look. "Murdered, you say? Who did it? Another black?"

"That is just what we are trying to determine," said the General, with a touch of impatience. "Now, Mr. Davenport, please tell me what you know about Julius's doings over the past weeks."

Davenport sat up in his chair at this command. "Well, sir, as you know, we don't have much to do with the farm up the road. They keep to themselves, as do we, no need for us to pay much mind to them, if you know what I mean."

The General nodded briefly to encourage the man.

"Still, when we did have to speak with him, he was downright rude and unhelpful to Ben and the men I sent. Or, at least, that's according to Ben."

"We will speak with Ben in a few minutes. Could you expand a bit on this incident?"

"Yes, sir." The big miller paused. "Well, sir. Um."

"Yes? What's the matter?"

The miller stared glumly at the floor, then raised his eyes to the General again. "Well, I suppose it's all got to come out now anyway." He took a deep breath and let it out. "I had my hopes of keeping this in the house and not bothering you with it, sir, but it's all come to nothing."

The General, mystified, frowned. "What on earth are you talking about, man? Out with it!"

"Yes sir. Well, sir, not to put too fine a point on it, there's been flour missing. Not a lot, just a few casks, but they've gone, and we don't know where. And some of the wood for the cooperage as well."

"Why was I not informed?"

"I didn't want to bother you with it, sir, until I knew more," said the miller, shaking his head. "I thought I could figure it out and get the goods back and nobody the wiser." At this confession, he stopped and his lips tightened. "I knew bloody well it was that bastard Julius and his crowd up to the farm. Knew it, by God! I worked over Ben and the coopers first, a course. They didn't know nothing at all about it, not even that anything was missing, they said. Not sure I believed that! But I watch 'em pretty close, and I think they are truthful about it all. I knew it was Julius even before I tackled them about it. Then I sent Ben up to the farm instead of going myself because I wouldn't be able to control myself, d'ye see? And that wouldn't help things. No, not atall."

"I can see that. Fine judgment on your part as far as it went, but you say it did not work out as you expected?" The General was at his most affable, though I knew from long experience that he must be quickly coming to the boil.

"I'm afraid, sir, that Julius just sent my men away with their tails between their legs. Ben ain't real strong minded, you know. Not like that bastard Julius."

"I did *not* know, sir. But please proceed. When was this?"

"Last week, sir. Last Wednesday. I was getting last year's flour saved for winter sale ready for the carts to Alexandria, and when I counted 'em up, they was 10 casks short. They'd rearranged the casks so I wouldn't notice right away! Then I looked around the yard to see what else had gone. We'd just got a new load of wood for the casks, ready to run up a new set for the spring. A quarter of the last load gone, and some metal hoops too. And geese too—I think there are a couple of them gone as well."

I suspected Davenport cared more about the geese than the flour, as their meat would have wound up on his own table and the feathers in his own bed. The General did not express his surprise, but I could see from his upright demeanor and from the set of his mouth that he was very near the boil now.

"Very well, Mr. Davenport. I do think my late suggestion to you about doing the counting up of the casks daily and keeping that record up to date would have helped. The whole point of my suggestion was to prevent or discover theft quickly."

"Yessir, sorry sir. I'll try my best. I been awful busy, sir."

The General was now at a full boil, his brow contracting and his face austere. He was very direct with Mr. Davenport. "I am sure. Mr. Davenport, you must realize that the mill and its flour contributes a goodly amount to the farm accounts, and having things go missing is not going to help me pay your stipend. Or to feather your bed, for that matter. Do you understand?" The General's voice was calm, but the words conveyed his frustration with his manager.

"Yes, sir. Sorry sir." Mr. Davenport looked down at the floor, not meeting the General's firm eye.

I had been working on the General's biography now for several years. I had observed that the General was always full of very detailed suggestions for improvement in the way things worked on the different farms, usually to no avail. The people working the farms were never quite good enough for the General's full approval, as his diligent efforts at improvement were often met with a wall of inaction. It was very much of a piece with his experiences in the war dealing with the dilatory Congress and the duplicitous local authorities, as he had wearily informed me on many occasions. I won't even mention the house carpenters and workmen at the Mansion House, who would be burning merrily in Hell had the General's comments been translated into action.

I had also observed that the General, while a man of strong opinion and decisive action, did not like to punish men; he preferred to persuade them where possible. Only when duty or imminent disaster forced his hand did he dismiss or punish a man or woman working for him, and that always with reluctance. Mr. Davenport was thus repentant but not particularly alarmed by the General's reaction to his admission of inattention to his duties. I was not optimistic about Mr. Davenport's future management of the mill.

The General arose and said, "I think the next step is to have a talk with the men." I laid a hand on his sleeve. Mr. Davenport did not appear very fond of his people at the mill, or indeed of Negroes anywhere.

"Your Excellency, I think it might be best for us to question the men separately, without Mr. Davenport. They will probably tell us more in his absence." I privately thought they would snap shut like newly dug clams were he there. The General nodded, so we left Mr. Davenport to his worries, his missing geese, and his Sunday dinner and pipe.

5

SUNDAY, MARCH 1, 1789, EARLY AFTERNOON

The coopers, having heard the arrival of the horses earlier, had gathered together outside their quarters to see what was afoot. As it was Sunday, the people were not at work. Ben, the miller, stood slightly apart from the coopers, waiting for us as we crossed the muddy yard. They had the look of irregular and unprepared troops ready to be massacred by a charge. Their women and children hovered behind them, looking out of the quarters with anxiety written all over their faces.

"Mornin', massa. Sir." Ben nodded to both of us and looked down at the ground.

"Good morning, Ben. Please don't be worried, we just have some questions," said the General. The men did not look reassured by this start, but drew together slightly, looking to one another without saying anything.

"We have just spoken with Mr. Davenport about the incident with the missing flour and supplies. I would like to hear your account of your visit to Julius at the Dogue Run farm last week, please."

"Well, sir, Massa Davenport, he told me to take a couple of other men and go to the farm to see if we could find the missin' casks and wood. He was right angry, Massa Davenport, so we went pretty quick. We went up to the house and saw Alice, but she says Julius out on the farm, so we look about awhile 'til we find him walkin' back from the field. I just says the word 'flour' to him, and he just gets crazy on us."

He shook his head.

"What happened then?"

"It ain't no good talking to him, he just told us to git away. So we git."

"And came back here with nothing to show for it all."

"Yessir. That about the size of it." The man paused, then said, "But Julius, he's dead now."

"Yes, that is true. Now, Ben. You have been living right here for years, you must know when things are going on at the mill, and even at the farm."

Ben shook his head, "No, sir, ain't nothin' goin' on to speak about. No sir. Goin' on? No sir."

The General, frustrated, motioned for me to try. I said, "Ben, you really must tell us what you know. You didn't like Julius, but we need to find who killed him, and it is likely that person is somebody who was involved with him in the thefts." I didn't mention that Mr. Davenport had as much reason to dislike Julius as anyone else and excellent opportunity to do something about it. As did Ben himself, of course. "How do you know of his death?"

Ben looked at the others, then looked down at the ground again. "That Julius," he said, "he ain't a good man. Folks don't like that man, 'cause he don't treat 'em good."

The General asked, "Do you mean about work? He worked them too hard or was unfair to them?"

"Nosir, just with people things. He kept to himself a lot, always had something goin' on somewhere else. We never go by there if we don't need to, sir. He didn't come to gatherings or nothing, didn't have many friends among the black folks. And he was a boss, which ain't gonna make him no friends. And he was just plain bad, sir. We heard he was dead from some people passin' by, 'cause they knew we'd like to know about it."

The coopers were nodding in agreement. The General asked, "But you did not see Julius or anyone else from the farm around here?"

"Nosir, not lately anyhow."

I asked, "How do you think the flour and boards were stolen?"

"Don't rightly know, sir, but it must have been while we was sleepin', 'cause we're always around the barrel house doing our work during the day. Woulda heard any wagons or anything, so they must have done it by carryin' stuff away quiet-like. At night, sir, must of been at night."

Skeptical, I pressed him. "Do you think Julius had something to do with it?"

"I don't know nothing about it, sir. All I knows is that Julius, he ain't no good."

The General grunted, then returned to his earlier point. "Ben, you and the coopers work with the flour and the cask wood every day. You must have noticed things going missing." He looked at the coopers one by one, questioning them with a firm eye.

They couldn't meet his look. They instead looked at the ground. I couldn't really tell whether they were withholding what information they had or whether they were simply frightened to speak of it. The General was treating them as soldiers, and they were not. I said, "Come now. You don't need to fear punishment from the General or me, we just need to know." I looked to the General for confirmation, and he nodded, though I could sense the rising anger in him.

One of the coopers finally decided to volunteer. "I guess I did see some boards gone, massa, last week."

"But you didn't tell Mr. Davenport," asserted the General, shaking his head.

"Nosir. Massa Davenport, see, he don't really like us to talk to him."

The General looked at me and said with exasperation, "How can he expect to know things if he will not listen to people?" I had no answer for this rhetorical query, and he switched his attention back to the cooper. "All right, man, tell me what you saw."

"See, we gathers up wood for the cask, to shape 'em, you understand, and I went back to the storeroom to fetch the wood, and the wood we put aside for the new staves, well it was gone. Just gone, sir."

"So what did you do then?"

"I look around, makin' sure them boards ain't nowhere around, then I moved the wood around and get some new staves for the casks, massa. Hoped Mr. Davenport ain't goin' to see the wood gone and think we done it."

The General shook his head at the ostrich-like logic but said, "Oh, very well. But next time, please tell Ben or Mr. Davenport. And has this happened before?"

Another cooper silently nodded. The first one said, "A couple times. Last month."

"And you have no idea how the boards went missing?"

"Nosir, no idea."

I asked, "Why does Mr. Davenport think Julius had something to do with it? Do you know?"

Ben volunteered, "Massa Davenport never like Julius, Julius gave him too much lip from time to time. But I seen Julius take things from the mill yard awhile back and told massa about it, had to 'cause I knew massa would see 'em missing, he had plans for 'em, and sure he blame me. They ain't big things, just eggs and such. Massa got mad, but he don't do nothing at that time."

I said, "And when bigger things went missing, Mr. Davenport thought of Julius and sent you up there to find out."

"Right, sir. I guess he think I might be better at getting some idea from that Julius, guess he was wrong about that." I sensed a bit of satisfaction in Davenport's being wrong, but I daresay it was my imagination at work. Or perhaps satisfaction that Julius had come to a bad end.

I asked, "Ben, do you think Julius was responsible for the thefts?"

Caught between his dislike for Julius and his dislike for expressing his opinion to his master, Ben opened and closed his mouth, nothing coming out, then croaked, "I guess so, sir, I guess so, but I ain't seen him do it and I ain't heard nothing about it."

The General, without outwardly reacting to this evasion, took his watch from his pocket. He said, "Colonel, I think we need to break off here and get back to the Mansion House to meet Mr. Cockburn and Colonel Hooe. Time is getting on. I think we have gotten all we can here for now." He turned to Ben and the coopers and said, "Thank you, you've been most helpful and honest, I will remember that." The men nodded uncertainly. The General continued, "But I must insist that you mind Mr. Davenport, and that you tell him when things are wrong. All right, that is all."

Leaving the little group of Negroes, we walked back to our horses in silence. The day warmed a little as we rode, as did the General's mood.

"Colonel, I would not say as much to anyone but you, but I am..." He could not find the right word to express his feelings. Our horses walked on. "How can I farm and keep a family and plantation in order if my servants and people hide all that is wrong from me? This cannot stand as a way of doing business. It is not right. My reputation in business will suffer. I will not have it. I could not tolerate it in the army, and I will not tolerate it on my farm."

As aide-de-camp to the General in the war, I had observed his obsession with details. He had insisted on everything being done at the right place and time. He would cope with emergences as challenges to be remedied by intelligent action guided by experience. A military reverse would drive him to consider ways to turn the situation into an advantage. If he could see no advantage, he would work with us to render the reversal inconsequential. When completely frustrated, he would become visibly angry, and it was the job of his aides to assuage that anger and find solutions. Every aide on his staff felt his anger as their own and wanted to help.

My observation of him on his farm over the last few years had confirmed this desire for control. Now, he had realized he was no longer in command of events on his own farm. His anger was apparent as we rode; but by the time we had reached the Mansion House, I had helped him to master it. Let me explain how.

6

SUNDAY, MARCH 1, 1789, AFTERNOON

I suddenly caught sight of a familiar hedge off to the right of the road. Memory flooded back. That was it.

"Your Excellency!" I exclaimed, pointing, "The hedge!"

The General looked around, saw the hedge, reigned in, and laughed. I joined in.

"The famous Humphreys Hedge," chortled the General.

In an earlier visit to Mount Vernon in 1786, I had learned quite a bit more about the General than I had gathered during the long years of the War as his aide-de-camp. After retiring from the cares of command during the War, he had assumed the responsibilities of a farmer and man of leisure—not precisely care free, but not heavily burdened, either. At Mount Vernon, his care extended to his family, his home, and his plantation, in that order. He was free to allow his mind to range over more light-hearted subjects—such as sport.

The General was very fond of fox hunting. The prominent gentlemen of Alexandria were forever frequenting the woods of Mount Vernon with him in search of the little creatures, all in the name of sport. The General possessed several hunters and many hunting dogs, of which he was justifiably quite proud. He has since given it up for lack of time, as his farming and political cares continually increased, but back then, he pursued the sport with enthusiasm.

The General was unquestionably the finest horseman in the state of Virginia, possibly in the United States, as any of his aides could inform you. Will Lee, his valet, who had assumed the name "Will" to replace the less dignified "Billy" as he got older, was nearly as good on a horse. Will particularly excelled in his role as huntsman.

One fine May day, we were returning from an energetic run with the dogs when we came to the hedge. The General drew up his horse on the road.

"Well, Colonel, you performed well today. But I fear there were no opportunities to jump, and I think you did not get the exercise you deserve from the effort."

"Sir, I have got all the exercise I desire, with the greatest compliments to your own fervor."

"Very well; still, I would have you undertake a bit more, if you are willing. D'you see that hedge?"

"Certainly, sir. It is very picturesque."

The General smiled. "Not just picturesque, Colonel, but the finest hedge on the plantation for jumping. Look how your horse is pulling toward it; he cannot resist it."

My horse was standing quietly, not making a move, but I deferred to the General's judgment as always.

"Colonel Humphreys, I formally issue to you a challenge: jump that hedge. I think you are ready to undertake such an adventure." Turning in his saddle to his huntsman, he asked, "Will—do you not think the Colonel's riding is up to that hedge?"

The Negro huntsman grinned widely, sitting easily in his own saddle. "Certainly is, sir. Certainly. I am very sure the Colonel will perform the feat with fine results. *Fine* results!"

"I am less sanguine, for I have not seen him jump a hedge while I have known him." The General smiled. "But I think you are ready, sir, quite ready."

Quite frankly, I was ready for an afternoon nap, but I could never resist the General's challenges. I had always found them instructive and to my ultimate benefit.

The General waved a hand. "Go ahead, Colonel; I will follow should you succeed."

I shook up the reins of my horse, rode down the road a bit, turned, and urged him to a gallop to take the hedge as I had been taught. The General in this case was misinformed; I had jumped many hedges before and during the war, and this hedge was no great thing, though a bit ragged at the top.

Well. As I easily cleared the hedge, I saw the lesson to be learned. I will say that I *absorbed* the lesson to be learned. I absorbed that lesson along with a great quantity of water and mud that resided on the other side of that hedge. As my horse floundered and I sputtered, in the middle of the mire, I could hear both the General and Will laughing unreservedly. Infectiously—I began to laugh, though rather more weakly.

The General rode over to the other side of the hedge, looked over at me, smiled, and said blandly, "Ah, Colonel, you are too deep for me."

My poor mount, up to his girths, struggled out of the mire onto drier land at my urging. Will, still grinning widely, dismounted and wiped off the chief of the mud. He grinned up at me, clearly enjoying the General's jest.

The General continued his raillery. "I shall in future call this hedge Humphreys Hedge, in honor of your rite of passage. I daresay Yale College offered little in the way of such depth of learning, eh, Colonel?"

"No, Your Excellency; I must say that the College taught me many things, but that Your Excellency is still capable of finding those things I still need to learn." I dripped, quietly, making hasty resolutions to *follow* the General in the future rather than simply obeying orders and charging ahead. The General perceived my resolution and nodded his smiling approbation.

"Well, sir, let us get you back to the Mansion House to get dry. I will ask Mrs. Washington to have a special pudding prepared to celebrate your Mount Vernon baptism, Colonel!"

It took me quite a bit of special pleading with Mrs. Washington to get my equipment cleaned by the house servants. She even scolded the General: "Mr. Washington, I should think you would know better by this time, indeed. Scandalous." The General's complacency in the face of criticism from higher authority made me suspect her, though, as did a certain twinkle in her eyes. Her pudding proved an excellent reward for my learning experience. The General remained in good humor for the rest of the week—as did I! I had become a full member of the Mount Vernon family.

I slipped the Negro maid a small amount of money to show my appreciation for her efforts, at which Will grinned even more widely than he had done at the sight of my immersion.

The General and I rode on toward the Mansion House. Humphreys Hedge had done its job, his smile showing his humor restored. I smiled to myself, thinking that a little mud was never put to better use.

7

SUNDAY, MARCH 1, 1789, AFTERNOON

When we left our horses at the stables, I noticed that John Fairfax's horse was in its stall; he must have returned from fetching Mr. Cockburn. As we approached the Mansion House, Mr. Fairfax came out of the storehouse.

He came up to us and reported, "Your Excellency, I found Mr. Cockburn at Springfield and informed him of the murder as you requested. He should be arriving at any moment. I sent Mr. Lear on the errand to Alexandria to fetch Colonel Hooe; he has not yet returned."

"Thank you, Mr. Fairfax, well done."

Fifteen minutes later, we had changed our clothes and were standing in the main passage of the house when we heard a carriage drive up the sweep. On going outside, we perceived Mr. Martin Cockburn emerging from the carriage, or so I was informed by the General; I had not previously met Mr. Cockburn.

He was a relatively tall, thin man with graying brown hair and a sharp nose that gave him a slightly disagreeable expression. As a man of justice—a county magistrate and justice of the peace—I had no idea what to expect from him, but his appearance was not encouraging. He approached the General with a smile, though a perceptibly cold one.

"General Washington, happy to see you again in such health, though one could wish for better circumstances, I suppose." He did not offer a hand, as he knew the General well enough to know that he did not like that custom. The two men bowed to one another.

The General responded with affability. "Welcome, welcome. Yes, a sad business. I hope your wife is well?"

"Tolerable, tolerable, thank you for asking."

"This is Colonel David Humphreys, my friend and guest."

"Pleased to make your acquaintance, Colonel."

I bowed without saying anything, and Mr. Cockburn returned the bow. The requisite greeting and social chat done, Cockburn's smile disappeared, and he said, "Well, sir, I suppose I should start by viewing the body." He lifted his chin in a silent question.

"Let me conduct you thence." The General extended his arm to show Cockburn the way.

We walked across the sweep circle, past the kitchen, and down to the ice house that overlooked the river. Two or three liveried Negroes stood around the door, but they scattered away at the General's approach, returning to their house business.

Even with the fresh ice the General had ordered from the river, the odor was beginning to be disagreeable as we opened the small door and entered. The ice house is small, and we were somewhat crowded. I stood in the doorway to give the General and Mr. Cockburn room. Cockburn wrinkled his nose but stepped over to the body laid out on the floor without further comment. He poked and prodded with his stick, muttering quietly to himself.

"A bit more light, Colonel, if you please?" he asked. "It is quite dark in here."

I thought of Diogenes and his student as I stepped out of the doorway into the open air, rather thankfully, giving him the light he requested, then peered back into the little room through the open wooden door. The General moved to a side wall. He had to stoop, as the ice house was not large enough to accommodate his height. It wasn't long before Mr. Cockburn had completed his inspection of the contusions and head wound.

"Washed?" he asked.

The General replied, "No sir, just as we found him. He was in the river, hence the waterlogged and bloated appearance."

"I see. Drowned, then."

The General replied, "I think not; I think the head blow killed him."

Cockburn stopped, then turned back to the body. "Hum. I suppose that's possible. Seems unlikely, though, given the slave was in the river. An accident? A fall?"

"I do not see how. You must realize he was away from his duty at the Dogue Run Farm and had no business being near the Landing."

"The Landing?" Mr. Cockburn cocked an eye at the General.

The General said, "Yes, my manager found him washed up on the bank at the Mount Vernon Landing, down behind the Mansion House."

Mr. Cockburn wrinkled his nose once again and stepped outside the ice house. The General followed and closed the door.

Mr. Cockburn rubbed his chin. "He'd been in the river. You say he's from Dogue Run? With no leave? He could not possibly have fallen into the Run there and washed up at your Landing, the river runs the other way. Could he have simply fallen and hit something? Perhaps someone pushed him? Perhaps one of your men here found him in suspicious circumstances and became overzealous? Or did you personally find him and punish him?"

The General responded in a calm voice, "None of my men have mentioned any encounter; nor would they have any reason to avoid doing so. I certainly did not find him and punish him. As for accident, I had my people investigate rather thoroughly: there is nothing there that might cause such a wound, I think, and nowhere to fall that would produce such an injury. We did not see any blood or other evidence of self-inflicted mischief around the wharf. We did not find any object that the murderer might have used, either, so he must have disposed of the weapon or carried it away."

"And you or your overseers had nothing to do with this?"

At Mr. Cockburn's insistent tone, the General frowned. "No sir; and I may say I am inclined to resent the implication of any involvement of my managers in so heinous a crime. Please do not let your political inclinations as an antifederalist affect your legal judgment."

Mr.Cockburn's face contracted, enhancing its disagreeable look. Sounding offended, he replied, "I am sorry, Your Excellency. I certainly did not mean to imply anything untoward. It is my duty as magistrate to clarify the facts as far as I can. Politics has nothing—nothing—to do with it. Justice must be done wherever it lies." But his eyes could not meet those of the General.

"Very well, sir. I agree with you that justice must be done. We must discover the murderer of my overseer and prosecute him in a court of law. What shall we do next?" prompted the General.

"I suppose my next port of call is the Landing, to see the actual scene where you found the body," Mr. Cockburn said. He looked back at the closed door. "You'll need to get him in the ground before much longer, I think, ice not withstanding. I will tell the Coroner to form a jury immediately so that they may inspect the body soon."

The General nodded and said, "Thank you, Mr. Cockburn. Colonel Hooe should also be here soon to perform his inspection of the body as Sheriff." I reflected that the General wanted his friend Hooe to have as much detail as possible to counteract the less friendly Cockburn. I could see that the situation was quite complicated by the local politics and relationships, as the General had earlier intimated, and that formal justice might be hard to find in the ensuing investigation if limited solely to Mr. Cockburn's efforts. His response had already proved he was not inclined to defer much to the General's opinions.

"I will leave the details of the investigation to Colonel Hooe, but I must see the actual scene, I suppose. Now?"

The General turned to me and said in his low voice, "Colonel

Humphreys. I will conduct Mr. Cockburn down to the Landing. Do you wait at the Mansion House for Colonel Hooe. Explain matters, show him everything, then bring him to us at the Landing. I must ensure Mr. Cockburn sees everything as part of his investigation." I thought "investigation" was strong language for the actual work Mr. Cockburn was likely to do, but I simply nodded, and they headed for the path down to the Landing.

I walked up the hill and entered the house through the Piazza door and went into the General's study to wait for Colonel Hooe. We had been in the study earlier in the morning when John Fairfax had interrupted us with his breathlessly imparted discovery of Julius's body. I picked up my book but had read only a few lines of poetry before I heard another carriage arriving. I went out to the front and found Colonel Hooe in all his blustery merchant's good humor exiting his fine carriage and Mr. Lear dismounting from his horse. Another man stepped out of the carriage after the Colonel.

Colonel Robert Hooe was the current Sheriff of Fairfax County and a leading merchant in the town of Alexandria. He was a genial, stout, red-faced man in his mid-forties, with greying hair and hazel eyes that always managed to look half asleep. He dined with the General regularly, and I knew him well. He greeted me. "Colonel Humphreys, good to see you. Terrible road from Alexandria just now. At least we have approachable weather, thank God." He looked around. "The General? What's all this about a dead slave? Is that Cockburn's carriage?" He grimaced, then smiled. "This is John Williamson, my clerk. Perhaps he can wait in the house?"

I turned Mr. Williamson, a short, self-effacing man in his late twenties with thin lips and brown hair, over to the House staff. I took Colonel Hooe down to the ice house and explained as we walked that the General and Mr. Cockburn had gone down to the scene of the event, and that he should examine the body before joining them. I summarized the situation for him. He entered the ice house willingly enough and spent a little more time than Mr. Cockburn had with the corpse, examining the head more closely with his fingers.

"Hit with something blunt, I'd say. Blunt and heavy. A rock? A club? Indeed." He took a handkerchief from his pocket and wiped his hands carefully, then tossed the dirtied cloth onto the floor. "All right, let us join the General and his nemesis down at the Landing. Phew!"

We walked past the House and stable, then down to the Landing, where we found the General and Mr. Cockburn examining the wharf and riverbank.

The General warmly welcomed Colonel Hooe, both out of friendship and, I think, out of some relief that he had no longer to deal with Mr. Cockburn alone.

Colonel Hooe then greeted Mr. Cockburn with apparent warmth, shaking his hand firmly and inquiring after his family. "Haven't actually seen you in a dog's age, Mr. Cockburn. Or at least a week or so." Colonel Hooe grinned.

Mr. Cockburn smiled briefly in return and extracted his hand from Colonel Hooe's as soon as he could. "I assume Colonel Humphreys has filled you in?" he asked Colonel Hooe.

"Yes, indeed, sir. Have you learned anything vital from your current inspection here?" Colonel Hooe managed somehow to remain genial while injecting doubt into his question.

"Nothing, unfortunately. There does not appear to be anything to find, as General Washington has informed me previously." Mr. Cockburn turned toward the river, looking up and down the bank. "I cannot see any reason for the body's being in the river other than that someone put it there, I am forced to agree with General Washington on that. Beyond that I have no opinion yet on the event." Mr. Cockburn looked at the General without expression. "You are doubtless aware of the laws, sir, on killing of slaves. The Act of 1669 is quite clear that killing a disobedient slave does not require assumption of prepended malice. Therefore, should disobedience be the situation, we might dispense with the legalities around murder. Are you certain that none of your men are responsible? They may simply say so and have no expectation of punishment should the man have been disobedient."

I was reminded of tales of the Devil tempting man with easy roads to happiness. Mr. Cockburn did not much resemble the Devil, and his tempting reward was not delivered in a voice likely to sway the General, who again frowned and delivered the same response.

"As I told you before, sir, I have had their assurances, and they are well aware of the laws."

"I suppose, technically, your slave Julius had not actually left the plantation, just that part of it for which he was responsible. Therefore, the legal status would not say that he was away without leave, hence disobeying. There would need to be some other factor to justify invoking the 1669 Act, I would think."

"Yes." The General regarded him calmly, still frowning. "Again, I doubt anyone here was responsible. Although Julius was apparently not well liked by his fellows or his masters, he was a reasonably diligent and respected overseer and did his work well." The General then described our foray to Dogue Run and the Grist Mill and the information, such as it was, that we had garnered during the morning.

Colonel Hooe said, "Missing flour, eh? Explains why I haven't seen your latest shipment yet in our warehouse, I suppose, Your Excellency?"

"Possibly, I will look into that with Mr. Davenport."

Colonel Hooe nodded. "Let my clerk, Mr. Williamson, know what to expect. We will hope for the best. Now, how shall we proceed, Mr. Cockburn?"

"I think at this point there's no need for my continued involvement, I will leave further investigation of the affair to you, sir, and then I will take all the information and decide how to proceed legally. Please report in full detail as soon as you are satisfied you have all possible information. Your Excellency, may we examine your people at Dogue Run?"

The General's face resumed its normally calm expression, and he replied, "By all means. I will inform the new overseer and Mr. Davenport that Colonel Hooe or his deputy may be stopping by. My people will of course be at work in the fields during the week, but I give you leave to speak with them as needed, Colonel Hooe."

Mr. Cockburn shook Colonel Hooe's hand and said,"Very well. Then I will take my leave." He bowed to us and walked off up the hill with little more ado. The General looked after him with arms folded and his most austere face.

8

SUNDAY, MARCH 1, 1789, AFTERNOON

The General led us all back up the path to the Mansion House. When he saw Mr. Fairfax near the stables, he stopped to ask him to organize the burying of the body in the slave graveyard down the hill after the Coroner's jury had completed their inspection of it. He then turned to Colonel Hooe.

"As long as you are here, Colonel Hooe, perhaps I can entice you to stay to dinner? I'm sure Mrs. Washington would be more than happy to see you; it is always a pleasure when you dine with us."

"Thank you, sir, I accept with pleasure, as Mr. Cockburn will not be there." Colonel Hooe smiled, looking after the rapidly disappearing magistrate's coach. "A bit of heavy going, there, eh? May I request that Williamson be allowed to join us? He is waiting in the house, we were just going out on a merchant errand when your man Lear rode up with his urgent notice, so Williamson came with me."

"Yes, certainly. I will inform Mrs. Washington of the happy addition to our family party."

After the General gave instructions for the stabling of Colonel Hooe's team and coach, we went into the house in search of its mistress. We found Mr. Williamson waiting patiently in a chair in the passage. Mrs. Washington was in the little parlor toward the back of the house with her two young charges, her grandchildren Nellie and Wash, along with Mrs. George Augustine Washington—the beautiful Fanny, if I might be so forward as to say so—and Mr. Lear, who was keeping them all company as they worked on their sewing. A fire burned in the fireplace. This was the family scene complete. Mrs. Washington looked up as the General entered, and said, "Is Colonel Hooe staying to dinner, Mr. Washington?"

"Yes, indeed he is, my dear. Along with his young clerk, John Williamson, whom I do not believe you have met." Mr. Williamson bowed.

Mrs. Washington smiled and said, "Very pleased to meet you, Mr. Williamson, and welcome to our house and table. Mr. Washington, I have already informed the cooks. I saw the carriages out of the parlor window, and I was quite sure there would be additional people at dinner today."

The General smiled in turn and nodded, then turned to me.

"Colonel Humphreys, while I dress for dinner, would you be so kind as to entertain Colonel Hooe and Mr. Williamson? While the Colonel is quite familiar with the house, I'm sure it will be of interest to Mr. Williamson, so I will show them around once I have dressed. Thank you." The General excused himself.

We gathered together in the central passage, and Colonel Hooe brought Mr. Williamson up to date on the murder, as the clerk was to be the primary investigator for Colonel Hooe. Once the Colonel had laid out the meager details, we turned to his real interests. Colonel Hooe was full of the doings of the Alexandria and Georgetown merchant crowd and full of misgivings about the state of trade, as the British were still being "bloody cats" as he put it. Mr. Williamson said little, but I noticed that his eyes were everywhere, making the most of this new opportunity to see how the great General lived.

During my long stays at Mount Vernon, I had seen similar reactions from the countless visitors that the household entertained. I think every American—indeed, every European—wanted to share the General's greatness. Being from Connecticut, where we Yankees tended toward parsimony, I was often astounded at the patience and generosity of the General and his wife at the innumerable people of all stations that descended on them without warning. The General informed me that Virginians regarded it as a sacred duty to offer hospitality to all that came by, no matter the cost or inconvenience.

The General's popularity magnified that duty beyond all reason, in my opinion, but there was no stinting in that house. And, indeed, the General and Mrs. Washington took no inconsiderable pleasure in accommodating the multitudes. Mrs. Washington's foresight and pleasure in ordering more dinner was not really surprising; the Washingtons had guests at dinner more often than not, sometimes every day of the week. Colonel Hooe was in fact a frequent visitor. It made for a lively social environment, despite the General's professed desire for peace and retirement.

"Sir," said Mr. Williamson, breaking into my reverie, "Perhaps it would not be too much to ask to see General Washington's study? As a clerk, the daily routine of the office is of great interest to me, and I would greatly appreciate the opportunity to see how the General organizes his matters of business."

I nodded and responded, "Certainly, sir, although it is not usual, I'm sure the General won't mind a brief look once he is done dressing there." Frank Lee went off to ask the General whether he would agree to the request. A few minutes later, Frank returned to say the General would be pleased to show the guests his private study himself. Frank conducted us all through the dining room and into the study, where the General awaited us with a welcoming smile.

Colonel Hooe was quite impressed with the study, with its glass-lined bookshelves and wood trim. He had never been admitted to this inner sanctum before. "A very nice, workmanlike room," he said. "One in which it would be a pleasure to spend all one's time. Do you perform all your business here, Your Excellency?"

"Yes, it is my headquarters complete," replied the General. "As on any farm, however, the real work is in the fields, where I spend a good deal of my time. Here is money, culture, and politics; there is the staff of life and the work to bring it to fruition."

Mr. Williamson walked around the room, carefully examining the library, then the desk and open account books. He made no comment, but his eyes were alight with the professional interest of an accounts keeper. After explaining the origin of the various items scattered around the room and extolling the virtues of a good private library, the General ushered us out through the dining room, across to the front parlor, and through that into the new dining room.

The General completed the New Room soon before my own visit began in 1787, and both the General and Mrs. Washington took a great deal of pride in the appointments of the room. A high, two-story ceiling, a large, elegant marble mantelpiece, and well-appointed furnishings and draperies provided a very elegant room for entertaining large numbers of guests for dinner and other social occasions.

The two gentlemen inspected the room and its furnishings with appreciation, Colonel Hooe admiring the mantelpiece and noting that the sideboards were just as he would have wished his own to be. Mr. Williamson simply looked at everything with interest but in silence.

The General commented, "I felt the house deserved an elegant space for entertaining, which it lacked. Once started, it was only right to appoint the room in the correct manner. I am quite satisfied with the result, sir, though it has been the work of many years."

We went out the back door onto the piazza and into the winter sun, with both men admiring the wonderful view of the hanging wood and the Potomac slowly flowing by. The General stood with his hands behind his back, looking at the river.

Turning to the General, Colonel Hooe said, "I must say, Your

Excellency, that the Mansion House is fully worthy of your residence in it!"

The General replied, "I have always felt it necessary to provide my family and guests with everything good and proper, sir. Whether I am worthy of such opulence I will leave it to others to determine. My intention is but to be happy here in my retirement."

Colonel Hooe shook his head. "As your retirement will soon be cut short by assuming the Presidency, Your Excellency, I suggest you enjoy it while you can."

The General was silent for a moment at this brutal attack on his happiness, then replied, "The uncertainties of New York or Philadelphia, and the large responsibilities of the position, make it very difficult for me to view the Presidency with anything but discontent. I have not yet decided whether to accept the offer, should the electors make it. I am quite undecided whether it would be a good or an evil. When I resigned my commission, I pledged to withdraw from public life, and I feel myself unqualified for the job. I am not persuaded that accepting the position is the correct course to take."

Colonel Hooe was shocked. "Indeed, sir, can there be any question? There is no one so well suited as yourself." He looked around at all of us, then continued, "You must accept, Your Excellency, the nation depends upon it."

The General looked at me, smiled wearily, and shook his head in dismay. I had been harping on this theme every day for the last year. I bowed, and excused myself to run up to my room to dress for dinner, leaving the others to admire the stunning, sunlit view of the icy river.

9

SUNDAY, MARCH 1, 1789, MID-AFTERNOON (DINNER TIME)

Mrs. Washington and the cooks had produced their usual wonderful repast: roast pork, roast goose, poached fish, cabbage, potatoes, pickles, and tripe. The General took his usual small plate of fish and glass of Madeira as the rest of us enjoyed the abundance. The family was all present at table: Mrs. Washington's two grandchildren, Nellie and Wash, and Major Washington and his wife Fanny. Mr. Lear and I joined the two guests, Colonel Hooe and Mr. Williamson, to round out the table.

The General usually played the role of genial host, but today he seemed preoccupied. I suspected that the events of the day were weighing on him. His wife, nephew, and niece, well attuned to his moods, perceived immediately that he was not quite himself. Of course, the murder was disallowed as a topic at dinner, so they could not directly address his concern with that event.

Mrs. Fanny Washington was the first to attempt to distract him.

"Oh, Uncle, the funniest thing happened today while I was walking in the garden, right after breakfast. Gardener was working away, planting some new bulbs I think, when what do you think happened?"

"I am sure to guess wrongly, my dear."

"Well, in ran two little Negro children from the quarters, a boy and girl, one chasing the other, both laughing as merrily as anything you ever heard! Around and around they ran. Finally, the girl ran by Gardener, who was kneeling down so she couldn't see him, and what do you think? She ran straight into his leg and went flying!"

"I hope the little one was not injured?"

"Oh no sir, not in the least! I think it was Gardener who was most surprised. When he saw what had happened though, he looked at me and smiled, then went to help the little child back to her feet and told her to be more careful. I was afraid for a moment he would scold them for being in the garden while I was there, but I made sure to smile and make everything all right."

Little Nellie said, "I never run in the garden even if Wash chases me, Grandmama doesn't like it."

Mrs. Washington smiled. "That is right, darling, perfectly right."

The General smiled as well. "And just where do you run when Wash chases you?"

Nellie realized that she was in deep water here, so she smiled bashfully. "I do not run at all, I tell him to stop, sir."

"And does he?"

At this point, Wash could not contain himself. "Never would chase such a silly little thing!"

Everyone laughed heartily at this avowal. The General then returned to his former gravity. Mrs. Fanny Washington began speaking in a quiet undertone to Mr. Lear, who was seated next to her. She laughed quietly at something he was telling her. Her husband, who was looking somewhat ill, interrupted them in a whisper. Fanny looked distressed, then nodded. Major Washington arose.

He said, "I fear I am somewhat under the weather this evening and must retire. I am very sorry, Aunt."

Mrs. Washington replied, "You just take care of yourself, dear. I will have the cook send up some broth later if you like."

Major Washington nodded, then bowed slightly and left the room. The poor man had been ailing for some time, probably with consumption. The General looked after him with dismay and set down his glass of madeira, untouched. His nephew was a favored member of the family. I understood that the General had made him the heir to Mount Vernon in his latest will. I wondered briefly what the General would do should Major Washington die suddenly; but this was also something we would not discuss at dinner. Mr. Lear and Mrs. Fanny Washington resumed their whispered conversation, which I thought to be a bit out of place, as did Mrs. Washington.

She cleared her throat. "Mr. Lear," she said, "Perhaps you could relate the story you were telling us the other evening? I daresay it would entertain the General."

Mr. Lear, embarrassed, nodded, and began.

"Well. Let me see. Yes, I think I remember the tale. Mrs. Fanny Washington had asked me about my good friend, General Benjamin Lincoln, and his experiences during the War. I was at Harvard at the time, of course, with his son, not with him in the War."

I smiled at Mrs. Fanny Washington, who grinned back at me with warmth. I was, of course, a Yale man, and as anyone will tell you, Yale men tell better stories than Harvard men. Especially about the War; and especially because Mr. Lear had not participated in the War while pursuing his education at Harvard, while I had seen plenty of action. I resolved to tell a few of my own stories to Mrs. Fanny to relieve her from the odious attentions of Mr. Lear.

The General was all attention to Mr. Lear, as he was quite familiar with General Lincoln's career and corresponded with him from time to time. My own interaction with General Lincoln came during the fearful time of Shays's Rebellion in 1787, the consequences of which led directly to our new Constitution. Perhaps that might be a good story with which to start with Mrs. Fanny. I turned my attention to Mr. Lear, however.

He began. "It was in 1780, I think." The General closed his eyes, shaking his head, remembering the unfortunate events of that year in the Southern Department, the Army designation for the Southern States of Virginia, North and South Carolina, and Georgia. Mr. Lear continued. "General Lincoln was in Charleston, South Carolina, with his army of fourteen hundred Continentals and a thousand more unreliable Southern militiamen. Having just learned of the approach of the British General Clinton's force of eight thousand seasoned British troops on 163 ships, General Lincoln politely requested reinforcements from Congress and the Southern States. He received back refusals to supply troops. He also received a Frenchman, the Chevalier de Laumoy, adept at engineering defense works."

The General smiled and added, "And a frantic emissary from my headquarters, John Laurens, proposing to enlist as many Negroes as could be, with pay and the promise of freedom."

Mr. Lear grinned. "Yes, sir; with the predictable result: the South Carolina legislature resolutely refused to entertain the idea. Now, Monsieur de Laumoy looked over the defenses of Charleston and came up with a wonderful plan of works that would protect the town. He told General Lincoln it would take sixteen hundred men to build it. General Lincoln looked around and decided he could not spare so many, so he requisitioned six hundred slaves and as many Continental troops as he could spare from other duties. The Southern militiamen refused to participate, as they could not envision themselves doing the work of slaves. On hearing this, General Lincoln, who was at the time suffering from a recurring fever and a suppurating war wound in his leg, rolled up his sleeves and starting working on the parapet walls alongside the slaves in the hope of persuading some of the militia to join in. Many did, but while they completed the works, they weren't enough to stop the British, unfortunately."

"And General Lincoln was forced to defend Charleston in the face of the British Navy sailing through his defenses. Yes, I remember the day clearly that I received his news." The General shook his head. "The picture of poor General Lincoln toiling away has stayed with me. I did not join with those who disparaged him after his surrender, Mr. Lear. He performed miracles with what he had." The General looked around at us and continued, "It was on his recommendation, of course, that I hired Mr. Lear. That alone certainly justifies admiration on my part." He nodded at Mr. Lear, who smirked in acknowledgement of the compliment. The man was a bit full of himself, it seemed to me.

Colonel Hooe said, "My own clerk, Mr. Williamson here, came to me on a similar recommendation, and I too have nothing but admiration for him and his work!" Mr. Williamson blushed and nodded his thanks. I had noticed that Mr. Williamson had drunk but little during the dinner, while his master had sampled the General's claret extensively. The Colonel had become progressively more merry and congenial as dinner had progressed.

"By the way, Your Excellency," continued Colonel Hooe, "to return to the topic we earlier canvassed, I should think it will be soon that the country notifies you of your election."

Mrs. Washington's lips were pressed tight; she did not enjoy conversing on the subject. Her peaceful days at home in Virginia would soon end should the General decide to accept the Presidency, as she would become the first lady of the land. The General, well aware of his wife's displeasure, without further response turned the subject to horses and hunting, to spare Mrs. Washington further distress on the subject. Colonel Hooe, for whom a wink was as good as a nod, did not seem to mind the quick change of topic, though Mrs. Fanny Washington seemed disappointed. She was not a horsewoman and had little to contribute, while the General's future was of great interest to her and her husband, as they would be in charge of Mount Vernon when the General was away. She resumed her quiet conversation with Mr. Lear, which seemed to cheer her up.

We finished our puddings, and Mrs. Washington arose to withdraw along with Mrs. Fanny Washington and the children.

"Mr. Washington, we will leave you gentlemen alone to discuss the business of the day. Colonel Hooe, please convey my regards to your wife, and please do not hesitate to dine with us whenever you like."

"Thank you, ma'am," replied the Colonel. "You are most gracious."

The ladies withdrew, and the Colonel turned to the General and said, "I must say, Your Excellency, I admire your family exceedingly. My own family seems all eaten up by the hustle and bustle of Alexandria in comparison."

"Yes, Colonel, it is indeed one of my joys in life to be blessed with an excellent family in a well-run, quiet home. Despite the trials and tribulations of daily family life, I have nothing but affection for them all."

Those trials and tribulations ran like undercurrents in the river of life at the Mansion House. I saw from the set of the General's face that he was perfectly aware of the undercurrents but wished to appear complacent and to stay on the surface to his guests. I knew the General had done everything in his power to ensure the happiness and prosperity of his family. I also knew of his ongoing concern that, especially if he became President, it might be out of his power to do much more.

10

SUNDAY, MARCH 1, 1789, LATE AFTERNOON

In the course of ordinary life, gentlemen have the right of privacy in their talk at the dining table after the women withdraw. Looking back on that afternoon, however, subsequent events override ordinary manners, and I will therefore relate the conversation in full. At the time, I took an interest only as a guest. Later events would involve me in these affairs of business as a participant and would prove of vital importance in understanding the full scope of the affair. The account I have made of our dinner with the family may have you believe all was easy and good; nothing could be farther from the truth. The affairs of business and politics I relate now must demonstrate the challenges and frustrations the General faced at that time.

Of course, the first topic broached once the ladies withdrew was the murder and its investigation.

"What are your next steps to investigate the murder, Colonel?" asked the General.

Colonel Hooe replied, "Well, Your Excellency, my next step is to turn the matter entirely over to Mr. Williamson, who is a much more capable investigator than I." He nodded toward his clerk and took a healthy draught of port. Mr. Williamson nodded and moved his own glass from one side of his place to the other.

The General nodded. "Very well. Mr. Williamson, I give my permission to you to question anyone necessary. However, I want to be sure you realize the importance of this investigation to me." The

General fixed his eyes on Mr. Williamson, commanding his attention. The young man sat up sharply and looking directly at the General, readied himself to take his orders.

"My first concern is simple justice. The murder of any man requires it. In this case, the man is my property as well. I do not require personal recompense for the crime, but I do require that whoever murdered my man must hang for it. And that sooner rather than later." The General's face took on that austere quality that meant he was deadly serious.

"Yes, Your Excellency. I am very sure we will hang the man responsible." Mr. Williamson's voice was low but firm as he confirmed his understanding of the General's concerns, and his eyes never left the General's.

The General added, "It appears to me that this murder and the chaos on my plantation will have a direct impact on my ability to respond to any invitation to become President, as my reputation for competence and integrity will vanish."

Colonel Hooe looked surprised. He said, "Williamson will make this investigation his top priority, I do assure you, Your Excellency. We will have justice."

"Yes, sir," said Mr. Williamson, glancing at his superior. "I will start first thing in the morning." He moved his port glass back to the other side of his place. I thought, from their manner, that both gentlemen seemed overly complacent about the crime.

The General, whatever his private reservations, nodded and smiled. "Very well, gentlemen, that should suffice." He relaxed and changed the subject. "Let us move to business. You know, Colonel, that we farmers are all distressed for cash, and the prices we are getting for our crops are little better than under the British. We are, indeed, at a crisis point in trade. Perhaps I can pick your brain on tobacco and other product prices in Alexandria? I understand that upstate shortages coming through Georgetown may increase the prices we might receive on our shipments here."

Colonel Hooe shook his head. "I have heard that the British government is being quite obstructive on trade terms, sir. Your higher prices will be all eaten up in carrying charges and duties. The British have always made sure our money flows into their pockets!"

The General responded, "I had thought to address these problems by promoting local trade here, but we are still very dependent on British commerce. With a stronger federal government, that may now change, but for now we still depend far too much on trade directed by British politics rather than by American needs."

"Yes, sir. My own trade suffers greatly from it. We all depend on your leadership as President of the Potomac Company to open up the Mississippi and Ohio to our Potomac trade. Making the upper reaches navigable will put paid to the British choking our trade through the Bay!"

"I am very grateful for that support indeed, Colonel," replied the General, smiling. "I am not sure the sentiment extends far enough to ensure the success of the project, particularly in Alexandria. I can detect some political factionalism behind this unwillingness to expand trade; it is otherwise inexplicable to me." He shook his head.

"As you know, sir," replied Colonel Hooe, "the town professes federalism down to the last man. No miscreant would dare to criticize the new Constitution on pain of a black, feathered coat."

"Indeed, I am happy to hear that, though I have my doubts," said the General. "The ratification last year of our new Constitution has made a difference in the neighborhood, but full support still seems uncertain."

"I must say, sir, I agree," replied the Colonel, contradicting himself. "Mr. Patrick Henry along with Colonel George Mason and his crowd are still stirring up trouble whenever an opportunity presents itself, as you know, and they are no friends to us merchants. It will be a relief when you take up the Presidency, sir!"

"*If* I do, sir," rejoined the General, "we must see what can be done with the Congress to promote trade more effectively."

"Again I say, nonsense, sir, you *must* decide for the Presidency!" Colonel Hooe was adamant. "If nothing else, our trade depends upon it, and upon you!"

The General leaned back in his chair and contemplated his glass. "I must decide, yes; but for or against—that is not yet clear to me. Certainly I see nothing but an ocean of frustration pounding me on all fronts, sir. Family, farm, business, politics, all seem to conspire to wash me out of retirement into public duty despite my disinclination." He drank off the madeira, and a servant refilled his glass from the decanter. The General seemed quite embarrassed at his own vehemence on the topic and desirous of changing it. He was not a man to suffer frustration happily, despite his stoic philosophy of life, but he did not like it when he showed his emotion to others.

Mr. Williamson excused himself at this point and went out to the passage, presumably to visit the necessary out by the garden. I contemplated telling a story to ease the General's emotion but never got the chance. Colonel Hooe took the opportunity to say again how much Mr. Williamson had added to his business since he was hired the year before.

"Indeed, I do not think I could adequately perform my duties as Sheriff without his assistance in both businesses. A God-send for me. I am sure he will get to the bottom of the current problem for you, removing at least one source of frustration, Your Excellency."

That led the General into another source of frustration, I fear. "And very much to your credit that you hired him, I'm sure," said the General, frowning. "One of my constant tribulations in running a plantation is the hiring of good men—carpenters, gardeners, and managers in particular. I have an excellent private secretary in Mr.

Lear and an excellent plantation manager in my nephew, Major Washington. Mr. Fairfax is proving himself as he learns the business of the Mansion House farm and is doing well. But I face difficulties in filling most other positions and frustration once I have filled them."

The General turned to me. "By the way, Colonel Humphreys, I have spoken with Mr. Fairfax about returning Morris as overseer at Dogue Run; Julius replaced him last year so that he could work with Mr. Fairfax here at the Mansion House. Mr. Fairfax, at least, can be counted on in an emergence such as this."

The door to the pantry opened, and Williamson unexpectedly reentered the room through that door, guided by the butler, Frank Lee, who then closed the door behind him. With a blush and an apologetic smile, Williamson resumed his seat without saying a word.

Colonel Hooe said, "Williamson, I was just telling the General how well I am served, and for God's sake man don't blush. "

As the hour was getting late, and the guests needed to return to Alexandria, we finished our drinks and sent for the carriage. I noticed that Mr. Williamson had not drunk any of his port; abstemious beyond reason, I thought. Mr. Lear disappeared in the direction of the parlor to join the ladies. Colonel Hooe reassured the General that Williamson would take all appropriate measures with respect to the murder on the morrow and that he would let the General know as events developed. Our guests took their leave, and the General and I watched their carriage roll off. The General disappeared into his study.

As I walked back into the passage, Frank stopped me to whisper, "Colonel Humphreys, I just thought you should know that the gentleman from Alexandria missed his way earlier. I found him lost in the General's study, looking for the dining room. I showed him the dining room door and brought him in."

"Thank you, Frank. I suppose Mr. Williamson came in from the necessary through the wrong door and failed to understand where he was."

"Yes sir, that's what I thought too, but I figured I'd better tell you about it." He paused. "If you don't mind my saying, sir, that gentleman don't seem to be entirely sure where his feet are. You understand?"

"I do agree, thank you, Frank." The butler then walked off to help with the clearing of the dinner table. They carried off Williamson's untouched port, doubtless destined for enjoyment in the quarters. I smiled to myself to think of Williamson's embarrassment at the social faux pas, so evident on his face as he reentered the dining room unexpectedly from his trip to the necessary. I began to have some doubt about Williamson's investigative abilities if he could not find the way from the necessary to the dining room in broad daylight. He did not even have the excuse of having drunk his portion of port.

I considered joining Mr. Lear and the ladies, but alas, I was due at my evening session with the General; his history and biography must take precedence over social dalliance. I would not lose any real pleasure, however, as I greatly enjoyed my discussions with the General on his past. As I went along to the study, I gave a thought to the ill Major Washington and what would happen on this plantation should he die prematurely. The General's situation at Mount Vernon was likely to give him pain, one way or another. The complexity of the public world he would confront as President would give him more pain. And yet, the country required that he endure that pain for the common good. Sadness and regret for his fate filled me as I contemplated the frustration he must endure in fulfilling the hopes of the nation.

11

SUNDAY, MARCH 1, 1789, EARLY EVENING

In his study, the General's somber mood so evident at dinner had returned. Tonight, he was interested in the Presidency, looking forward by looking backward.

As I took my seat by the fire, he said, "Colonel Hooe's insistence on my accepting the Presidency has shown me that it is more vital than ever to gather all the information and advice at my disposal. It will not be an easy decision. I must thread my way through many arguments to arrive at an honorable decision. Here," he said, walking to his desk and handing me a letter he lifted from it, "is your very kind letter of advice from 1787 regarding the Constitutional Convention. I was this very morning reviewing it to have it fresh in my mind for our daily talk. The to-do over the murder of Julius interrupted that perusal, but I think we may resume now." He sat in his own chair and moodily watched the crackling fire.

I glanced through the letter, my own handwriting and flawless logic reminding me that every man has days when his stupidity eclipses his genius. In my case, it was the day I took my pen and wrote this carefully reasoned letter of advice to my friend and benefactor on the subject of the Constitutional Convention. Advice, I may say, that had he taken, we would now be residents of the small nations of Virginia and Connecticut. I had insisted the chaos in the country was so severe, and the conflicts between parties so fierce, that nothing he did would help, and that he would damage his reputation irretrievably by associating himself with the attempt to change the government through a new Constitution. Oh my Lord, I thought to myself: how wrong had I been.

The General, on seeing me look up from my letter, said, "Mr. Lear's anecdote at dinner about his uncle has reminded me of some other past events in which General Lincoln participated. I wish to go back with you over those events and their dramatic consequences, as they directly impact my decision on the Presidency."

I groaned. "Captain Shays."

He smiled a grim smile. "Indeed, Captain Shays. But let us first consider the issue of my withdrawal from public life at the end of the War. I sent a circular letter to all the states to communicate my intention to resign my commission as Commander-in-Chief and my promise to withdraw from public life. And you were there, Colonel, in Annapolis when I fulfilled that promise and reiterated it to Congress in 1783."

"Yes, sir, I remember it well. Cincinattus personified! But, Your Excellency, the situation we face is now so very different." Listening to the General's calm summary of his early commitment to retire like that quintessentially virtuous Roman general, I felt the hot fear growing in my breast: that he would refuse the Presidency. That could not, must not happen. I stared into the fire, the crackling sparks exploding into showers of heated conflict, but only in my mind.

The General, calm as ever, replied, "Indeed, the world has changed completely. And yet, I made the promise."

"I believe strongly, having spoken with many public men, that no one in this country wishes to hold you to that promise—very much the opposite."

"That is the advice I have received from my other correspondents—Colonel Hamilton, for example, was quite warm on the matter. The man twists it around—he thinks that just by having led the creation of the Constitution, I am in fact pledged to take part in the creation of the government. And yet, I made the promise."

I could see that the General felt the barrier of his word and honor, and I searched my mind for ways to overcome it. There were few things more important to the General than his honor and his word. But I felt the fear growing.

"I will fall back on duty, Your Excellency—public duty. I cannot feel quite as Colonel Hamilton does about a pledge being made, as you did not make it but remained silent. I think the situation does require your participation. When considering men to lead us forward under the new Constitution, who is there beyond yourself? Mr. Patrick Henry, the famed orator, whose leadership is just words, and words that are strongly against the new Constitution? Mr. John Adams, whom everyone respects and no one likes? Governor Clinton of New York, who leads the antifederalist faction and nearly destroyed the chances for creating the new government through his machinations about the Convention? That would be truly putting the fox into the henhouse, sir. There is only yourself."

"Very well argued, Colonel. And yet. Surely any of those men or an as-yet-unknown gentleman with a strong sense of public duty might lead as well as I. But then, there is my retirement itself to consider."

"As we have seen today, sir." I smiled, remembering the dinner conversations that demonstrated the General's affection for his family life and his strong attachment to his farm. "When I wrote that letter two years ago, I was very sensible of the universal desire among your acquaintance that you would have some peace in your life. The Good Lord knows you have had enough trouble and battle in that life to account for several lifetimes of service to your country. I remember that as we rode from Annapolis to Mount Vernon after your resignation in 1783, I could see how much pleasure you took in being again a gentleman farmer, and during my visit with you then, and the visits later, I have seen how you have grown into your retirement. As your friend, I have every desire that you should remain at peace. As an American, I know you cannot." My voice failed me for a moment. "I am very sorry to have to say it, sir. I know you will feel regret for it, but I know deep in my heart that you cannot remain at peace. I despair for the country if you do not take on this burden."

The General said, "A pretty speech indeed. You are an excellent friend to me, Colonel, and I am sorry that the Union has put you in the position of expressing an opinion that gives you pain. Yes; I will admit to a good deal of pain myself in such considerations. Am I to put aside all this," he waved a hand in the air to indicate Mount Vernon and his life of peace, "for a life that promises little but trouble and endless toil? But I do acknowledge the public duty, and I will consider it. What about the British influence, Colonel? There were always rumors...."

"British or Tory influence might have sowed some of this discord in Massachusetts. Sir Guy Carleton, or Lord Dorchester as he now styles himself, no friend to America, had become the chief Governor of Canada. I am sure that he did everything he could to disrupt the peace treaty he had so opposed. Rumors abounded of secret meetings in taverns and so forth, but nothing ever came to hand to prove such influence as far as I am aware. The rebels always denied it. Still, the possibility of a malign British influence is ever present."

"Mrs. Washington would certainly think so. You may recall that, during the War, British ships anchored in the Potomac off the Landing," he said, pointing out the window to the river. "It took Colonel Mason's persuasion to get her to leave Mount Vernon for her own safety, but she stayed away for only a day, and the danger passed. The British do seem to have a never-ending ability to interfere in our lives, whether we are at war or at peace with them. Putting the British aside, there remains the issue of my reputation, which is showing serious signs of disrepair."

"How can you say so, sir?"

"Any man in public life understands the fragility of reputation. A man with my experience understands the importance of it—you cannot get anything done without reputation. You might think that position would guarantee results. I found that, as Commander-in-Chief of the Continental forces, my every action was challenged and debated. No man, especially in these new United States, has the final say just as a result of the power of his position. In fact, with the new Constitution, the separation of powers renders such power as a King has obsolete in this country. What remains? Reputation and the character on which it is based. It is the only way to persuade people to their duty. I fear its loss more than anything."

"Every passing day renders such a loss more improbable, Your Excellency. Your reputation now can move mountains!"

"Perhaps, yet I see only fragility. A slave murdered on my plantation, mismanagement everywhere, constant political attacks from antifederalists such as Colonel Mason and Mr. Patrick Henry— neighbors, mind you, not just politicians. I cannot long maintain a character destined for strong leadership if I cannot even lead my people on my own plantation. These republican mountains may choose not to move for me."

"I do see that, sir, but I am confident that Colonel Hooe and Mr. Williamson will find the truth."

"I wish I were as sanguine."

"A very few days will see the result of their investigations, and we can spend those days working with Major Washington and Mr. Fairfax to bring the management of the plantation better under control."

"So much for peaceful retirement," said the General with a rueful smile. "Well, Colonel Hamilton also feels strongly that, were I to decline the Presidency, my reputation would suffer from *that*. Joined to the damage from an unsolved murder and a plantation in chaos, I can only conclude it would finish me entirely."

"It is all very well to joke, sir. I must also say, in all seriousness, that I believe your character to be stronger than you may think. When I wrote my letter, I feared you would damage your reputation with some part or other of the public, or that the assemblies and bulk of the people would simply ignore you, as they did when you were Commander-in-Chief. I was wrong about that. You served as the President of the Convention and used your reputation and character well to marshal those very disputatious men into a semblance of order to produce the new Constitution."

"And very hard work it was, too. I sat upon the dais looking down on everyone with a stern face, saying nothing, and it seemed enough. How hard it was to do nothing! How hard would it be should even doing nothing constitute a pledge to abandon everything I value in my life here."

"The ratification of that Constitution came about because everyone knew that you would be the first President and would make it work. I doubt not that ratification would have failed had you not been a constant presence in everyone's mind."

"I am as susceptible to flattery as the next man, but I think that will suffice for this evening, Colonel. Again, thank you for your friendship. We will see what the morning brings."

"I think, sir, you must also consider the alternative to your becoming President, and recollect the events that were occurring even as I wrote my letter."

"Ah, yes. The Rebellion."

"I think that the causes and consequences of Shays's rebellion are still very relevant. You know they led directly to the success of the Constitutional Convention. Those causes have not yet resolved in our new nation, and without your leadership, we could yet see more conflict. As I said in my letter, if men will not have the wisdom to govern themselves, it is in vain to compel them to be happy and free contrary to their inclination."

"Let us review those events in detail. Would you be so kind, sir, as to find Mr. Lear? I think he may add insight to our discussion on this."

"Certainly, sir." I went out through the dining room to the passage, and hearing Mr. Lear's mellifluous voice, went into the little parlor. He was sitting with Mrs. Fanny Washington and reading to her and Mrs. Martha Washington from Shakespeare—*A Midsummer Night's Dream,* to be specific. Puck, loose among the fairies.

I said, "I am loathe to interrupt your entertainment, ladies, but the General needs Mr. Lear for a time."

"Pardon me, ladies; I will return and resume our entertainment as soon as possible." He bowed to the ladies, then came with me. We entered the study to find the General seated at his desk.

"Mr. Lear, I wish you to take part in a conversation that the Colonel and I are about to undertake. We are to discuss Shays's Rebellion. Could you find a copy of General Lincoln's letter, please? You know the one."

Lear found the letter in a copy-book and handed it to the General. The General scanned it, then said, "Thank you, Mr. Lear. Now, please get yourself a glass of madeira, if you will, and pull up a chair to join us around the fire."

After we had all resumed our seats, the General tapped the letter in his hand. "Colonel, I believe you have not seen this letter from General Benjamin Lincoln about the Shays affair."

"No, sir, I have not."

"It is a most complete summary of events in Massachusetts from late 1786 through the end of the rebellion. To my way of thinking, we are perhaps not in so different a place with a Constitution as we were with a Confederation, and that weighs heavily on my mind when I think about the Presidency. Shays's Rebellion illustrates that."

12

SUNDAY, MARCH 1, 1789, EARLY EVENING

The General asked me, "Why, in your opinion, Colonel, did Captain Shays and his troublesome yeoman farmers become such a thorn in the side of the government?"

I replied, "It was rather the reverse, Your Excellency: the government had become a thorn in *their* side, or worse. The Massachusetts government at that time was nearly all men from Boston or other trading towns on the coast. They were merchants, and they owed massive debts to creditors in Britain."

"Those debts are yet another tie to a Britain that we all thought we had cut."

"Yes, sir. The British flooded our markets with goods after the War, making it that much harder for our own merchants to succeed in paying off their debts. The Massachusetts legislature itself had War debt. The Confederation government, having no money and no power, was completely unable to help them pay it. You know the result."

"Taxes."

"Yes, Your Excellency. But being men of substance and power, and having their own debts, the legislature dominated by merchants decided that the farmers should pay off the government debt. They imposed and enforced those taxes ruthlessly. The farmers did command a few legislators from their counties, and those legislators responded with attempts to create a new paper currency."

The General nodded. "But that debt required payment, having been incurred in good faith. And we all know what happens to paper currency—it devalues immediately. That is good for debtors but only through magicking away the debt through financial means. If you lend someone a dollar, and a dollar becomes worth only a shadow of itself, the money you lent disappears."

"Yes, sir. The yeoman farmers had their own debts. Most men had gone away to war and financed their long absence from their farms with loans—from the merchants of the East, of course. So those merchants decided at the same time to collect and enforce that collection ruthlessly, to better be able to pay their own debts—and devaluing the currency would not help them, so they simply refused currency as payment, requiring coin. Then the farmers tried to change the legal tender laws to force them to accept currency, and the legislature rather ruthlessly refused."

"You seem to like the word 'ruthless,' Colonel." Mr. Lear smiled. "Was the debt not owed?"

"Certainly, sir, I meant nothing more than that the legislature did not design its actions to help the situation. I certainly regard it as a moral duty to pay one's debts. Nevertheless, the farmers became distressed for money, and unfortunately not all of them were as nice as you and I. These men were levelers, not just simple farmers responding to tyranny. They took up arms to forward their interests, not to help others."

The General had assumed his austere expression and drummed frustrated fingers on the arm of his chair and expressed his greatest fear. "They were indeed levelers. And many of their interests have not changed since. What they then did they may do again."

"Yes, Your Excellency. They formed a rump militia of their own armed with pitchforks and muskets and descended on the Courts of Common Pleas that were enforcing the debts, in many cases running off the judges."

"A frightful prospect for a new country, Colonel," said Mr. Lear. The General nodded his agreement with this opinion.

I continued, "It became more than frightful when the Massachusetts governor heard rumors that the farmers were moving on the federal arsenal at Springfield, Massachusetts. They styled themselves 'The Regulators,' a name they misappropriated from a group of patriots in North Carolina before the War. Armed with the weapons from the arsenal—rifles, pikes, and artillery—they would be more than a thorn. The Confederation government then failed again by failing to send troops to protect its own arms."

"And that is when my good friend formed his army!" cried Mr. Lear, clapping his hands sharply.

"His—militia, yes, sir." I held the letter up and read aloud from General Lincoln's account of the matter: "General Lincoln 'went immediately to a club of the first characters in Boston who met that night, and layed before them a full state of matters, and suggested to them the importance of their becoming loaners of part of their property if they wished to secure the remainder. A Subscription was set on foot in the morning, headed by the Governour. Before night the cloud which twenty four hours before hung over us disappeared as we had an assurance of obtaining the sum we wanted.'"

"I remember," said the General. "I think you too were forming a militia, Colonel."

"Trying to do so, Your Excellency, rather like your own efforts in your youth. I, unfortunately, do not belong to a club. Massachusetts had requested aid from Connecticut. I remember rushing out for the latest papers to understand what was happening. I finally raised only two companies by advertising and promises of good pay and marched them to Springfield, but by then the action was finished, so I left my companies to do guard duty at the arsenal, resigned, and went home."

"I was just returned from the West on the General's business," said

Mr. Lear. "I contemplated going to join General Lincoln's army! But I knew I would not be needed given the lack of real opposition. Daniel Shays was no real soldier."

I was about to retort that the opposition was enough to stir the country, and that a man who had never served was not the best judge of soldiery, but the General got his own emollient remark in first by saying, "Well, Mr. Lear, I am quite happy that you did not—for I do not know what I would have done here without you." The General glanced at me, and I took the hint and remained silent.

The General said, "Colonel, perhaps you could briefly summarize the action from General Lincoln's account and your own memory."

"General Lincoln marched his troops quickly through the snow to Springfield to confront the Regulators, but the local militia commander, General Shepard, had already fired cannon from the arsenal, killing several Regulators, and dispersing them briefly. Then General Lincoln arrived and harried them upstate to Pelham, Shays's home town, surprising them there after a hard march. Negotiations produced nothing but delay. General Lincoln then discovered the Regulators had retreated to Petersham, to where he pursued them and surprised them again on February 4th, capturing many and dispersing the rest. And that was it: the formidable insurrection had resulted in little more than a few deaths and a lot of cold feet."

"There," said Mr. Lear. "As I thought—no real opposition." He had a smirky sort of smile on his face as he stated his approval of his own opinion. I bit my tongue.

The General gave him a gentle rebuke. "Do not say so, Mr. Lear. An armed force, even a lightly armed and poorly led one, can achieve wonders through luck and persistence."

"Yes, Your Excellency." Mr. Lear wisely said no more, as he must have understood quite well that the General was referring as much to his own army and efforts during the War as to those of Daniel Shays.

A detail tweaked my memory. I said, "I believe Shays was just the name the merchants in the East decided to put on the leadership." I smiled. "In fact, several men paid for their joint leadership of the Regulators with their lives, either by hanging or by exile. Shays was but one of these men, and perhaps not even the most effective of them. I believe he is now in exile in Vermont."

"That is what made it all the more worrying to those of us looking on from a distance," said the General. "That so many leaders should emerge spontaneously in unified violation of law is an extraordinary thing. There is nothing more dangerous to a fragile state than such violent, lawless protest, other than the corruption or misfeasance of those men responsible for governing. These concerns are what led Madison and others to propose the Constitutional Convention. It drove me to participate in that Convention, despite your opposing advice, Colonel. We thought about those concerns and the Rebellion every day as we worked on the compromises for the new Constitution, and our concern drove us to a successful conclusion. Now we face the actual implementation of the new government; and I face the decision of whether to lead it against any more such rebellions. I must carefully evaluate the state of the country in making my decision. If I am to break my word, I must assure myself that the nation really needs my leadership. But I shall not do that tonight."

I looked at the clock: time was getting on, as the General and his lady usually retired early at 9 o'clock. The world outside the windows had grown dark, shutting us into the study and reflecting the lights of the fire and candles the servant had brought in as the weak winter light disappeared. The chaos and fear of the Rebellion and the quicksand of the new Constitution receded from my mind, replaced by the warmth and calm of the General's study.

The General understood my change of mood and sat back in his chair. "I will continue to think on all this, Colonel, possibly even until we receive formal certification of the electoral results. And thank you, Mr. Lear, for interrupting your evening to join us." This was a polite dismissal, and Mr. Lear arose and went back to his congenial duties with the ladies. The General and I moved on to discuss some remaining issues in our biography.

After a time, Mrs. Washington entered from the dining room. "Well, you gentlemen are certainly going at it tonight." She smiled at her husband and said, "It is already time to retire, Mr. Washington."

"Why, so it is, my dear." The General arose. "We have indeed been quite engaged, both upon today's sad event and upon both past and upcoming decisions."

Mrs. Washington grimaced, her worry resurfacing. "I wish with all my heart you had no such decisions to make, you deserve your rest after all you've done, as Colonel Humphreys well understands. And our home is so lovely just now, after all the building; to start anew is not to my pleasure, Mr. Washington."

"I am very aware of it, my dear; events may compel us to action, however unwelcome."

"Yes, I know. But I cannot take pleasure in such untoward events."

"Yes. Well, my dear, let us ascend and leave the Colonel to his remembrances."

Mrs. Washington smiled upon me and said, "Good night, Colonel Humphreys. Sleep well." The General and his lady exited the study to the privy stairs.

I yawned. Lately I had been restless at night. My poetry benefited from my wakefulness, but I could not say my mind was at ease. I could see the General still pulled in many directions, and I worried for our new country without him at the helm. Now, I had the additional concerns about the murder of Julius and the thefts at the farm and the Grist Mill. I wondered how well the General and Mrs. Washington slept these days; I had heard no complaint, but they were not complainers. I could only hope that Mrs. Washington would grow more fond of the idea of being the first lady of the land, despite it taking her away from the home she loved. I feared that it would take another, minor, revolution to effect this, however. I hoped that, as in most other things, the General would eventually find the strength and leverage to do what was right, but the possibility of his declining the Presidency reinforced my increasing despair.

I replaced the letters on the General's desk and found my way up to my room. Little Wash, with whom I shared the room, was already asleep. I quietly undressed and lay down to get what rest I could before the exertions certain for the following day. I remember that I dreamt long and badly that night, the despair in my soul for the General's decision and the brutal image of dead Julius guiding my dreams down paths I would rather not recall.

13

Two days later, I awoke from a restless sleep to the breakfast bell. I dressed quickly and went down to the dining room to break my fast with a soothing meal of hoecakes and honey washed down with chocolate. The General was again preoccupied and was mostly silent through the meal, while Mrs. Washington and Mrs. Fanny Washington politely made conversation.

As we were finishing up, Frank Lee entered. "Your Excellency, Mr. John Williamson has arrived and wishes to speak with you."

"Thank you, Frank. Please ask him to wait in the passage, and offer him refreshment if he will have it. I will attend to him shortly." The General proceeded to finish his cakes and chocolate with some dispatch, then, rising, said, "Colonel, would you join us, if you please?" I stuffed the last of the hoecakes into my mouth and rose to join him.

We walked out into the passage to find Mr. Williamson, in riding clothes, waiting patiently on a chair.

"Ah, Your Excellency," he said, standing and bowing. "I have this letter for you from Colonel Hooe reporting on our progress."

The General read this letter over twice, with darkening brow. He assumed his most upright posture, towering over the smaller man.

"Indeed," he said. "Mr. Williamson, is it indeed true that you have found nothing of interest in your investigations?"

"I fear that is so, sir," replied the clerk apologetically. "I have worked with Major Washington, Mr. Fairfax, and your overseers to question everyone I could find who might know something but have uncovered no new information and no motive for the crime. I will continue my investigations, of course."

"I am very concerned about Colonel Hooe's report in this letter of his conversations with the merchants of Alexandria." He fixed a stern look on Mr. Williamson.

"Erm—yes, sir, it is indeed...troubling," stammered the unfortunate Mr. Williamson.

The General turned to me to explain. "Colonel Hooe reports that he has questioned several of his friends in Alexandria about thefts from plantations. He discovered that not only were they well aware of a breadth of theft unprecedented in this area, they were unconcerned. They were, in fact, quite willing to take what they could get at the lower prices offered."

I mulled this over, then said, "I would have thought better of them."

The General said with some asperity, "Colonel Humphreys, these revelations are what I feared. I found, on questioning the overseer at River Farm yesterday on my ride out that he, like Mr. Davenport, concealed from me the disappearance of a large amount of produce. He thought he could find the culprit and deal with it before I noticed."

He shook the letter in his hand. "But this—how can these merchants be as vicious in their habits as any English merchant or factor in London, that heart of iniquity? What did we fight for, to achieve such a result? Colonel Hooe uses the phrase, 'just business'—I find nothing *just* in it at all!"

The General turned back to the clerk. "Mr. Williamson. Colonel Hooe says that he has given you the task of following this up with the merchants. Have you done so?"

The man looked apologetic. "I have not yet had the opportunity, Your Excellency, as I have been engaged in the inquiries hereabouts. On my return to Alexandria today, I will see what I can find out."

"Very well. Please keep me informed—without fail. All right, Mr. Williamson, I think that is all. Please give Colonel Hooe my thanks and my regards." The General made a slight bow of dismissal.

The clerk nodded, bowed, and escaped to his horse. I followed the General back through the dining room into his study. He tossed the letter onto his desk, his brow showing his displeasure.

"While I appreciate Colonel Hooe's broaching this matter with us so quickly, on reflection I doubt that he was as uninformed as he says. He is, after all, one of the most successful and wealthy merchants in the town and did not get that way by paying more than the common price for goods. He is both canny and ambitious."

"Do you believe him to be honest?"

"As far as it goes for an Alexandria merchant, yes. But I am even more concerned about his further discoveries. Colonel, his last paragraph intimated that he had found more antifederalist sentiment in Alexandria among the merchants than he expected. They apparently feel that a strong federal government will make it just that much more difficult to do their business. Those feelings balance against the possibilities of increased trade due to the reduction of chaos in government. The more pressure we bring to bear with the law upon this illegal trade, I fear, the more sentiments will swing toward political opinions opposed to the new Constitution and its implementation."

I replied, "Is it possible that Colonel Hooe himself harbors antifederalist opinions?"

The General considered this possibility gravely, then said, "No, I do not believe so. He is a friend, proven over many years of acquaintance."

"What about Mr. Williamson? He seemed assiduous enough just now."

"I know nothing of Mr. Williamson's politics. I daresay Colonel Hooe would not otherwise employ him or laud him as he does."

"We must hope that Mr. Williamson will prove himself then." I thought back to the young clerk's inability to find his way back from the necessary to the dining room. I supposed that if he could find his way back to Alexandria today, he might well have enough wit to find a thief or two, or possibly a murderer. Events would tell.

The General saw my doubt. "I am not sanguine, as I have said before, but I think we must allow him to finish his investigation. In the meantime, I must myself address the problem of theft from my own plantations, because I simply cannot afford to lose the money! You said the other day that we would have the opportunity to improve management of the farm; now that simple task has become a matter of necessity. I have cajoled and persuaded and promoted care in my managers and overseers, apparently to no avail. I have avoided punishment of my people and dismissal of my managers as a matter of principle, and as common sense: punishment simply reduces productivity, and dismissal simply means hiring yet another manager who needs cajoling and persuasion. However, the scale of the problem we have uncovered induces me to think that the problem lies not in my people but in influences outside my farm."

I saw that the General would consider any alternative before being forced to punish his employees or his people. Admirable, I thought, but I had my doubts that his forbearance would bear fruit in the long term, as the chaos on his farms would persist as long as the people creating it continued unchecked.

"What can we do, Your Excellency, to block these influences?"

"I think the merchants are but the end of the chain that enables the hidden trade. No, I think there must be an organized effort across the region, perhaps a single person or group that is corrupting the managers and workers. A small theft then flows into a larger stream, much as Dogue Run flows into the Potomac. Let us see if we can dry up the stream so that it does not become an ocean."

If it were anyone other than the General proposing the existence of this conspiracy, I would think this theory outlandish. The General's restraint may have produced a need to see such a conspiracy rather than the simplest explanation: indolence and obstinacy in both managers and workers. Colonel Hooe's information, however, contributed some evidence to the possibility of an external source for the chaos.

But I was skeptical. "Sir, do you really think such a conspiracy could exist without being generally known?"

"My own experience of conspiracy has shown me that men are quite capable of hiding even the blackest deeds under a blanket of trust, and what is there in mercantile affairs but trust and more trust? Only the rule of law and the order imposed by effective government can underlie such trust, and I fear we do not yet have such an environment. We must find and dig out the roots of this blight to rid ourselves of it."

14

TUESDAY, MARCH 3, 1789, MORNING

The General and I donned our cloaks and walked out of the Mansion House in search of Mr. Fairfax. We found him coming up the path from the Landing, looking dissatisfied.

"What is it, Mr. Fairfax?" asked the General.

"I was just looking around down there, sir," replied the manager. "To see if I could find something. I was down there with Williamson an hour ago, explaining things to him."

"To any avail?"

"Not so far as I could tell, sir," said the plain-spoken young man. "To be honest, Your Excellency, I have my doubts about Mr. Williamson's investigation. So I went down to see if I could find anything we missed earlier."

"To no good result, I conclude."

"No, sir, couldn't see anything."

"Well, do not worry about it, Mr. Fairfax—that is the job of Mr. Williamson and Colonel Hooe, after all. It is their investigation. I want you to spend your energies getting my farms running well, if you please."

"Yes, sir. Of course, sir. About that, sir..." The young man stumbled to a stop, unable to articulate his fears.

The General smiled. "Let us take it one day at a time, Mr. Fairfax. Let us see if we can find ways to reduce the embezzlement and misuse of my property; that is the place to start. I have already given you instructions for the farms. Simply put more energy into managing the people on them, if you please."

"Yes, sir."

As the General was delivering this instruction, I noticed a rider in the distance coming down the driveway from the road—galloping, in fact.

"Sir!" I pointed.

We turned to look as the rider came down around the circle and stopped in front of the Mansion House. We walked up to him. His horse snorted and blew out steamy breaths into the cold air from hard riding.

"General Washington?"

"I am he."

"Express from Mr. Cockburn, Your Excellency. I have just ridden from Springfield." The man took a letter from a leather bag hanging at his side and handed it down to the General. The General looked at Mr. Fairfax, who dug around in a pocket and gave a penny to the man. He tipped his hat to us and urged his horse around, then he was gone.

The General broke the seal on the letter and read. He then read it again, lips tight.

"Well, Colonel, this is the end." He shook the letter at me. "Look at this!" He handed me the letter. It was short and not at all sweet:

> Springfield, March 3, 1789.
> Sir,
> I am in receipt of a letter from Colonel Hooe, the Fairfax County Sheriff, dated today. That letter informs me of a complete lack of any evidence of homicidal intent toward your overseer, and a similar lack of any information about his death other than the meager facts we already have. From the absence of any other possibility, I must therefore conclude that someone on your plantation, or yourself, probably committed this act.
> The Coroner's inquest has handed down a verdict of murder by person or persons unknown.
> I desire to inform you that I have decided, in my capacity as investigating magistrate in a preliminary hearing, that it

is incumbent upon the County of Fairfax to examine your actions under the Act of 1669 related to the homicide of your slave Julius.

The act is clear: "Whereas the only law in force for the punishment of refractory servants resisting their master, mistress, or overseer cannot be inflicted upon Negroes, nor the obstinacy of many of them be suppressed by other than violent means, be it enacted and declared by this Grand Assembly if any slave resists his master (or other by his master's order correcting him) and by the extremity of the correction should chance to die, that his death shall not be accounted a felony, but the master (or that other person appointed by the master to punish him) be acquitted from molestation, since it cannot be presumed that premeditated malice (which alone makes murder a felony) should induce any man to destroy his own estate."

Therefore, I must ask you to attend an examining court that I will call to determine, under oath, whether a felony has been committed either directly by you or through joint enterprise, should said slave not have been in a state of resistance to your authority, thus requiring referral of the case to the grand jury and then to the General Court of the State of Virginia. I will notify you of the time and place of such court. With Great Respect, I am &c.

Martin Cockburn, Justice of the Peace, Fairfax County, Virginia

I read through this letter, then addressed the General with simulated facetiousness to try to lighten his mood. "It appears that Mr. Williamson visited Mr. Cockburn before coming here, Your Excellency. I do wish we had put that Bill of Rights into the new Constitution, sir, it would now prove useful!"

The General laughed and frowned simultaneously. "Yes, you may be called upon to compose a new ode to my achievements, though in a far different realm than the battlefield—that of the General Court of Virginia. Or perhaps even to my glorious execution by hanging. Let us see whether we can find a way to avoid having to write such a poem, Colonel; I doubt it will prove as popular as your others." He paused, then said more seriously, "I cannot fathom why Mr. Cockburn would think that I could, personally, punish a slave, much less kill him and dispose of the body in the river. I continue to resent his assumption that I or one employed by me committed this act. I can only imagine that this is a political ploy of some kind. He is Colonel Mason's friend; he is himself antifederalist in sentiment."

"You think this decision is political?"

"I do, as otherwise he would have had the common decency to treat me with the respect my position and reputation deserves. With this development, it has become very clear to me that the authorities are not going to be of much help in this situation. I have the choice of answering to Mr. Cockburn in court or managing affairs myself. With a decision imminent on the election, time presses. I cannot accept high office with a murder investigation hanging over me. I cannot afford to allow organized theft from my plantation to continue. I cannot allow the authorities to ignore the need for justice for this murdered man. I must therefore undertake to investigate the murder and thefts myself."

15

Tuesday, March 3, 1789, morning

The General said, "Let us consult Mrs. Washington as to where we might find Alice." Mrs. Washington was in the garden. She was quite an energetic manager when supervising domestic tasks, and the gardener and his people were hard at work moving the last year's leavings and preparing the soil for its new life. Her dark brown shawl and her mob cap kept her warm and looking stout and pink-cheeked as she directed the laborers in their work.

"Ah, there you are, Mrs. Washington," said the General. "May we interrupt you for one moment?"

"Certainly, Mr. Washington."

The General surveyed his wife's domain with approval. He asked, "We must speak with Alice again about the unfortunate Julius. Where can we find her?"

Glancing at the sun, Mrs. Washington said, "I should think she will be in the kitchen. I did try her on sewing yesterday, but she proved to be utterly unskilled in those talents, I am afraid. I put her to work helping the cooks for now until we can decide how best to train her."

"Excellent, thank you. We will look for her there."

"Mr. Washington."

The General turned back to his wife. "Yes, my dear?"

"Do you know, I think you might find it easier to get information from Doll."

"But, my dear, Doll was not at Dogue Run. She did not know Julius and has no information about why someone murdered him. And she is very old, you know."

His wife smiled. "Men are always so direct, a frightful mistake. Look here, Mr. Washington. When Alice came to us yesterday, she was practically mute. Terrified. Alone. All hope had vanished from her world. I spent some time with her to see what she knew how to do, and, satisfied that she knew almost nothing, turned her over to Doll. You will find that Doll knows everything about her now that is to be known. And my suspicion is that you will have less effort getting it out of Doll than you would getting it out of Alice. Alice is not...communicative."

The General, much struck by this advice, said, "Thank you, Mrs. Washington. It would appear there is always something I can learn about my people." His wife nodded and turned back to her gardening.

Doll was the matriarch among the Negroes at the Mansion House. If a servant was not her daughter, son, granddaughter, or grandson, it was a rare event. She acted as godmother to all the people at the Mansion House. Lucy, her daughter, had married Frank Lee, the butler. Once a cook, Doll was now assigned little work, but she was still the major force in the quarters. She was also the person from whom the General and his wife bought their poultry, and on whom they depended for making the various home remedies required by daily life on the plantation.

We found Doll in the servant quarters, supervising a group of women mending clothes. The old lady was short and fat, grey-haired, with a flat nose, thick lips, and very sharp black eyes. The General exercised his power and told the rest of the women to take a short break from their labors while he spoke with Doll.

"Ginr'l, I guess this ain't about chickens."

The General smiled. "Not this time, Doll; Mrs. Washington has all she needs, so I need not buy any from you today. No; the Colonel and I need some information about Alice."

The old woman nodded and said, "Umph, that one. Piece o' work, she is, Ginr'l. A real piece o' work."

"Perhaps you can tell us her story as you know it."

"Her story is jus' pitiful, sir, jus' pitiful." The old woman shook her head. "She done married this donkey Julius, I know'd him from a babe, sir, he wasn't no good then and wasn't no good when she took up with him, and now a' course he ain't good for nothin' at all, bein' dead and all."

"But Doll, everyone told me Julius would be an excellent overseer, when the time came to choose someone for Dogue Run."

"A 'course they'd a tell you that, Ginr'l, 'cause that what you want to hear. They people got no sense atall. Puttin' that fox in charge of all the henhouses at once, Ginr'l. An' I bet you don't ask no womenfolk 'bout it." The old woman grinned toothlessly.

The General's face was a picture. I could only imagine what was going through his mind, but it clearly wasn't pleasant. I was fascinated; this was much like being lectured by your old great-grandmother who had nothing to lose from being honest about the family. My own great-grandmother...but no matter.

The General said, "All right, Doll. But Julius was murdered, and we must find the killer. Has the Sheriff's man spoken with Alice? Or you?"

"Ain't no Sheriff's man talkin' to us women. That little feller was around talkin' to some o' the men, for what good it do him."

The General shook his head dubiously. "So do you think Alice killed her husband?"

"Well, the Lord knows Alice got reasons to kill that feller, but she ain't done it."

"But does she have any idea about who did do it, Doll?"

"Ginr'l, that woman ain't got but one idea in her small head, and that's to stay alive 'long as she can, sir. Swear to God, I ain't never heard such shit comin' out a woman's mouth as she done. All she got is 'they goin' to kill me' and 'he tole me to keep quiet' and 'I ain't got no one in the world for me now' and such like."

I said, "So she didn't confide any secrets to you, Doll?"

"That woman got secrets up her bum, but she ain't lettin' 'em go to us, sir. No sir."

The General asked, "What about Julius? Did she say anything about what he was doing? I understand he would leave Dogue Run on his own business a great deal."

The old lady looked down at the ground, "Don't know nothin' about that, Ginr'l. Nothin'."

I said, "Come now, Doll, she must have said something about who she thinks killed her man."

"She do, sir, she do. 'That white man,' she say, 'he done it. He'll kill me too now, sure.' That what she say. I asked her, a 'course, 'What white man?' and she jus' close up like a clam on a Chesapeake beach, sir, jus' like that."

The General considered this for a few moments. "Did she say where Julius would go during the day?"

"She said he spent a lot of time down to Occoquan on Colonel Mason's place, and goin' to Alexandria for tradin' and doin' business."

"Quite a ways from where he was supposed to be."

"Yes, massa, but she say he make a lot of money on them visits. He make a lot of money just doin' what he do 'round here, too."

The General shook his head. "Money? I found none in Julius's house."

I thought back to the poor, dilapidated overseer's house. I could not imagine that anything might be concealed anywhere there, it was so thin and sparsely furnished.

The old woman laughed. "We don' keep our money in our houses, Ginr'l. Sure it be buried somewhere 'round Dogue Run, you never find it. Alice couldn't find it, she looked like hell after that Julius be dead, but didn't find nothin', nothin' at all."

The General replied, "So she knew about his death before we told her?"

"We all done, Ginr'l, soon as the boys down to the Landing found him face down onna strand. Massa Fairfax come along shortly after, but *we* all know 'fore that."

"I see." The General shook his head in despair. "I would have won the war in a year had I a communication network as good as that."

"She did say one thing, massa. She say Julius always brought back somethin' good from Occoquan, like a chicken or corn flour or somethin', and he ain't traded nothin' for it that she knows about, so she's afraid all that stuff is just took from Colonel Mason."

This bit of information appalled the General. "We cannot have that; we cannot have theft from our neighbors by our people. Frightful!"

"Yessir, that what I thought too. That Julius, he just weren't no good." The old lady shook her head. "No good atall, alive or dead."

16

TUESDAY, MARCH 3, 1789, MORNING

The General was as angry as I had ever seen him on our walk back to the Mansion House. "Theft from my neighbors! Such an act would be the worst possible thing for my reputation and for my farm!"

I made no attempt to assuage his anger, as I knew there was little I could do. In the social world of plantation Virginia, the murder of a slave paled in comparison to stealing from one's neighbor. A feud started with such behavior would likely end only in the complete destruction of entire families on one side or the other. That said, I felt the General's rage—in a man who eschewed the more usual emotions— was excessive, and I did not understand why.

As we entered the passage, the General said, "I must go to Gunston Hall immediately to see Colonel Mason about this, although there is nothing I am more loathe to do. I must explain the situation in such a way that he will unbend enough to condescend to help our investigation. Can you ride with me there directly, Colonel?"

"I am completely at your disposal, Your Excellency."

We rode out shortly thereafter, up the drive to the Fredericksburg road, then down it toward Mason's Neck, the peninsula downriver from Mount Vernon. It was a relatively long ride, as we had to ride past the abandoned plantation of Belvoir, the Fairfax estate, then most of the way down Mason's Neck to the house, Gunston Hall. I had met Colonel George Mason on several occasions, though never at Mount Vernon. He was a quiz: I could not reconcile the polite but eccentric individual I had met with the importance the General gave him.

"Your Excellency," I said as we rode, "perhaps you could fill me in on your exact relationship with Colonel Mason so that I fully comprehend what we are about to do."

The General wore a grim expression but condescended to tell me of his history with Colonel Mason. "As you know, I resided with my brother Lawrence at Mount Vernon after my father's death, and became acquainted with the Fairfax and Mason families. As I grew into my inheritance from my brother and assumed the legislative duties of a Virginia Burgess, I began to work closely with Colonel Mason, who was at the center of many webs of political action in Fairfax County. Between the wars, he and I worked to present various proposals to the Burgesses that would forward our position with the British government."

"So the Colonel is a lawyer?"

"No, he has never formally studied the law and has not been called to the bar. He is a farmer. He has read widely and has the mind of a lawyer but no great affection for the profession, I think."

We rode along for a brief while, the General silently recollecting those old days before the great War. He continued, "One of the first indications I had of Colonel Mason's true character, I believe, was an incident that occurred in 1775, just as things were heating up with the British. I had advanced some funds to buy ammunition for the militia, along with the Colonel, and we were to be reimbursed by collecting the monies from those able to pay in the district. I had to write to him to accuse him of pocketing the money he collected for us; he wrote back that of course he had intended to share equally, he had just not gotten around to it yet. The Colonel stood very much on his dignity, I am afraid. We smoothed over both the miscommunication and the offense, and he conducted himself well as a member of the Virginia House of Delegates during the War."

I noticed the General frowning. "Was there a problem during the war, sir?"

"Indeed there was. Many of the key Patriots wanted Colonel Mason to exercise his abilities as a member of the Continental Congress. His character again asserted itself by his absolute refusal to consider such service. He refused in the end to leave Virginia at all!"

"I believe you told me that the Colonel was not a well man? Was that the source of his reluctance?"

The General grunted. "Stomach gout. Colonel Mason was always a valetudinarian, though he often managed to overcome his gout before and during the War. Afterwards, however, as he grew older and fancied himself sicker, he withdrew even more from public life. By 1785, he had essentially retired to his farm, as of course had I, though for very different reasons."

The General reined in his horse suddenly. We had reached the drive to the ruined Belvoir, the Fairfax mansion that was the hub of the social world of his youth. His reflections on his past had clearly made him think of that bygone society with regret. His Fairfax neighbors had long returned to England, and their mansion had burned to a ruin last year. Our own John Fairfax was a distant relation from the Maryland branch of the family.

Shaking off his melancholy remembrance of the Fairfaxes, we rode on. The General continued his account of Colonel Mason. "In 1787, both Colonel Mason and I were called upon to represent Virginia at the Constitutional Convention along with Governor Edmund Randolph and Mr. James Madison, among others. For once, he acquiesced in the call to duty, despite his gout. He came with fire in his eye, perhaps enhanced by the fire in his belly. He became one of the most outspoken proponents of individual rights at the Convention. And then, at the end, after all the compromises and agreements were done, he again stood upon his dignity and refused to sign the document." The General shook his head.

"That must have frustrated you, sir."

The General nodded. "And it grew worse. Then began the long, prideful opposition. By the ratification convention in Richmond last year, his misplaced pride had gone so far as to push him into a leadership position in the opposition to the Constitution, those now called the antifederalists. The Colonel led the moderates, while the more volatile former Governor Patrick Henry led the radical antifederalists. For someone claiming to be a moderate, however, Colonel Mason did everything he could to muster opposition to ratification, working closely with Governor Henry. He was impervious to reason. He continues in his opinions to this day, while most others including Governor Henry have come around to an understanding that we must move forward as a unified nation to preserve our liberty. It was my final realization of the extent of his pride and lack of candor that led me to cut him socially after the convention."

I had seen such feelings before in the General, during the War. He formed strong attachments to his aides and his generals. When they went astray, became disloyal, or proved unreliable, he often took the slight personally. His attitude toward Colonel Mason reminded me of Colonel Hamilton's abrupt departure in 1781 from the General's staff as a result of clashing personalities. Fortunately for us all, the two recognized the value in each other, and their pride did not exceed their common sense—they wrote to each other and respected each other's opinions greatly in the years since their separation. But Colonel Mason's pride appeared to indeed exceed his sense.

"And does the Colonel oppose your Presidency, Your Excellency?"

The General smiled, his eyes on the road ahead. "He must, though he does not say so. He is ever the polite neighbor. Indeed, that is the only reason I would try to enlist him in our investigation. His pride in his beliefs on the rights of the people, on the evils of slavery, and on the fight against tyranny must lead him to help us. I will appeal to his sense of justice. But I must tell you that visiting him goes against every grain of my being."

"Is it possible that the Colonel might somehow be involved in the thefts, Your Excellency? Or, indeed, in the murder?"

The General smiled again. "Quite unlikely. Colonel Mason's probity is not in question, just his judgment on political affairs." He then thoughtfully added, "But in today's world, I suppose anything is possible. We should not make any assumptions."

"Did you say that the Colonel opposes slavery, Your Excellency?"

"Yes, indeed, Colonel, he does. He has said so, both verbally and in his published writings. He regards the slave trade as an evil with which we must dispense as soon as possible. It was one of the things that he said prevented him signing the Constitution—the acceptance and even promotion of the slave trade in that document."

"Has he freed his own slaves?"

The General smiled even more widely. "No, indeed, Colonel, he has not. Colonel Mason is a man of many parts, sir, as you will see. One is never quite sure, when looking at one of his hands, what the other may be doing." He became serious again. "If we are to get anywhere with the Colonel, we must navigate the shoals of his excess pride, or it will get the better of him, and he will intensify his opposition to us. I have my doubts," sighed the General, "as to whether Colonel Mason will submit to any sort of interrogation of himself or his people, given his extreme pride. But we must try if we are to unearth anything from his people."

"I do find his attitude toward slavery very curious, Your Excellency."

"I would not mention slavery at our upcoming meeting, Colonel. Let us keep our attention on the simple crimes of theft and murder, if you please, and leave the topic of slavery to the future."

17

TUESDAY, MARCH 3, 1789, AFTERNOON

The ride took us three hours, Gunston Hall coming into view as the sun neared its azimuth. We rode down the lane through Colonel Mason's four-rowed alley of cherry trees, leafless and bare in the winter sun, stretching down along the road for what seemed forever, up to the house on a little hill overlooking the Potomac. The Hall was outwardly quite similar to Mount Vernon but constructed of red brick, with a more regular design.

We dismounted before the Hall, giving our horses to a servant and announcing ourselves at the front door to the Negro butler, who showed us into the passage, took our hats and cloaks, then took us through to the front parlor.

"My master is somewhat indisposed, gentlemen, but I will tell him you are here." He nodded to us and left us sitting by the fire.

After a goodly wait while the Colonel dressed himself for us, we heard creaking steps on the passage stairs, and Colonel Mason joined us. He was an old, somewhat stout, full-fleshed man in his early sixties, with grey hair and what I could only call a sour expression, as though the lines of his face had permanently set into a fierce rejection of the world. That was presumably the effects of his recurring stomach gout, but it did not make him any more likable at first sight. His manner proved more courtly than his looks, however, as he greeted the General.

"Welcome, Your Excellency, welcome; it has been too long since you graced Gunston Hall with your presence. Please excuse my delay in greeting you, a resurgence of my old complaint has laid me a bit low recently."

"I am very sorry to hear that, sir, and please accept my best wishes for your early recovery. Also, you may remember Colonel David Humphreys, currently a guest at my residence."

"It is a very great pleasure to welcome you to my house, Colonel," said Colonel Mason to me.

"Thank you, sir."

Mason indicated the chairs, and we all sat. A small silence developed, then the General said, "You must excuse our abrupt appearance, Colonel Mason, but we come here on business that cannot be delayed."

Mason looked warily at the General and responded, "Indeed; and the nature of that business?"

"I do not know whether you may have heard lately from Mr. Cockburn?"

"No sir, we have not spoken in a week."

"Ah. Then you are probably not aware of the unfortunate incident that occurred a few days ago at my Landing."

"No, sir, I am not. I hope it was nothing untoward?"

"Very much so, I fear. One of my people, Julius, my overseer at the Dogue Run plantation, was found dead; brutally clubbed and murdered, then put into the river."

Mason shifted uncomfortably in his chair. "I am sincerely sorry for your trouble, sir."

The General compressed his lips, then went on. "Mr. Cockburn, for reasons best known to himself, seems to have taken it into his head to start court proceedings against the possibility of my personal involvement in the death. He has initiated an examining court which will require me to defend myself against a murder charge." The General smiled briefly. "Given the current political situation, I am forced to conclude this matter may be an attempt to damage my reputation for political purposes, or to sway my mind against certain decisions I may be forced to make regarding my retirement."

Mason shook his head. "I know Mr. Cockburn well, sir. I cannot believe he would allow his political beliefs to interfere with his judgment in such a manner." He paused and thought, then said, "I am sure there is some mistake. You are aware that the law protects a master—"

"Yes, I am fully aware of the law; I am not consulting you legally but rather on matters of fact. Colonel Humphreys and I have been looking into the matter, and we have made some discoveries that are troubling."

"Discoveries." Mason frowned, rendering his face more dyspeptic than ever. "Inferring from your presence given the unfortunate breach between us, I must infer that those discoveries involve myself, or Gunston Hall."

"The latter, sir, or at least the part of your plantation at Occoquan. I assure you, we have learned nothing at all to your discredit. Our political views are too well canvassed to bring up, and I hope you can set aside our conflict as a matter of simple justice, as a magistrate yourself. No, we are here to ask whether we may speak with your overseers about some matters that may bear on the matter."

"What matter?" The Colonel's question was sharp; clearly the General had pricked his pride.

The General was conciliatory. "Nothing untoward about your farms or your people, sir. My own people have apparently had interactions with yours that may require explanation."

"I fail to comprehend what these 'matters' or 'interactions' might be that would assist you in freeing yourself from suspicion in the matter of your man's murder."

The General chose his words carefully. "It would appear, sir, that the man had some dealings with your people at Occoquan, and at least from my perspective those dealings are unexplained. Your people may be able to shed some light on them."

"What kind of dealings?"

Colonel Mason's legal mind was clearly centered on getting all the facts before committing himself to anything. The General tried again.

"I am really not certain I know, sir; that is why I wish to ascertain the facts in the matter. My information is that my man would go to Occoquan and come back with goods for which he did not trade."

"He stole them, I conclude?"

"I do not know, sir, but I must find out."

"As you must know, slaves cannot testify in court, and thus are not material witnesses in a case at law against a white man. It is a useless exercise."

"Yes, sir, but they can give information that may lead to witnesses that *can* testify. You must see, Colonel Mason, that I will do anything I can to clear my name."

Colonel Mason smiled somewhat coldly. "I think your name needs little clearing, Your Excellency, and I would not choose to have you attempt it by blackening mine."

The General sat back, clearly exasperated but controlling himself. "I have no wish to blacken your name, sir, just to question your people about the thefts."

This was a misstep, and the General realized it immediately upon uttering the word, but he could not take it back.

Mason arose, his countenance rather black. "If I understand you, sir, I must insist you do no such thing. While I am aware that Virginian hospitality extends to many things, questioning one's servants about putative theft certainly does *not* qualify. I am honored by your visit, of course, but I think at this point I must ask you to leave me in peace."

He winced, then said, "Or at least with my gout, which I do believe is taking a turn for the worse. I give you good day, gentlemen."

The General looked a little startled at this early termination of his business. I thought to myself that Colonel Mason's reaction seemed too strong for the General's rather mild insinuations, and that perhaps the Colonel knew more than he was willing to admit to us.

Before the General could respond, there was a bustle outside the house. Through the window, we could see Mr. Martin Cockburn jumping down from his horse. The General and I arose simultaneously. We all moved toward the parlor door. In the passage, the butler was opening the door to admit Mr. Cockburn. Mason walked through to the passage as the butler was taking Mr. Cockburn's hat and cloak.

"Mr. Cockburn, welcome. These gentlemen I believe you know. They are just leaving." Mason signed to the butler, who turned to retrieve our hats and cloaks.

"General Washington, indeed." Cockburn did not smile. "And Colonel Humphreys. I did not credit my man's information that he had seen you on the road, but it is true." He pursed his lips. "Colonel Mason, may I ask whether these gentlemen are here on particular business? I ask as a magistrate rather than as a friend."

"Yes, sir, and you already know that business, apparently. I have asked them to leave without further pursuing it."

Cockburn turned to the General. "You must be aware, sir, that given events, your appearance here on such a quest is highly improper and prejudicial. Your direct interference in this investigation must have little other construction than an attempt to dissuade me from further proceedings. Such an attempt must only reinforce my resolve to continue. I must reiterate Colonel Mason's request for you to leave at once, only adding that any further efforts to exonerate yourself should be left to your appearance before me at the magistrate's court."

The General, with the determined expression I knew hid darker passions, said, "I make no assurances, Mr. Cockburn. I must defend myself against your insinuations with every means at my disposal. I am sorry that Colonel Mason does not see fit to assist me at this time." He turned to Mason. "I can only assure you, sir, that I do not hold this against you, but rather against the party to which you belong. Partisanship and its excesses will be the death of this new country, I fear. But enough of this; you have asked that we leave, and we will comply." He took his hat and cloak, and I took mine, and we stepped to the door as the butler opened it for us. The General strode more quickly than usual to his horse and was in the saddle before I even reached my horse. He waited, a little impatiently, for me to join him, then we rode off down the alley the way we had come.

18

Once we were out of sight of the Hall, the General slowed his horse and stopped. I caught up with him and stopped as well.

He said, "Colonel, several of Colonel Mason's people were loading a wagon at the side of the house. I noticed a Negro overseeing them. While it may not be the most gentlemanly thing to do, I believe I must ask you to return there without attracting further notice from the Colonel or Mr. Cockburn and speak with the overseer. We really must know what the people here know and do. Colonel Mason's abrupt dismissal of our request...I cannot but think the Colonel knows more than he is telling." The General's voice was calm, but his eyes reflected his hidden resentment at such treatment. He looked off toward the river, then up the road. "I will go on, and you can catch me up."

"Yes, sir." I had undertaken missions during the war that had pleased me more than this, but I obeyed. I trotted back down the alley toward the house and dismounted out of sight of it, tying my horse to one of the cherry trees off the drive. My own feeling as a Yankee was that Virginia gentlemen might be less forgiving than the British for transgressing hospitality; but also as a Yankee, I was not in a mood to care that much. Such treatment! If the General's blood stirred, mine boiled.

I walked carefully down the outer alley trees, trying to ensure that I stayed invisible. I was wearing a brown cloak, luckily, that blended in nicely with the dark trees. As I came to the end of the alley, I saw a

Negro supervising the loading of some barrels onto a wagon parked by the side of the house. I looked carefully at the house and saw no curious faces at windows. Noiselessly, I walked quickly over to the wagon and quietly saluted the overseer.

"Hello; my name is Colonel Humphreys, an acquaintance of Colonel Mason's."

He turned and replied in a deep voice, "Yes, sir. What can I help you with, sir? Keep up loadin' that stuff, you, while I talk with this gentleman."

"What is your name?"

"Nace, sir."

"I am staying at Mount Vernon, and we've had some problems there with things disappearing. The General would appreciate any information you might provide on this sort of thing."

"Well, sir, don't know nothin' at all about that." Nace regarded me calmly.

"Has the Dogue Run overseer Julius ever been here to see you?"

Nace scratched his beard, then said, "Sure, Julius come by sometimes, trading or whatnot. His job, ain't it? Hasn't been by awhile, though." His face was noncommittal.

"Do you think any of these others might have some more information for us?"

"I think you got all the information you gonna get, sir. More than my life's worth to say different. Sir." He smiled, looking past me.

A hand fell on my shoulder, from behind. Nace stepped back a pace.

"And just exactly who might you be?" I turned to face a white man with a scraggly beard and with no friendly look in his eye, the hand slipping off my shoulder. "And whyever are you talking to my people?"

"Are you the farm overseer, sir?"

"Damn right I am. I asked you who *you* were."

"Colonel Humphreys, staying with General Washington."

"Doesn't give you any purchase to come by and talk with my people, taking up their time. This ain't Washington's property."

"Nevertheless, I had some questions that required answers."

A thick finger poked in my chest. "Don't give a good goddamn what you think is required, you should not be here. Colonel Mason don't like interference with his people. Git."

"But—at least can you tell me your name?"

"Thompson; George, that is. If it's any of your business. Which it ain't. Now git before I get these boys to toss you."

I got. With some dignity, I hope, but not without a bit of speed, as I did not like the look in Thompson's eye, and I did not want to attract attention from the house by knocking him down if I could avoid it. Call it a tactical retreat. I retrieved my horse and trotted up the lane.

I caught up with the General after about 15 minutes of trotting, and we resumed a normal pace. I reported my lack of success, and the General thanked me for my effort, though I could see his disappointment.

"I will endeavor to perform better next time, sir."

"Your performance was excellent, Colonel; never mind. One learns as much from a negative result as a positive one, I think. Your opinion of Nace's denial of knowledge?"

"Almost certainly lying, sir. For a slave, Nace was particularly confident in his reply to me, which seems unusual for Virginia slaves. I have found in the course of my military career that the more confident a man's reply, the more certain you may be that he dissembles. And as for Thompson, he was clearly interested in ending my questioning. Whether that intent was motivated by the need to hide information or simply by anger at my intrusion I do not know, but I think they know more than they are willing to say."

The General made no comment other than to say, "Very well, Colonel. And your impression of Colonel Mason?"

"It seems to me that Colonel Mason was straightforward in his address to us, sir. He was quick to take offense at your question, but, forgive me, that seems in accord with the behavior of Virginia gentlemen with whom I have interacted. I doubt he is hiding anything."

"A bit irascible as a class, are we, eh? When challenged. True. It is part of our Cavalier heritage, I suppose. Still, Colonel Mason's response seemed to go a little beyond the usual offended honor, even taking his gout into account. Perhaps all that in combination with our estrangement has excited his ire, or his gout, to a higher degree than usual. But I must not discount the possibility that he knows something he is not telling us. And I am still very surprised at Mr. Cockburn's lack of courtesy."

The General, being one of the foremost Virginia landowners, was not used to any discourtesy at all, and he clearly resented it.

I replied, "I am sure, sir, that he did not mean to be discourteous but only correct in his behavior given his beliefs about the situation."

The General eyed me from his horse with a dour expression. "Perhaps. I will again just say that my position and reputation in this county deserve a better treatment."

"Yes sir."

The General was quiet for most of the long journey home, only pointing out some interesting trees as we passed by, telling me he was always on the watch for additions to his plantation. He actually marked one tree near Dogue Run as we passed for later transplanting at the Mansion House. We arrived there just in time for dinner; Mrs. Washington had set Frank Lee on watch for us, and he informed us dinner would be served as soon as we were dressed. As orders from Mrs. Washington superseded even those of the General, we addressed ourselves to our toilet with alacrity, all worries and resentment set aside for the nonce.

19

WEDNESDAY, MARCH 4, 1789, MORNING

The next day, the sky filled with threatening clouds and the temperature dropped 5 degrees. The General rode out on his rounds to Muddy Hole and the River Farm. Thinking to have a nice day by the fire, I went to the study to fetch my book of poetry. There I found Major Washington holding a sheet of paper. The Major had not appeared at breakfast, so I greeted him.

"Good morning, Major. I trust you are feeling well?" He did not look well, but rather pale and drawn.

"I'm all right, Colonel. Just didn't feel much like food this morning." He smiled, but his eyes were tired and his face pinched.

"You should take care of yourself, sir," I replied.

"The General has laid out my day." He raised the sheet of paper he was consulting and smiled again. "Cannot very well be a manager if I don't manage, now can I?" Even his voice sounded tired.

"What are you intending to do, then?" I asked.

"Ride out to Ferry and French's, sir, to see about fencing and livestock management. Then up to Dogue Run to check on the new overseer."

"It is very cold today, perhaps you should defer—"

"No, sir. Thank you for your concern, but no; I must do the General's bidding."

"Perhaps Mr. Fairfax—"

"No, sir." He straightened up and squared his shoulders. "I will dress warmly; my wife has seen to that," he said, pointing at a pile of clothes on a chair. "I was just getting ready to go out."

I made a quick decision. "May I ride out with you, sir? I am interested in how the plantation works, but I am also anxious to hear about Mr. Williamson's investigation, which I believe you observed over the last couple of days."

Major Washington rolled his eyes but made no further comment. "Certainly, Colonel, I would welcome your company. It is a very cold day indeed, a little company will set me right."

We rode out within the hour. I wore my warmest great-coat and cloak and hoped for the best. We rode up the drive to the road, then turned down toward Ferry Farm.

"You did not seem to exhibit much faith in Mr. Williamson's investigation, Major," I said.

"I did not, sir. I spent all day Monday with the man questioning the people and servants all around the Mansion House." He shook his head. "Mr. Williamson is an excellent clerk, I am not saying otherwise. I work with him every week. But I do not see that his superficial questioning moved things ahead at all, and his curiosity seemed limited to the simple fact of where people were during the last week and whether they had any problems with Julius. He seemed at the end in a rush to finish and get home." He passed a hand across his brow, pushing his hat up. His face was more pale, if that was possible. I felt as though I were riding with a ghost.

"And did they?"

He looked at me from his horse as though I were speaking Greek. "Sorry?"

"Did any of the people at the Mansion House have a problem with Julius?"

"No, no one that would admit it at any rate."

"What about Alice?"

"Who?"

"Alice, Julius's wife."

"Oh...yes. I did not see her, we did not question her."

"Why not?"

The Major was silent for a time, thinking. "I do not recall coming across her during our investigation, Colonel. I think she may have avoided us. And Mr. Williamson questioned only the men, of course." He ran a finger around his collar, as though it were too tight.

He had confirmed, at least, that the Williamson investigation was less than thorough. I made a mental note to talk about this with the General, as we would need to consult with Colonel Hooe if Mr. Williamson did not make any progress in a reasonable amount of time.

Major Washington was quiet as we rode. I became a bit alarmed, as he was swaying in his saddle.

He mumbled more to himself than to me, "It's too much, too much. It is so hot, I'm sweating! Uncle has been so good to us, good to us. The money...how will we pay him back? I'm ill.... What will Fanny do? And that bastard Thompson, and Julius, and Hooe, and murder, and death everywhere.... Too much, too much."

"What was that about Thompson, Major?" I asked.

The Major was swaying even more alarmingly in his saddle. He looked at me with glazed eyes. "Thompson? Son of a bitch.... I knew there was something up when I saw him at Dogue Run.... Can't trust him, knows too much. Julius too, bloody black bastard knows everything about everything. Uncle would be furious, can't tell him...." The Major's eyes focused suddenly on mine, and he looked appalled at what he had said. "Colonel, please...I can't...." His eyes rolled back in his head, and he fell off his horse directly into a mud-hole by the side of the road.

"Bloody hell!" I could not restrain myself, both because of his accident and because of what he'd let slip. Just how far and how deep had the Major gone with Thompson and Julius? But he was obviously out of his head, and obviously completely loyal to his uncle.

I jumped off my horse and tied him to a bush, did the same with the Major's horse, then ran to the Major and lifted him up. He was unconscious. I felt his forehead: it was wet and hot.

I stood up and looked around. We were just at the boundary of French's Farm, and I saw some field workers within hailing distance. I called them over, and they came running.

"Major Washington has taken very ill. Can you help me get him up on his horse, please?" The two men grunted as they grabbed both ends of the major and heaved him up across his saddle, face down. I mounted my own horse, and one man gave me the reins of the Major's. The other man picked up the Major's hat, wiped some of the mud off of it, and handed it up to me.

I thanked the workers and slowly walked the Major on his horse back to the Mansion House. When I drew up in front, Frank Lee stepped out, and seeing the situation, called for help. We got the Major into the house and into the ground floor bedroom, which was currently unoccupied. The servants took off his muddy clothes, then gently laid the Major out on the bed, propping him up with some pillows behind him.

Mrs. Fanny Washington rushed into the room, having heard the disturbance.

"What happened? Oh my dear, what happened? Is he dead?" She stood stock still in front of the bed, her hands over her mouth.

"No, no, Mrs. Washington," I replied. "Just very ill, I am afraid. We were riding...." I found I could not give voice to the vile suspicions that the Major's delirious confessions had raised in me, not to this sweet woman, his wife.

She cried, "I told him, *begged* him, not to go out today, he was so ill." She was in tears by this time. I stood there tongue-tied. I did not know what to do, I could not comfort her though it was my warmest desire to do so. Mrs. Martha Washington arrived at this point to rescue me by taking Mrs. Fanny in hand.

As she led Mrs. Fanny to a chair, the General's wife commanded me, "Colonel, please send for Doctor Craik. And Doll, find Doll and tell her what has happened. Please hurry!" Once she had settled Mrs. Fanny, she turned to tend to her stricken nephew.

I found Mr. Fairfax and asked him to fetch Doctor Craik from Alexandria, and he rode off immediately. I went to the servant quarters to find Doll, and they directed me to the kitchen, where I found her stirring some potion or other over the fire.

"Doll, Major Washington has been taken ill and is unconscious. Can you help?"

The old woman grinned, a bit toothlessly, and said, "Po' massa Washington, he got the 'sumption real bad now. I kin help, but ain't nothing I kin do gonna fix it." She took off her apron and we walked into the house through the pantry. There, she stopped and got a large bottle and shook it vigorously. It was a light colored liquid with a bunch of some kind of plant soaking in it.

I said to her, "We have sent for Doctor Craik, but it will be some time until he comes."

She shook her head. "That Doctor, he a good man, but he don't know nothin' 'bout how stuff works. He can set a bone jes' fine, but sure as shit he gonna bleed him or sompin'. Nothin' I kin do 'bout that, but I kin help po' young massa 'fore the Doctor gits here."

She shook up the bottle. "Sweet Annie tea, Colonel. Made it myself. Best thing for 'sumption. Cuts the fever." She carried the bottle through to the bedroom, where the two Mrs. Washingtons were huddled over the bed, chafing Major Washington's hands.

"Oh, Doll," said Mrs. Martha Washington, "Thank the Lord. Can you do something for him?"

Doll put the bottle on a small table and took a spoonful of the liquid from it, inserting it between the Major's flaccid lips and down his throat. He swallowed and groaned, nearly conscious. His eyes opened and he looked around wildly.

"Where...? What...? Oh. Fanny, Fanny, I'm so sorry. Oh, God...." he groaned. His wife held his hand in both of hers.

"Now, massa, you jus' calm down now and sip some more of this tea." Doll gave him another spoonful of the Sweet Annie tea.

"Bitter." But the Major took the tea and swallowed. Doll followed with more tea. When the Major had recovered his senses to some extent, he looked around and, seeing me, said, "Colonel. Did you bring me here?"

"Yes, Major. From French's."

He closed his eyes and said, "Thank you. Had you not been there...."

"I am sure the people on the farm would have helped you, sir, but it was my privilege to do so."

"Thank you. Please....don't tell my uncle."

"I should think it unavoidable, sir, with all these friends knowing." I smiled. "Somebody's bound to let it slip."

Mrs. Martha Washington leaned over the bed and said, "George, your uncle will be more distressed than you know if he is not informed. I will tell him when he returns. Now, rest."

The Major's head relaxed on the pillow, his eyes closed. "Very well," he said. "Fanny...."

"I'm here, darling, I'm here," said his wife, still holding his hand.

"I'm sorry," he whispered. "So sorry."

His wife looked perplexed. "Sorry for what, dear?" He just shook his head on the pillow, eyes closed. "Now just you rest, dear. Sleep now, I'll stay here by your side. Rest. Please don't worry. I'm here."

Major Washington held her hand and said nothing more. I looked at his suffering countenance and felt compassion for him and his wife; but

I could not get past what he had said about Thompson and Julius, and my dismay at what the General would feel when he understood it. I looked at the two distraught women and hoped with all my heart they would never need to know it. The bedroom suddenly seemed very crowded; I eased myself out the door to consult my feelings in private.

20

WEDNESDAY, MARCH 4, 1789, AFTERNOON

The General found me alone in the parlor at about 1 o'clock in the afternoon, reading. The parlor had provided me with a haven from all the female hustle and bustle about the house as the distaff side of the household dealt with the issues of the day. Mrs. Fanny Washington took time out from tending her husband after Doctor Craik arrived. She had come to sit with me for a few minutes, mostly to tell me how grateful she was for my actions earlier in the day. She was much distressed, and I comforted her as far as I could, my own feelings quite as afflicted as hers but for different reasons. Mr. Lear, who had just returned from a morning errand to find the house in turmoil, tried to comfort her as well. They had left me in peace an hour ago to recover from the morning's events.

"Well, Colonel," the General said, "it appears to have been quite a day. May we have a short conversation in my study?"

"Certainly, sir." I closed the book and laid it on a table, then joined the General in his study. He closed the door.

Once we were alone, the General surprised me by allowing the worry to show in his countenance.

"Colonel, I am very concerned by my wife's report of my nephew's illness. She said that you were present during my nephew's attack. Would you tell me what happened?"

I told him about the increasing illness and fall, but hesitated when it came to Major Washington's revelation. His confession, to my mind.

The General said, "What are you not telling me?"

It was hopeless to keep anything from my friend. He usually showed few feelings of his own, but his perception of the feelings of others was acute.

I said, "Your Excellency, I am sure it means nothing. Your nephew was very ill, and I daresay his touch of brain fever got the better of his sense."

"Brain fever?" His face showed his anxiety for his nephew. "Tell me, please. What transpired?"

I took a deep breath and let out a sigh. "We spoke of his experience with Mr. Williamson. Your nephew did not think the investigation thorough. Mr. Williamson and the Major failed to find and question Alice, among other things. But then the Major started rambling, speaking nonsense, as he became more ill. He spoke of you, of money owed, of his wife. He spoke of—forgive the language, sir—'that son-of-a-bitch Thompson' and 'that black bastard Julius,' and about their 'knowing everything,' and he also mentioned Colonel Hooe. He then mumbled the words 'murder' and 'death' and said it was all too much for him. That's when he fell off his horse."

The General looked appalled. He fixed his gaze on me and slowly sat, nearly missing the seat. "George...said that? But you say he was feverish?"

"On his last legs, sir; completely out of his mind."

"Well." He considered, his face grim. "I cannot believe my nephew is involved directly in the murder or the thefts, not on such evidence. Surely not, no, surely not. I know him well. I think—yes—he worries himself to death—unnecessarily—though we all try to reassure him. Surely not. He must recoup himself now, but I will speak with him on the matter when he is recovered. Yes, that is the right of it, I am sure." He looked at the door that led to the bedroom. "Doctor Craik is with him now."

"Did Mrs. Washington tell you, sir, about Doll?"

The General sighed, "Yes, Colonel. Mrs. Washington places great faith in Doll and her old remedies, though to my mind Doctor Craik has a more scientific approach. I am sure that between them they will restore George, if not to perfect health, then at least to coherence and rationality. Until that time, however, I think we must let his fevered ramblings lie."

I am afraid I was frustrated enough to pace up and down before the General. Taking a chance, I said, "Your Excellency, I really believe it possible that Major Washington knows something vital. Can we not just ask him? I understand that you care for him, but I think you are too nice in this instance."

The General frowned. "You go too far, Colonel." He stopped, then reconsidered, his face lightening. "I am sorry. I know you are concerned for my welfare as a friend, but you may not understand the deeper feelings and duties in my family situation. George is my closest relation, my...well, yes, practically my son. My wife and I love him and Fanny beyond measure. My wife has lost all her own children, and I have not been blessed with any. My brother...." The General paused and closed his eyes for a moment. "My brother Lawrence died after a long illness very similar to this. I felt his loss greatly then, and I feel it now looking at George. I have not yet learned to ignore such feelings, Colonel, even to save myself from a charge of murder. Really, I think we are following the right course for now. We must give him some time."

I replied, "We seem to face brick walls at every turn, Your Excellency. Is there nothing we can investigate ourselves?"

"Well, Colonel, you heard Mr. Cockburn. As he is the magistrate in charge, his telling us to keep ourselves out of it would appear to preclude any more effort on our part. And just now I have much to do in preparation for removing from Mount Vernon to New York should I accept election to the Presidency. As I must set off immediately on acceptance, I must prepare now regardless of my decision, or it will take weeks before I assume the office. General Knox has written from New York that Congress does not yet have a quorum, that many new Congressmen have not yet answered their call to duty. But it may happen at any moment."

"Can you do nothing to remove these restraints, Your Excellency?"

After a long pause for thought, the General smiled. "Perhaps you can help, Colonel. I must remain at Mount Vernon with Mr. Lear to deal with the loans that I am negotiating with Mr. Conway in Alexandria, to provide myself with the cash I need for New York. Then on Saturday I must travel to Fredericksburg to visit my mother, who is near death."

"I am sorry to hear that, Your Excellency. How can I help?"

"You can go to Richmond for me to consult with Captain John Marshall. I trust him to know the law more than any other lawyer I know, and I am sure he can propose a solution to our problems."

"I would be happy to do that, Your Excellency."

"Good. I will write a letter of introduction. I will leave Fredericksburg on Monday morning. If you come to my mother's house on your return from Richmond, we can ride back together in the coach and discuss matters."

"Very well, Your Excellency. I will be off for Richmond first thing in the morning."

21

Saturday, March 7, 1789

After 2 days of travel and a good night's sleep at the Eagle tavern in Richmond I walked two very dirty blocks to Captain Marshall's house. I found that it was quite new; so new, in fact, that the family had not yet moved in. I walked up to a carpenter standing in front of the house.

"Good day, sir. Is this Captain Marshall's residence?"

"Aye, sir, but the Captain don't live here yet. As you see, we are just in the way of finishing it up, like." He waved at the workers laying on various pieces of trim and going in and out of the house holding plastering tools.

"I see. Where can I find him, then?"

"See that little house down there, sir?" The man pointed down the street. "That's it. You should find him there, sir, 'less he's gone out. Wonderful social gentlemen he is, sir, for a busy lawyer man." The carpenter grinned. I gave him a penny and he thanked me.

I knocked at the door of the little house, and a maid-servant answered. To my request to see Captain Marshall, she seemed uncertain. Then a voice from behind her said, "Well, sir: I am at home only briefly; but is this legal business?" I looked past the maid and saw a young man, about 35, with a broad face, strong black eyebrows and snapping black eyes, and a ready smile. He was a bit disheveled considering his status as a prominent attorney.

I extracted my pocket-book and a card. "In a way, sir. I am Colonel David Humphreys and I come to you on a mission from General

Washington. Here is his letter to you." I handed my card and the letter to the maid, who curtsied and handed them to Captain Marshall.

"Thank you, Letty, you may go." The smile grew wider, showing excellent teeth, as he read the General's short note. "Do come in, Colonel Humphreys. Or, better yet, will you not accompany me to my club? I am sure you will find it entertaining, and we can do our business when we get back later this afternoon. Do you have the afternoon free?"

"Yes, certainly, if it is not too much bother."

"Do you have a horse?"

"Yes, at the Eagle."

"I know Mr. Formicola, the owner, quite well! Let us repair, then, to the Eagle and retrieve your horse."

He led me to his own stable, where a lad had his own horse ready. Captain Marshall led his horse and walked with me the two blocks to the tavern, where I called for my horse.

The club was at a farm a short ride out of town. As we rode, he explained, "Ordinarily our club meets from May to November to celebrate and enjoy ourselves outdoors. Today, though a little cold, is a special celebration for the success of one of our members whom we have elected to the new Congress."

"Should the man not be on his way to New York?" I knew from General Knox's letters from New York that the Congress still did not have a quorum due to the dilatory men that made it up. "How is the General to become President if there is no Congress to approve it?"

"Now, now, sir, a time and a place for everything. We could not possibly let our friend leave without celebrating, and quoits provide an excellent excuse."

"Quoits?"

"Quoits, sir. Ever played?"

"Certainly."

"Any good?"

"My strengths are in the poetic realm, sir, not the athletic."

"Indeed. A pity. Still, I am sure you will enjoy it. Do you mind a trot? We're a bit late for the festivities." We urged our horses into a trot and made excellent progress.

We shortly arrived at a meadow called Buchanan's Spring, where about 20 men had already gathered. They welcomed Captain Marshall as a prodigal son and me as the son's best friend. I gathered that the punch bowl had already been refilled twice, and the bonhomie was overflowing.

The afternoon passed quickly, with quoits taking up only a part and a great deal of drinking and back-slapping taking up the rest. They made me welcome, and I imbibed more than I would usually do on a Saturday afternoon, but it was very cold and the punch was very good. I fear I recited my own poetry at their demand. My Connecticut friends had received my poetic efforts with acclaim; the Quoits Club reception was stupendous, especially on the new verses I had composed at the end of the War. Captain Marshall grinned widely and congratulated me on my success. Well.

I saw the Captain perform at quoits and at law simultaneously. He took off his coat, loosened his arms, carried his right hand and right foot to the rear, then put his full strength into tossing the ring onto the meg, a short spike driven into the ground some distance away. The next player then did the same, to cheers, and that started the legal argument.

Captain Marshall was quite persuasive, though more disheveled than ever. "My ring, sirs, is the first occupant on the meg, sirs. By common law, of course, the first occupant owns the rights of the land extending up from the ground to the vaults of heaven. If my opponent has an adversary claim, sirs, he must apply for a writ of ejectment, and I am fully confident no judge here will grant such a thing." The point was his by acclamation, and indeed, the several judges present and even his opponent made no objection.

Over the course of the afternoon, I spoke with just about every person there. Lawyers, merchants, and other prominent citizens: to a man, they supported the federalist cause and the new Constitution. The Congressman, rather the worse for drink, said he would moot a bill to make the General President regardless of election if he could. The group picked up the new Congressman bodily and bundled him off in his carriage with cheers. The party had by then run out of drink, and as a result, broke up without further ado. The Captain and I rode back to his house. After we had warmed ourselves at his parlor fire, I inquired after his wife.

"Mrs. Marshall is afflicted with the loss of our child, Colonel, and does not mix in society."

"I am sorry for your loss, sir."

"That's all right, Colonel. I am as sorry for society, for she is the bright fire that warms my life." He smiled. He was clearly of an optimistic and sanguine temperament. "Now, sir, what can I do for the General?"

I explained the history of the murder to Captain Marshall, then took out my pocket-book and the Cockburn letter. He read it over and smiled. My heart sank; surely Captain Marshall did not approve of the judgment of the magistrate? Surely this warm, social man would come to the General's aid?

He said, handing the letter back to me, "This Mr. Cockburn must fancy himself quite a lawyer, to cite the Act so readily in his supposed preliminary hearing to commit the General to an examining court."

"He is really just a farmer and magistrate."

"These county magistrates are mostly just jumped-up yokels, sir, with little real acquaintance with the law, despite their title as justice of the peace. I would say, in Mr. Cockburn's case, that he has little real acquaintance with the General either."

I rallied. "He is the next-door neighbor and a close friend to Colonel George Mason, sir."

Captain Marshall smiled again. "Indeed. And so, presumably, he holds similar political leanings as the good Colonel?"

"Yes, and that is the source of this accusation, as the General thinks."

"I agree with him." He smiled again. "I do some little legal business with the Colonel, and he is what most lawyers would term an impatient client. He knows the law and, because he has no practical experience of its application, cannot see why it should take so long to apply it to his benefit. I daresay the same is true of Mr. Cockburn. But Mr. Cockburn seems to feel no compunction in using his small legal knowledge for political advantage."

Time to plead. "The General would appreciate anything you can do to help the situation."

Captain Marshall leaned forward toward me and tapped my knee with his finger. "Sir, I would do anything in the world to assist the General, who is the foremost figure of our time. I admire and respect what he has done for our country without limit, and I know he will be the first and finest President of this land. I would follow him through the gates of Hell, should he decide to go there, just as I and my father followed him in the War."

"Then you will write a letter of support?"

Captain Marshall sat back in his chair, showing me the grin I had seen on winning his quoits match. "The proper course would be to initiate a case at law to remove Mr. Cockburn as a magistrate." He rubbed his hands together in what I could only call lawyer-like glee. "The legislature just this last year passed a law taking that power away from the Governor's privy council and requiring a judge to rule on the request. It was I who insisted on such a law, having seen what tyranny can do. But legal action in the courts may be as effective as executive tyranny when the cause is just. And this cause is more than just. Perhaps simply the threat of such an action may be enough."

He steepled his hands and looked up at the ceiling. "Dear me, let me see. What can we do about Colonel Mason?" He looked at me. "Colonel Mason and I have been acquainted since the ratification convention last year, and he and others were impressed enough with my performance there to send their legal business my way. I cannot, as a lawyer in good standing, disavow the relationship, but I think I might, hypothetically of course, give the good Colonel some advice—in confidence—about his participation in what might be considered in certain quarters a political conspiracy against the General. Yes, that might do the trick." The lawyer eyed me with a smile. "Hypothetically, of course."

He got up and sat at his desk to write out a letter and sealed it. He handed it to me.

"Please deliver this to the General, who may give it to Colonel Mason. I am sure that the Colonel on reading this letter will extend his influence to his friend Cockburn. The letter lays out in full the dangers of their position. As the Colonel is a client, I cannot reveal its content because of client confidentiality, but please be assured I am confident that the General will be satisfied with the result."

I smiled. "Thank you, sir."

"As you saw today, I have many friends, and they are mostly as well-disposed toward the General as am I. I am prepared to lose Colonel Mason's business, and indeed his friendship, if it helps the General. Now, should Mr. Cockburn refer the General to a circuit court for trial, I will defend him to the utmost of my ability, and I will certainly persuade the court to find him guiltless. Of course, I could also undertake to shepherd a case against Mr. Cockburn under the 1788 law through the Virginia circuit courts should events require it."

I was relieved and overwhelmed by this remarkable support for the

General and thanked him effusively after stowing the letter in my pocket-book. He shook my hand and told me he was happy to make my acquaintance and to look him up any time I returned to Richmond, and to give his very best respects to the General.

"And tell the General to let me know," he finished, "whether to proceed with the application to the district court. I will stand ready to plead at any time for him."

I took my leave and rode back the short distance to the Eagle, where I had a fine supper courtesy of Mr. Formicola, who was very happy to serve a friend of Captain Marshall. I fell into bed a satisfied and happy man, my mission complete.

22

MONDAY, MARCH 9, 1789, MORNING

On Monday morning, I joined the General at breakfast with his sister's family. His mother's house was on Charles Street in Fredericksburg. Mrs. Elizabeth Lewis, who cared for their mother, was a cheerful widow of 56, one year younger than her brother, and you could see the resemblance to him in her face. Their mother did not appear at breakfast.

"What brings you to Fredericksburg, Colonel Humphreys?" Mrs. Lewis asked while pouring me some chocolate.

"I am here at the General's request, ma'am, having undertaken a mission in Richmond for him."

She turned to her brother. "Is this about the cruel murder you were telling us about?"

Apparently, talk of murder was not forbidden at the Lewis family breakfast table. The General looked a touch uncomfortable but answered, "Yes, Betty. The Fairfax County magistrate is being a bit obstreperous and dare I say magisterial, and I am taking legal advice from Captain Marshall, whom you know."

I did not elaborate on my mission, as I thought the General might not appreciate the extent of his business being known to his sister's family. I also felt that I was not up to explaining my afternoon among the leading citizens of Richmond or explaining the complexities surrounding the game of quoits. My head still ached, two days later.

Mrs. Lewis picked up her original topic, not being deterred by her brother's reticence. "But what are you going to do about your people, George? Surely a murder like this is going to make them restless?"

"Very much so, I am afraid, Betty. I am relying on Colonel Hooe, the Fairfax County Sheriff, to investigate and find the culprit. His man has spent several days at Mount Vernon apparently to no avail, but I must depend upon them for now."

"I know you, George. You depend upon no one but yourself."

The General smiled at his sister. "I suppose that is true, as a rule. You do indeed know me, Betty! But at the moment I have nothing to do but to wait for information. I consulted Captain Marshall to discover whether I have any standing to do something myself, d'you see."

"Speaking of waiting, sir." Robert Lewis, the fresh-eyed 18-year-old son of the General's sister, addressed the General. "What is the state of the election? When are you going to New York?"

"Bob! Now I told you not to distress your uncle about that," Mrs. Lewis admonished her son, though in a kindly tone.

Abashed, the young man said, "Sorry, uncle, I did not mean to pry."

The General merely nodded in acknowledgement and smiled at his nephew. "Bob, I have not yet decided whether to accept the Presidency. Knowing of your interest, I will keep you and the family informed, of course, as events develop. They appear to develop extraordinarily slowly at the moment, with little glory to be had."

"Well, George," persisted Mrs. Lewis, "I think you really must take a hand in this murder before your people start disappearing, as they surely will if they think they are all to be murdered."

"Now, it is not that bad, Betty. Indeed, we have found the murdered man not much liked by the other Negroes, and it would appear that he was involved in some kind of organized larceny. We must allow the Sheriff to complete his investigation, as this matter may extend to neighboring plantations in the county."

"Not Colonel Mason's, surely." Mrs. Lewis seemed to know

everything about her brother.

"Indeed, yes."

She looked at him with compassion. "George, no one of our acquaintance has a life as complicated as yours. I think you do it deliberately," she said with good humor. "Oh, that reminds me: did you get the chance you wanted to talk with Mother about the Presidency?"

The General grimaced. "Yes, Betty. It was painful, very painful, to have the same discussion over again, but after these long months of opposition to it, she has grudgingly accepted that I may be elected and that I may accept the election."

"Oh, George, how wonderful! That must be a great relief to your troubled mind."

The General cut and ate a piece of ham, chewing with what seemed extra deliberation. He swallowed. Having had time to consider his response, he decided on a joke. "The sermon we attended yesterday mentioned the trials of Job, Betty. I think that, while I am not quite challenged by Providence to such an extent, the removal of my mother's disapproval is not likely to make much of a difference to my troubled mind. It does certainly make my decision about the Presidency easier, but I have enough else to be getting on with still."

His sister laughed and agreed with him.

After we had finished breakfast, we gathered in the parlor for a leave-taking. I asked "May I ask, Mrs. Lewis, how is your mother?"

Mrs. Lewis replied, "Thank you for asking, Colonel Humphreys. I fear she is not doing very well."

The General then said, with little emotion in his voice, "She is near death. It cannot be many weeks."

"Oh, George. You know we can always hope." Mrs. Lewis reached out to touch her brother's arm.

"I think it best to be ready for the inevitable, Betty. It is only to be expected; she was given a longer life than most in our family and has struggled through it with many painful events, starting with the deaths of our father and Lawrence at too early an age." Mrs. Lewis looked as though this reflection was not of much comfort to her. I knew the General was expressing his strong belief in the Stoic principles he espoused, but I also knew enough of his history with his mother to understand his feelings, or the lack of them. His mother was not a kind and considerate woman, to say the least. But he knew his filial duty and performed it.

The General was sitting watching his grandson Wash playing with his toy soldiers. Mrs. Lewis said, "Before you leave, George, I think we must talk a little about Mother's will. Will you join me in the library?"

"I think we might as well talk here, Betty. I think Colonel Humphreys and I are intimate enough so that I do not mind his hearing it."

Mrs. Lewis smiled at me. "Very well, George. I have gone over everything, and I think there are really only a few things you must know. You are executor, you know."

The General replied, "I thought that might be the case. To be honest, I do not think I can do it if I accept the Presidency. Yet another reason not to accept, I suppose! Ah well. No, if I am to become President, move myself far from here to New York, then create a national government *de novo,* out of thin air—how can I handle the details of Mother's estate as well?"

Mrs. Lewis, rather taken aback, said, "I hadn't thought! True, true. Well, you must use your own judgment on that, of course, but I should think being President more important than managing a small estate. Now, about that, in fact. She's left you the Accokeek land and some furniture. But you know Mother has been struggling with her slaves."

My ears perked up a bit at this; I was not aware Mrs. Mary Washington was also a slave owner.

"No, I did not. Struggling? How?" The General's voice was resigned.

"I mean, what to do with them. I think she wanted to leave them all to you."

"What!"

"It cannot come as much of a surprise, George, you know she thinks the world of your management abilities."

The General's countenance told me clearly he knew no such thing, but he remained silent.

Mrs. Lewis took no notice of his reaction and continued. "But she has decided to leave you just that one man you have working at Mount Vernon, what's his name?"

"George; his name is George." The General thought for a moment. "Yes, that would be good—well, not good, I do not wish to encumber myself with more people, but George—he has married a woman at Mount Vernon, and if he were left to some other person, he would be split from his family."

"Could not his wife just go with him?"

"No, she is a dower slave."

Mrs. Lewis looked puzzled. "What does that mean?"

The General explained, "My wife's late husband died intestate, without a will. She thus inherited his estate but with all its assets entailed on the other Custis family heirs. That means that any slaves she inherited cannot be sold or freed, either by her or by me, but must pass to the other heirs on her death. My wife gets only the income from the property and work from the people during her lifetime."

"My goodness, how complicated." Mrs. Lewis smiled again. "But not your fault this time, George, unless by your marrying Martha."

The General laughed. "I will not say I did not value my wife's estate on my marriage, but it has proved such a wonderful thing in itself that I almost regret the inheritance."

"Well, I suppose George is better off with you, then, George." She smiled: two Georges in one sentence. I wondered whether the complexities of the free George's life matched up to the complexities in his slave's life; that George might not find his problems so easy to resolve as those of the General.

"All right. What else?" The General was ready for anything.

"Well, now. She has divided up all the other Negroes among her other heirs, one by one. But I was thinking that if any of the heirs die or refuse the inheritance, those Negroes will all be part of the residual estate and go to you again."

"We will just have to see what happens, Betty."

A servant then announced the General's carriage, and he, Wash, and I assumed our places after tearful goodbyes. I gave the General Captain Marshall's letter and explained his hypothetical strategy, and the General expressed his satisfaction.

I could tell, after just a few miles, that the General was not quite himself. He said but little and made only half-hearted efforts to help Wash organize his toy army on the seat across from us. Catching my look of concern, the General smiled and said, "I am sorry, Colonel, I am not very good company today. That business of the will—I could not say as much to my sister, but I do indeed recoil at the idea of inheriting more Negroes."

"But I collect that you are not yet ready to rid yourself of them? Could you not refuse the inheritance?"

"No, I cannot. It is my filial duty to accept it, if only as a memento of parental affection. It would not be right."

The intricate web of family, property, law, and social duty was a trap for the General, a never-ending cycle of dependency on this evil. But I could not help it, I spoke my heart. "Sir, you must acknowledge the simple moral evil of slavery."

He grimaced, then said, "I am perfectly willing to acknowledge it, Colonel. I feel the evil very much, every day. The murder of Julius has brought the matter much forward in my mind. The more we learn, the more it appears that the slaves on my plantations, and on other plantations such as that of Colonel Mason, are forced in many ways to do things they ought not, as a matter of survival. Julius may have been a villain, but his enslavement simply made that situation worse by creating a moral vacuum."

"I cannot agree more, sir. But surely you can do something yourself?"

"I have been racking my brain over the last few months, and today's revelation pushes me to a conclusion: If I accept the Presidency, I cannot. As President, I will be able to do nothing to solve this moral dilemma."

"How so, sir?"

"You were not privy to events during the Philadelphia convention two years ago. I sat for interminable hours as President of the convention listening to the southern gentlemen argue about ways and means of preserving their way of life. Hamilton and other northerners would spout abolition; Pinckney and other southerners would fulminate in response, and nothing would be done."

"Why, sir?"

"The southerners realized that there were more Negro slaves in their states than freemen; should those slaves count only as property, those states would have far smaller delegations to the new Congress, as the number of members from a state is proportional to the number of people in the state. So slaves are now people, but only three-fifths of a person—a compromise."

"But you, personally, sir—can you not just set an example with your own property?"

The General smiled, but his eyes were sad, and his tone was fatalistic. "What example would you have me set, Colonel? This is exactly what I have realized this morning. Consider George, and his wife. Would you have me break up that family? Remember, I cannot free the dower slaves. It is impossible. I could turn down the Presidency, of course; but then, I would still have nearly insuperable issues in freeing my people."

"I cannot admit the idea that you might refuse the Presidency, Your Excellency. But as a leader, sir, you must set the example."

"Again, I realized this morning, if I freed my own slaves, as a leader setting an example, the gentlemen of the South would comprehend that they did not have a leader they could follow. To free their slaves is to pauperize themselves, or even to create potential voters that might disrupt their hold on power. They would abandon me, and the Union, entirely. America as a nation would cease to exist. I would be President of nothing."

I shivered, suddenly. I felt a great foreboding wash through me, as though hundreds of thousands of men looked at me from beyond the grave, from beyond history. I pursued my point no farther with the General that day, or for many days to come.

23

MONDAY, MARCH 16, 1789, MORNING

The General spent the next week riding out to his farm, managing his managers and overseers, and preparing to leave Mount Vernon for an extended period as President.

The General's patience wore thin as the week progressed, as we heard nothing about the murder and nothing about the electors. By Sunday, his restlessness took him to church with his wife and family and myself. The General attended church rarely, but as during the War, when confronted with complex decisions, he earnestly prayed for the guidance of Providence. I do not know what answer he may have received that Sunday, but on getting home that day, he wrote to his sister in Fredericksburg offering her son the position of junior private secretary to the President, should the General decide to accept the office. A little of the despair I felt dissipated—the General was increasingly serious about New York. After telling me of his letter to his sister, he then asked me whether I would serve him as a private secretary for a time as well, and I quickly agreed.

Monday morning dawned bright and cold. The General and I were up at the usual hour of 5 a.m. for breakfast.

"Colonel Humphreys." The General swallowed a bite of his hoe-cake. "I find myself unable to wait any longer for events. Will you join me on a ride out to Springfield Farm this morning? I think it is time to acquaint Mr. Cockburn and Colonel Mason with Captain Marshall's very cogent legal opinion on the situation."

"I am entirely at your service, Your Excellency." My own patience had run out before his.

The General arose from the dining table and said, "Last evening, I sent a note to Colonel Hooe requesting that he attend a short meeting at Mr. Cockburn's farm with us today, as early as possible, and he has agreed to it. We will meet him there."

Springfield Farm sat on Mason's Neck a short ride away from Colonel Mason's property and Gunston Hall. Colonel Mason's properties stretched above and around this farm. As we rode down the Neck three hours later, the General and I said little. We drew up at the house behind a coach which I recognized as that of Colonel Hooe.

The butler showed us into the front parlor, where Colonel Hooe and his clerk Williamson rose to greet us. The passage floor creaked, and Mr. Cockburn entered the room.

"It is always a pleasure to welcome you to my house, gentlemen," he said with a cold kind of politeness, "even under the current untoward circumstances." He remained standing, so everyone stood as well.

The General said, "Thank you, Mr. Cockburn; it is precisely about those circumstances that we have come. First, may I ask whether anything has changed about the situation since your letter to me of two weeks ago?"

"I am afraid that the only thing we have learned is that there is significant unrest and dissatisfaction among the Negroes on the Mount Vernon plantations. Colonel Hooe, have there been any new developments in your investigations since Mr. Williamson reported to me last?"

"No, sir, none," said Colonel Hooe. "We have been unable to find anyone at Mount Vernon or beyond who will admit to any knowledge or information about the tragedy. Williamson?" The clerk nodded his agreement.

Cockburn resumed, "While I cannot discuss the details of our investigation, I can assure Your Excellency that everything is being done to resolve the questions in this case."

"And so I remain under a cloud of suspicion." The General's voice was calm as he looked Mr. Cockburn in the eye. "And you still wish to drag me in front of an examining court."

"Yes, I am afraid that is unavoidable, sir, given the information we have received about unrest on your plantation and the utter lack of motive for anyone else." The magistrate was unmoved. "And so, I think there is little more to say today."

"A moment more of your time would be appreciated, sir." The General used his most commanding tone for this mild request.

"Certainly, Your Excellency." The magistrate masked his obvious irritation with his politeness.

"I have taken legal advice on the matter, sir. I think the first step we must take to resolve it requires us to consult with your good neighbor, Colonel Mason."

The magistrate eyed the General narrowly. "Colonel Mason? What has he to do with it?"

"As my nearest neighbor, Colonel Mason's plantation appears to have been the locus of some very strange events. Colonel Humphreys and I have found evidence that my overseer, Julius, had commerce with people on Colonel Mason's farm that may have strayed into the illegal."

"Evidence? What evidence?"

"I would prefer to discuss that with Colonel Mason directly, if you do not mind. Some of my people—"

"Slaves? Your evidence is from slaves? You must know that is inadmissible." The magistrate's tone was dismissive.

The General looked nettled at being interrupted. He began again. "Some of my people have reported a good deal of theft of goods and provisions from my farms, as I reported to Colonel Hooe, who has determined that such thefts are widespread. I daresay your own farm must suffer such depredations as well. In any case, I propose we visit Gunston Hall now and talk out the matter with Colonel Mason. I feel sure that with his aid we may resolve this situation."

Mr. Cockburn reluctantly agreed to this reasonable proposal. "I will accede to your request, as long as it will not take up too much of our time."

The General replied, "Thank you, sir; I strongly appreciate your candor in this regard, Mr. Cockburn. I can assure you that I intend to find the truth of this affair, if for nothing else than to obtain justice for my slain overseer."

"I will ride with Colonel Hooe, gentlemen," said Mr. Cockburn. The General's stride was long and confident as he walked to his horse, mounted, and led the way to Gunston Hall. Colonel Mason himself emerged from the front door of his home to greet us on his large porch.

The General said, "Good morning, Colonel Mason. We are very sorry to disturb you, but we have urgent business."

Looking at the little crowd of people before him, Colonel Mason said, "Good heavens. Have the British resumed their offensive?" His attempt at humor showed his gout was, if not gone, at least easing.

The General replied with a smile, "No, sir, I am happy to say there are no British soldiers closer than Canada. We come on an errand related to the recent murder of my overseer."

"I see. This is not a social call. Well, I suppose you had all better come in and sit down."

As we entered the parlor, the General took a letter from his pocketbook and handed it to Colonel Mason. He said, "Colonel Mason, this letter is from Captain John Marshall of Richmond. I requested advice from him on the matter of my murdered overseer, and he was kind enough to supply me with this letter to you. He considered you to be the person most likely to understand the nature and scope of his advice. As you see, I have brought Mr. Cockburn and Colonel Hooe with me to participate in this conference."

Colonel Mason broke the seal on the letter as we all took our seats and read it through with an unreadable face. He then read it through again. He stared at the General, his mouth a tight line and his mind clearly churning through a range of thought, good and bad. After a few moments of such reflection, he said, "Captain Marshall certainly demonstrates his ability to write compelling legal argument. I think it is quite appropriate to share this with Mr. Cockburn; do you agree, Your Excellency?"

"I do indeed agree, sir. Please," said the General, waving a hand at the magistrate. Colonel Mason handed the letter to Mr. Cockburn, who read it through quickly, his face alternately paling and turning red. He, too, took some time for reflection, which allowed his face to resume its natural coloring.

He opened his mouth, closed it again, then said, "Captain Marshall is...quite convincing, sir. Quite convincing. I may have gone too far, sir, in proposing a general inquiry on the evidence I have." He gnawed his lower lip, then continued, sitting forward in his chair. "I am willing to acknowledge the General's reputation and honor and accede to Captain Marshall's suggested course of action. I am perfectly willing to cooperate with the General in this investigation to follow the evidence to a just conclusion. Without any...political...considerations." The magistrate closed his mouth firmly and sank back into his chair.

"Quite, quite." Colonel Mason, the leading antifederalist opponent of the General, spoke in a perfectly bland tone. "Colonel Hooe, what is the state of your investigation?"

"I must admit, sir, that my investigation—or Mr. Williamson's—has found very little of any use. We have not identified a suspect in the crime, we have not identified the murder weapon, and we have no witnesses that can tell us why the slave was at General Washington's

Landing. Does that sum it up, Mr. Williamson?"

The quiet clerk nodded.

The General said, "You may recall, sir, when we were last here, we explained there were signs of collusion between your people and mine in a matter of theft. While this may not seem related to the murder, it would appear that the murdered man, Julius, had dealings with your own overseers and people. Our only request is the chance to speak with your overseers to see what they know."

"I see. I am sorry I was so short with you a week ago; I fear my gout got the better of my temper. I have no objections to your speaking with Mr. Thompson."

"There is more, sir." The General hesitated, then said, "When we were last here, we had an opportunity to question one of your Negro overseers." He looked at me.

I said, "He was working with Mr. Thompson: a large, well-built man of about 30 years of age with small ears, a large, flat nose, and a ready smile."

"That would almost certainly be Nace, the overseer at Occoquan. When was that? Never mind—it must have been done in secret after you had left." Colonel Mason's face flushed. "After, indeed, I had made it clear that I did not wish you to engage in any such activity."

"Yes, that is so," replied the General. "I apologize for the intrusion into your affairs, but it seemed a necessity. It still does." His words apologized, but his voice was firm and commanding.

The choler rose even further in Colonel Mason's face, and his eyes bulged. Instead of giving his choler expression, as he normally did without reservation, he closed his eyes and held himself back, lips pressed tight, the red gradually becoming mottled. The silence lengthened while he battled with himself. In the end, diplomacy won. He opened his eyes and looked at the General calmly but with disfavor.

He said, "I accept your apology, sir, however reluctantly. Did you discover anything to the point at all?"

"We did not discover anything, sir, except that Nace was not willing to speak with us in the presence of Mr. Thompson, and that Mr. Thompson did not want to speak with us at all."

"What do you wish me to do?"

"If you might facilitate a conversation with Mr. Thompson, that would be extraordinarily helpful, Colonel. As well, we would like to speak with Nace alone, out of the presence of Mr. Thompson and yourself."

"Very well." Colonel Mason passed his hand over his face with exasperation; but, committed, he realized he had little choice but to accede to our request. He looked impatiently at Mr. Cockburn, who drew back into his chair as though to disappear in it, then looked back at the General. "Let me see; it would be best to talk with Mr. Thompson at his house rather than having him come in here. And I must summon Nace from the Occoquan Quarter where he lives and works."

Colonel Mason asked James, his butler, to send a horse to Occoquan for Nace. We then went outside to a brick building in the yard, where Colonel Mason knocked at the door.

He called out, "Mr. Thompson! A word, if you please, sir."

The door opened and Mr. Thompson looked out at us, beard bristling. His eyes narrowed as he saw the group of men: authority in mass, come to weigh on him. He focused suddenly on Colonel Hooe and Mr. Williamson and his eyes widened. "Colonel Hooe. Mr. Williamson, you here?"

Mr. Williamson quickly replied, "In my capacity as clerk and deputy to Colonel Hooe, sir, not as merchant." The clerk stared at the shirt-clad overseer without blinking. I thought the clerk's obvious suspicion might warn the overseer that something was up; then I reflected that a crowd of people including one he had previously run off the property—me—had probably already done that.

Mr. Thompson replied, "Looks bloody damn serious. Just give me a moment, gentlemen, I will get my coat—I reckon the house is too small for this brawl." Mr. Thompson stepped back inside and shut the door. We all waited with varying degrees of impatience.

Eventually, Colonel Mason tired of the wait and stepped up to the door again. Knocking loudly, he called out to Thompson to hurry. We waited. After a short time, I had a sinking feeling in my stomach. Simultaneously, the General said, with some urgency, "I think, Colonel Mason, that Mr. Thompson is not coming out. Perhaps we should go in?"

Colonel Mason said with exasperation, "I suppose so." He turned the door handle and we crowded into the house and found—nothing and no one. The back window of the house was open to the cold air, and the house was empty.

24

MONDAY, MARCH 16, 1789, LATE MORNING

"Well, gentlemen," said Colonel Mason, "I do believe I feel a resurgence of my gout. Damn the man! What is he thinking?"

The General, taking command, said, "Colonel Hooe, you must chase down this man Thompson as quickly as possible. He cannot have gone far. Mr. Cockburn: I trust that everything is now clear and easy between us?"

Mr. Cockburn was subdued. He nodded and said, "Yes, Your Excellency."

"Thank you, sir. Now, Colonel Hooe, please proceed."

"Very well, Your Excellency. Colonel Mason, do you have a good tracker here?"

"Yes, sir. James, my butler, will assist you in finding the right man."

"Thank you. Will you join us, Cockburn? Come along, Williamson. We have started the fox, let us loose the hounds!"

Williamson bowed to us, then followed his employer and Mr. Cockburn out to the yard to consult with the butler. The General and I stood in the passage with Colonel Mason, who said, "Nace will come soon. Would you care to refresh yourselves, or would you prefer to wait in the parlor?"

The General replied, "Thank you, no, sir. We will wait here; there is no need to trouble yourself further."

"Then I will retire to coddle my gouty stomach without further ado, sir. Good day." He stamped off up the stairs. We sat down in the passage to wait for the Occoquan overseer.

The General said to me in a low voice, "Colonel, we must quickly determine what Nace knows about the connections between Thompson and Julius. If you would be so good as to lead the questioning? I find that I can sometimes be...intimidating."

I reflected that intimidation may sometimes be the best way of getting information, but said, "Certainly, Your Excellency. It seems likely that Thompson is very much involved given that he has absconded when confronted with the law."

"Yes, though I think the detail of what he knows would be more useful than just the fact that he is involved. I truly regret that we have lost the opportunity to confront him directly. We must trace this conspiracy back to its source. This overseer Nace is probably up to his neck in it as well; but I will not make assumptions, and nor should you."

We waited patiently for a time until we heard a stirring in the side passage. James came up to us and said, "Gentlemen: Nace is here. Would you care to step into the yard?"

"Thank you; yes, we will come out now," said the General, rising from his chair.

We stepped outside into the cold day once again, this time to find Nace awaiting us in the yard. He looked quite as calm as the last time I had seen him. Though not dressed as warmly as us, he appeared impervious to the cold.

I said, "Hello, Nace. You may remember me—Colonel Humphreys. This is General Washington."

"Sirs. James said you wanted to talk to me?" Quick brown eyes shifted from me to the General and back. The slave overseer did not seem particularly afraid of us, just curious.

I said, "Yes—on the same topic as before, I fear."

"Julius." The slave's deep voice sounded resigned.

"And now Mr. Thompson."

"What about Massa Thompson?" Nace looked around for the overseer.

"He has absconded, run off. I think he is no longer master here."

Nace grinned. "Got to agree with you there, sir, if he done run away. Guess Colonel Mason gonna try to get him back?"

"Colonel Hooe and Mr. Cockburn are endeavoring to trace him now."

"Good luck to 'em. Massa Thompson, he can move pretty quick and quiet when he need to. Anyhow, about Julius."

"Yes—what do you know about Julius and the thefts from the Mount Vernon plantation?"

"Not much."

"Come now, Nace, nothing to fear from us—you can speak freely." I tried to put as much candor and friendliness into my voice as I could. The General kept his face calm, though I am sure he was irritated at the reluctance of the overseer to say what he knew.

Nace grinned. "Honest, sir, I don't know nothin' about Mount Vernon. Just met Julius a couple of times, aways back. Julius did meet up with Massa Thompson and other white folks, though, back in January. Last time I saw him was then." He looked down, looked at the General, looked at me. "I only know about Colonel Mason's farm, that's where I work, sir. Occoquan."

"Nace, first let me ask, is there much theft here? On Colonel Mason's farms?"

Nace smiled, slowly. "People got to live, sir. Always a bit of stuff going out the wrong door. You know how it is."

"Perhaps there is more than a bit of stuff, though? And is Mr. Thompson part of that?"

"Cain't say no, sir. Massa Thompson, he always did have more money than sense."

Of course, Thompson being gone and not likely to come back, I had no way to check that.

"And does Mr. Thompson have a lot of money, Nace?"

"Yes, sir, he do." Nace smiled again. "Massa Thompson, he kind of foolish about his money. I can show you where he keep it." He turned and led us over to Thompson's house. We went in through the open door and invited him to come in, as he had stopped at the threshold. He walked over to the fireplace, and showed us a hole. A piece of brick was lying on the floor below it.

Nace said, "He keep his money behind that brick, take it out with a poker or some such. He got a lot of money, maybe 20 pound or more."

The General picked up the brick and carefully reinserted it into the fireplace. "Then he has more cash than do I at the moment. I think it unlikely he came by it honestly." He turned to Nace. "Did Mr. Thompson gamble? Could this be a loan?"

Nace said, "I been workin' around Massa Thompson quite a while, sir, and he ain't never borrowed a penny. He got money from Julius and other people like that. Didn't like games much, either—quick way to lose what you got, he'd say. He was a close man. No, Massa Thompson got that money from folks doin' his business, sir, sure did."

I asked, "How did you know about the brick?"

"Another thing about Massa Thompson, he like his whiskey. Couple weeks past, I got some from a friend of mine over to Occoquan, no need to say who. Gave it to Massa Thompson so's I could spend a little more time on a trip I was gonna take. He's so happy about that whiskey, he drank it all right off while I was there. A little later, he was so happy, he took that brick out of the fireplace and counted that money, clean forgot I was there. That how I know how much he got. I left kind of quiet, then, so's not to disturb him. Have to say, that brick is a devil, temptation after temptation. I hope you gentlemen understand. Them ten commandments are right powerful commandments."

So Nace was a good Christian.

"You go to church, Nace?" I asked.

"Yes, sir, every sabbath. Black church, a course."

"Of course. So you do not steal yourself, but I think you have not informed Colonel Mason about Mr. Thompson's possible transgressions?"

"If I understand you, sir, then no sir, like I said—more than my life is worth. Massa Thompson, he pretty quick with the whip, and he know how to use a knife too. And he got other friends, too."

"Other friends?"

"Yes, sir. In Alexandria and Fredericksburg. They's a lot of action between here and Alexandria, lot of money changing hands. Massa Thompson sometimes meets up with folks up the road or down to Log Town, back down there." Nace pointed off to the south. "That's where Massa Thompson met up with Julius."

The General explained to me, "I remember that Colonel Mason built some cabins from logs down out of sight of the main house, Colonel. Log Town. For his people."

"That's it, sir. Massa Thompson liked to meet up with his white friends there so nobody at the house would see. Course, *we* all saw, but that weren't no account to Massa Thompson 'cause he knew we wouldn't tell on him."

The General shook his head slowly, and said, "I cannot quite believe Colonel Mason's plantation is so out of control. But then, I had little suspicion that mine was either. At least I can trust my nephew George and Mr. Fairfax and the other managers." He paused, perhaps thinking about his nephew's ramblings, then continued. "Perhaps the Colonel's gout has somewhat inhibited his ability to oversee his staff effectively."

"Plantation works fine, sir. We all just get along with our work and get things done, don't pay much attention to the white folks, cause they don't work much."

The General was taken aback by this very remarkable statement, but he saw the humor in it.

"Indeed. I am happy to hear it, for Colonel Mason's sake. Oh, and by the way, Nace, are Colonel Mason's chickens in the habit of finding their way into pots on my plantation?" The General's tone was jocular, but his eyes were sharp on the overseer's face.

Nace, unafraid, grinned. "That Julius, he sure did like his chicken. Got Massa Thompson to give him part of his share of the doin's in kind, sir. We all know that." The smile disappeared. "Jus' took our chickens, he did, and didn't pay us for 'em." The resentment was clear in his voice.

"And Colonel Mason knew nothing of this?"

"I don't think so, sir. But Massa Mason, he ain't so happy with Massa Thompson anyway. He give him the rough edge of his tongue quite a bit, sir—specially when Massa Thompson got ahold of a cask of whiskey. Now Massa Thompson done run off, I think that be the end of him round these parts."

"Indeed. And what about Ben the miller? From the Mount Vernon Grist Mill?"

Nace nodded his recognition. "Yes, sir, that man come by a lot to visit the girl Chancey at Log Town, I seen him there. As for stealin'—I don't know the man enough to say, but I never liked him much. Did not seem like a solid kind of man to my mind." Nace's face was inscrutable. I looked at him, and he looked at me, and I judged that, for better or worse, he would not tell me what he really thought. My poet's imagination sensed that, should Nace somehow translate himself into a fantastical world where black men could be politicians or diplomats, he would be a strong one.

The General picked up on this undercurrent from Nace and said to me, "I think it is time to pay Ben another visit, Colonel. All right, thank you, Nace. You may get back to working with your people, now."

Nace walked off down the road toward Occoquan, and we rode off to the Grist Mill.

25

MONDAY, MARCH 16, 1789, AFTERNOON

We arrived at the Grist Mill after a two-hour ride to find Mr. Davenport in his house. The General asked him to find Ben, and the miller went off to the mill to get him, as he was working there to get it ready for its spring work. We walked down to the mill quarters where we would talk with Ben.

The coopers, attracted by our presence and having no work at the moment, gathered together in a small group, muttering to each other quietly. Mr. Davenport came down from the mill with Ben.

The General said, "Since you are all gathered here, I will tell you all what I was going to tell Ben. We have just come from Gunston Hall, Colonel Mason's plantation. We went there to ask some questions of Mr. Thompson, the overseer there. Unfortunately, before we were able to do that, he disappeared."

The Negroes in front of us moved uneasily, not liking talk of disappearing overseers and theft.

"It would appear that there was more interaction between Mr. Thompson and you, Ben, than you have previously revealed, so we have come today to get a deeper understanding of what was really happening. I cannot stress enough the importance of your being completely honest. I do not intend any punishment or severe measures, but I must insist on knowing what was really happening."

Pigs in the animal paddock squealed at some hidden alarm, and all the men jumped in surprise. Ben looked dejected and said nothing.

Mr. Davenport, who had been shifting from foot to foot, suddenly shouted, "Damn your eyes, you bloody arsehole! Talk, and talk now!" The men jumped again, and the pigs squealed in new alarm.

The General, looking a little shocked, said, "Mr. Davenport! Be quiet, if you please." Mr. Davenport subsided, and the General turned back to Ben. "Ben, I have heard that you were Mr. Thompson's primary contact here. Is that true?"

Mr. Davenport rushed over to Ben, laid hands on him, and dragged him forward, the small Negro stumbling a little as his shirt ripped.

"Mr. Davenport!" The General reached and grabbed Mr. Davenport by the shoulders and dragged him back, away from the Negro, who was struggling to regain his footing. I reached and wrapped my arms around the swearing white man to keep him away from the Negroes, who had moved back a step or two as a group, leaving Ben isolated between them and us. The General loosed his hold, then stepped over to Ben and steadied him with a strong hand.

"Ben, no harm will come to you if you tell us the whole story."

Ben cleared his throat. "Yes, massa." He cleared his throat again and gulped air as he steadied himself, recovering from the sudden attack. "Very sorry, massa, sorry."

"All right, all right, man. Just tell us." The General stepped back from Ben and fixed him with a stern look.

"Well, it's like this, sir." He paused and looked up at the General with a pleading look. "Massa Thompson and Julius, they come by one day, summer of last year, sir. I'm working alone in the mill; Mr. Davenport, he's gone to Alexandria for the day. They knew that, and they come to t-t-torment me." The small Negro stuttered to a stop.

"Torment you how?"

"Well, sir, massa, they know about a girl I kind of know over to Log Town, just somebody I know."

"A girl. That would be Colonel Mason's Chancey?"

"Yes, sir. We, erm, see, we kind of, erm, got together from time to time."

"I collect that, Ben. I conclude that Mr. Thompson knew you were seeing this girl; I know the overseer at Occoquan did. At night? Without leave?"

"Yes, sir, just like that."

"Damn your bloody fucking eyes!" sputtered Mr. Davenport, struggling against my pinning arms.

"Be silent, sir!"

"But damn it to hell and gone, sir!"

"I daresay. Be quiet now." The General was frowning and his voice was low but commanding.

Mr. Davenport subsided again, but I could feel the tension in his body and held him tightly.

"Ben, what did Mr. Thompson and Julius say?"

"They told me they knew about us and all and if I didn't want Mr. Davenport or anyone up to the Mansion House knowing about it, to do what they said." He looked around wildly, then continued, "And they said they'd hurt Chancey, and I couldn't do nothin' about it!"

"And what was it that they wanted from you?"

Ben looked at the ground, then back up to the General's probing eyes. "Stealing stuff, sir—from the mill and all."

"Arrr!" said Mr. Davenport, rendered inarticulate with fury. I held him more tightly.

"And so this has been going on for this long while?"

"Yessir! Very sorry, massa, but I couldn't help it. Mr. Davenport, he'd-a killed me dead."

"I'll damn well kill you dead now, in a minute, you bloody fucking little devil!" The man struggled against me to free himself.

"Silence, sir!" The General's bark silenced the miller. "Perhaps, Colonel, you could escort Mr. Davenport back to his residence for the time being, as he is not being of much help to us here. If you please!" He waved his hand toward the miller's house.

"Yes, sir." I dragged the protesting miller back up the hill to his house, opened the door, and pushed him inside. "Wait here, sir, and cool off, until the General requests to see you. At your peril?"

"All right, all right." The man was sullen but resigned.

As I walked back down the hill, I could see Ben waving his arms around as he explained himself to the General. The other Negroes had taken another step back. I imagined that they would shortly disappear into the ground if they could find a way to do that.

The General was saying, "And so you would give the flour or other materials to Julius, who would take them away. And he gave you nothing in return? No money?"

"No sir, just promised not to tell about me and Chancey, sir. And not to hurt her."

"And did you ever see Julius with any other white men?"

"Nosir, I tried to stay away from that man lest he come to torment me even more. He weren't no good, no good atall, sir."

"Now, let's go back to the time that Mr. Davenport sent you and the others to Dogue Run to confront Julius about the theft of the flour. Tell me what happened."

"I had to g-g-go, Massa Davenport whup me otherwise, but Julius, he just laughed and c-c-cussed and told us to git out. I couldn't do nothin' else but git."

"Where were you that Friday and Saturday?"

"Which ones, massa?"

"The days on which Julius was killed. The last few days of February."

"Here, sir. Maybe at Log Town, part of the time."

"Will the other men back you up?"

The General looked at them. They nodded and one said, "Yes, sir, that's right. Ben was here."

"And can Chancey back you up for the time at Log Town?"

"Yes, sir, but please, sir, don't get her whupped! Just for being with me that night!"

"We will be careful with her and Nace, Ben. I am sure Nace will understand."

"Sir," wailed the Negro miller, "that man want her for himself! Nace ain't no thief, but he ain't my friend neither!"

"Did you kill Julius?"

Ben looked thunderstruck, then terrified. "Nosir, nosir, no, I did not. I never done that!"

"Do you know who did?"

"Honest to God, sir, no I don't! Ain't got no idea, sir! First we heard was when you told us, sir!" The other Negroes were as vocal in their agreement with this statement.

Ben's voice had gone up in pitch, his fright showing in his body and eyes. I hoped he would not expire on the spot with terror. The General seemed to be thinking along the same lines as he said, "All right, Ben, thank you for finally telling the truth. I am very sorry for your trouble, but you must realize you brought it on yourself through your illicit actions."

"Sorry, massa, very sorry."

"And no more night walking, to see your girl or anyone else." The General's face was austere and his tone admonishing but not angry as he calmed the man down. "If we talk with Chancey, we will avoid involving Nace. All right?"

"Yes sir, yes sir. Thank you sir. Sorry, sir." Ben nodded his head so furiously I was afraid it might pop off.

The General looked at the little group of gawking coopers. He gestured at them with a gloved hand and ordered, "Now, you all get back to your work."

The little knot of men vanished in an instant, as if by magic.

"I think, Colonel," said the General, as we walked back up toward the house, "that we must speak with Alice up at the Mansion House. The more we find out, the more we discover Julius's many transgressions. Surely he could not have lived that long with the woman without her being fully aware that he was up to something nefarious."

"I agree, sir."

"Let us first speak with Mr. Davenport to understand perhaps a little of his point of view, as I remain uncertain as to his actual role in all this. What do you think, Colonel?"

"You mean, was Mr. Davenport involved in the thefts?"

"Yes."

I thought about the man and his actions. "I doubt it, sir. He strikes me as a man of passion, not of guile. And he reacted explosively to Ben's admission of theft. I think he may just harbor dark thoughts about dark men."

"Poetically put, Colonel, I must say. I concur. Still, we must ask."

We walked back up the hill to the house. Knocking and entering, we found Mr. Davenport with a bottle, calmer but redder of face. The smell of whiskey was strong; he had been fortifying himself. There was no sign of his wife.

"I wish to apologize, General Washington, for my uncontrolled behavior." The man was being excessively formal, but his actions had been so extreme I was not surprised.

The General's voice was very firm. "I do not tolerate swearing and physical abuse of my people, sir. Please think carefully in the future before allowing yourself to lose control. It does not help in any situation."

"Yes, sir, no sir, I will sir."

"Now, Mr. Davenport, I must ask—were you aware of any of this? Is your anger generated from surprise or from fear of exposure?"

Mr. Davenport was nonplussed. "Exposure?" He suddenly realized what the General was asking. His face paled. "No, sir—never! I was just taken by surprise by that devil's words. Night walking without leave, stealing, outsiders coming in while I was not here—it's too much, sir!"

"You have served me without major issues arising since 1785, Mr. Davenport. I hope to retain you, but I cannot conceive of doing so if you continue to behave this way. You are on parole, sir. And do try to stay away from the strong liquor."

"Yes, Your Excellency, yes. I understand. You have my word." He looked at his bottle with longing and sighed.

"Very well." The General looked around at the meager furnishings. The simple life and belongings of the miller told us he was not spending large amounts of ill-gotten monies on himself and his wife. Nary a loose brick in sight. "I will want you to account for everything here monthly to Mr. Lear, or to my manager at the Mansion House in our absence. Every penny, sir; every penny!" He stared down at the miller with hot eyes and an intimidating frown.

"Yes, Your Excellency."

"Come, Colonel, let us return to the Mansion House—Mrs. Washington will be waiting dinner on us."

We left poor Mr. Davenport with his forbidden bottle and his parole and trotted back to the Mansion House just in time to assuage Mrs. Washington's fears that the General might go hungry.

26

THURSDAY, MARCH 19, LATE AFTERNOON AND EVENING

On Monday, Mr. Williamson sent a note informing us that the hunt for Mr. Thompson had come up empty. On Tuesday and Wednesday, the General sent for information from Alexandria, but there was little progress in identifying any leads in the murder investigation. Late Wednesday afternoon, Mr. Williamson sent another note advising us that one of Colonel Mason's horses had vanished on Monday and turned up Tuesday morning in a field near Alexandria, leading the authorities to believe that Thompson was somewhere in the vicinity of the town; but as yet they had not found any trace of him.

Major Washington had recovered somewhat while we were traveling, but the General had not found an opportunity to speak with him about what he had said during his recent attack of illness. I perceived the Major was deeply embarrassed and ashamed of his illness, and that he kept himself as much out of sight of the General as possible, and the General himself was very busy managing his own affairs.

On Thursday, the General sent a servant to town at first light, then rode out to visit the Ferry farm just down the river from the Mansion House. Early in the afternoon, he found me reading on the piazza, where I enjoyed the midday light and brisk temperature, a counterpoint to the warm poetry.

"Good afternoon, Colonel Humphreys." The General regarded the river, hands clasped behind his back, his face thoughtful. He had received the response from Alexandria. "This morning the authorities in Alexandria again reported no progress in their manhunt. I think it is time to make use of our newly acquired investigatory powers. However, there is much we do not know, and I am reluctant just to charge ahead without understanding the terrain. We must consult with our friends in Alexandria in person, not by proxy. If we leave soon, we can be at Wise's Tavern for dinner."

Within the hour, the General and I were on horseback accompanied by our servants, heading for Alexandria at a fast pace. The General brought two servants, the young Negro Christopher and another man, saying that Christopher needed exposure to the wider world.

A little under two hours later, we pulled our horses up at Colonel John Fitzgerald's house in Alexandria. Colonel Fitzgerald had been one of the General's original aides-de-camp in the war and was a great friend to the General. He had been wounded in the Battle of Monmouth and had retired before my time as an aide, but I had met him several times in the General's company. Colonel Fitzgerald had joined with the General in forming the Potomac Company, the enterprise that was to promote commerce in the West by linking the Potomac River to the James and Ohio Rivers with a canal. The General had a standing invitation to stay with the Colonel if he needed to be in Alexandria for extended business. Colonel Fitzgerald, like Colonel Hooe, was one of the chief merchants in the port city as well as serving as a director of the Potomac Company.

Colonel Fitzgerald and his wife made us welcome and accommodated us, our horses, and our servants for the night. The General suggested that Colonel Fitzgerald accompany us to dinner at Wise's, and the Colonel agreed immediately.

While Colonel Fitzgerald was preparing himself, the General apprised me of his plan for the evening.

"Colonel, Wise's Tavern is the center of social activity for the merchants and important men of Alexandria. I know many of them, of course, and Colonel Fitzgerald knows many more. I want to socialize with them to understand what the merchant community in Alexandria thinks about the political economic situation. It will also give us an opportunity to see what they know about Mr. Thompson and his doings."

"Do you want to bring up the matter of larceny, Your Excellency?"

"Yes, but let us do it diplomatically, make it emerge from conversation, perhaps guided by subtle hints on our part. We can then discover what people really think is going on without accusing anyone of anything."

This was a side of the General I had not seen before. During the War, as Commander-in-Chief he commanded his men and pleaded with Congress for support, money, and supplies. I realized that, as an elected President and executive chief of the government, he must rely on the support of his followers to get things done.

"What do you wish me to do, sir?"

"Listen well, form opinions of the men with whom we speak, and if you see opportunity, bring the conversation around to Mr. Thompson and the problem of theft on the plantations hereabouts."

We entered the tavern, immediately engulfed by the noise of the crowd. The room was warm and smelled of beer and wine and roasting meat, very pleasing to hungry travelers such as ourselves. John Wise emerged from behind the bar and welcomed the General and Colonel Fitzgerald with great fanfare and many bows; I'm sure his business did not suffer for being the consistent choice of the Great Man. As it also happened to be by far the best tavern in Alexandria, a town full of taverns, it was always a pleasure for me to dine there with the General.

Naturally, the Great Man was also the center of attention. Many of the town's leading lights were present, and all of them wanted to socialize with the General. John Wise sat us in a prominent corner and kept them at bay during our dinner, but with the pudding consumed and the postprandial madeira glasses in our hands, we were fresh meat to the hungry crowd.

Colonel Fitzgerald introduced us to every member of the small crowd that the General did not already know, and we circulated in good humor, the General at his most affable. I made mental note of their names while I am sure they immediately forgot mine. After a time, the crowd grew so dense around us that Wise and his barmaid pulled together a few of their tables and we all sat for a general discussion.

"The damned British are making our lives impossible," said one portly gentleman, moodily swirling his glass.

"And when was that not so, sir?" replied the General. "As in the war, we must make the best of it."

"But Your Excellency, there must be something you can do about the restraints on our trade. After all, if there is no trade, there are no customs fees, and the federal government will be as bereft of funds as the Confederation."

The General replied, "As I have not yet finally decided to accept the Presidency, I have not yet contemplated the commercial and diplomatic measures the new nation will take. I do think the nation may do something to create a more independent commerce. It may not be primarily with Britain, of course. Mr. Jefferson, and indeed Colonel Humphreys here, have made great strides in France and the rest of Europe."

I interjected, "Indeed that is so, sirs. Why, the whole world is open to us. After the War, I joined Mr. Jefferson in France to promote commerce there and in Germany, with great success! We should not obsess over the tribulations imposed by a small island nation." I compressed the air with my hands to show how small it was.

There was a burst of laughter from the crowd of merchants at that characterization of the great Empire, but I could see they were really not convinced.

"Thing is, Colonel, that our trade is with Britain, it has always been with Britain, and with Britain it almost certainly will remain." A tall, thin man with fire in his eye spoke. "France has little money and a great deal of political trouble. The German states export people, not goods, and those people come here to buy the British goods we sell, they don't buy our goods at home. Britain may be weakened politically, but they are the major trading partner for all the world. And their Navy can easily prevent us from carrying on trade with other countries. And with all due respect to Your Excellency and Colonel Fitzgerald here," he continued, "the Potomac canal and the Ohio are not likely to bring us trade from the interior in our lifetime."

"Even the slave trade is at stake now!" exclaimed another merchant. "I understand from my correspondents in London that there are serious political discussions around legislation to abolish the trade! Ruination, if so."

"I thought things were difficult before the War, but now the uncertainty we face is twice as bad."

The General listened to all the concerns and comments, occasionally responding with questions and support. I noticed he carefully avoided the topic of the slave trade and slavery itself; I believe he felt it was simply too divisive for his purpose with these men. I also noticed him grow progressively more thoughtful as he took on board the many issues raised among the social set most likely to support him as President.

The General gradually worked his way around to his immediate problem: George Thompson. He introduced the topic of plantation management, then moved to his neighbors' management and how hard it was to obtain good managers. He briefly described for the crowd Mr. Thompson's abscondence from Colonel Mason's plantation and asked about the merchants' opinion of Thompson.

"Thompson, eh? A disreputable man, I'm afraid. I've had dealings with him over some of Mason's produce, and frankly I bloody well despise the man."

"He always had an aura of dishonesty about him. Given what you tell me, I think it deserved."

"Bloody arsehole, if you ask me, always out for the main chance."

"To be fair, though, the man had excellent prices for his goods." A couple of the merchants eyed the man who said this warily, but said nothing. I suspected Mr. Thompson had good prices because his only costs were the small amounts paid to the slaves who stole the goods for him. I also suspected most of the men in this room were well aware of that simple fact.

I said, "As a guest of the General, and as a city man rather than a farmer, I have been amazed at the complexity of the management of a plantation of his size. Preparing the land, organizing the people, acquiring the right seeds and livestock, preventing theft—all these things require the most diligent oversight. Mr. Thompson did not strike me as a well-organized man, unlike the General's managers. Even they seem to have problems with larceny. Why is such dishonesty rampant among the people on the farms?" I tried to sound as naive as a city man could be.

There was general hilarity over my lack of sophisticated understanding of the issues of Virginia plantation management. There were several theories about the high rate of theft: that the Negroes were natural thieves was most prominent, unsurprisingly given the general attitudes toward Negroes I had seen in Virginians, though some were more harsh on the general dishonesty among overseers and managers. Some men cast knowing looks at each other when others talked about honesty among merchants, then turned the conversation to the complete lack of integrity and honesty in London merchants and factors, about which there was loud and general agreement. I came away from this part of the discussion with the clear idea that the great men of Alexandria knew and accepted the high rate of larceny on plantations, and that they preferred not to talk about where the fruits of such lawlessness wound up. The General listened and learned.

"You know, gentlemen," I said, throwing out a net to see what fish would catch up in it, "all this talk of integrity and honesty reminds me of the political corruption in the North, where every man seems to be part of a general conspiracy to extract money from the people. Is that situation replicated here in Virginia?"

The thin man who had lectured me on trade spoke up. "Used to be, Colonel, when the British government controlled everything. We were somewhat upset with that, you know; I think the Patriots in Boston may have had similar feelings. We did something about it." He smiled at the General, who laughed. The man continued, more soberly, "There is always an undercurrent in any center of commerce. There are always men—present company excepted of course—who see more advantage in taking what they can get than in promoting liberty and honest commerce. I know Colonel Hooe is much concerned with such men; they should beware. They will find their conspiracies quite short lived."

"To liberty!" Another man raised a toast, and the conversation changed again. I was somewhat dissatisfied with the vague intimation of corrupt conspiracy, but I suspected we had learned all we could that evening.

After a couple of hours, the mood was very jolly, and Mr. Wise looked very happy with the business he had done in port, madeira, and other liquors. The conversation moved into a short series of toasts, with the General receiving the loudest one of all. His affability and willingness to listen to their complaints had generated good feelings all around and a universal demand that he accept the Presidency. He thanked them and said he valued their support and would take their recommendations under consideration.

As the hour grew late, the merchants slowly dispersed. Replete with beef, claret, and madeira, we staggered back to Colonel Fitzgerald's in good humor, or at least Fitzgerald and I did. The General does not stagger, he strides. As we walked, the General said, "Do you know, gentlemen, I have badly misunderstood the politics here. While focusing on the Constitution and the large issues that concern men like Colonel Mason and Colonel Hamilton, I have missed the everyday. Federalism and antifederalism are not the issue. These men here are suffering badly from the lack of a unified nation and government. They do not feel prosperous, and they do not feel safe. They are desperate for leadership, and they are willing to demand it even from a man with no government executive experience whatsoever, such as myself, as long as they see that man as someone who can do a job of work. They do not care much for how government is organized, just that it works for them and their families. Perhaps honesty and integrity and a clear vision of the right thing to do are yet the best qualities required in a President. I must reconsider some of my preconceptions."

27

FRIDAY, MARCH 20, 1789, MORNING TO AFTERNOON

After breakfast the next morning, the General, Colonel Fitzgerald, and I walked down to Colonel Hooe's place of business on the strand. We found Colonel Hooe and his clerk hard at work on a shipment of fittings and furnishings lately received from England.

The General said, "Good morning, sir. Hard at work, I see."

"Yes, Your Excellency. Trade has been brisk lately—a new phenomenon since the British cut off our trade with the West Indies! Williamson is far behind in his usual duties, I fear, due to his efforts on the murder."

"May we draw you away for a time to consider the Thompson situation?"

"Certainly, sir. Williamson, keep at it, I will return shortly."

"Yes, sir." The diligent Mr. Williamson continued with his book-keeping without looking up.

"Come to my office in the back, it will be a bit more quiet there," said Colonel Hooe.

We followed Colonel Hooe to a small office at the back of the warehouse. I closed the door after we all entered, and the busy noise of the warehouse diminished.

The General asked, "Is there any further report on the whereabouts of Mr. Thompson?"

"None whatever, sir. Williamson was about the task all day yesterday, to little avail."

"Mr. Williamson appears to be preoccupied with matters of business. Is that so?"

"Yes, Your Excellency! I am afraid I cannot spare him indefinitely for County work." Colonel Hooe was apologetic. "You see, our work would grind to a halt. All this fuss—the murder and larcenies, absconded slaves—we do not have people enough to do everything."

"I understand, Colonel. However, we seem to have made little progress toward finding the murderer, and I feel strongly that Mr. Thompson is the key to that. How can we bring more resources to bear on the search for him?"

Colonel Hooe pondered this question, then said, "Well, Your Excellency, I suppose we could form a posse. I have not had occasion to do that before, nor do I believe my predecessors have done so in recent memory."

"It might prove easiest to form the posse from our collected servants."

"Yes, that would work nicely, sir." Addressing Colonel Fitzgerald, Colonel Hooe asked, "Is that agreeable to you, sir? How many servants would you provide?"

"I can summon six good men, sir."

"And we have two," added the General.

"I myself can supply another dozen from my personal servants and some of the men working for me, though I cannot send them all or Williamson will fall even further behind on his duties." said Colonel Hooe. "Will you take charge of the posse, Your Excellency?"

The General smiled, acknowledging the compliment. "Certainly, sir, if my two aides here will agree to lead them?" He indicated Colonel Fitzgerald and myself, and we both agreed with good humor, returning to the roles we had played in the War as aides-de-camp.

An hour later, we had assembled the group in Colonel Fitzgerald's ballroom. The General addressed his new troops briefly to impress upon them the importance of the search, then turned things over to Colonel Fitzgerald and myself. Colonel Fitzgerald fetched a good map of the town from his library. He was good enough to use his better knowledge of the streets of Alexandria to organize the men into teams of two to conduct the searches, then dividing up the town into search areas and marking it on the map.

The General said, "Time is of the essence. You should start with this area around the port, as Thompson may be contemplating an early removal from the town by sea, which we must prevent at all costs. Alert the ship captains and ferrymen and have them search their ships for stowaways. Go to all the warehouses in the port and alert them as well. We must then go to every commercial establishment and tavern in the town, as well as all residences. Ask to search any buildings where the man might conceal himself without the owner's knowledge. Say that you have authorization from Colonel Hooe to conduct these searches as a posse. Colonel Humphreys, can you describe the man for everyone?"

"Yes, Your Excellency. He is middle aged with the appearance of someone who has done a good deal of labor in his time. He has grizzled hair and beard. He is about six feet tall and rather thin. When we last saw him, he was wearing farm clothes, though obviously he may have had an opportunity to change those by now."

Colonel Fitzgerald added, "As a reminder, this man is certainly desperate and dangerous, so if you discover something suspicious, obtain assistance rather than confronting anyone. Do not alert the man to his danger. We will then arrest him and any accomplices."

The General nodded approvingly as we sent our minions out to their searches. "Please report back to Colonel Humphreys or Colonel Fitzgerald as you complete a search area. Thank you, and good hunting!" All the teams set off, eager as hunting dogs to find their fox!

Colonel Fitzgerald then showed us to his parlor and asked us to make free with his substantial library. The morning progressed toward dinner with little response; three of the teams returned from their initial searches at the port with no information and were sent out to additional locations. The General and the Colonel settled themselves with the day's newspapers, and I selected a volume of Freneau's poetry from the library. Teams returned intermittently through the day without any new information. I feared this search would occupy us for days. As comfortable as I was in Colonel Fitzgerald's parlor, I would rather we made progress on our murder.

As the dinner hour approached, the General arose, having finished the last of the newspapers, and walked to the window to look out upon the town, hands clasped behind his back, frowning at the lack of progress. After a few minutes, he started, then turned to me and said, "Colonel, I think there is information coming our way." I put down my book. Colonel Fitzgerald looked up from his newspaper.

Indeed, within a minute, noise and bustle ensued at the back of the house, and the parlor door burst open, with our two servants spilling into the room, Colonel Fitzgerald's butler close behind. The two men were gasping for air, having apparently run from another part of town.

"General, you must come quick! Down at the strand!" Christopher Sheels, the young servant from Mount Vernon, was literally hopping up and down in excitement.

The General asked, "Have you located Mr. Thompson?"

Christopher grinned and said, "Oh, yes, sir! We done found him all right. Down at the strand, right near Colonel Hooe's warehouse. You need to come quick, sir!"

"Why quickly, Christopher? Did you alert him? Is the man in danger of escaping again?"

Christopher was nearly beside himself. "Oh no, sir, he ain't going nowhere at all. He's dead, his head is all bloody and his brains out all over the floor. Somebody shot him, massa, shot him dead!"

28

FRIDAY, MARCH 20, AFTERNOON

The General and I followed Christopher down to the strand after dispatching one of Colonel Fitzgerald's servants to fetch Colonel Hooe to the murder scene. Christopher led the way into a drab little warehouse a block away from the Colonel's larger and brighter place of business. The place stank of tar and an undefinable smell that reminded me of a swamp. Christopher took us into the back, and there we found the missing overseer.

He had indeed been shot dead, at what appeared to be rather close range. In the dusty light, I could see that the ball had entered his head at a slight angle and had exited the back taking most of the man's skull with it. His brains and a bespattering of blood spread out on the wall and on the floor around his slumped body, and the pattern of blood on the walls indicated that he had been shot standing up and facing the door. He must have died instantly.

The General briefly knelt to examine the body, then arose.

"Colonel, Thompson must have posed a severe threat to his murderer, as this place, while obscure, is not particularly private. The man took a great risk shooting him so close to the public area of the strand. We should be able to find a witness who heard the shot."

He stepped over to the wall, took out a handkerchief, and dabbed at the spatters. He took the handkerchief over to a window to examine it.

"Mostly dry, but not completely. I suspect he was killed at some time earlier in the day today."

Christopher ran over from the other side of the warehouse, where he had been poking around some barrels and boxes. He plucked my sleeve. "Colonel, come look over here, sir!"

We walked back over, and he shoved a barrel aside to reveal a small space behind the barrels. I saw a straw mattress with a tattered blanket and some clothing, along with a metal plate with some crusts on it and some bottles, and a chamber pot. I picked up the one bottle that contained liquid, which was open, and sniffed: gin. Bad gin. Extremely bad gin. Christopher grinned at my expression.

"Your Excellency," I shouted. "Would you come over here, please?" My shout seemed to disappear into the high space above, but the General heard. He came over and examined the find closely, picking up the clothing gingerly. It was a coat. I could smell the gin on it from where I stood.

"The body was dressed in the clothing we saw on Mr. Thompson at Gunston Hall," he said. "I would imagine he took this coat when he absconded through his back window." The General dropped the coat back on the floor and looked over the remains of Thompson's lodging. "He must have been staying here for the last few days. Unless he spent a short time very drunk, the number of bottles indicates several days. Mr. Williamson said that Colonel Mason's horse was found near the town on Tuesday." His mouth set firmly. "This murderer seems always one step ahead of us."

I girded myself, held my breath, and opened the chamber pot. A quick look confirmed that there was enough excrement to say with some assurance that Mr. Thompson had been alive and shitting for some days. I closed the thing. I took a breath, then nodded at the General, who smiled and said, "Thank you, Colonel; that is truly going beyond the call of duty."

I stooped and picked up a filthy leather bag lying on top of the straw mattress. I looked into it, then emptied it onto my palm: a single penny.

"I think we've found Mr. Thompson's money, Your Excellency, or what is left of it. Perhaps he paid for his board and lodging, though it seems he did not do very well for his money. Or perhaps his murderer is now wealthier than he was before he killed Mr. Thompson. And now we will never know what Mr. Thompson knew." I put the penny back in the bag.

"Yes. We must gather as many facts here as we can, then we must return to Gunston Hall to see what we can find there. Christopher, could you please search that mattress to see if anything has been concealed there?"

Christopher gingerly took up the cloth bag stuffed with straw as though it might harbor hot coals, or at the very least poisonous snakes.

While he was rootling around in the straw, Colonel Hooe appeared at the door.

"Your Excellency, Colonel. Fitzgerald's man told me you would be here." He came in with a questioning look, coming over to us. "What on earth is your man doing there?"

"Searching the mattress, sir," replied the General, who was observing Christopher's efforts with interest. "If you would come this way?" He moved back toward the corpse, and Colonel Hooe followed with the puzzled look still on his face. That changed to shock when he saw the body. He leaned over it.

"My God, what a mess. It is Thompson, certainly. The same clothes, too."

"Yes, shot once with a pistol at close range."

Colonel Hooe looked back at us after briefly inspecting the body. "And a mattress? Here? Meaning he was sleeping here?"

"Yes, we think so. We think he was shot sometime in the early hours this morning." The General folded his arms. "I think the next step is to find out who owns this warehouse."

"Well, that will not be hard," said Colonel Hooe. "I do."

The General stared at him.

"I acquired this place at auction two weeks ago, from a merchant who had gone under. Bankrupt," Colonel Hooe added as he perceived the perplexity of the General.

"I understand the notion of going under, sir. What I do not understand is how a fugitive wound up in a warehouse you own, and subsequently was murdered there."

"Nor do I, sir, nor do I." Colonel Hooe seemed not to be particularly concerned by the revelation.

The General asked, "Do you have any idea how Mr. Thompson might have gained access to this place, Colonel Hooe?"

"No, sir, I do not."

"Colonel Humphreys," the General said to me with a touch of impatience, "Could you please check the locks on the door? It is possible they have been forced."

I walked over to the open door and closely inspected the locks. I returned to the General. "Nothing sir. There are no signs of forcing upon the lock, and the door is not damaged other than by long usage."

"Very well, sir."

"Nothing, Your Excellency," reported Christopher, coming over to us. "Just straw in that thing. And bugs. No money or nothing."

"All right, thank you, Christopher. Did you find the door over there unlocked earlier?" The General pointed at the door through which we had entered.

"Yes, sir—we just walked right on in and started looking around."

"And, Christopher," I said.

"Yes, sir?"

"That gin will kill you if you drink it. It certainly didn't do Mr. Thompson any good, but I suppose he's past caring."

The boy shamefacedly extracted the bottle from his pocket and handed it to me.

The General said, "Colonel Hooe. I think we must proceed without delay to find any witnesses to the event. I would like to propose that we redirect our posse to that effort."

"That seems advisable, Your Excellency." The Colonel was subdued at the General's rather commanding tone but proved amenable to his taking charge of things.

"I will coordinate the search from Colonel Fitzgerald's house, and I will keep you informed of anything we find." The General's tone conveyed a polite dismissal.

"Very well. If you need any more authority, I will be happy to provide it." Colonel Hooe looked again at the corpse. "I will instruct Williamson to coordinate the removal of this dross with the coroner." He smiled, bowed, and walked out.

The General stared after him.

"Are you concerned about something, sir?" I asked.

The General smiled briefly, then said, "You know very well I am, Colonel. I feel that we should not depend on Colonel Hooe and his staff for disinterested investigative work at this point. At least not until we have a better idea of how Mr. Thompson came to be here." The General frowned down at the body. "Colonel Hooe is my good friend. I do not want to believe evil of him, but I cannot ignore the possibility that I know him less well than I thought. This situation is becoming worse and worse every day."

We gathered up our servants and went out of the old warehouse. As we walked back to Colonel Fitzgerald's house, I poured the gin into the street, resolving at least one of our multiplying problems.

29

SATURDAY, MARCH 21, 1789

The General reconvened the posse at Colonel Fitzgerald's house the next morning. Reports trickled in throughout the morning from the various servants as they scoured the strand and surrounding houses and establishments for anyone who had seen anything, but they reported nothing of consequence. As the day wore on, the General paced the floor in Colonel Fitzgerald's very nicely appointed parlor, while I continued with the book of Freneau's poetry, but the distractions proved too much for me. I did not pace, but I spent a good deal of time staring into the fire and thinking about the family at Mount Vernon. I spent too much time thinking about Mrs. Fanny Washington, I fear; I was much too self indulgent.

Finally, in the early afternoon, the posse proved successful. Two of Colonel Fitzgerald's servants had been questioning the captains and crews of the various ships docked at the port. One of them came back to the house with the information that they had found a seaman who thought he had heard something.

Both the General and I were quite ready to be doing something other than pacing the floor and watching the flames flicker, so we took our cloaks and followed the man back to the port, a short walk from Colonel Fitzgerald's house. He took us to a small trading vessel docked among several more just like it, all very busy loading and unloading barrels and crates of goods.

The captain was from Massachusetts, as was his ship. He said he was proud to shake the General's hand, which he did with both of his. The General disengaged his hand as quickly as he could; he hated shaking hands.

He said, "Captain, I understand one of your seaman heard something that may be of interest to us relating to a murder that took place last night."

The captain beckoned, and Fitzgerald's servants came over with a rather bedraggled-looking seaman. The captain said, "Johnson, give His Excellency any information he may require, if you please."

"Aye-aye, sir," replied the seaman, bobbing his head in acknowledgement of the order. He turned to us. "Are you really General Washington, sir?"

"Yes, I really am, Mr. Johnson," replied the General with a smile. "I wish we could meet under better circumstances, and we are in a bit of a rush, so...."

"Aye sir, sorry sir. Just I never met anybody as important as you, sir."

"Get on with it, man." The captain said this with a degree of humor in his voice.

"Aye sir, sorry sir! Well, Your Excellence, it was like this." He passed a hand across his brow. "I was on shore leave last night, along with a couple of me mates, and we was out a bit late, kind of past the time we was supposed to be on board." He looked anxiously at the captain, who remained impassive. "Well, sir, not to put too fine a point on it, we was drunk as lords, excusing the expression, Your Excellence."

"But you heard something? How and where?"

"Well, me mates was a bit under the weather, see, and I couldn't rouse 'em, so I figured I'd better take care of meself and get back to the ship before worse things happened, since I was still on my feet. I was coming along the street here," he pointed to the street along the strand, "when I heard a shot, like the crack 'o doom, sir, it was."

"And where were you?"

"Down there, sir," he said, pointing back along the dock toward the warehouse where we had found the body.

"And what did you do?"

"Well, sir, I jumped a few feet in the air, sir, as I recall, then looked about me. I couldn't see nothing amiss, couldn't see nothing I needed to worry about, but then a fright took hold of me and I kind of rushed back to the ship. I wasn't up for an adventure, sir. In fact," he continued, "I bloody well emptied my stomach over the side once I staggered on board, sir."

"Yes, I fully understand. And you didn't see anything or anyone about?"

"No, sir, it were the dead of night and they wasn't nobody about at all, just the ships creaking. Spooky enough, then this shot—I ran for it, sir, and that's about the size of it." He rubbed his brow again; I thought it was probably hurting him with the hangover. The captain did not look overjoyed at Johnson's story.

"No carriages or anything out of place?"

The man looked abashed and said, "I can't say I was paying a lot of attention, sir, not after the noise. Didn't notice nothing before that, though." His eyes darted from the deck to the General and back again; the man was clearly nervous and apologetic about what he had not seen.

"All right, thank you, Mr. Johnson." The General turned back to the captain. "And no one else on board heard anything?"

"I did not, sir, and to my knowledge the other seamen did not. Your men questioned them, I believe." He looked at Fitzgerald's servants, who nodded in affirmation.

"Very well, sir, thank you." The General looked around the deck of the ship, then asked, "And when are you to sail, sir? In case we need to ask more questions of Mr. Johnson?"

"Two days, sir, at the tide."

"Very well," said the General again. "I think we must again consult Colonel Mason to understand Mr. Thompson's affairs better before we can again trust Colonel Hooe's investigation. Let us get back to Mount Vernon for dinner, Colonel Humphreys; then, first thing tomorrow morning, again to Gunston Hall—and Log Town."

30

SUNDAY, MARCH 22, 1789, MORNING

James, the butler, stepped onto the porch of Gunston Hall, took our cloaks and hats, and showed us into the front parlor. Colonel Mason joined us almost immediately, with no sign of gouty dyspepsia.

"I wish your visit were under better circumstances, Your Excellency," he said. "I have had a letter from Colonel Hooe by express this morning, informing me of Mr. Thompson's untimely demise. I suppose we can count as a success your finding the fugitive, even though dead. Colonel Hooe did not give many details."

The General nodded and said, "We must get more information about Mr. Thompson's life here. Knowing more about him might give us a clue about his murder, and about the murderer of my overseer."

"Very well, sir." Colonel Mason waited for his interrogation with no sign of impatience.

"Had you any reason to suspect him of larceny or other criminality?"

"No, sir. I am afflicted often with men who cannot truly perform their work. He was one of them, I fear. I had admonished him repeatedly after finding him drunk and incapable of performing his duties, but I had no indication he was involved in anything criminal. My only regret at his absence is my need to hire another overseer, always a difficult task." The Colonel did not seem overly concerned at the death of Mr. Thompson.

The General nodded, no doubt empathizing with his neighbor, then changed the conversation to our reason for coming. "We have discovered that Mr. Thompson would meet with outsiders down in your quarters, Log Town, to avoid notice. Your overseer Nace told us of that practice when we questioned him. Perhaps if we questioned the people who live there, we can learn something fresh about Mr. Thompson's activities? Or, even better, we might learn details about the people with whom he conducted those activities."

"Certainly, Your Excellency. I should be going to church; but I will assist you. I would prefer to be present when you question my people. But would it not be better to send for Colonel Hooe and have him conduct the questioning? Or perhaps Mr. Cockburn?"

The General considered, then said with care, "We feel, sir, that it may be necessary to investigate independently of Colonel Hooe for the time being."

Colonel Mason frowned and replied, "Surely you do not suspect your friend Colonel Hooe of double dealing?"

The General pursed his lips, then said, "I find the coincidence of his owning the warehouse in which Mr. Thompson met his end unsettling to say the least. I would prefer to understand as much as I can about Mr. Thompson and his doings without involving Colonel Hooe until it is absolutely necessary."

"You did not answer my question, sir," said Colonel Mason sharply.

"You are always quite perceptive, sir," the General replied.

"Hmph. Very well." Colonel Mason, still frowning, gave his attention to the initial request. "Now, sir, most of the people living down in Log Town are house servants. How do you wish to question them?"

The General considered for a moment, then said, "If you could suggest two or three servants that might contribute the most, that would be very kind, sir. I fear we do not have the time to question all the servants here."

"I will consult with James." Colonel Mason arose and left the room. After five minutes or so, he came back. "James has suggested our housemaid, Lucy, and one of the carpenters, and two or three other servants. James is fetching them. How do you wish to question them?"

"One at a time, sir, so that we may reassure them that their answers will be kept private."

"Very well. Let me just see my wife and family off to church, and I will join you."

We waited another five minutes, then James ushered a tall, middle-aged Negro woman into the room. Colonel Mason rejoined us at the same time. James said, "Your Excellency, this is Lucy. She spends a lot of time between the house and Log Town. Now, Lucy, you just tell the General here anything he wants to know."

"Please sit down, Lucy," said the General. She sat. "We are looking into matters relating to Mr. Thompson, the late overseer here. We understand he was in the habit of meeting people down in Log Town. Have you observed such meetings?"

Lucy gulped and stammered something unintelligible, then cleared her throat and said, "Yes sir. They was various folks, some black folks from other farms around, some white folks. He talk with Nace from Occoquan a lot."

"I see. Do you know Julius, the overseer from my Dogue Run plantation, Lucy?"

"Yes, sir, he come by a few times, met with Massa Thompson once or twice down there."

"Did you hear what they were discussing?"

"No sir, Massa Thompson didn't like us near when he talk with folks."

"Not very surprising, I suppose. These white people, do you know who they were?"

"Don't know they names, they just outside folks, not from this farm."

"How were they dressed? Gentlemen or servants?"

"Sorry, sir. Guess I ain't real sure, guess they was just regular folks, not gentlemen like you and your friend or the massa, sir. Just folks, sir, nothing special."

"I see. Is there anything else about Mr. Thompson that you think might be of use to us?"

"No, sir, can't think of nothin'."

"Very well, you may go." Lucy arose and left the parlor, and James then brought in a rough-looking man of about 25 years dressed in coarse brown clothes.

He said, "Your Excellency, this is one of our carpenters, Daniel. He works most days at Log Town. Now, Dan, do like I told you."

Daniel shot a look at the butler and nodded, then turned to the General.

"Please sit down, Daniel," said the General.

Daniel looked at the elegant chair, then shook his head. "Better stand, sir, my arse ain't the cleanest right now."

The General smiled and nodded. "We're looking for information about Mr. Thompson's activities in Log Town, and especially any meetings he would have there with people from off the plantation. What have you observed, Daniel?"

The carpenter thought for a minute. Finally, he said, "I done see Cujo from massa Cockburn's house down here once with massa Thompson. I believe they was talking about some barrels going over to Alexandria from the massa's storehouse here, or maybe massa Cockburn's store, didn't really hear much, sir. Jus' that it a little strange, you understand? And a course merchant-men from Alexandria and Fredericksburg, sir."

"Merchant-men?"

"Yes, sir, they come to the farm a lot, talk with Mr. Thompson all the time about they business. A few times they come down to Log Town to talk with Mr. Thompson, quiet-like I guess."

"Hmm. Anyone in particular?"

Colonel Mason broke in and said, "We trade with many merchants and their agents, Your Excellency, their presence here is constant and normal."

"I suppose so, sir—but I wish we could learn what 'quiet-like' discussions were had between them and Mr. Thompson."

"Don't know any names of the merchant-men, sir, not my business," replied the carpenter.

"Anything more you'd like to tell us, Daniel? About Mr. Thompson?"

"No, sir, nothing more."

"Very well, thank you; you may go."

After showing Daniel out to the yard, James showed in three more servants, but none of them yielded any more specific information than we had already received from Lucy and Daniel. On James's telling the General and Colonel Mason that he didn't think any of the rest of the servants would have more information, the General asked, "Is there a girl named Chancey here?"

James stared at the General for a moment, then frowned and spoke. "Chancey. Why, yes sir. She's down at Log Town right now, taking care of her sister."

The General arose. "I think we should walk down there. I would like to see the place to understand just how Mr. Thompson saw it. And we can speak with Chancey there."

Colonel Mason arose. "I will accompany you, sir. James, I suppose you should come along." We all walked out and down the road past the lawn and a wooded area to the little collection of log cabins. Colonel Mason walked slowly, but he persisted without complaint. The cabins were in two rows, looking as neat and orderly as log cabins could look. I heard the cackling and honking of some chickens and geese from a pen down at the end of the lane, and several vegetable gardens peeked out from behind the cabins. The trees, just turning green, would provide reasonable shade in the hot summer. I looked over my shoulder and saw that indeed we could no longer see Gunston Hall, even with few leaves on the trees. This would have been a good place to have unobserved discussions. Many of the people that lived here would be out and about during the day, with only a few women and children present.

James led us to one of the cabins and called out, "Chancey! Come out here, now."

A young woman emerged from the cabin, looking at us in surprise. She was about 17 or 18 years old, middling black with a full figure and very regular features, giving her a pleasing and expressive countenance. As she absorbed the white faces in our group, she stopped and stared, then looked down at the ground and clasped her hands nervously.

"You are Chancey?" asked the General.

"Yes, sir," replied the girl nearly inaudibly.

"Speak up now, Chancey! This is General Washington." said James.

She looked up at him slowly and nodded, "Yes, Papa."

The General asked, "She is your daughter, James? This is your cabin?"

"Yes, sir."

The General hesitated, then asked him, "Are you aware of Chancey's relationship with my miller, Ben?"

The old butler said, "No, sir." Nothing moved in his face. He had erased his frown.

"Relationship? What relationship?" asked Colonel Mason sharply.

"The usual kind, I would imagine, sir," replied the General.

The butler stared straight ahead without saying anything. Chancey looked at the ground.

The General said, "Colonel, could you...?" He waved at hand at Chancey.

"Sir." I walked over to the girl and led her out of earshot of the group. "Chancey, please tell me what you know about Mr. Thompson and Ben. We will not tell your papa anything about it."

The girl muttered, "Done got out now, don't it? All of it."

"Yes, I suppose so. But don't make things worse by hiding what you know. It's important that we find out who killed Mr. Thompson, and who killed Julius."

"Damn that Julius, he a real bad man! He deserve to die!" Her eyes were furious.

"I understand, but that doesn't help us much. What about Mr. Thompson?"

"He ain't no good neither, sir, no good." She folded her arms, erecting a barrier to fend off my questions.

"Yes, but what did he want from you and Ben?"

"He and that Julius, they got Ben where they want him, you understand?" The girl looked straight at me, concentrated and angry. "They don't take no. They want him to steal stuff, they want me to steal stuff too. Please don't tell Massa Mason I done that, he sell me off!"

"Don't worry, we won't tell him."

"Julius even got Ben spying up to the General's place."

"Spying? Spying how?"

"Watchin' out for people and things so Massa Thompson and Julius could steal. And they always talkin' politics too, about the new 'lections and the General. Real interested in that, like Massa Mason. Papa says Massa Mason talk about the General all the time."

"Did you hear what Thompson and Julius were talking about?"

"No, Ben told me some, Nace told me some. Ben real mad at Julius, thinks Julius gonna get him sold off. I don't know nothin' about no politics anyhow. Sir."

Ben had been less than forthcoming about all his worries, it would appear.

"And what about Nace?"

The girl looked at me defiantly. "You done know it all, sir. But that ain't nobody's business but Nace's and mine." She looked away into the forest. I looked back at the group of servants. James had moved a little ways toward us, looking at us talking, his face a dignified mask.

I thought the girl was perhaps too young to understand the nature of her relationship with Colonel Mason, and his interest in her 'business,' but I felt I could not disabuse her.

"I'm not concerned about your relationship with Nace, Chancey, just with his involvement in all this. Is he part of the larceny? Or the spying?"

"No he ain't, and you ain't got no call to pull him into this! He a good man!" Her voice was low and hissing. She faced the wood, and I realized she did not want her father to see her emotions. I smiled at this realization, because her arms akimbo and stiff body showed her emotions to all. She was not reserved.

"So Mr. Thompson didn't make use of Nace for his activities?"

She looked a bit confused, then said, "No, sir, Nace done got somethin' on him, he let Nace alone." She smiled. "Nace made Massa Thompson stop botherin' me, beat up that Julius too when he started botherin' me. Wish Ben had the backbone that Nace got, but he got other things."

If I interpreted the nature of "bother" correctly, I thought the girl lucky to have Nace around.

"And your papa won't help?"

"Cain't tell Papa, Mama dead and gone. Papa way too close to Massa Mason, this break him, you understand? Won't do the massa any good neither. Please don't tell Papa." She was again looking at me anxiously.

I asked, "Do you know the names of any of the white men Mr. Thompson brought round here?"

"No, sir, I don't. Don't know nothin' about 'em. Massa Thompson and Julius thick as thieves, fuckin' *were* thieves! Nobody tole me nothin'. Nace and Ben maybe know, but you gotta ask them, not me!"

"All right, thank you, Chancey." I decided to give her some advice. "I think you should tell your papa about your relationships, though, he'll be wanting to know now."

She rolled her eyes. "Yes, sir, he will." She clamped her lips and stared at me again. I led her back to the group. James took her hand.

I said to the General, "Some more information of relevance to us, Your Excellency, I will tell you later."

He nodded. "Very well."

By this time, Colonel Mason was shifting his walking stick from one hand to the other and frowning with impatience, so we all walked back to the house. James stayed behind, standing by his small log cabin with his daughter, holding her hand but saying nothing. Chancey stood straight, all angles, looking out at the woods rather than at her papa or at us. A younger girl, presumably the sister that Chancey had been minding, joined them and took her other hand. The other slaves dispersed among the cabins or followed us back to the house to their daily work.

We took our leave. Colonel Mason bowed and said, "I hope you have found what you were seeking, Your Excellency. I fear, however, you may have found it at the cost of bringing new troubles to my people. But that is my concern, not yours."

The Colonel stood on the porch looking after us as we rode away up the cherry alley, which was showing signs of the massive bloom to follow. As we rode, I described my conversation with Chancey to the General. He mulled it over, then responded, "Mr. Thompson seems to have been a thoroughly objectionable man. If he were killed here, I would be pursuing Nace and Ben, or even Chancey and James, but he was killed in Alexandria, five hours away by horse."

"Yes, sir. My guess is that he was a danger to his confederates, one of the 'merchant-men' he met with here. From Lucy's description, it would not appear that Colonel Hooe was one of them."

"No; Colonel Hooe is nothing if not a 'gentleman' in dress. Perhaps another of the merchants from Alexandria? Or a representative of Colonel Hooe? Williamson? He dresses for riding, not for town, when he rides out on business for the Colonel. Thompson sounds like the kind of man who would not generate trust in a confederate, and perhaps that is why he is dead."

"Plausible, Your Excellency. But there is no evidence for any of that. I fear we have not narrowed down our list but have rather expanded it greatly."

"I agree, Colonel. I fear that Mr. Thompson's demise has made things much more difficult for us. I am also intrigued by this 'spying' that the girl Chancey mentioned. It is beginning to sound as though Julius and Mr. Thompson had a larger operation and a deeper game than was at first apparent to us. I will ask some questions of my overseers to see whether they had caught wind of anything. I see nothing in all this that persuades me to abandon our independent investigation, however. We have clarified the terrain, at least, though not much in our favor. Now we must get information about the enemy. I think we must remain wary of giving information to Colonel Hooe or to Mr. Williamson. And perhaps Colonel Mason and Mr. Cockburn had something to do with the 'politics'. They are political men."

We navigated a small creek, after which I commented, "Colonel Mason seems surprisingly cooperative, Your Excellency, given his politics."

"Yes, I find it refreshing. I doubt it will last."

I debated with myself whether Colonel Mason's cooperation reflected a deeper political game or simply the improvement in his health but came to no real conclusion. Time would tell. I said nothing to the General on the subject, as it would not improve his humor or his knowledge of Colonel Mason.

31

MONDAY, MARCH 23, 1789

Shortly after breakfast on Monday, the General and I rode out together to Muddy Hole to inspect the work being done there, as well as for the exercise. The people at Muddy Hole were diligently working away at preparing their lands for spring planting, to the General's satisfaction. He took the opportunity to question the overseer there, Will, about Julius. Will had had little to do with Julius or Dogue Run, and even less interest in people passing through Mount Vernon. He kept himself to his own business at Muddy Hole, he told us. The General gave his approval of this management policy but admonished Will to take special care in tracking produce and to report to him immediately any stolen or missing produce or livestock. This incited a certain amount of resentment in Will, who felt a little insulted. The General soothed this reaction by explaining the nature of the larceny conspiracy that we had uncovered at Dogue Run and the Grist Mill. Will fell silent, looking at the ground and shaking his head in dismay, and said nothing else.

We rode back to the Mansion House shortly after noon to find Major Washington waiting for us as we walked up to the house from the stable. I anticipated something dramatic as we saw him approaching. He'd been avoiding us ever since his recovery from his attack of brain fever. But I was wrong: it was a simple matter of business.

He said, "Uncle, there is a man to see you about a position as coachman. I asked him to wait, as I remember you expressed the thought that you may need an experienced coachman before much longer. He is in the passage."

"Thank you, George. I will see him after I change." The General gave no hint of the terrible suspicions we harbored about his nephew. He would again defer talking with him about it out of delicacy and unwillingness to harbor such suspicions, I supposed. The General went in the side door directly to his study and dressing room. The Major and I walked into the main passage, where a man waited. He was dressed in livery, and the Major informed me in a whisper that it was Colonel Mason's livery, which piqued my interest: why would a servant of Mason's come to the General for work?

The man looked at us expectantly, but the Major signaled him to wait. He sat on the edge of his chair, clearly not at his full ease. I held my tongue with the man there; I could not air our concerns with a stranger present.

After a few minutes, the General came through the dining room door to the passage and said, "Now, sir, what is this all about?"

"General Washington?" The man arose from his chair.

"Yes, I am he."

"Well, Your Honor, I wish to apply to you for the position of coachman." The man's accent was heavily German, an unusual characteristic in a Virginia servant.

"I perceive by your livery that you belong to Colonel Mason, is that so?"

"Yes, sir."

"Your name?"

"Gustav Stein, Your Honor." He ducked his head.

"Well, Mr. Stein, I am indeed wanting a coachman. However, it is not my custom to treat with anyone in the service of another unless a separation is about to take place, and unless there are sufficient testimonials to sobriety, skill, honesty, and industry in the occupation that is to be followed."

"Oh, Your Honor, I have told Colonel Mason last fall that I intend to leave; I was going next month to the North to better myself, until I heard that Your Honor needed a coachman."

"Where did you hear that?"

"From one of the other servants, Your Honor."

"Indeed. And why do you wish to enter my service rather than going North to better yourself?"

"Oh, Your Honor, everyone knows that Your Honor's service is the best in the country, and I could not do better for myself, and when you are the greatest man in the land you too will be in the North, so I came quickly to apply."

"I see." The General nodded.

"And, sir, the Colonel has me training another servant as coachman, as he sees that I am no longer necessary to him for his coach."

"And what about your character?" The General clasped his hands behind his back and fixed the man with a sharp eye.

"Your Honor, I am very sure Colonel Mason will give me a good character for my years of service."

The General nodded again. "All right. I cannot converse any farther with you, Mr. Stein, until I hear from Colonel Mason as to your parting from him, as a matter of delicacy toward his feelings. I will write to him today, if that is satisfactory, sir."

"Oh yes Your Honor, that is very good of you." The man bowed several times to show his thanks, then the Major gently took his arm and showed him the door.

The General stood looking after him as the door closed, his hand rubbing his mouth as though it pained him, which it may very well have done. He turned to me and asked, "Colonel, what do you make of that?"

"Sir?"

"Do you not find it curious that a servant of Colonel Mason's just shows up asking for a position the day after we confront the Colonel about the murder of another servant? Look here. I suppose I must be explicit. I think there is every chance this man is meant to be a spy inserted into my household by Colonel Mason. Spying seems all the thing these days."

The good Lord knows the General understands spies, he was certainly afflicted by them up to his waistcoat in the War, but as we were no longer at war, I could not see it and told him so.

He shook his head dubiously, frowning and walking up and down the passage while considering the problem. "I mean to plumb this to the bottom to make sure we are not under political or personal threat, Colonel." He paused, then asked, "Colonel, supposing, just supposing, that this man were a spy—what would you do to uncover it?"

I thought about it, then suggested, "We could ask the other servants at Colonel Mason's about the man." The General shook his head, and I quickly realized that would not do: the servants would certainly support Colonel Mason whether or not the coachman was a spy, and we already knew that the Colonel did not like outsiders questioning his servants. Trying again, I had an idea. "Perhaps Colonel Mason himself, sir? A kind of liar's paradox?"

The General smiled. "Ask a man whether he is lying, you mean? Or a variation on that. Yes, that might work. I shall simply apply to Colonel Mason for a reference for the man, and if he supplies a good reference, I will assume he is lying until proven otherwise. If he gives a bad reference...unless Colonel Mason is deeper than I believe he really is, it would mean he has no ill intent. Yes, that will do. Thank you, Colonel." He nodded, then went back through the dining room to his study. I looked about me, and I realized that the Major had evaporated once again; I was now alone in the passage. A few minutes later, the General returned, folding a letter.

We went out to the yard and found John Fairfax, and the General gave him the letter and asked him to carry it immediately to Colonel Mason at Gunston Hall and to wait for a reply. Fairfax rode off at a gallop.

After dinner, the General and I were in his study discussing some material to add to his biography. I had a draft of a paragraph extolling his virtues which I intended to add just before the end. He read it over, then said, "Well, Colonel, as an eulogy, this works very well, and I think you may reserve it for that sombre purpose. For a biography, I would prefer something a little less fulsome, if you please."

"Very well, sir."

"And let us not descend too far into hagiography; I do not believe it will serve either of us well. I am already a martyr to politics; I have no wish to become the first American saint."

"Yes, Your Excellency. I will leave sainthood to my poetry."

"Thank you, Colonel. Ah, here is Fairfax!"

A little breathless, John Fairfax joined us in the study, slapping down a folded letter on the General's desk.

"Any verbal message?" the General asked.

"No, sir; Colonel Mason merely smiled and wrote this out immediately without further comment after he had read your letter."

"Let us see." The General unfolded the letter and read it through quickly, then read it again more slowly. He smiled widely, then handed me the letter.

The letter is too long to include here, but I thought Colonel Mason performed very well as a writer, a trait which did not contradict what I had heard about his abilities. He started out, "I thank you exceedingly for your very candid & friendly letter," and ended with "I beg my Compliments & Mrs. Mason's to your Lady & Family; and am with the greatest Respect and Regard, Dr Sir Your Affecte & obdt Sert." The Colonel was certainly trying hard to be congenial, and there was not a single reference to politics in the letter.

The coachman was a German Redemptioner, a man who paid for his immigration to America by indenturing himself for a period to a master who paid the passage.

Colonel Mason praised Mr. Stein as an excellent coachman but otherwise painted a darker picture of him as quarrelsome, misbehaving, idle, and neglectful of his other duties, especially when drunk, which was apparently quite often. "...tho' when he leaves me, I shall be without a Driver, I am not at all desirous of keeping him; as well on account of the above mentioned Faults as that he is a man of such restless & dissatisfied Disposition, that no Dependence can be placed in him." Other than that, Colonel Mason thought highly of the man. Indeed. "If therefore you chose to employ him, I have no objection to parting with him, as I am sure will be the Case soon, if you do not."

"Somehow, sir," I said after my laughter at the Colonel's irony subsided, "I do not think Colonel Mason is particularly warm on the idea of your employing Mr. Stein, as a coachman or as a spy."

The General turned and smiled. "I have seen better reports of men I had hanged for desertion, Colonel."

"Yes, sir; I enjoy his ironic style. But about the idea of this man being a spy..."

"I think it is clear that the man is not a spy, just a bad coachman. I shall not hire him. I must say, it is a relief to remove suspicion from at least one man. Perhaps I create goblins where none exist; and yet, I think we must be alert to the possibility of unwanted interference in our affairs." He grimaced, shook his head, then picked up his spectacles. "Now, if you would be so kind, Colonel, send in Mr. Lear. I must give him the monies he will need to travel to New York, and also the monies for Mrs. Washington to use in my absence. I have just received my loan proceeds from Mr. Conway in Alexandria."

32

THURSDAY, MARCH 26, 1789

The General had turned his mind to leaving Mount Vernon. He felt the country's business would not wait, so he judiciously prepared to go, even though he had not made a final decision. I had turned *my* mind to convincing him that decision was inevitable. This proved easier than I expected as events progressed that week.

We rode around the farms on Tuesday, Wednesday, and Thursday. The General considered carefully each farm's plans for the next year so that he could issue full instructions to his managers about what to do in his absence.

The General took the opportunity to question each overseer carefully about Julius; all disliked the man, but none with enough heat to suspect a suitable First Murderer. We also questioned them all about theft, covering it under the other questions we were asking about plantings, fencing, and cattle.

We did not learn anything of consequence—other than that the overseers, to a man, knew nothing at all about larceny on their farms despite the clear evidence of produce going missing. They did not associate theft with Julius and knew nothing of George Thompson. They were either blind or unwilling to acknowledge the scope of the problem on their farms. The General spoke with each man, admonishing them and explaining how to better track the produce of the farm.

I will spare the General's feelings by not relating the small flood of emotion I witnessed later in the day on Thursday, as we rode back from the River farm. No man, stoic or not, can contain himself when pushed beyond endurance. But enough of that. I will just say that the tensions arising from this exercise were later instrumental in convincing the General that his acceptance of the Presidency was inevitable.

Dinner provided a chance for the General to regain his equanimity. Dr. Craik and Mr. Lund Washington, the General's cousin, dined with us. The party was convivial, and it cheered the General immensely. Dr. Craik, who had come to check on Major Washington's health, left directly after dinner, as he had business in Alexandria, and Mr. Lund Washington went to bed early as he was to leave very early the next morning.

Before he left, Dr. Craik told the General that Major Washington was recovering but not yet well. The General determined, after the doctor left, that it was not yet time to speak with the Major about his ramblings. The General and I had just sent Mr. Lund Washington off to his rest when Frank Lee came up to us in the passage with the day's mail, which had just been sent down from Alexandria from the Post Office there.

Looking at the letters, the General sorted one out and said, "Well, Colonel, here is a missive from my good friend Colonel Tom Marshall."

"The father of Captain Marshall?"

"The same. He served with me at Valley Forge and proved a most resolute soldier. He took up residence in the West, in Kentucky, several years ago. Come, let us go to the study for our nightly session of hagiography."

We walked through the dining room to the study. The General tossed the other letters on his desk but held the Marshall letter up and broke its seal, eager to see what his friend had to say.

"My goodness, dated the 12th of February. The letter must have been lost for a time in the post."

The General read the first few lines, and his face changed. He took the letter over to the window to take advantage of what light remained of the day, and his face set into lines of anger and mortification. He read the letter carefully several times.

He said, "You had better read this, Colonel; I need your advice once more." I stepped over to him and took the letter. I soon saw what had upset the General; this was not a letter of friendship and local news. It was a letter warning of signal events in Kentucky that involved not only our nation but others as well.

I exclaimed, "Wilkinson! I had last heard of him resigning from being the tailor of the Continental Army!"

The General smiled, despite his concern, and said, "Now, Colonel: such personal disparagement is surely beneath you. General Wilkinson may have been in charge of clothing an army in rags, and he may have failed at that task, but I have not learned to disparage the generals of my command for failure at tasks that are beyond the capability of mortals."

"But Wilkinson was an idiot, sir; and he was part of the Conway Cabal against you."

"Never proved, Colonel, never proved. I would not have advanced him as far as I did if I had not respected his loyalty." The General was no longer smiling. "Which, according to this letter, was a respect seriously misplaced."

"The man is a traitor. He is negotiating with Spain over the control of the Mississipi and promising to use his influence to create Kentucky as a separate country!"

"I have often wished that France had kept its influence over the Mississipi; our current alliance with the Most Christian King would have certainly simplified our future there, had the French not delivered Louisiana to the Spanish before the War. But now Wilkinson and his party of antifederalists thinks to deliver Kentucky to them as well!" The

General paced across the study and back again. "It is unconscionable, Colonel. We cannot be losing bits and pieces of the country to European powers after expending so much blood to obtain our independence!"

I glanced again at the letter. "But Colonel Marshall goes on to say, Your Excellency, that the story does not end there: two parties, one dedicated to a new country allied with Spain, another dedicated to a state of the Union. No, indeed: the Colonel says that the British want a piece of it as well!"

Colonel Marshall led the party in Kentucky that wanted the region to become a state of the Union separate from Virginia. Shortly after Wilkinson's folly, an agent of Lord Dorchester, the British governor of Canada, approached Colonel Marshall. Having learned of the Spanish proposals, Dorchester proposed arms, ammunition, clothing, and money for the support of troops that would enable Kentucky to become its own country, separate from the Union, but allied to Britain rather than to Spain. Colonel Marshall indignantly refused, telling the man that Kentucky hated the British and their Indian allies with a passion. But he feared that events were assuming an alarming character, and he felt that he must make the General aware of the serious nature of the situation.

I read this part of the letter again, in amazement and distress. I looked up and saw the General's gaze upon me in its full austerity, not a trace of humor in his face.

He said, "Colonel, you must realize the implications of this. Colonel Marshall is not one to exaggerate. I believe him without reservation. What is your opinion?"

I stared at him, my brain awash with the enormous consequences of these events. I finally said, "There are so many evils I do not know where to start, Your Excellency. Evil upon evil! The Spanish are bad enough. And yet, one thing is clear: the British government is intent on making our lives as difficult as they can."

"Indeed they are! We have seen it over and over in the last few years. And we cannot permit it. Should Kentucky go its own way, other parts of the Union will come to believe they would be better off with such allies. If Britain or Spain controls the Mississippi, it would mean an America fenced in by its enemies: Britain controls the seas, and should they control the rivers as well, the new country will break apart. I feel myself back in the time of war!" He paced back and forth, hands behind his back.

I felt a cold fear stealing over me. Was it to be another decade of war to separate us all from our families and friends and to water the valleys of the West with what blood we had left after the barrels already shed?

The frustrations of our investigations earlier in the day then combined with those created by the letter, but not in a flood of emotion. The General stood for a moment with a faraway look in his eye. His countenance assumed the calmness I had seen descend over him on the battlefield. Clearly he had crossed a visceral Rubicon.

Before I opened my mouth, the General said, "Do not say it, Colonel. I must decide for the Presidency, and I must lead our new country out of this abyss. The press of events makes it clear. I still feel myself unequal to the task, but it appears I must acquiesce in the general opinion that I am indispensable. But we still have these murders hanging over the decision."

He went to his desk. As he sat writing, he told me, "Although I cannot yet finally decide on the Presidency, I must write to Colonel Marshall to set events in motion. The situation is too desperate to hesitate. I will explain my thoughts to him and ask him to keep me informed through a secure information channel, or even ciphered communications."

The General sealed the letter, then wrote out another one, very short. He enclosed the first letter in the second. He said, "I shall send my response to Colonel Marshall through Captain Marshall, who will be sure to get the letter to his father securely and confidentially."

We went out and found Mr. Fairfax. The General gave him instructions to get the note to Captain Marshall in Richmond as soon as possible. Having relieved himself of his immediate need for action, the General stopped for thought, arms folded, the darkness settling around us as the evening took over from the afternoon.

Looking at his house, he said, "I believe that, having come this close to my decision, I must now speak seriously with Mrs. Washington on it." I knew he would rather face British guns than tell his wife her life at Mount Vernon was to end, at least for a time. He hesitated, then said, "Please join me, Colonel. You have been present at most of the difficult moments of my career. This, one of the most difficult, will be the better for your presence behind me."

I hesitated, as I did not wish to intrude on the General and his wife, but his entreaty for my friendship and support was too exigent to decline. We went back into the house in search of his wife.

33

Thursday, March 26, 1789, evening

We found Mrs. Washington in the back parlor, instructing her young maid in some sort of complicated needlework.

The General approached her and asked, "My dear, may we speak with you for a moment?"

"Certainly, Mr. Washington. Oney, would you please excuse us?"

"Yes'm," said Oney, curtseying. She left the room. We sat down in the parlor chairs.

A small silence developed, which the General broke with his news. "My dear, I must tell you that it is all but certain that I am to be President."

Mrs. Washington, taken aback, said, "President?"

"President, Mrs. Washington. I am afraid it is...unavoidable."

"And all this," she said, waving her hand, "is to come to nothing? We have been so happy these last years since the war."

"Mount Vernon will always be here for us, and we will surely return soon. You have made our home a very happy place indeed."

Mrs. Washington, not to be diverted, lamented, "Years away in the heat and squalor of big cities."

"Yes, I am afraid so. My duty—"

"I do understand, Mr. Washington. I know you too well. If there is public duty to be done, you will do it regardless. It is just that I had anticipated that we would continue this life, that we would be left to grow old together in solitude and tranquility." She carefully put down her sewing materials. "Living a secluded life with little more than the weather to give us trouble."

I thought to myself that a woman who entertained five or six visitors a week was not very secluded. Despite the social activity, however, the tranquility of Mount Vernon was certainly something to be lost. It was that, after all, that prompted my own visit of over two years, that and the General himself.

The General said, "I too anticipated such a life; I am very sorry it is not to be."

"Is there yet no hope of their finding someone else for this great honor?"

The General smiled at this irony and replied, "Apparently not, my dear, despite my best efforts to inform all and sundry both of my unfitness for the exalted position and my unwillingness to forego the quiet of retirement. They insist. And there are events...emergences... that will require my prompt attention."

Mrs. Washington looked as though she did not much appreciate the will of the people. "Well, it is all for the best, I am sure, that you do your public duty as you see it. You and I must sacrifice, but our compensation will come with the knowledge of the good you do for the country. Pray do not tell me about your *events;* I daresay I will learn about them soon enough, Mr. Washington." She looked at me. "And what are you to do, Colonel Humphreys? Back to Connecticut?"

I smiled and told her, "The General has asked me to become his private secretary, along with Mr. Lear. I will join you in New York. I am very happy to be of further service to the General."

"Indeed. A familiar face will be most welcome at dinner. Wonderful!"

The General relaxed a little. "There are some practical issues to consider that we must discuss, my dear. I have instructed Mr. Lear to aid you in organizing your household for your absence."

"When is it to be?" Mrs. Washington's voice was quiet and resigned.

"I am not sure; surely the Congress will meet soon, if they have not already. General Knox tells me he is yet waiting for a quorum. There is the lingering problem of the murders—forgive me for mentioning it, but we must deal with those as well. However, I feel that should the notice come, and should the electors entrust me with the office, and should we have resolved our legal issues, I will need to leave immediately, as events appear to be overtaking the new country. I have prepared myself for that eventuality over the last month. You, however, do not need to accompany me immediately. Please take as long as you like to get ready—though I am sure I will be distressed for things to do of an evening until you join me in New York."

"Mr. Washington, you know very well that I will travel anywhere to be with you, as I did during the war. I daresay the social round will be more pleasant than it was at Valley Forge."

"Much more pleasant, I should think. It will be, at the very least, warmer. I will depend upon your ability to charm the politicians in New York as you charmed my officers in camp."

His wife considered for a moment, then said, "We might take Hercules, if you think fit. You have doubtless noticed that the quality of dinners has improved remarkably with his being made cook here." Mrs. Washington looked earnestly at the General. I believe she wished to recreate as much of her home life as she could in her new surroundings.

The General demurred. "I believe we must wait on that, my dear; the uncertainty over where we will stay, and the difficulties associated with establishing a household routine, may make it difficult to accommodate any other than our personal servants and postillions. It may be best to hire temporary household servants in New York." The General paused, then said, "There is a topic that the Colonel and I have been discussing lately, that I think I must also raise with you. I have mentioned to you several times that my views on my people have been undergoing change."

Mrs. Washington smiled and said, "Mr. Washington, you have decided enough for one day, I believe. I am aware of the progression of your thinking, and the Colonel has always been very forthcoming on the subject of our people. I do not see the force of it, to be honest. We have always had slaves and cannot do without them. I do not see what freeing them would achieve. And I do not want to worry about it with all this fuss going on. Let us solve that problem when we come to it."

The General said, gently, "We may come to it unexpectedly, Mrs. Washington. Providence may not provide me with much time on this earth, you know. I anticipate four years as President, but Providence may not permit even that."

Mrs. Washington lost her smile and looked down at her lap. "I do not like to speak of such matters, you know that."

"I do, my dear. I feel the press of time, however, and I must consider what I may do for my people before that time runs out for me."

"I have lost nearly all my loved ones," she said, her voice shaking a little. "Mr. Custis, first; then all my children. I cannot contemplate the worst. I cannot. You must not make me."

The General relented. "I understand. But I want you to realize that I must take these decisions soon, along with everything else I must do. I will delay on this decision, though it pains me. I will speak more of it with Colonel Humphreys and Mr. Lear, and when you are ready, we can talk."

"That will do, Mr. Washington; I can go on with that."

"Very well." The General arose, and we left Mrs. Washington to her needlework, and to her people.

34

FRIDAY, MARCH 27, 1789, AFTERNOON

The next day, after the General returned from his daily ride out, he said to me, "All this talk about slaves and duty reminds me: Alice. We now have two murders. While Doll's information was useful, we must talk with Alice directly, given what we have learned about her husband."

We walked out through the front door and over to the kitchen, where Hercules was busy preparing the dinner.

The General said, "Hercules, we must speak with Alice, if it is not too much trouble."

"No trouble at all sir, 'cept maybe for Alice." The big cook smiled and pointed toward the back of the kitchen. "She ain't much use to us here in the kitchen. She out in the scullery."

The General nodded his thanks. We turned into the scullery and found Alice scrubbing pots and dishes.

The General said, "Alice, we must speak with you again about Julius."

"Yes, sir." The small woman put down the plate she was cleaning and wiped her hands on her apron.

"We have learned that he went about with Mr. Thompson, the overseer at Colonel Mason's plantation, and that he and Thompson threatened the people at the Grist Mill, among other things. Can you tell us what you know about Julius and Mr. Thompson?"

Alice remained silent, her lips pressed tight and her eyes very big in what could only be fear.

"Come now, Alice, there is no need to fear us. Mr. Thompson is dead, killed in Alexandria. Julius is dead. Your only responsibility now is to me," said the General.

This assertion did not have its desired effect on Alice. "They all dead, all dead, and I be next!" she cried. "If that man don't kill me, you-all will!" Tears dripped down her face and she hid it in her apron. She was shaking. Her fear grew large, into terror.

I asked, "Who is 'that man', Alice? Who is trying to kill you?"

She shook her head violently, still concealed in the apron.

"You must answer us, Alice," said the General.

I asked, "Do you have any friends among the house servants we can bring to help you get the strength to talk with us?"

She kept shaking her head. "No, no friends at all, no friends at all." She dropped the apron from her face, then said in a frantic voice, "Shouldn't never have gone to live with that man Julius, he was no good then and no good to anyone now! Didn't have no one else. No one else. Ain't no one wanna know me or help me! I jus' trapped here. Gonna whup me for sure now! Sell me off!"

"Who is your mother, Alice?" I thought that her mother might make her calm enough to be sensible. The General started and raised a hand, but it was too late to stop me.

She laughed bitterly through her tears. "My mama done got sold off long ago, never knew her. Got no one! Gonna sell me too!"

The General looked away, shook his head, and said, "A complicated story, Colonel. Her mother went shortly after Alice's birth, many years ago. Before the War." Before the General had begun to think of his people as people rather than as just slaves, he meant.

"I cannot say I am your friend, Alice," I tried again, "and your master is your master, but he and I are kindly disposed to you right now, and we must have an answer."

The General added his own entreaty. "Alice, this is vital for us. Colonel Humphreys is correct: you must answer us. No one will punish you." The General's voice was as compassionate as he could make it, but he was not a compassionate man.

She shook her head again, violently, and said, "Cain't say nothin', he just kill me dead!"

I replied, "Mr. Thompson? He's dead himself."

"Julius told him off, he got murder in his eye. Julius jus' laugh. I ain't got much, sir, but I got my life and I want to keep it."

"You are safe here at the Mansion House, Alice," said the General. "There is no need to be afraid."

"That's all you know! They everywhere! He come here or wherever, just to find me and kill me! All them smiling, bowing people here, got to be some that have hearts as black as they are," said Alice. "They'll tell. Can't trust no one, no one. Black folk tell on you, white folks sell you down, then they kill you!"

"Are you saying there are people here that were in league with Julius?" I asked. I thought about what she had said and realized she was not referring to Thompson. "Who is there besides Mr. Thompson? Another white man?" Unbidden, a picture of Major Washington flashed through my mind, though I instantly dismissed it.

Alice just cried more loudly, nearly screaming with her terror.

Recoiling, the General said, "This is absurd!"

"Well, Your Excellency, it might explain a good deal about the pervasiveness of the thefts. Mr. Thompson could not have done this alone." I thought about the perniciousness of slavery and the chaos it caused, and I wished the General would see it that way too. But I knew he had sold slaves who caused him trouble; I did not know whether he had gained enough perspective yet to see that selling a slave was not the best way to address a troublesome servant.

He said, putting his stoicism up as a barrier to the heavy emotion in the room, "I suppose so. It sounds as though Alice knows who this person is and will not tell us." He looked at her without expression. "I am not sure how to proceed."

"I expect we'll need to question all the slaves, and probably the white servants as well, to see if we can identify anyone." I said. "Somebody must know something. Somebody must have seen someone."

"But there are hundreds of Negroes and servants on the plantations!" The General was appalled at the prospect. "There isn't time! We cannot possibly question everyone before I must leave for New York." He paused, then amended his words, "Should I get the summons to do so."

Alice's screams subsided, though her tears still flowed. The General asked her, "Did Julius ever say who else on the plantation he was working with to steal things? We know about Mr. Thompson, but who else?"

She shook her head without saying anything.

"Who were his good friends?"

She sobbed, "Didn't have no friends, he was the overseer, just drove people and drove people. Told 'em what to do and when to do it. Don't be nobody friends with a man like that. No friends to me, either, 'cause I with him." She sniffled. "Just me, now he dead and he going to make me dead too." She started crying hard again and lifted the apron to her eyes.

"All right, all right, Alice," said the General in his calmest voice. "We will leave you now. Please try to gather yourself together, all these tears are most unseemly. Take some time off in your quarters, I will tell Hercules you are ill." It appeared the General was willing to forego additional information to free himself from Alice's excess of emotion. The General was not compassionate, but it was very clear to me that he was not willing to use his power over Alice to get what he wanted. He could have had her whipped; instead, he gave her time to recover from her terror.

"Yes, sir, thank you sir," mumbled Alice through her apron.

"And please, Alice, reconsider, and when you feel better, tell us what you know. Come to the house and get Frank to fetch me at any time."

We walked out of the scullery. Hercules was standing in the middle of the kitchen holding a large spoon, but not doing anything with it. How much had he heard?

The General said to him, "Hercules, Alice must take the rest of the day off to recover herself. I hope that will not discommode you."

"No sir, not at all." He waved the spoon, expression inscrutable. "Mima, she take over on pots. Dinner on the table directly, sir."

Taking the hint, the General nodded. "Thank you, Hercules, I will let you get back to it. I am very sorry for the disruption."

We walked out and back to the house. The General was silent and contemplative, but whether he was thinking of Alice or of the large task ahead of us, I could not tell.

35

Saturday, March 28, 1789

Once the General understood the need for action, he wasted little time. The science of logistics was an open book to him, and he could not tolerate any more days of doing nothing.

"Colonel, today will be a full day," said the General to me before breakfast the next morning, "We must question the overseers and slaves at all the farms systematically. We must enlist my nephew George, Mr. Lear, and Mr. Fairfax as well." He asked Major Washington and Mr. Lear to come to his study after breakfast and sent Frank Lee to fetch Mr. Fairfax.

When everyone was present, the General stood facing them and organized the hunt.

"Gentlemen: I need your help with our murder investigation today. We have found the murders to be intertwined with systematic theft from the plantation. We need to get a complete picture of how much produce has gone missing, how that produce can disappear on a regular basis, and whether there are any intruders appearing on the farm that might be engineering this theft. To accomplish this, we must question all of the people on the farms individually about these things. We must not leave any stone unturned."

The men exchanged incredulous glances but said nothing.

"Clearly this task is beyond the capabilities of Colonel Humphreys and myself working alone, so I must form my own posse: you gentlemen. Each of us five will ride out to a specific farm and question everyone there, today. Mr. Fairfax, you must go to Dogue Run; Mr. Lear, you take on Muddy Hole; George, if you please, go to Ferry Farm; Colonel, please go to French's; and I will take the River Farm and the Mansion House. You must ask each person to think carefully about visitors they have seen on the farm, and you must press them on things that have gone missing. Any questions?"

The gentlemen looked at each other a bit helplessly. The General smiled. "I know this sounds futile, but we must learn what is happening, and I believe this is really the only way to do it. I rely on the old Scottish adage, 'Many mickles make a muckle.' A little vigor applied to collect information from many sources may provide that one solid fact that will be the end of our quest. Thank you. George, may I speak with you briefly? And you, Colonel Humphreys?"

Major Washington lingered after Mr. Lear and Mr. Fairfax had left.

The General asked, "George, do you think you are sufficiently recovered to be up to this task at Ferry farm?"

The Major was not the picture of health; he looked pale and drawn. Nevertheless, he said without hesitation, "Certainly, Uncle. I have been up and around for several days now. Not quite ready to run races, you know; but I'm all right for this."

"And is there nothing you wish to tell me? About your attack?"

The Major passed a hand over his face and said, "Fanny and I would like to forget those days, Uncle. I felt ashamed to be so weak. I will do my best to regain my full strength and be of use to you, sir."

And that was all. The General, still feeling on delicate ground, let Major Washington go to his tasks.

"We must wait a little longer, Colonel," he said to me. "George is clearly not yet ready to talk about his experience. When he is fully recovered, I will speak to him seriously about it."

I shook my head but said nothing, not willing to push my already overburdened friend beyond his limits. He clearly was not willing to think ill of his nephew, and his mind was occupied with other things.

The General informed Mrs. Washington that she might need to postpone dinner in favor of a late supper for us all. I rode to French's, riding part way with Major Washington, but we made only ordinary conversation, and he rode off into Ferry Farm without incident.

The five of us gathered together in the General's study in the late afternoon to report. Despite the many mickles, we made no single muckle of any worth other than to understand the scale of the problem.

The General, after hearing all the reports, found only excuses. A quite extraordinary number of deaths afflicted the cattle and hogs, and the number of chickens taken by foxes proved that the General was neglecting his fox hunting to such a degree that it might prove the ruin of him. And one might have thought there had been a drought to have caused the fall in production of tobacco, wheat, and corn. But no one would admit to knowing anything about any intruders. Major Washington was as puzzled as the others. If he were involved, he was a better actor than he had any right to be. He retired early, without supper, to recover from his exertions during the day.

The General and I stepped out onto the piazza after hearing the reports to watch the sun set over the river.

"I am troubled by the scale of it all, Colonel, and by the willful ignorance of my people," said the General. "We have probed and questioned to no avail, even though many of the people on the farms must know what has been going on. We are completely blocked by their intransigence."

"I suspect, Your Excellency, that their interests must oppose yours in these matters. They will take advantage of anything that makes their lives easier, and they will resist telling you things that make their lives harder."

"I have tried as their master to make their lives as easy as my duty and resources permit."

"But they are not *free,* Your Excellency."

"No, they are not; and now I must consider more drastic methods, which I have little wish—"

The central door opened, and Mrs. Washington emerged followed by Mr. Fairfax. Both looked worried and agitated.

"There you are, Mr. Washington! The worst thing. Alice has absconded!"

"What!" The General gazed at them in astonishment.

Mr. Fairfax related his sad tale. "Hercules came to me just now and reported that she never came to work in the kitchen today, and we have gone to the quarters and she is not there!"

The General asked, "Have you instituted a search, Mr. Fairfax? It is possible that this murderer has claimed another victim."

The manager responded, "Yes, Your Excellency; but it is clear from the other slaves that she was preparing to abscond, and her possessions are missing."

I said, "Her terror yesterday must have led her to this unhappy step, sir. She fears death here more than the risks and consequences of running away. At least, if her possessions are gone, she is still alive—for the moment."

The General nodded, then said, "I was wrong yesterday to allow her to remain silent. We must find her and learn what she knows. Mr. Fairfax, start the search for Alice immediately. She is a valuable witness in the murder of her husband, and her flight will impair our investigation. Please send servants to Georgetown and Fredericksburg first thing in the morning to advise the authorities of her flight and to advertise for her recovery—I think a bit more than the usual amount for salvage, say 15 dollars in addition to the amount allowed by law, 10 shillings? That should provide strong motivation for her prompt recovery."

Mr. Fairfax agreed. "Yes, sir. What about Alexandria? That's the most likely place for her."

"I intend to go for Alexandria tomorrow morning myself to handle that end of it." The General looked at me. "I shall visit Colonel Hooe and see about the details of his investigations so far, then I shall initiate the search for Alice. Will you come, Colonel? We should get there before Colonel Hooe is off to church."

I shook my head in dismay. "I am very distressed by all this, Your Excellency. The business of slave-catching is not much to my taste. But I will accompany you despite my feelings."

"It is not to my taste either, Colonel. Yet it must be done. Compassion has its place, but duty often makes it impossible."

We went in with Mrs. Washington to a cold supper as darkness descended on Mount Vernon.

36

SUNDAY, MARCH 29, 1789, MORNING

At cocks-crow on Sunday morning, the General and I rode to Alexandria at a trot. We stabled our horses at Colonel Fitzgerald's house and walked the two blocks to Colonel Hooe's, arriving just as the Hooe family was finishing breakfast. Colonel Hooe had us shown into the parlor, then joined us after a short time, accompanied by Mr. Williamson.

"I apologize for disturbing your Sunday, Colonel Hooe," said the General.

"Oh, that's all right, Your Excellency. A Sheriff keeps odd hours at the best of times, sir."

The General smiled, then said, "I fear I bring more trouble for you, Colonel. It has been a month now since my overseer's death, and we have not reached a conclusion. I find myself completely stymied. Despite our best efforts, all we have is two dead bodies and now a runaway slave. Time presses more than ever, as Congress may achieve a quorum any day and force my decision on the Presidency."

"A runaway, sir?" Colonel Hooe picked out the new element in the General's summing up of the situation.

"Yes. Alice, Julius's wife, has absconded. We found her missing late yesterday at Mount Vernon. We have come to start the search for her as well as to consult with you on the status of the murder investigation. I have heard little to nothing from you about that recently." I heard the General's frustration, as did Colonel Hooe.

Colonel Hooe shifted uncomfortably and defended himself. "We have put forth our best efforts, Your Excellency, please be assured. Williamson?"

The quiet clerk cleared his throat. "I am really very sorry, Your Excellency, to have to report so little progress. I have again questioned the seaman who heard the shot that killed Thompson, but he had nothing to add. His ship sailed two days ago. No one I have spoken with in town has had anything to add to what we already knew."

The General rubbed his mouth. We had strong grounds to suspect Colonel Hooe of involvement in the Thompson murder, as he owned the warehouse where Thompson was killed. Striving to gather more information, the General said, "Perhaps we should look more deeply into Mr. Thompson's flight. I am not yet fully acquainted with what occurred on the search for him."

At this probe, Mr. Williamson looked questioningly at Colonel Hooe, who nodded. The clerk said, "Well, Your Excellency, we engaged a servant of Colonel Mason's who was an experienced tracker. He was able to trace Thompson to the south of Gunston Hall, heading toward the river. Mr. Cockburn and I accompanied the man through the wilds of Mason's Neck on horseback, following traces of his flight. We shortly came to a creek, where the trail vanished. The tracker thought that the man had used the water to obscure his flight, a common trick. We cast around for quite some time, up and down the creek, but we could find no other trail. We then returned to Gunston Hall."

"I recall hearing something about a horse found later that week in Alexandria?"

"Yes, Your Excellency. When we returned to Gunston Hall after our fruitless search, Colonel Mason reported that a horse had gone missing from an outlying farm. On Wednesday a week ago, two days later, a farmer came to us to report finding a stray horse wandering in one of his fields just to the west of town. It was Colonel Mason's. My conclusion then was that Thompson doubled back to the farm, stole the horse, and rode out along the road to Alexandria while we were hunting fruitlessly in the forest. I redoubled my efforts here on hearing about this, but to no avail. And then, on the Friday, you found his body."

"Bloody man was in that warehouse the whole time!" ejaculated Colonel Hooe. The General frowned at the language but nodded in agreement.

The clerk looked down at his feet. "Yes, sir, I feel quite embarrassed about that, and I apologize for it. Someone knew about the derelict warehouse and took advantage of that knowledge."

The General said, "Seneca said that memory recalls the stab of fear, Mr. Williamson. We must adapt ourselves to the present rather than being tormented by events of the past. But sometimes paying attention to what those past events can tell us may help to direct our attention in the present."

"Thank you for your understanding, Your Excellency." Mr. Williamson's voice was nearly a whisper, and he continued to look at his feet.

"How many people knew about that warehouse?" asked the General.

Mr. Williamson's eyes lifted toward the General's. "I would say most of those who spent their days on the waterfront, sir, which means most of the town." Mr. Williamson shook his head in apology. "I am afraid I cannot identify any individual more likely than any other to have known about its availability as a hiding place."

"What about those few days here in Alexandria? Did anything happen here that might be relevant?"

"I do not believe so; business transpired very much as usual for me. I also consulted with your nephew about anything I might have overlooked at Mount Vernon, but he could suggest nothing further for me to do there."

The General, surprised, asked, "When did you consult him?"

"On the Tuesday, Your Excellency, when he came to Alexandria on business."

The General and I looked at each other. Tuesday? The General said, "I was not aware that he had come here on that day." I shook my head in agreement. Tuesday was the day George Thompson first found his way into a disused warehouse in Alexandria, which he never left alive.

"Oh, yes, sir, Major Washington was here on Tuesday afternoon. He appeared at our main warehouse. He seemed...quite ill. I was concerned, but he disclaimed any concern for his own health. He seemed very worried over some small matters of business underway at that time, none of which warranted his presence here. I reassured him and recommended that he return home to rest himself." Mr. Williamson paused. "In short, Your Excellency, I could not understand why he had put himself to so much trouble."

We could see this information about his nephew was surprising to the General. Thus far, he had been resolute in trusting Major Washington unreservedly. Surely this information about his nephew's movements and presence at the scene of the murder must give him pause?

He turned quickly to Colonel Hooe, a frown deepening on his brow. "Were you aware of this visit, Colonel Hooe?"

"No, Your Excellency. I was away from Alexandria at the time."

The General looked at me, but he was looking through me, his mind clearly on his nephew and Mount Vernon and the consequences of such a betrayal for his family. After a moment, he recollected himself and said, "I see. I will consult with Major Washington when I return home today. Was there anything else, Mr. Williamson?" His face regained his usual calm expression as he turned back to the clerk.

"No, Your Excellency."

"Then I think it high time to turn our attention to the warehouse."

37

SUNDAY, MARCH 29, 1789, MORNING

The General cast his eyes steadily at Colonel Hooe. By prompting him to tell us about the warehouse, we could press for details that would confirm our suspicions of him—or remove them, which would be a much preferred outcome.

Colonel Hooe said, "I must say, I feel quite put upon that this murderer decided to use my warehouse as his playground. The impudence!"

"When did you purchase the warehouse?"

"Let me see. I believe it would have been toward the beginning of February of this year. Williamson? You handled the purchase."

The clerk responded, "Yes, sir. The auction was on the first Wednesday in February, in the Market Square. I learned of the availability of the warehouse, so I attended and acted without consulting you."

"Yes, that's right."

The General smiled. "I assume your motive was to expand your capabilities for shipping here in Alexandria?"

Colonel Hooe smiled in return. "I am confident that the new administration that you will lead, Your Excellency, will produce such trading conditions as have not been seen in decades, especially as Alexandria is your home port, so to speak."

The General replied, "I certainly hope to enhance trade, and particularly trade from Virginia, of course, but I cannot favor particular ports—or individuals, Colonel Hooe. You are doubtless aware of the efforts to create the national capital here."

Colonel Hooe replied, "I know you will do your very best for the whole country. You know, a rising tide lifts all boats. And boats contain trade goods."

The General reverted to his original concern. "What was the state of the warehouse? Who owned it, and why was it up for auction?"

Colonel Hooe looked helplessly at Mr. Williamson, who said, "An elderly merchant owned it, Josiah Brown. Mr. Brown's increasing infirmity had led to the demise of his trading business in recent years. Mr. Brown having recently died without issue or will, the County auctioned off his house and warehouse to pay the debts of the estate."

"You did not consult Colonel Hooe on the purchase?"

"No, sir, as the Colonel has given me authority to make even large purchases along the lines he has established. The firm is currently pursuing expansion in many ways due to the increase in business in the port. I immediately saw the opportunity to expand our warehouse area to prepare for future needs, as the warehouse is right down the street from our main warehouse."

The General nodded, then asked, "But you did not use the vacant warehouse during February and March?"

Mr. Williamson nodded, and Colonel Hooe said, "I have more irons in the fire right now than I can manage, I fear." He pursed his lips. "I am also expanding in Georgetown, and most of my work lately has been there."

Mr. Williamson said, "And much of my time has been taken up with the firm's current affairs, and now with these investigations into criminal activity in the County. I was thus unable to supervise any improvements to the property. I have been much away from town in recent weeks."

"As have I," added Colonel Hooe.

The General smiled. "Indeed. Both Alexandria and Georgetown are quite lively ports at the moment, I think."

"Yes, indeed. Lively and growing! Georgetown is already the hub of the tobacco trade from farms to the west, and when the Federal government establishes itself in the area, the port can do nothing but expand."

"So you did not visit the warehouse during the week before the 20th of this month?"

"No, sir, it would have been quite difficult. In fact, you were lucky to find me here on the 20th when we found Thompson's body—I had been in Georgetown. Directly after our adventure with Thompson at Gunston Hall, I organized the search for Mr. Thompson, put Williamson in charge, then went directly to Georgetown to attend another auction there. I came back late on the 19th. After all that work and travel, I slept like a log that night; my wife tells me I was nearly impossible to rouse the following morning."

So Colonel Hooe could not have been the person to whom Mr. George Thompson ran on the 16th when he fled from Gunston Hall. How could we determine whether this was truthful?

The General smiled. He said, "That reminds me of something else, sir, about that day at Gunston Hall. May I ask a few questions of your coachman before we depart for Colonel Fitzgerald's house?"

"Certainly, Your Excellency." Colonel Hooe arose. "Come this way and we will find him. Williamson, you may join the family to prepare for church. I will be along directly." The clerk nodded and left the room. The Colonel led the way to the stables in the back of the house, where we found the coachman standing and talking with one of the stable lads about a bruised foreleg on one of the carriage horses.

The Colonel introduced the man to us, then said, "I must leave you here, gentlemen, as my family awaits me and I must dress." Colonel Hooe bowed and walked back into the house. The coachman looked a little awed to be speaking with the famous General.

The General asked, "Do you remember the trip to Gunston Hall on the 16th of this month, sir?"

"Yes, Your Honor, brutal cold day that was, sir."

"Did you happen to catch sight of the man who fled that day from the back of the Hall?"

"No one crossed my path then, Your Honor. Wherever he ran, he didn't run past me in the front of the house, sir."

"I understand Colonel Hooe went from there to Georgetown almost immediately."

"Oh, yes, Your Honor. I was rare put out we couldn't stay for the hunt, I dearly love a hunt. That bloke Williamson gets all the fun."

"So you drove Colonel Hooe to Georgetown, then?"

"Yes, sir, I did. Right from Gunston. We had to make a quick run, too, as His Nibs was late for a big meeting of some kind."

"I see. Thank you, and here is something for your trouble." The General handed the coachman a penny.

"Thank you, Your Honor, pleasure doing business with you." The man bobbed his head and clutched his reward.

We walked back to the house. The General smiled and said, "It would appear that Colonel Hooe lacked the opportunity to have been the moving force in our little tragedy."

"Yes, sir; though I suppose he might have organized it."

"I am unpersuaded the man could organize getting out of bed without his clerk or his wife at hand. He is, nevertheless, an excellent man and a good friend; I am very glad to have no reason to distrust him now. Very glad indeed! But as he and his clerk are not making progress on the murders, we must continue our own investigations."

"Yes, sir." I knew the General held men to a high standard on matters of logistics and organization. Colonel Hooe was as well-organized as anyone of his class, I supposed, but he certainly relied on

Mr. Williamson more than the General relied on Mr. Lear or myself.

"Just one more thread to tie down," said the General. I followed him back into Colonel Hooe's house, where he stopped a servant and asked to see Mrs. Hooe before she left for church. She came bustling up, a portly woman with good sense shining out of her face, in her Sunday best.

"So nice to see you again, Your Excellency."

"Yes, ma'am, though I wish it were under better circumstances. May I ask a question of you?"

"Certainly, sir."

"Do you remember the night on which the Colonel returned from Georgetown? The night of the unfortunate event in his warehouse?"

"Yes, indeed sir I do. That tragic event happening so close to our house raised quite a lot of concern among the servants and neighbors."

"Colonel Hooe says he heard nothing of it until we summoned him, is that correct?"

"The man would not have heard the house collapsing around him, he was that soundly sleeping, sir." She laughed. "He is ordinarily a sound sleeper, which helps me sleep next to him, but that night he was so worn out by his travails in Georgetown and the poor conditions of the roads coming back that he was barely able to get his nightclothes on before he collapsed into bed with me, and he did not wake until we shook him awake at your summons the next morning."

With such testimony, we could not further doubt Colonel Hooe. The General thanked Mrs. Hooe, and we bade her goodbye.

As we walked the two blocks back to Colonel Fitzgerald's house, the General gave me my next task. He said, "If you please, Colonel, there is a man I use here to handle the recovering of absconding slaves from my plantation, William Hutchison. While I confer with Colonel Fitzgerald, I would like you to approach him about recovering Alice. He is by far the best of his type in Alexandria: he has no record of abuse or unnecessary killing in the process of recovery of the property. I would like you to emphasize the need to recover Alice without harm or insult to her in any way. It will be difficult enough to persuade her to talk without that."

My feelings rebelled at this request, however, conflicting with my intense loyalty to the General. I replied with what I hoped was an even tone. "I cannot refuse you, Your Excellency, much as I might wish to do so." Could it be that David Humphreys was to assume a new career, that of slave catcher? I forced myself to add, "But you must know that I would prefer any task to that."

I felt that "recovery of the property" hardly did justice to the horrors of taking an escaped slave on the run. The General might be referring to an escaped barrel of fish. I could not accept the task without at least letting the General know how much I opposed it.

The General replied, "I would spare you this trouble, Colonel, if I had anyone else I could trust as much to accomplish the task. I would attempt it myself, but I feel that your diplomatic abilities far exceed my own, and Mr. Hutchison—well, you will meet him. I must admit that he and I have very different personalities and preferences, and yet he is the best man at what he does. I hope I have not overstepped the bounds of friendship. I feel that Alice's recovery is vital. I would ask Colonel Fitzgerald, but he is full of his own business and his family and would not be able to concentrate his attentions fully on the task."

I said, "Then I must undertake it, Your Excellency, however reluctantly."

The General replied, "Thank you, Colonel. I cannot say how much I appreciate your trouble in this, as it removes all worry from my own breast." He gave me Hutchison's address.

An ugly task indeed. I would need to steel myself to it, but I would obey. We desperately needed Alice as a witness in the murder investigation, and I felt I must consider it in that light. And, as much as my heart rebelled against the task, it rebelled even more at refusing my friend and benefactor a service he needed from me. My sense of loyalty to the General and my commitment to helping him in this case outweighed my objections to slavery.

38

SUNDAY, MARCH 29, 1789, AFTERNOON

William Hutchison resided on Alfred Street near Prince, a goodly walk from Colonel Hooe's house near the waterfront, so I mounted my horse and rode up there. I tied the horse to a railing and knocked on the door. The maidservant who answered was a young Negro woman in a homespun brown dress, no frills. The house was small but neat and clean on the outside. There was a small front parlor into which the maidservant showed me to wait for her master, who she said was out on a short errand. I gave her my card.

After ten minutes or so, a bustle indicated the return of Mr. Hutchison. I stood as the parlor door opened, and in walked a young man, about 25, tall with a strong physique, a short beard, and twinkling brown eyes. He was dressed rather in the manner of a backwoodsman than in the formal style most Alexandria residents adopted. He eyed my card.

"Colonel Humphreys? A matter of business, I presume?"

"Yes, sir."

"Let us sit and discuss it, then."

We sat, and a small silence developed while I formulated my request to him.

I said, "Mr. Hutchison, I hope—"

"Hutch, please sir. No need to stand on formalities here."

"As you will, sir. Hutch it is." This disarmed me, so I got right to the point. "I am a guest of General Washington at Mount Vernon, and one of his slaves has absconded. He has worked with you before to retrieve absconding slaves, I believe; he has given me the task of finding Alice if she is present in Alexandria."

"Description?"

"She is a dark Negro woman with black eyes, about 21 years of age. Her face is thin, with a high, furrowed forehead, a broad, flat nose, and prominent cheekbones. She has thick lips, always without a smile and downturned. She has a small stature and a very thin build, and she hunches as though expecting punishment at any moment. Her hair is black and bushy and she does not tie it back. She was wearing a simple brown dress."

"When did she flee?"

"We discovered the flight yesterday afternoon; she must have absconded some time yesterday or the night before. I have just come from the Sheriff, no one has recovered or seen her and reported it to him."

"That's all right then, we should be able to turn her up pretty damn quick, I'd think, if she came here—and most of the runaways from Mount Vernon do, you know. Good. And the reward?"

"I am authorized by the General to offer 15 dollars in addition to the amount allowed by law."

He grinned. "Must be bloody valuable to the General. He's usually less generous."

"She is a witness in a murder investigation at Mount Vernon. We need her information."

The grin disappeared. "Murder? Well, then, let's get cracking, sir." He arose.

"A moment." I hesitated, then said, "Both the General and I must insist that no harm comes to Alice. She is a witness whom we must persuade to divulge what she knows." I hesitated again, then firmly said, "I am rather resolute in my opposition to slavery, Hutch, and have much compassion for the woman, who has not had an easy time of it after the murder of her husband. I am doing this as a personal favor for my friend, but reluctantly." There: I was on the record.

Hutch sat down and scratched his beard thoughtfully. "By your voice, sir, you are from the North?"

"Connecticut, sir; Hartford and New Haven."

"Ah. Well, as the General's guest, I must assume you have come to a compromise with your feelings about slavery? I believe he has upwards of 300 men, women, and children. Some of whom I have personally recovered after they ran."

I closed my eyes, then opened them and said, "Yes, I have the honor to be a great friend of the General, and though I cannot condone the practice of slavery, I value his friendship and am loyal to him above all else."

He nodded and grinned. "With reason, I should think, him being a hero and all. We shouldn't have a problem, then, sir. And I am not in the habit of abusing people, slave or no. Come, let us talk as we walk. Is that your horse outside?"

"Yes, sir."

"And where are you staying?"

"Mount Vernon."

"I meant in Alexandria, sir."

"Oh—we are here only for the day. The General is at Colonel Fitzgerald's house, if that helps."

"Indeed it does, sir; I am great friends with the Colonel. We will send your horse back to him, then; we'll be walking." He got up and went in search of his servant, whom he tasked with getting my horse back to Colonel Fitzgerald's house.

We walked out into the cold sunshine. Hutch said, "We'll visit some taverns, sir; not to drink, necessarily, but to ask for information. I have many sources in taverns around the town."

I nodded, and we walked. Alexandria, for a small town, had enough taverns to house, feed, and slake the thirst of a multitude. I could see that knowing the tavern-keepers would provide a man with bushels of information.

Hutch told me, "Runaways gravitate toward the south side of town, sir; they find it more amenable for food and shelter than the areas with high class residents such as Colonel Fitzgerald." So we walked southward down Alfred Street, stopping in several taverns on the way to ask about the runaway slave, with no luck.

In snatches between taverns, Hutch related his life story. He had grown up on the Western frontier, and with the early death of his parents at the hand of hostile Shawnee Indians in a British raid during the War, his Alexandria relations had taken him in and raised him. He had found that a liking for hunting acquired from long practice with the local, friendly Shawnee had formed in him a natural talent for the hunt; and in Alexandria, one either hunted rats or men, and he had chosen men. They proved more lucrative. All this was said with such grace and humor, that I formed an immediate liking for the man despite myself. I commented on this to him.

Hutch said, "I understand the practice of slavery is not common up North, Colonel. It is quite common here, and most of us have grown up with slaves in one way or another and are comfortable with it. The General is certainly comfortable with it; we have a good relationship, though I think he does not find me much to his taste socially. Hence you are here?"

"Yes, he said something to the same effect. I am sorry if my views offend you, Hutch, but I am resolute in my opposition to slavery, and I do not relish my current task."

He smiled widely. "Your views do not offend me, sir, I perfectly understand them; it is just that I do not feel the strength of them. And I hope that does not offend *you*."

Strangely, it did not. I must admit, a warm man with good intentions, even though a slave catcher, is yet a warm man. And, after all, here was I, following him around, chasing slaves. At the General's behest.

"It would be hard for me to be offended considering my task, sir. But I do not like it." And I would not do it for anyone but the General.

He looked at me shrewdly as we walked. "It would seem the General cares little for your feelings, Colonel, even as a good friend."

I shook my head. "No, sir, he merely trusts me to get the job done— as a loyal friend. You are wrong about his views, I think. He is very conflicted himself but finds himself quite trapped by circumstance. I do feel that he thought I would be a more suitable emissary to you, for whatever reason."

Hutch smiled again. "Well, as long as he has the cash to pay me, I have little concern for his conflicts, I suppose, or his aversion to me. Though I must say," he added thoughtfully, "I do admire his exploits greatly and am very happy to be of assistance to him in a time of trouble." I imagined that having the General as a client would do him no harm in the community. But I saw that he genuinely felt the honor of serving, as did I. Another example of the unwavering support given the General.

After another couple of taverns, we reached Franklin Street and turned down toward the waterfront. Hutch said, "There's a fine barmaid at the Spring Gardens, Colonel, who has a finger in every pie, or at least every pot of ale. Shall we try her next?"

We entered the Spring Gardens tavern, which bustled with activity; it was lesser known than Wise's City tavern, but it had the patronage of many of the townfolk.

Hutch motioned me toward a bench. "I'll find Lizzie, sir, and I'll stand us to an ale."

I smiled and agreed, and he went off toward the bar. Shortly he returned with a young barmaid with black hair, a pert nose, and two ales. She gave me a piercing look with her lively black eyes.

"He'll do, then. A gent."

"Certainly," said Hutch. "Didn't I say?"

I felt rather like a prize hog being evaluated at market. I opened my mouth in protest, then shut it again as I saw the laughter in those eyes. I was suddenly a young man again, in a tavern looking at barmaids.

"An Irishwoman, I would guess," said I. Her voice had the lilt of a recent immigrant.

"Bloody right, sir, Irish I am. Or American, now, sir."

"We're all Americans now."

"Bloody true, sir, and the ale's on the house for that."

"Well, thank you—Lizzie, is it?"

"Lizzie Casey, Your Honor. County Cork by way of Georgetown."

Hutch sat down next to me. "Now, Lizzie, the Colonel here and I need your help. Colonel Humphreys. He's a-looking for one of General Washington's slaves, run away yesterday."

Her eyes got big. "General Washington? I've seen him about the town, a great man he is, sir, and no doubt about that. Comin' up in world, are we, Hutch?"

Hutch grinned. "Damn right. There's a large pot of money to be made here, Lizzy. Now, she's a young 'un, small and thin, black and bushy, high furrowed forehead, thick lips, broad nose and cheekbones, brown dress. Anything else, Colonel?"

I thought a bit. "She's quite a timid person, I suppose. Her mouth never smiles, and she wears a hunched, fearful look about her. And quiet, often won't say a word. I think she's afraid—more than afraid, terrified—of punishment and death. Her husband, an overseer at the Dogue Run Farm, was murdered." I was slightly surprised by my feelings. I realized I had sympathized with Alice more than I had understood.

"Bloody hell, I've seen her!" Lizzie's eyes opened wide.

I sat up. "Where?"

"How much?" She fixed me again with her eyes and grinned.

Hutch smiled. "Time to pay the piper, Colonel."

I looked up at those pretty Irish eyes and said, "I'm lost, aren't I?"

"You are, sir. You are." She was quite composed but smiling.

I got out a half-dollar and gave it to her, and it disappeared into her bodice.

"Thanks awfully, sir, I have three screaming brats and a worthless drunk of a brother to feed." I didn't believe her for a minute, of course.

"What do you know, Lizzie?" asked Hutch, hunching forward to better hear.

"What I know, Mr. Hutchison, is for me to say and him to hear."

"It's all right, Lizzie, Hutch is my Virgil."

She looked the young man up and down. "A virgin he is not, sir, by no means."

My classical education was quickly being revised by experience. "No matter, tell me about Alice." I sipped my ale, thinking moodily about slave catching. Here I was, enjoying Alexandria tavern life with a man who devoted his life to a practice I abhorred and a barmaid who clearly was in it for the money.

Lizzie leaned closer and lowered her voice. "Well, sir, I saw a black girl like that just this morning, right outside the tavern, struggling with a white man. Something familiar about him, but I couldn't place it. Not a regular here, anyway. Dressed down, but not a farmer or anything; maybe a gent—not like old William here!" She whacked Hutch on the head, and he whacked her back on her behind.

"That's enough of that, Mr. Hutchison. Honestly, can't serve a man a beer in this town without paying for it."

"You've been well paid this time, Lizzie," said Hutch, grinning. "As I will be once we catch this girl." Lizzie gave him a pitying look and resumed her story.

"So he drags her off down the street, she's barely walking with fright, just stumbling along. I thought it was just a master having troubles with his servant, but I almost called out, she looked so scared. Blacks on the run usual look scared, but she was in a bad way. He had a pretty firm grip on her arm. He was as much helping her walk as dragging her along."

"So, she's here in Alexandria, and someone has caught her."

Hutch scratched his beard again. "If she ain't turned up at the gaol or a fuss been made, I don't think it's quite normal, sir."

"And you have no idea who the white man was, Lizzie?"

"Not a clue, sir, sorry." She paused, then said, "Seen him around Alexandria, I must have, sir, but never had him in here."

I thought this over and found I had no questions to ask. "Thank you, Lizzie. I trust I have treated you well?"

"Bloody right! And thank *you* very much, Colonel. Any time you need anything, just come along here and find me. And the General, too, anything at all." She nodded, gave me a wink, then walked off to the bar. I gazed after her.

"Close it up, Colonel, you'll catch flies."

I grinned despite myself. "Where on earth did you come up with her?"

"Alexandria has its landmarks, and Lizzie Casey is one of 'em. You need to get out more, sir."

"I do indeed. All right, what's next?"

"Next is we find the bastard—and the girl." Hutch lifted his ale and drank it down. "And I get my fee."

I came down to earth. The hunt was on. Whatever my feelings about slavery and slave catching, and barmaids, it was time to get on, before Alice suffered the same fate as her husband, if she were not already dead.

39

SUNDAY, MARCH 29, 1789, AFTERNOON

As Hutch and I walked out of the Spring Gardens, I felt a touch on my sleeve. I turned; it was Lizzy Casey, looking very serious.

"Colonel Humphreys, may I speak with you for a few moments? Alone?"

Hutch grinned, slapped my back, and said, "Go to it, Colonel. I don't need you for this part. I will find you at Colonel Fitzgerald's when I have news." He strode off in the direction of the waterfront.

Lizzy was even prettier in the sunlight than she had been in the tavern. She led me inside and up the stairs to her room. She turned her head to me as she opened the door.

"Now don't you go getting ideas. This ain't business, Your Honor, this is serious."

"I never have ideas, Lizzy." And how I wished that were true.

"More's the pity. But it's not the time or the place. Come in, please, sir."

I went into the little room, furnished with a bed and a dressing table. There was a single chair against the wall. Lizzy closed the door and said, "Pull up that chair, I'll sit on the bed."

A small silence developed while Lizzy worked out what she had to say.

"Sir, this may be nothing, or it may mean something important. I can't decide, so I'll just tell you about it."

"This all sounds very mysterious, Lizzy."

Lizzy looked at me for a minute then rushed into it. "I think there is a British spy here."

I blinked and was tongue-tied. Whatever I had been expecting, that was not it. I looked hard at Lizzy, but she was perfectly serious, not a twinkle in sight.

"A British spy? In Alexandria?"

"Yes, sir."

"But we are not at war."

"No, sir, but let me tell you the story, and you can decide."

"Very well, I'm listening."

She shut her eyes to gather her thoughts, then started. "Well, Your Honor, I was up here in this room, having just taken care of some business—if you take my meaning, sir," she said. "My customer had just left, leaving me to relax a bit before getting back to the tavern, you understand, sir?"

"Yes, please go on." I do not know whether I blushed, but I felt my face grow a little hot.

"I heard voices in the next room, sir. Now, usually, that's 'cause Susan, the other barmaid here, is, well, entertaining."

"Get on, Lizzy, I take your meaning." I definitely blushed.

"But I knew Susan was down below, 'cause she'd taken over for me when I came up with my customer, see?"

"Yes," I said.

"So I thought there might be something wrong with it. Now these walls ain't too thick, sir, and with a little effort you can pretty much hear everything that goes on. And there's this eyehole, see it sir? That's for some gentlemen as likes to watch others rather than doing it themselves, see sir?"

"Yes, Lizzy." I smiled despite my blushes, then added, "Do go on, you're riveting my attention."

"Well, I could see the one gentleman, it was an officer, like, from a ship, I could tell by his clothes, sir. He was talking to another gentleman, sir, who I could not see through the hole. I think he must have been sitting right underneath it, sir."

"I see. This was just talking?"

"Yes, sir, nothing else going on." She smiled, then went on. "I could hear most of it, sir, and it troubled me greatly. The one man was talking in a soft voice, so I could catch only a few words, but he was saying how he had written up all his findings and wanted the officer to take it back to London."

I had a sudden doubt. "Could this have been commercial information? Did they speak of trade or tobacco, anything like that?"

"They talked about militias and arms, sir. And the defenses of the port here. And how everything was so chaotic here now; he used that word, chaotic. And the other man said his report had details about his successes in sowing more chaos."

An agent of chaos, a British spy. My stomach twisted as my mind went of its own volition back to the War with its spies and its death and its duplicity. I thought we'd left all that behind us. I wrenched myself back into the moment.

"When was this, Lizzy?"

"Tuesday week, it were."

My God, that had been a busy Tuesday in Alexandria! Thompson arrived, Major Washington arrived, and now a spy meeting with his British contact. I will admit that my mind reeled.

Lizzie continued with her story. "So, the two gentlemen finished up their conversation, and the soft-voiced man said that they should leave separately so as not to be seen together, just as they had come."

"Did you see them at all? After they left the room?"

"Well, Your Honor, as I hadn't seen the second man atall, I made sure to be in the hall when he left. He was a smallish man but he'd covered his face with his hat and a scarf, and he kept his face turned away from me when he saw me. He wore a shabby cloak, but I could see his shoes and hose were of the best quality. He went down the back stairs and out, and I saw no more of him. Susan said that officer was a friend of hers from a British sloop, *HMS Harvey,* and told her he wanted the use of her room for a short time, and he gave her two shillings for it. But she hadn't seen any other man, she told me. I didn't tell her what I'd heard, but I said she should be more careful about strange men alone in her room." She grinned. "All she said, the trollop, was what you don't want to hear about, sir."

I thought a moment. "Lizzie, do you know Major George Augustine Washington?" Major Washington could be thought a small man, thin and hunched as he was with his illness.

"No, sir. Erm, a course I know who he is, sir, but I haven't ever seen him."

Bloody inconclusive, the whole thing. Nothing but Lizzie's tale to go on, and no names.

I asked her, "Why didn't you take this to the authorities?"

"Well, to be honest, sir, the authorities and I don't get on as well as I might like, now. But I been stewing about it for days, sir, and you seem like a good sport, and Hutch is all for you, and the General, well, he's the man to do something about it." Her eyes got angry. "I'm Irish, sir, and I came to America 'cause there weren't nothing doin' in Ireland for a girl, so I indentured myself and worked myself free. Can't abide those British, sir, specially the soldiers. Fucking animals, some of them." I heard the echo of a century of discontent in her lilting Irish voice.

"All right, Lizzy, I'll take this to the General." I brought out my pocket-book to get some money for her, and she took it gratefully.

"Thanks, Colonel Humphreys," she said. "It takes everything I've got to just stay alive in these times. But I want the new country to be safe. You tell that to the General."

"I will," I replied, putting my pocket-book away.

She shivered and looked around her small room. "It ain't much, here, and things are bloody tight right now. At least the bloody British are gone. Maybe the General can make a difference." She stood up, then smiled and said, "Now you go on, get out of here, and tell the General."

40

SUNDAY, MARCH 29, 1789, AFTERNOON

The General would want Colonel Hooe to be present when we came to grips with my news of British interference in our affairs, as he represented the legal authority in the County and would need to authorize any action the General decided to take. I doubted he would be of much use in giving the General counsel, but one never knew from where good information and advice would come. I directed my steps to his house to ask the Colonel to come with me. The Hooes were back from church, and the Colonel was quite willing to accompany me once he understood the gravity of the situation.

He turned to his clerk, who had come into the passage while we were talking. "Williamson, could you get our coats?"

I raised a hand. "Just you, sir, if you do not mind coming without Mr. Williamson. I would like to keep the details of this to as few people as possible for now. No offense, Mr. Williamson!"

The clerk smiled and bowed. "None taken, sir. I will get your coat for you, Colonel Hooe."

We were soon at Colonel Fitzgerald's house, where we found him and the General in conference. I summarized Lizzie's story for the little group of men. After the first few words, the General's attention intensified, and by the end, anger filled his countenance at this blatant violation of American sovereignty. His brow contracted and his lips were tight, but he said nothing.

The other two men, however, expressed themselves volubly in their dismay. Colonel Fitzgerald reacted as a soldier, sitting forward in his chair with an exclamation and a look of anger. Colonel Hooe, who already knew the basic facts, said, "We cannot allow the British to disrupt our business and trade in this way, Your Excellency!"

The General brought everyone to order and declared a council of war. His anger settled into a grim determination to act.

"Gentlemen, it would appear that events are hurtling us toward a major crisis. Although Colonel Humphreys and I came to Alexandria this morning hunting for a slave and a murderer, we have apparently been thrust into a much more serious morass by this surprise."

I asked, "What do you think we should do, sir?"

"Think, Colonel; sit for a time and think. We are all aware of the constant din of complaint from various quarters about the unreasonableness of the Constitution. Mr. Henry and Colonel Mason have made it clear that they think the new government will run roughshod over the people of this country. They think it is but a continuation of the tyranny of the British. This has created a crisis of confidence in the new government and has gone far toward persuading me to assume the mantle of leadership. Our country's own politics created all this chaos without reference to foreign parties, only to our own foolishness."

"And now the British engage to create more chaos, Your Excellency," said Colonel Fitzgerald.

"You two gentlemen are not aware of the letters I have received from Kentucky. My correspondents there tell me of plots by both the Spanish and British governments to persuade the Kentucky parties to declare independence from the Union rather than becoming a part of it as a state."

Colonel Hooe's mouth opened and closed in astonishment. Colonel Fitzgerald just smiled. He said, "I too have interests in Kentucky that have informed me of this, Your Excellency. It is very worrying, but I cannot see it happening."

The General shook his head and contradicted his friend. "You are overly optimistic, Colonel, as I was until Colonel Tom Marshall informed me of British interference in Kentucky. And now Colonel Humphreys's barmaid tells us that there is British activity in Alexandria itself—creating chaos in the very heart of Virginia! We have uncovered a major conspiracy on our plantations that not only damages our businesses but creates unrest and dissatisfaction among our Negroes. Is it not possible that the British are behind it all?" The General's forceful assertion erased Colonel Fitzgerald's smile, which yielded to a thoughtful silence as he considered the General's remarks.

Colonel Hooe, however, dismissed the danger. "A bit far-fetched." He paused and realized he challenged the strongly held views of his friend the General. "Well, a possibility, of course, Your Excellency, of course it is, sir. Indeed...." He stuttered to a stop.

The General smiled. "Come now, Colonel. I convened a council of war, and I do not expect my councillors to agree with me. I need counsel, not flattery."

"Well, then, Your Excellency, I just find it difficult to believe in this spy, or in his creating such chaos here. How were we not aware of such a thing? Consider the source: a bloody barmaid!"

I responded with some heat. "We did not see it, sir, because we were not looking for it! We have been far too complacent, I fear. You, Colonel Hooe, have yourself seen the unrest among the merchants of Alexandria, as I have seen it in the taverns of central Virginia and the quarters of Mount Vernon. If that unrest is a result of active British agents as well as our own volatile politics, it is more understandable. As for my source, I have in my life found many men less reliable than that barmaid." The General glanced at me quizzically, interested by my heated defense.

Colonel Fitzgerald leapt in to agree with me. "I was expecting something of the sort in Kentucky because of the value of the Mississipi for trade and because the Canadian government still occupies the northwest forts. But here? I certainly wasn't looking for such a thing here."

Colonel Hooe looked as though he did not much like being told he had been blind, but he accepted our opinions without further comment.

The General sighed, then said, "We may not have been looking, but it has found us. We must now confront this gathering storm of conspiracies before the British manage to undermine the liberty for which we all fought so hard."

Colonel Fitzgerald asked, "What must we do, Your Excellency?"

"We must look a little harder, now that we know he is active. We must uncover the true facts here and in Kentucky so that we may act with a better understanding of the situation. One barmaid's tale is perhaps not enough; we must get confirmation. Colonel Hooe, you must add this search to your current list. We must find this spy, if he really exists, and we must discover his mission and his accomplishments and co-conspirators. Then we will know how to counter them."

"I will happily engage to do that, Your Excellency," replied Colonel Hooe.

The General sighed again and said, "Thank you, Colonel Hooe. I think that Colonel Fitzgerald, as the one of us with the most contacts in the West, should mobilize all of them in aid of discovering and rooting out any local conspiracies there. I have asked Captain John Marshall in Richmond to coordinate communications with his father in Kentucky. Perhaps you can follow up with him and others with whom you work as part of the Potomac Company to better understand events in Pennsylvania and the Ohio as well as in western Virginia and Kentucky. But please, use discretion and secrecy and keep the situation as confidential as you can."

Colonel Fitzgerald responded, "I will write immediately, Your Excellency!"

Colonel Hooe looked at me. "Did your barmaid give any useful details about the man, Colonel Humphreys?"

"She did not see his face, and he kept his voice low. She said that he was a smallish man, that he wore a shabby cloak, and that he wore good shoes and hose, indicating at least a man of some property."

The General suggested, "Perhaps it would be best to canvass the wealthier men of the town, particularly those involved in the militia and the arms trade? And those involved in the defense of the port? They may have encountered someone asking unusual questions."

Colonel Hooe looked thoughtful. "Williamson and I will start on this immediately, Your Excellency. You do not mind," he added, "that we suspend our other investigations? Time is of the essence, and Williamson has too much on his plate as it is."

"I think we must suspend them, although I think all this chaos may stem from the same source. This spying is a threat to our liberty and independence, which must come before my own legal woes. And I have already convinced Colonel Mason and Mr. Cockburn to let me do as I wish. I must again consider the issue of the Presidency. Perhaps assuming that office now takes on a completely different and necessary character for me, even with the murders unresolved. I suppose I must also inform General Knox in New York, as he is Secretary of War." The General arose and began pacing the room, his hands behind his back and his brow furrowed in the familiar profile I had seen as his aide-de-camp so often before a battle.

Colonel Fitzgerald arose and, looking at the clock, suggested, "You can stay for dinner, Your Excellency, while we start sorting things out."

The General stopped his pacing and said, "No, Colonel, we must get back to Mount Vernon. The sooner I am there, the sooner I may act on these matters. And, should that not be motive enough, my wife is expecting us for Sunday dinner!"

Colonel Fitzgerald acquiesced and smiled. "An urgent task indeed! Very well, Your Excellency; then I will bid you good afternoon."

The sanctuary of Mount Vernon beckoned, and we hurried on our way.

41

SUNDAY, MARCH 29, 1789, LATE AFTERNOON

The General and I trotted our horses along the Alexandria road toward Mount Vernon, enjoying as much of the sunshine as we could given our preoccupation with the discoveries in Alexandria. The first signs of spring adorned the bare trees along the road, and the sun had successfully defeated the cold morning. We talked in snatches as we rode.

The General said, "Conspiracy in Kentucky, British occupation of our northern forts in violation of the peace treaty, and now spies in Alexandria! These events force me toward the Presidency."

"I agree, Your Excellency."

We were silent as we negotiated a creek. The General abruptly changed the subject.

"I am very concerned about my nephew George. I cannot understand why he did not tell us he was in Alexandria Tuesday week."

"It could be just coincidence, sir." But I was sure it was not.

"I daresay. He is ill; goodness knows there was a lot going on over the last two weeks for him. Perhaps it simply slipped his mind. Still, I must question him about it. Until today I would have trusted him with my life. He is, after all, part of my immediate family—my favorite nephew. I cannot believe him involved in theft, and certainly not in murder! He would not betray my trust."

"Is he in want of money, sir? Could he have fallen into the scheme bit by bit and got in over his head? Could he have struck a blow with unintended consequences?" I had little question in my mind that to shoot someone in the head while hiding them in a disused warehouse was not likely unintended, so I did not distress the General further with that idea.

The General said, "Consider the harm to his family. He would not do anything that would harm his family." Though uttered in his usual calm voice, the statement had the ring of a plea to Providence. I remained silent, unconvinced. We trotted along a stretch of road that would soon have us near the General's Muddy Hole Farm boundary. The General was thoughtful and silent as well, thinking about this unexpected pain. I therefore tried to change the subject back.

I said, "Your Excellency, do you really think it possible that this spy is himself related in some way to the murders?"

"I am not certain, but something about all this disruption makes me suspect a wider conspiracy, Colonel."

As we rode around a curve in the road, I heard a familiar click. I shouted a warning to the General and threw myself down along my horse's neck. There were two nearly simultaneous explosions from the woods to the right of us, and I distinctly heard a ball passing close by my head. I drew one of my pistols from its holster on my saddle and looked up. The General had lost his hat but looked otherwise unharmed and was reining around his horse. I caught a movement in the trees, aimed and cocked my pistol, and fired. I holstered that pistol and drew the other one. The General charged his horse into the brush and trees. I heard the men running noisily through the brush as they escaped the General's counterattack. I urged my horse forward after the General, and we both crashed through the trees in pursuit. I caught another glimpse of white among the leafless trees and fired again.

After a minute, we stopped our horses, as the trees and brush became too thick to pursue the men any further on horseback. The noise of their running died away. The General sat tall on his horse, hatless, staring keenly through the trees, trying to catch sight of our prey. But they had gone.

We turned our horses back toward the road, picking our way through the brush. As we approached the road, I saw a musket on the ground under a bush. I dismounted and picked it up; it was an old musket with rust and discoloration all along the barrel, though the action was well oiled and in good working order. I then noticed a drop of red, then saw more blood on the ground.

"Sir, over here! I think I did for one of them, he's dropped his musket, and there is blood on the ground!"

The General rode over and looked down at me from what seemed an enormous distance. I could quite clearly see the fire in his eye that I had often seen during battles, and his horse was stamping the ground and shaking his head with excitement. The General calmed the horse with his hand. I handed the musket up to him, and he examined it, turning it around in his gloved hands, then returned it to me. I tied it onto the back of my horse, then remounted, and we regained the road in short order. The General stopped his horse and looked about, then rode over to the other side of the road and dismounted. I followed on my horse.

The General reached into a bush and pulled out his tricorne hat and dusted it off, then poked a finger through a bullet hole in one fold of the hat and showed it to me, wiggling the finger. He laughed; I shuddered. This was too close a call.

"Well, Colonel, just like old times, eh?"

"Too much so, sir."

The General replaced his hat on his head, adjusted it, remounted, and we trotted off toward Mount Vernon. The incident had restored his good humor, as battle often did, and we reminisced about incidents we had shared during the War as we rode.

We stabled our horses, and I gave my pistols to one of the stable lads with instructions to clean and oil them carefully as soon as possible. We would need them, I wagered to myself.

When we entered the Mansion House passage, the General asked Frank Lee to find Mr. Fairfax. Mrs. Washington, hearing the bustle, emerged from her parlor and greeted us. She cocked an eye at the General.

"Do you want to delay dinner for your business with Mr. Fairfax, Mr. Washington? And just what has happened to the pair of you?"

The General smiled. "I could never conceal anything from you, my dear. The Colonel and I had a small incident on the road near Muddy Hole Farm, I fear." He handed her his hat. She examined it and gasped as she saw the hole.

"Mr. Washington!"

"As you can see, my dear, things have got complicated again. Do not worry yourself about it, however. The Colonel is an excellent life-guard."

Mrs. Washington looked at me wildly, then made a strong effort to compose herself.

"And in answer to your first question, Mrs. Washington, yes; please delay dinner for fifteen minutes while I set Mr. Fairfax to work on the matter. Here he is!"

Mr. Fairfax walked into the passage through the front door and cast an enquiring look at the General, who told him to proceed to the Study. The General addressed his wife, who was still holding his hat. "Mrs. Washington, you might see if the thing can be salvaged."

"I will do that, Mr. Washington. And we will please have a little discussion later about all this, will we not?" Her tone was light, but her look I could only call steely.

"Yes, my dear, we will," replied the General with resignation. "Come along, Colonel." We walked through the dining room to the study, where Mr. Fairfax awaited us.

"Mr. Fairfax," he said, "we have just encountered two brigands along the Alexandria road who did not first ask but just shot." He described the incident in detail, and Mr. Fairfax injected suitable exclamations of dismay. "Now, what I would like you to do is to ride to Alexandria as fast as you can and inform Colonel Hooe of the incident. Tell him that the discovery we made earlier may be generally known and may be behind the attack, and that his task has assumed some urgency."

"Discovery, sir? Task?"

"Just tell him that, Mr. Fairfax, no need for you to know more at this time."

"Yes, sir," said the young man, a little disappointed.

"Do not despair, Mr. Fairfax, you may yet get an adventure. Do you take full precautions on your ride. Here are a pair of pistols for you; do you know how to use them?" He took a box from a cabinet beneath his collection of farming books, opened it, and extracted two pistols, giving them to Mr. Fairfax along with shot and powder.

"Oh, yes, sir!"

"Good. Ask the stable lad for holsters. These men have fled, but it is certainly possible that they or others may wish to prevent you from reaching Alexandria. Take care and be alert on your ride, and do not linger."

"Yes, sir!"

I said, "The musket we found is in the stable. You can take that with you as well, sir, and give it to Colonel Hooe. He may be able to use it in his investigation."

Mr. Fairfax nodded. The General dismissed him, and Mr. Fairfax ran out of the study, and we heard his horse after a few minutes tearing up the drive toward the Alexandria road.

"Well, Colonel, shall we dine? I suspect the conversation will prove a little more interesting tonight for the family. I think we should avoid confronting my nephew until tomorrow. You saw my wife's reaction to our news already. She has reluctantly accepted my decision, but this emergence may prove too much for her, further complicating things. I shall speak with her later tonight."

"It seems the more we progress in understanding of events, the more difficult it gets."

"Indeed it does. Now we must confront personal attacks as well. I am reluctant, I must confess, to put you in danger. I must also consider whether such danger could extend to my immediate family." The General sighed, then added, "Retirement has certainly proved a taxing proposition. Could the Presidency present worse challenges than we have already experienced? And thank you, Colonel. What I said to my wife was true: I could not ask for a better life-guard."

"You are quite welcome, sir."

The General turned toward his dressing table, and I ran up to my room to change for dinner. I was ravenous and did my duty well to Mrs. Washington's excellent viands. And the conversation was, indeed, quite exciting, especially for little Wash, who couldn't believe that he had missed the whole thing. He felt quite out of luck!

42

MONDAY, MARCH 30, 1789, MORNING

Breakfast the next morning was subdued. Mrs. Washington eyed her husband with concern and remained silent where she would ordinarily have guided the polite conversation. Major Washington did not appear. At the conclusion of this strained meal, Mrs. Washington drew her husband aside, took him into her parlor, and closed the door.

After a good half hour, the General came out to join me on the piazza.

I said, "Mrs. Washington was very concerned at breakfast, Your Excellency."

"She was indeed, Colonel," replied the General, sitting down next to me and contemplating the river. "Though I feel certain her concern should be greater than she is aware." His eyes moved restlessly over the spring-awakening Maryland shore across the river, green appearing more and more among the bare, grey trees. "We have discussed my— how did she put it—my excessive reliance on my own good fortune."

I smiled at the General's tone, but I knew he had a deep faith in that good fortune. He had never once in all his military career acquired so much as a nick from a bullet despite being in the thick of many actions, though his clothes and his horses were at times less fortunate than he in that regard.

"And the consequence, sir?"

The General, still studying the Maryland shore as though it were the site of massing British troops, said, "I have agreed to take measures to prevent any recurrence of yesterday's trial of my good luck, Colonel. The situation here has grown much more menacing with the emergence of espionage and its consequences. No man of sense would court disaster."

I shook my head. "My head whirls with possibilities, Your Excellency. We are all at sea. Was this an attempt to dissuade us from our murder investigations? Did the spy in Alexandria discover our interest? Is it possible the source of the attack is in Mount Vernon itself? Was it just a pair of highwaymen trying for our purses?"

"We are indeed at sea," the General agreed. "Livens things up a bit, though, Colonel." He continued to contemplate the river, apparently perfectly content doing nothing more than admiring the scenery.

Frank Lee came onto the piazza from the passage door, holding a letter.

"An express from Alexandria, Your Excellency." He handed the letter to the General and went back inside the house.

The General held up the letter in the morning light, looked it all over, then dropped it onto his lap, unopened.

"Are you looking for a secret message, Your Excellency? Invisible ink?" I joked.

He looked at me with humor. "I am looking for anything that will prevent me from having to get out of this chair and do something, Colonel, as I am thoroughly enjoying this view. As you very well know. Ah well."

He unfolded the letter and read it. He said, "Colonel Hooe reports, perhaps unsurprisingly, that he and Mr. Williamson have found no trace of the two assailants in Alexandria. They continue their efforts on all fronts. Perhaps I should indeed check for invisible ink, as there is little else of import here."

The General tapped the fingers of his right hand on his chair arm in frustration while he read once again over the short letter he held in his left hand.

He grunted, then said, "Colonel, the situation is intolerable. We cannot permit murderers, spies, and thieves to run roughshod over the Virginia countryside. If it were a time of war, I would understand the situation; in time of peace, such peace as we have only known briefly, I cannot comprehend it. It is not *right*." He stared at the river, holding the letter on his knee. He continued, "Mrs. Washington is most upset. She feels the danger to my person much more than she comprehends the danger to her own, or indeed to the entire family and household."

"She did not seem complacent this morning, sir."

"No; but her displeasure centers on my continuing participation in political affairs, which she blames for the hole in my hat. And other things."

"While you believe the danger is more than just to your person, Your Excellency?"

"You must feel it yourself, Colonel, though fortunately the bullet intended for your heart missed its mark." He stopped tapping his fingers and arose from his seat. "I must inform the family of the true extent of the danger, and I must persuade Mrs. Washington. If I am to accept the Presidency, I must gain her acceptance first. She has acquiesced, but this new danger has made her retreat. I must find a way to persuade her to abandon our retirement here in favor of the rigors of public life. I can do that only by resolving the current mysteries and removing the immediate danger. Until then, I must have everyone aware of that danger. I must protect my family and farm while I protect my country."

The General gathered together the family and all the servants in the New Room and addressed them, summarizing the situation and asking them to take care in their excursions outside and especially off the farms, and to report anything remotely suspicious or untoward. Major Washington suffered a return of his illness due to the stress and excitement, and the General and his wife joined Mrs. Fanny Washington in assisting him.

43

MONDAY, MARCH 30, 1789, MORNING

I had narrowly observed Mr. Lear during this conference, and toward the end I found him to have a slight smile on his face as he observed Major Washington's distress. My feelings rose against this, and I decided that while I could do little to aid Major Washington, I might be able to help his wife.

I persuaded Mr. Lear into the front parlor, leaving the General and his family to their compassionate efforts with Major Washington. I shut the double doors behind us, then went across the room and shut the door to the passage. I turned and faced Mr. Lear.

"Sir. It pains me to have to confront you with this, but I feel I must. What are your intentions toward Mrs. Fanny Washington?"

"Sir?" Mr. Lear was amazed and discomfited.

"You heard me."

Mr. Lear's face turned red, and his expression changed from amazement to anger.

"Colonel Humphreys, what do you mean by this? How dare you!"

"Come now, Mr. Lear. I have watched you with the ladies over the past few weeks. Your attentions to Mrs. Fanny Washington are becoming too obvious to ignore. I daresay her husband has noticed and it is contributing to his illness. I would not be at all surprised if the General's wife has noticed. What do *you* mean by it?"

"I have the highest regard for both Major Washington and his wife." Mr. Lear decided to stand upon his dignity. He said very coldly, "I have done nothing to earn this reproof, sir, and I very much resent it."

"I will bear your resentment without much effort, sir. But if what you say is true, you must modify your behavior before it affects the General and his family. I am sure that, had the General noticed, he would have already dismissed you from his employ. He has, perhaps fortunately for you, been quite distracted lately."

"Again, sir, I resent your unjust accusation." He folded his arms with defiance, standing stiffly in his anger. It occurred to me that it would not be out of the question for him to challenge me to a duel, if he were angry enough. I had breached his walls, now it was time to sue for terms.

"Look here, Mr. Lear. It appears that we must work together when the General takes up his office. Can you not simply step back and examine your behavior without prejudice and change it to suit me? If you can do that, I will be quite satisfied."

Mr. Lear, still red in the face, stared at me. "I am not blind, Colonel. I know you harbor affection for Mrs. Fanny Washington, I have seen your attempts to engage her notice. Is that affection at the base of this baseless accusation?"

I felt this blow very much; the touch struck true, though it was badly expressed. I felt that honesty would serve me best. "Prettily worded, sir. Mrs. Fanny Washington is indeed a very attractive woman. She is, however, part of the General's family and married, and I can control my impulses to foolish action, whatever I might feel for her. Surely you can do the same? Can we not work together? She will, of course, remain here at Mount Vernon with her husband when we go to New York. And what about Major Washington's feelings, and what about hers for him?"

Mr. Lear closed his eyes as his face became more mottled.

I said, "Let us sit down, sir, and discuss this as two rational men." I pulled up two chairs, and we both sat. Mr. Lear rubbed his chin with one hand, staring at me, gathering his thoughts and deciding how to respond.

"Colonel, I will admit to an attraction to Mrs. Fanny Washington. She is young and happy, she has a sunny personality, and she flirts shamelessly with us all. I do see that my attentions to her might bear the construction you place on them; I will forgive you that. Nevertheless, those attentions stem only from the desire to please the General's family and from my own need to get away from the General's business, if only for a time. To take some pleasure in her company. I am nearly engaged, sir, to a young woman in Portsmouth, New Hampshire."

I mentally changed the word "please" to "ingratiate", but I saw that Mr. Lear was at least trying. I wondered whether, even if we resolved the current contretemps, I could work closely with him as the General's private secretary. The man had limitations that I found troubling. He seemed to have little insight into his own actions and to their effects on others. While he was a great help to the General in organizing and conducting his affairs, I could not help but believe that he might turn his work to his own account rather than to that of the General and his family.

Mr. Lear continued, "And I certainly would never do anything to harm Major Washington. He is both a good man and a sick one deserving of our respect and support. His affairs may be...somewhat involved at present, but I am sure he and his wife will continue in the greatest happiness for as long as Providence permits."

Mr. Lear's comments about Major Washington distracted me from my main point. "Involved? Involved in what way? Financially? Politically?" I felt the General must know the truth about his nephew, and that if he would not ask directly, I must find out that truth and tell him.

Mr. Lear looked away from me. "I have said too much that was told to me in confidence. I will not say more."

By Mrs. Fanny Washington, no doubt.

"As I conclude your source must be Mrs. Fanny Washington herself, I must ask: do you think she knows and understands her husband's affairs well enough to trust her conclusions?"

Mr. Lear was puzzled. "I think she does. Although she is young and possibly somewhat naive, she is close to her husband and cannot have failed to understand him. Why do you ask?"

I realized I would need to speak with her directly to form my own opinion, but I did not need to burden my relationship with Mr. Lear further. I again became conciliatory but did not answer his question. "All right, Mr. Lear. I will accept your assurances about your intentions, though I will hold you to them. I trust you realize my concern here comes directly from my concern for and loyalty to the General? And from the fact that he will employ us together in his service as President? We will continue on as before, then?"

"Colonel, I do know the General values both your friendship and your loyalty highly. If you can find a way to be my friend, I can certainly find a way to reciprocate that feeling, as long as we both work for the General. That work is too important to allow any personal feelings to interfere with it."

"Thank you, Mr. Lear, I agree; I believe that we can proceed on that basis. Now, I must speak with Mrs. Fanny Washington about her husband myself."

"Why?"

I said, aware of the possibility of misconstruction, "Purely to obtain knowledge of her husband related to the events to which the General referred just now. From your remarks, I think it may be relevant."

"I see."

"Would you send her in to me here?"

Mr. Lear was alarmed. "You are not intending to tax her with this...

matter, are you, Colonel?"

"No indeed, that is closed between us. I merely need some information from her in private. About her husband."

"All right. Then I am satisfied, though less than happy." He arose and offered a hand. I took it and shook it as warmly as I could given my mixed feelings. He turned and went out to the New Room. Soon, Fanny herself entered with a questioning look at me. I closed the doors, then indicated the chairs, and we sat.

"Thank you for seeing me, Mrs. Washington."

"You're being excessively formal and mysterious, Colonel. Mr. Lear seemed somewhat odd when he requested that I attend upon you. He said that you have some questions about my poor George? Now, what could I know that you gentlemen do not?" She smiled and blushed. "I do so enjoy your company, the two of you enliven what might otherwise be a quite staid life here. And you were so kind in helping my poor husband when he was ill!"

Nothing about this was easy. I said, "We...that is, I, feel that you may know some things about your husband that might be of use."

She was puzzled. "My husband? Surely you can ask him?"

"Well, no. We need independent information, and you are best placed to be able to provide it."

She was even more puzzled, and a little worried. "Information?"

"The General and I learned that Major Washington was in Alexandria the week before Mr. Thompson was killed."

"Mr. Thompson?"

"Mr. Thompson, yes. Colonel Mason's overseer."

"I am very sure my husband knows Mr. Thompson. But you say he was killed?"

"Yes, that is one of the murders to which the General referred just now."

She continued to look somewhat confused and blushed even more.

"I am sorry, I'm afraid I did not listen properly, my husband's illness distracted me. And the General speaks so very quickly!"

She was a very young woman, and her blushes did her complexion no harm. As I said, nothing about this was easy for me. I soldiered on, however.

"Mr. Thompson's murder was a week ago Friday, and we found that Major Washington visited Alexandria earlier that week. Rather than distressing him more at present than need be, I would like to know if he said anything to you about his visit."

"Oh, I see, of course. Well, let me think." Her brow contracted as her eyes lifted to the ceiling. I noticed they were dark, a perfect match for her hair. "Oh, yes, I remember. Two weeks ago, I think you said?"

"Yes, that's right."

"Yes, I remember. George had been very ill that weekend, as you know, but had recovered enough to be up and about. I remember remonstrating with him that he should not overexert himself so soon, but he was adamant. Yes, I remember. He was very concerned about the General's problems and felt he needed to visit his contacts in Alexandria to make sure all his business was going ahead well. When he returned, he had of course overexerted himself again and had to retire to his bed for a day. I kept him company, and we talked extensively about the General and how good he is to us. George worries that the farm will exceed his capabilities due to his illness, you know, though he doesn't complain about it. The General has reassured us that he finds George an excellent manager despite his illness. And the General has several times got Dr. Craik in from Alexandria to give advice. We live, you know, with a small income from our inheritances and by the benevolence of the General, and we do so desperately want to be of use to him."

She did not mention the will, and I thought it beyond my power to mention it myself. Those dark eyes...perhaps she was naive, perhaps not, but I felt strongly that she was not lying, either to me or to herself.

"And Major Washington has not had problems with things happening here on the plantation, or with his contacts in Alexandria?"

"No, everything seems fine. It is just that George worries so. His illness prevents him from the energetic care of the plantation that he would like to exercise, and he feels he does not get out enough to the farms on business, and he feels his dependence on the General excessively. We speak of it often."

"I have not spoken extensively with Major Washington about politics. I assume his interest makes him a Patriot?"

"Oh, yes, we are both Patriots! The General and his wife have been so kind to us, how could we be Tory or anything like it? And I know that George feels strongly that the new Constitution will help us all to a better life. We will miss the General when he goes to New York, but we know he will lead the country well!"

There was a knock on the door from the New Room, which opened to admit Mrs. Martha Washington. "Oh, hello, dears, I am sorry to interrupt you. Colonel, the General has requested your attendance upon him in the study." She smiled, then said, "I do hope there is nothing amiss?"

"Other than the complete state of chaos, do you mean, ma'am?" I smiled.

"Quite right. We are all at sixes and sevens! You go and assist my husband, Colonel. The two of you will put things right in no time."

"Thank you for your confidence in me, ma'am. And thank you very much, Mrs. Washington," I addressed Fanny, "for being of assistance. I do very much appreciate it, as will the General."

"You are quite welcome, Colonel," replied the young woman with a smile. "Really, any time. I do so enjoy talking with you, though I am not sure what it was all about."

"Come along, my dear," said Mrs. Washington, touching her arm. "I daresay your husband could use some comfort."

I bowed and left them, going out through the passage door. I suspect I left a portion of my poetry behind, figuratively speaking. As I walked through to the study, I formed hasty resolutions to keep my emotions under control, as I had requested of my good friend Mr. Lear. I, too, wanted the General to be happy, whether in retirement or in office, and upsetting his family arrangements would play no good role in that endeavor.

44

MONDAY, MARCH 30, 1789, MORNING

I found the General in his study, sitting at his desk and contemplating the wall, his spectacles dangling from his hand. I knocked and entered, and he handed me a letter from his desk.

The letter was from General Knox in New York, dated March 23rd. He expected the arrival of several members of the House and Senate any day, and then the Congress could act on the electoral vote and send for the General as President-elect. Mr. Charles Thomson, the secretary of the Continental Congress, was to have the task of summoning the General to his fate; and the General's friends were planning the welcoming delegation.

"General Knox is quite certain of your election, sir," I said, "and of your acceptance."

"Just as I am now certain that I will accept the Presidency as a duty, Colonel." The General stood up from his desk and walked over to the window to look out at the spring morning. "You know, Colonel, after all these events, after having to tell my family that we are under siege, I feel quite inadequate to what I must do for the nation."

Surprised, I asked, "Inadequate? In what way, Your Excellency?"

"Every day of delay in the Congress is to me a reprieve. You may not believe me, but the idea of sitting in the seat of power, being President, leaves me with nothing but feelings not unlike those of a man going to the place of his execution. Mr. Cockburn does not need to indict and try me; my punishment will be severe enough as it is."

"Come now, sir; surely ultimate power is not to be despised." I was not entirely joking.

The General looked at me and smiled and took me seriously. "I do despise such power, Colonel, and have no intention of exercising such. Indeed, no ability! Between the limits placed on the office by the new Constitution and the ocean of difficulties I face, there is little doubt that I lack the competency of political skill, the abilities, and the inclination for politics that would be necessary to manage the helm of this ship of state."

"I see no reason to doubt, sir; I see only your modesty."

"Thank you for your kind words, Colonel. I can promise integrity and firmness, the only qualities I may bring to the voyage, based on the voice of my countrymen and my own good name. What returns I may bring to those countrymen, Heaven alone can foretell. I can say that should the voyage be long or short, I will not lose those qualities, though my countrymen desert me."

"They will not, sir, no more than would I."

"I suppose that, whatever my misgivings, I must summon all my confidence in Providence and forge ahead, and that is what I will do."

The General returned to his desk and sat, putting on his spectacles and taking up his pen and a piece of paper.

"I will write all this to General Knox to assure him of my resolve, no matter my lack of inclination. I will add a short note advising him of our current situation, as well."

The General wrote for a time, scratching out portions and writing new ones, then copied out clean versions of his letter and his note, the latter of which he handed to me to read. He asked General Knox to destroy the note after reading. He advised him of the presence of a British spy in Alexandria and of the situation in Kentucky, then detailed some of the antifederalist rumblings we had uncovered over the last month in Virginia. He asked General Knox to counteract such attempts to damage the new Constitution and his own reputation, knowing that Knox and his other friends in New York would not abandon the voyage or allow the ship to be scuttled. I smiled at the naval metaphors from a man who had barely ever been to sea, but I knew *this* man well enough to be sure of his command of the ship.

I handed the note back to him. "A good start, sir, on your Presidency. And, sir, I must convey some information I gained just now from Mrs. Fanny Washington."

The General motioned me to a chair by the fire, then joined me.

"After your conversation with Mr. Lear?" The General's gentle probe let me know that he had noticed my drawing Mr. Lear aside, even while concerning himself with his nephew's condition.

"Yes, Your Excellency." I paused, then said, "I would prefer not to discuss what Mr. Lear and I spoke about, as I have given him assurances to that effect."

The General nodded briefly, but I felt his eyes fixed on me. Mine were studiously examining a spot on the floor. I put aside my memory of Mr. Lear, then lifted my eyes to his and said, "My conversation with Mrs. Fanny Washington, sir, was not confidential."

The General closed his eyes.

I summarized what we had said, then stated my opinion of it all. "I believe Mrs. Fanny Washington when she says her husband visited Alexandria purely on business. I will admit I harbored very uncertain feelings toward him given my experiences. But her high opinion and superior knowledge support his innocence, Your Excellency. Nevertheless, I think you should ask him about his very unusual speech that day at French's Farm."

The General sighed and opened his eyes. He said, "Thank you, Colonel." He paused, then said, "You may think me distracted or blind to others, Colonel, but I assure you I am not. I have been reluctant to press George on this out of concern for his health and from a firm disbelief in any guilt on his part. I thank you for your kindness to Fanny and her husband." He paused, then looked at me directly. "I know that both you and Mr. Lear are unreservedly loyal to my family and to myself. And I trust both you and Mr. Lear will remain close companions when we are in New York."

He had decided to ignore Mr. Lear's attentions to his niece—and probably my own attraction to her as well—by assuming that our loyalty would guide our actions toward his family. We were not moths for a small flame to beguile. Overwhelmed, I simply nodded and thanked him. I reflected that the subtlety and candor he evinced would stand him in good stead as President.

The General decided to send for Major Washington, and that gentleman knocked and entered the study shortly thereafter. He walked with the aid of his walking stick, which concerned the General.

"Ah, George, sit down and rest yourself. Are you recovered from your earlier setback?" He pulled over a chair and ushered the still pale Major Washington into it.

"Yes, Uncle, it was just a shock. I am recovered enough, sir, to apologize."

"Do not distress yourself; but I am happy to hear anything you have to say, George."

"My wife has told me of her conversation with Colonel Humphreys, Uncle." He looked at me reproachfully. "About Alexandria and all that."

"Ah. Perhaps you would care to elaborate on her information, George?" the General asked in a kindly tone of voice.

"Just to say that I am sorry for my weakness and any misunderstandings, sir. I do realize the gravity of the current events as you outlined them. I have inferred from the extraordinary effort of Colonel Humphreys—no offense, Colonel, I am sure—in questioning my wife that you may feel a disgust toward my behavior. I can only assure you myself, Uncle, that my visit to Alexandria and my efforts here on the plantations are only examples of my full devotion to your business."

The General steepled his fingers. "Colonel Humphreys has related to me your distressing language that day you collapsed, George. We have both been very concerned over it. If you are up to it, may we speak of that time?"

The Major passed a hand over his brow but squared his shoulders and said, "Yes, Uncle. However, I am not confident that I remember everything about that delirious day. Perhaps, Colonel," he addressed me, "you could remind me of what I said that was of concern?"

I said, "All right, Major, I will try. I think the first thing you mentioned in your delirium was money and paying it back?"

The Major smiled weakly. "Yes, I remember that part. Uncle, you have been extraordinarily generous and kind to my wife and me. Indeed, you have showered us with largesse. I have been worried for some time how to best pay you back for it all."

The General, surprised, said, "Pay me back? George, you are welcome to everything I have. Indeed, under my will you will inherit Mount Vernon. Mrs. Washington and I feel as though you two are our own children."

"I..." Major Washington cleared his throat. "I suppose, sir, I just felt the dependence too much."

"Say not one more word on that subject, George. You owe me nothing other than the loyalty you have already demonstrated."

The Major again looked at me. I said, "Then came a troubling series of references to Mr. George Thompson and Julius, how they 'knew everything'."

"Insufferable—" The Major clamped his lips before he spoke the words he knew his uncle would not like. "Sorry, Uncle. I do not remember what I said, but I can imagine it. My interactions with Mr.

George Thompson—may he rest in peace, if that's possible—have been quite difficult. He seemed to feel that he understood farming far better than I and that I was no better than a dilettante pretending to manage your farms, Uncle. He would encounter me on the road and make jokes about it. I could not stand the man."

"And Julius?"

"I remember that you asked me about Julius that day, Colonel, I suppose he was on my mind. I do not remember what I said about him, but I have always disliked him. I encountered him one time on the road past Dogue Run, talking with Mr. Thompson, so I told him to go about his business. He gave me quite an evil stare, sir, for a man in his position. I stared him down and off to his right position and work. Thompson took the occasion to laugh excessively, which did not endear him to me. He said I needed to learn how to use a cane properly." The Major shut his eyes with remembered pain.

That did sound like just pictures of both Julius and Mr. George Thompson. "So your feelings toward those two were purely based on those interactions?"

"Yes, Colonel. Well, and from other, similar occasions." The Major eyed me with some concern.

The General cleared his throat and said, "And that day in Alexandria? You went there, Fanny said, because of business? Even though you were ill?"

The Major grimaced. "I think it was *because* I was ill, Uncle. I wanted to be up and doing things. I wanted to be about my business. But I fear my head was not as clear as I might have wished."

"And what was the business?"

"I was concerned about a number of shipments from New England, we will need them for the spring plantings. I wanted to check with Mr. Williamson on them, and I did so. He had not received anything yet. I must say, Mr. Williamson was extraordinarily kind, taking the time for me when he was so busy with affairs. He sent me off in short order with very kind words. He has since made sure the shipments were sent as soon as they arrived." The Major's eyes were downcast as he said all this, showing his shame at his weakness and poor judgment in going to Alexandria under such circumstances. Seeing him and hearing him, I could not help but believe him about his feelings and actions.

The General pressed him. "And you saw nothing of Mr. Thompson in Alexandria?"

"No, sir. Why?"

"That very day was the day he must have arrived there and hid himself. You were probably within steps of him that day. We found him dead later that week."

Major Washington's eyes got large as he understood the full implications of this information. "I am so very sorry, Uncle, I did not know. I can see why...." His voice failed him. "Williamson...Mr. Williamson will testify to the fact that I was too ill that day to see anyone, sir." He shut his eyes in dismay and put his hand over his mouth. Again, I saw nothing but truth in his manner.

"Do not be concerned, George. Although the appearance was against you, I did not choose to believe ill of you, knowing you as well as I do."

I said, "I will admit to a good deal of doubt on my part, Major, which I hope you will not hold against me. I understand you better now." I felt that the Major had allayed most of my earlier suspicions of his behavior with his explanations, which confirmed his wife's account.

Major Washington arose from his chair. "I and my wife are very grateful to you, Colonel, for your efforts on our behalf on that dreadful day when I was taken ill. She said so just now. I can see how...but no matter, no matter. Thank you." He shook my hand. I noticed his walking stick leaning against the wall and handed it to him.

"A new stick, Major?" I asked. The stick was a beautiful thing, inlaid with ivory with brass ferrule and a weighted head.

Major Washington smiled wanly and replied, "Yes, Colonel, to replace an old one I lost. I had Thaddeus make it; he is quite adept at the metal tooling and inlay work required." Thaddeus was one of the slaves attached to the Mansion House farm. I smiled. Should these men be freed and turn their efforts to commercial purposes, we need have no fears in our new country of continued dependence on Britain for such things.

The General said, "Now, George, please go find your wife and tell her to take proper care of you until you are ready to resume work. And please, do not worry yourself. Everything will be for the best." The General embraced his nephew, then ushered him to the door.

When the Major had gone, the General turned to me. "I need air, Colonel, fresh air. I want to talk to Nace at Colonel Mason's Occoquan Farm. Based on what Ben has told us, Nace would have had as good a motive as any to kill Julius—and perhaps Thompson as well. We must find out more about him and his movements. And the ride will provide us with some needed exercise!"

45

Monday, March 30, 1789, afternoon

The day was cold but fine and warming, and the General and I made good time to the Occoquan farm on Mason's Neck. The quarters were near the bay that formed the outlet of the Occoquan River, to the west of Gunston Hall.

"I do not believe I have ever visited the Occoquan farm, Colonel," said the General as we reined up in the small cluster of cabins that made up the quarters there. "From its workmanlike appearance, I think it likely that Nace is an excellent overseer."

We dismounted and gave over our horses to a boy who came out to see what the noise was about.

I asked the boy, "Where might we find Nace?"

"He's over in that field today, sir."

We walked over to the field, where we could see the people bending to their work in the warming March day. Tall and motionless, we saw Nace standing and looking on as three men built a fence on the other side of the field.

We approached, and the General said, "Hello, Nace. We have come to ask a few more questions. Do you have a moment?"

"Yes, sir, sure do. Let me just tell the men what needs doin'." He conversed with the workmen for a few minutes, then turned to us.

"Perhaps we could remove ourselves to somewhere a little more private," suggested the General, looking around at the working men and women.

Nace grinned and said, "Ain't nowhere round here private. Just my cabin over yonder, but that ain't too private neither. Sorry, sir, we just have to talk here. Now don't you worry, none of these folks will pay no attention to what you got to say. At least, if you don't want 'em to."

A little taken aback, the General said, "Very well, then. I have some questions about the relations between you and the girl Chancey at Log Town."

"Chancey told me she done spilt all them beans."

"Yes, she did, and what she withheld, my miller Ben spilled. We wanted to follow up with you to see what you are intending to do, and to see if you have any more information for us."

"In-tending to do?" The big man looked a little puzzled. "Not real sure what you mean, sir."

"About Chancey. What are you intending to do with her?"

Nace smiled and said, "Pretty much just what I been doing with her but more so, sir."

The General smiled a little, embarrassed. I fear I had a larger smile.

"All right, Nace. I hope you intend to regularize the position?"

"We getting married in a couple of weeks, sir, then we gonna just be a whole family, 'cause she got a baby comin'. Chancey will move over here. We ain't told her daddy yet. Or Massa Mason."

I asked, "And what about Ben?"

"What about him?"

"Chancey seemed uncertain—"

"Not any more she ain't, take my word, sir." The big man smiled again. "We's going to do the deed in the black church, make it all legal like. Soon as I get up to the Hall to talk to her daddy and the Massa. Been kinda busy here."

I said, "I think James is expecting you." Nace grinned at me and nodded.

The General asked, "Have there been any more signs of thieves or other unusual goings-on since we last spoke with you, Nace?"

"No, sir. All that seem to have come to a dead stop now. Bastards musta got the wind up when Massa Thompson got pegged."

"And nothing more about Julius? Or, indeed, Mr. Thompson?"

"Nothin' here, anyways."

"And have you been to Alexandria lately?"

Nace again seemed puzzled. "Got no cause to go there, sir. Most of my business is Fredericksburg, I don't get up to Alexandria much. Ain't set foot there since last year some time."

"But you know that Mr. Thompson died there?"

"Yes, sir, that news came quick last week. Once the Hall knew, we all got the news."

The General paused, then got to the point. "Then, one last thing, Nace. Please do not misunderstand me, I am all but certain of your innocence, but I have to know. From Chancey's story, and from what we learned from our miller, it would certainly appear that no one had reason to kill Julius more than you, given his behavior towards Chancey."

"Thought you might see it that way, sir." Nace grinned again and looked around at his domain. "Kin I be real frank, sir?" he asked the General, who nodded with a smile.

"I been thinkin' a lot on this since Massa Thompson run off, and since you-all come by and say things so fucked up at Mount Vernon. I got to say, frankly, sir, I don't like being a slave, sir, and that's the truth of it. Hard life. Being an overseer, that life ain't quite so hard, you understand? Than just workin' with my hands, like these fellers." He waved a hand at the men working around us. "Massa Mason ain't bad as massas go, beggin' your pardon, sir. And being a Negro and a slave, I got nowhere to go but here, lest I want to run off and take my chances, which ain't good, really. I got no reason to fuck all that up, you understand? By killing a donkey's turd like Julius. No reason atall, sir."

The General said, "You make out a good case for yourself, Nace."

"Yes, sir. Now, Chancey's a good woman, but she ain't worth what would happen if I done somethin' like that. And yeah, I'm a good talker, but all you folks are smart as a whip, and whips is real smart, they don't fool easy. I ain't gonna fool you very long. So, I ain't gonna fool with killin' at all. I just marry the girl, tell Ben to stay on his own farm, give him five good reasons why, and that be that. You understand?" He balled his fist and held it up in the air. "And I was round here most of the time when Julius died, but can't back that up real well 'cause it's been quite a while now, near a month."

The General nodded. "Yes, that makes sense. And you were here when Mr. Thompson was killed in Alexandria?"

"You bet. Got lots of folks here who'll tell you that." He shook his head. "I'm some glad Massa Thompson's gone, makes my life easier; but I got less reason to kill him than I do Julius, you understand? Specially once he run off."

"Well, then." The General looked at me. "Any questions, Colonel?"

"Nace, it would seem that Julius had a different outlook on life than you. Why do you think he did what he did?"

Nace shook his head. "I don't know, sir, not really. Some people just bad. Some just want a short cut. Most black folks just run away if they unhappy. Julius musta thought he had another way out. Maybe he thought he could get enough money to buy himself free. Ain't likely, though. You gentlemen woulda asked him where he got it, and what he gonna say? Angel of the Lord came down from on high and give it to him? Ain't likely, no way."

I stretched a hand out. Nace looked at it, then took it and shook.

"Thank you for being honest, Nace," I said.

He nodded to us. "Got to get back to my work, now, gentlemen. If you don't mind."

"We will just speak to some people to verify what you have said."

"No problem, sir, no problem. You go right ahead." The big man walked back to the people working on the fence.

The General said, "Your suspicions seem allayed, at any rate, Colonel."

"Yes, sir; he seems an honest man."

We spoke to three men as we crossed the field; all agreed that Nace was here the week of the 15th. We asked if he was here after Mr. Thompson had run off, and the men all said yes, he'd been around the farm all those days. They were less sure about the beginning of the month but couldn't remember anything unusual happening around that time.

As we walked back to our horses, the General said, "We must stop off at the Grist Mill on the way back to Mount Vernon, Colonel. Let us put some additional questions to Ben, given these developments. I am quite sure he has not been completely truthful with us."

46

Monday, March 30, 1789, afternoon

On hearing our arrival at the Grist Mill, Mr. Davenport came over from the stockyard, covered in dirt. He came up to us looking of all things apologetic.

"I am very sorry about this, Your Excellency. Nor did I think it could happen, didn't think to keep watch as well as might be."

The General looked at him, perplexed. "I am sorry, Mr. Davenport. Of what are you speaking?"

"The slaves, a course, sir. My people here."

"The slaves." The General was still perplexed. "What about them?"

"Ain't you here 'cause of my message?"

"What message?"

Davenport stuttered out, "It's just, sir, that is, it's like…"

"Mr. Davenport! Get a grip on yourself, man, and tell me what the matter is. I have received no message."

The man braced up and spit it out. "Well sir, not to put too fine a point upon it, two of the coopers have run off. Tom and Davy."

"What!"

"Yes, sir, very sorry to say it, sir. Sent a message up to the house by Ben earlier today."

"We have been at Mason's Neck much of the day."

"I see, sir, sorry sir to have to tell it to you this way."

"Well, let us not worry about the telling so much as the doing, Mr. Davenport. What has been done?"

"Waiting for you, Your Excellency."

"How did you learn of this?"

"They two didn't show for work this morning, sir. Not in their cabin. Asked Ben, he a course had no bloody idea about it, nor did the other son-of-a-bitch. So I sent up to the Mansion House."

"The message must have just missed us."

"Yes, sir."

"Where are the other men now?"

"Over to the mill house, sir."

"Get 'em out here." The General cleared his throat, recollected himself, then added, "If you please."

"Yes, sir!" Davenport ran over to the mill house and in short order had the miller and the remaining cooper, Jack, lined up in front of us. Davenport stood between them, gripping their arms in a tight hold. Both looked a little the worse for wear, and Ben had a disturbingly bruised eye.

"Now, you bastards tell the General what's what." He shook them by the arms he held.

"A bit more address, sir, please," said the General. Turning to the two Negroes, he said, "I would like to hear your stories from your own mouths. About Tom and Davy."

The two men looked at each other and at the General, then at Mr. Davenport and back again to the General. They did not say anything.

I said, "Perhaps if Mr. Davenport will excuse us, it might be better to speak with the men alone."

The General nodded. Mr. Davenport loosed his hold on his people, and I saw him off to his house. The General had begun questioning the men.

"And then?"

"Well, sir, no one come out of the cabin. I go inside, nothing and no one there. I come out and tell Massa Davenport, he make me run to the

Mansion House to report it. I tell Massa Fairfax and come right back here."

"Did the men say anything yesterday that might have led you to think they might be intending to abscond?"

The two men looked at each other, then down at their feet.

"Come along, man, just tell me."

"Mr. Davenport, he whupped us something terrible couple of days past. Them two had it worse'n us two. They give him lip." Ben grinned with little humor. "Mr. Davenport, he don't like lip."

I remembered the clear instructions to Mr. Davenport about punishing his people. The General had been quite clear in putting the man on parole. The General's face was now austere in its disapproval of this revelation of Mr. Davenport's maltreatment of his people. I remembered the resistance I had felt in the man as I held Mr. Davenport back from his frenzied attack on his people a few days earlier. I was sorry I had been so gentle to the man and resolved to speak to the General about the man's parole.

The General was silent for a few moments, considering, then asked, "Was this whipping so bad that Tom and Davy absconded as a result of it?"

Ben and Jack again looked at their feet.

"Well?" The General was fast losing patience.

"No sir." Ben looked up at the General.

"Then why?"

"I guess I g-g-got to t-t-tell it all, then, sir." The miller was stuttering with fear. Perhaps the General's manner was indeed intimidating, though I could not see it. I felt the miller was afraid for reasons of his own, not because of his fear of his master's reaction to whatever he was about to say.

"Yes, you do. Now."

"Well, it was like this, sir. Julius had this hold on me over Chancey, sir, like I said b-b-before...." The miller's voice petered out, as though his throat was not letting the words through.

"Yes?" the General barked.

"Well, sir, it all went a bit further than I said, with Tom and Davy. See, Julius made a special deal with them. Jack, he didn't want no part of it, his wife wouldn't let him." Jack was nodding his head furiously at this. "Nor I did. More than my life was worth, and I got a good job here now, no need to fuck it up. You know, sir? No need. And Julius had already fucked up my life real good."

The miller's throat had loosened and the words were flowing. The General said nothing, letting it flow.

"Well, sir, Julius said if they two could tell him info'mation about things round here, comings and goings and such, people who come to the mill to buy, as well as stealing stuff, he'd pay 'em more, and maybe they'd get a chance of going free. I asked Julius why he thought that, he just smile and say that his white man deeper than just a thief, he got a lot going on and there was a lot of money to be made and a lot of chances for him, Julius that is, to make it. He kept saying working for the massa was for fools. Well I can tell you that scared me down to the toes, sir, so I just shut up and walked away. Whatever that man had going on was not something I wanted any part of."

"White man? Mr. Thompson?"

The miller shook his head. "No, no, sir, he talking about the man who paid Massa Thompson and him to steal. Ain't never seen that man, sir!"

"What specific kind of information did Julius want?" I asked.

"Don't know, sir, Tom and Davy never said nothing more about it. I just knowed what I just said, sir, nought more. Sorry, sir."

The General rubbed his face in frustration. "It is like following a track through loose mud and water, no scent and very little trace to see. There is truly a fox, I think, but we will need to run him to ground in

Alexandria." He turned to Ben and looked carefully at his face.

"Now, then, Ben—I would wager good money that Mr. Davenport is not responsible for that eye."

Ben looked down again. "No, sir. He just whupped us."

"Nace?"

Ben looked up sharply.

"I think Nace has resolved the competition between himself and you, am I right?"

Ben was downcast. "Yes, sir. He done that all right."

"And I will ask again: did you kill Julius because of Chancey?"

"No, no, sir, I didn't. I couldn't do nothing like that, sir." His voice was pleading.

I asked, "Ben, do you think Nace had anything to do with Julius's schemes, or with Tom and Davy's spying? Could he be responsible for Julius's death?"

"Naw, not him. He take one look at Julius and tell him to go fuck himself. No, sir, I don't exactly like Nace, but he's a good man, better 'n me, way better than Julius. He know what he can do and what he cain't and what he wants and what's right. He wouldn't never do nothing like that." A remarkable testimonial from Ben, who might stand to gain a good deal from Nace's downfall. Ben seemed to have learned some hard lessons from recent events.

The General dismissed the pair back to their work. "All right, you two, you get back to work now. Take heed: we will find Tom and Davy, and their lives will not be as pleasant as they were. Do you mind your behavior and your work. I will talk with Mr. Davenport about the whipping, I do not countenance such behavior in my overseers without justification. Did he have justification?"

"Just lip, sir, from Tom and Davy. And he just whupped us two for good measure, we didn't give him no lip at all. We's just there when he got the frenzy on him."

"All right. Now please return to your work, and it would be well for you to keep to your work alone in the future. No more larceny, no more night walking, no more misbehavior of any kind."

"Yes, Massa Washington! Yes sir." The two trotted back into the mill building and disappeared. The General turned and walked up to Davenport's house, and I followed.

Mr. Davenport greeted us at the door, slumped against the door frame, watching us as we came; he had presumably watched us as we questioned the men. His wife was again tending to the livestock in the pen.

"A word inside, if you please, Mr. Davenport," said the General. We all entered the little house and stood in the main room.

"Among other interesting things, Ben told us you have whipped the men, especially Tom and Davy. Is that so?"

"Damn right I did. Bloody little bastards, doing bloody little work and a lot of back talking. Sir."

"I thought I had made it very clear when I engaged you, Mr. Davenport, and just two weeks ago again, that punishing of the people on the farms and mill was to be done only when fully justified, and preferably with the approval of myself, Major Washington, or Mr. Fairfax. I received your parole. Did I make that clear at the time?"

Davenport looked down at the floor. "Yes, sir."

"But you whipped them without getting such permission? You could not restrain yourself?"

"Yes, sir."

"And why did you do that, specifically?"

The miller looked up at us and exclaimed,"They two, Tom and Davy, they were responsible for most of the thievery, I was certain of it, sir. And such disrespectful language you never did hear, sir. I whipped them up good, damn little sons-of-bitches, I wanted to make sure they knew they could not get away with such things with me." He shuffled his feet. "I guess I got a little hot, sir, I am sorry about that. I will mind your instructions in the future."

"You had best do so, sir, at peril of your job. I cannot have overseers creating unrest among the people by inappropriately harsh punishments. I must insist that you consult with the Mansion House before doing so again. Do you understand clearly?"

"Yes, sir." Mr. Davenport was sullen.

"And Negroes are men, Mr. Davenport. Treat them as such, not as horses or oxen. For God's sake, man, wake up."

I thought from the rather mulish look Davenport aimed between us that it would be a long while before he took on opinions that would allow him to treat his people with justice and reason. He was not that kind of man, or mule.

The General turned and walked out the door without bowing, his shoulders rigid with anger.

"You realize, Colonel," said the General as we rode down to the Mansion House, "that this sounds very much like the actions of the last British Governor of Virginia at the beginning of the War. He tried to get the plantation people to revolt by promising them their freedom if they abandoned their masters, thus creating chaos in our ranks. And you will remember that the British under Lord Dorchester were intransigent about returning the people that had absconded during the war. He pretended it to be against his principles, having promised them their freedom, but I detected a continuing desire to disrupt the treaty. I despair at the depths to which the British will sink to harm us, even now."

"Yes, sir. I can see that the British would try anything to disrupt political events here, including aiding and abetting runaways. I will be frank, sir: this is yet another reason to free them, as holding them as slaves simply creates opportunities like this. You are as dependent on them as they are upon you, and thus you both sink into the mire. And the whipping—you cannot really expect people like Davenport to treat them with basic humanity."

The General just shook his head. "Not now, Colonel, though I thank you for your advice. We will go to see Colonel Hooe tomorrow to follow up on what we have learned today, and to see what Mr. Hutchison has done about Alice, and to see what he might do about Tom and Davy. Three people gone! The British should be overjoyed at their success, as my plantation is certainly in complete disarray. Perhaps Colonel Hooe or Colonel Fitzgerald will have some new insight into who might be fomenting rebellion among my people as well as murdering them."

47

The General found himself quite disconcerted by all these events and revelations. On Monday morning, as he finished his breakfast, he said to me, "Colonel, if I am to assume the Presidency in New York, I must set my plantation on a path to normalcy, despite all this nonsense. Our summons may come at any moment."

He closeted himself in his study to draw up his plans for his nephew and Mr. Fairfax. I took the opportunity to walk down to the river to throw a few stones while considering the events of the last few days. My brain buzzed with annoying insects: all the questions and concerns we had uncovered. I needed to get my thoughts straight. I had no plantation to manage, just a disordered mind. I walked out on the wharf at the Landing and thought about Julius and who might have killed him, to little avail. Vexed at my inability to make sense of it all, I walked back up the path to the Mansion House about 10 o'clock to find that I might as well not have bothered. Events had moved on.

I found the General standing in the drive in front of the house talking with Mr. Fairfax, Major Washington, and a mulatto man whom I recognized as the overseer at Muddy Hole Farm, Will. The man's horse breathed hard from exertion.

"Oh good, here is Colonel Humphreys now!" said the General, turning toward me as I came around the corner of the kitchen.

I quickened my pace and came up to the little group. "What has happened, your Excellency?"

"

Mr. Fairfax answered. "At Muddy Hole, Colonel; the slave Caesar killed this morning, shot in the head."

"And a horse gone too." The General's face was grim. "We were just going to send for you, Colonel, before getting details."

Chaos upon chaos.

The details came in bits and pieces as we questioned the overexcited Will. He related an amazing story. He had just sent his people off to their daily work when a white man walked up to him from the road along with the man Caesar, who ought to have been working in the fields. The man surprised Will by taking out a pistol from under his coat and clapping it to his head.

While Will stayed motionless with fear, Caesar got the overseer's horse and saddled it up. The white man mounted the horse, made as though to give Caesar a hand up behind him, then shot Caesar in the head at point blank range as he leaned down toward him. Then he galloped off down the road toward Belvoir and Fredericksburg. Davy ran after him but soon lost sight of the man. Will then rode one of the farm horses down to the Mansion House in haste to let us know what had happened.

Mr. Fairfax and Major Washington stood with their mouths agape, not able to comprehend the meaning of these events. The General had assumed the posture he usually took when getting very bad news from his generals during a battle: feet apart and firmly planted, hands behind his back, and a furious frown on his face.

I felt as though I were a disembodied observer looking on at some kind of fantastic Greek tragedy; I expected a chorus to emerge from the Mansion House to explain things to me as the Gods looked on and laughed while all the characters in the play met their tragic ends. I decided I did not really like Greek tragedy all that much.

Sounds from the drive brought me down to earth. We saw another Negro on a horse galloping toward us.

"That's Davy Gray, the River Farm overseer, Your Excellency!" cried Mr. Fairfax.

"What now?" muttered the General, staring at the approaching Davy.

Davy rode up and dismounted, his breath heaving almost as much as that of his horse.

"Massa, massa, a terrible thing! Gabriel's been murdered!"

"Catch your breath, man, then explain what has happened!" The General steadied the man as he stumbled in his rush to report his news.

"Oh, sir, it was just awful. Jessie went to find him, she found him in a pool of blood in his cabin. Somebody done cut his throat and left him to die!"

"When did you last see Gabriel?"

"Last night, massa, just before bedtime. He's fine then, sir, jes' fine. Now he's dead in his own blood! Wife Jessie screamin' all over the place! She said she went out early to get wood, come back and found him. She damn sure a haunt took him and tore his throat out!" The overseer was gasping for breath.

"Erm...take a breath and calm down." The General turned back to Will.

"Was there any warning that Caesar might have troubles?"

The overseer stared at the General, then looked down.

"What is it, then?"

Will stumbled a bit on the telling of it. "See, massa, I didn't like to say before when ya come around askin' on Saturday, but I got my ideas about Caesar maybe bein' the kind of man ya lookin' for, 'cause of the thefts. I didn't like to say anything 'til I was sure, though, sir. I just got my ideas about it, you understand. I was goin' to watch him close and see what was what!"

"Hum." The General studied the man's face for a moment, then turned back to Davy Gray, who had gotten his breath back and was looking on, pop-eyed at learning of Caesar's death. "What about Gabriel?"

"Yes, massa, just like what he done said jus' now, jus' like that. Sorry I didn't say nothin' before to you when you come by Saturday. Yeah, I think Gabriel got something to do with all that theft too!"

It was too easy to pin the blame on dead men; they can no longer answer to the charge, and they can no longer reveal their accomplices. The overseers could easily be covering up as much as they were revealing truth. I carefully examined the faces of the defensive Negroes but could find nothing but fear and horror in their countenances. Then an idea presented itself to me.

"Your Excellency, I think our spy and murderer is cleaning up after himself!"

"Explain, Colonel, if you please."

"While setting up the ambuscade for us, he commissioned the murder of these slaves as well. He wanted to silence them before they gave us more information that might lead to him."

The General turned back to Davy. "Can you describe this white man?"

"He was tall and thin, sir, with a mess of hair and beard, a fierce look on him, sir, a hard man. Had a musket slung along his back, but he never touched it. He got that pistol on me 'fore I knew what was happening, you understand? Couldn't do nothing about it. He weren't no gentleman like you, massa. Looked kinda like he been sleepin' rough, sir."

The General shook his head. "That doesn't sound like our spy: one of the brigands who attacked us, perhaps? He might have gone from the ambush to River Farm to find and kill Gabriel, then back to Muddy Hole to finish the job by killing Caesar and escaping by horse. Why the devil did he go toward Fredericksburg? I must send Mr. Fairfax to Alexandria to tell Colonel Hooe about these new killings."

The General gave instructions to the overseers about the bodies of the dead slaves; they were to bring the corpses to the Mansion House ice house for later inspection by the Coroner's jury. Mr. Fairfax ran off to the stables on his way to Alexandria to report the murders to Colonel Hooe.

48

WEDNESDAY, APRIL 1, 1789, MORNING

The next morning, as we all assembled to break our fast, Frank Lee delivered a note that Colonel Hooe had entrusted to Mr. Fairfax the night before.

> Alexandria, Mar 31, 1789.
> My dear General,
> This short note is to inform you that we have found the man that Cl. Humphreys wounded! The man is feverish and cannot walk, but he does not appear to be in danger. At his request, we brought him to the local gaol & have him under guard by my servants. The man is febrile not only in body but in mind; he insists he will speak only to Your Excellency & will tell nothing to anyone else. We can get nothing out of him. I have sent for Dr. Craik to treat his wound.
> At your earliest convenience, if you would please come to Alexandria, we may make some progress in the matter of the attack on you. I suggest caution, as it is not out of the question that this may be a prelude to another ambush, as we have not identified the other man involved, nor the person or persons who instructed them, & the new murders you have reported are not reassuring. I am as always, yr. Obed. Servant, Robert Hooe

After gulping down some gruel and chocolate, we chose two white servants, Thomas and Edward, who had experience under arms, and then equipped ourselves with enough firepower to see off an attack by British regulars. The General, surveying his troops, sighed and said, "Ah, to have Billy Lee once again under arms. We grow old, Colonel."

Mr. Fairfax appeared, bleary-eyed from lack of sleep. The General gave him the letter and said, "Mr. Fairfax, I fear you must ride at all speed to Springfield Farm to fetch Mr. Cockburn. Please advise him that we have found one miscreant from our adventure, and we may need him to start legal proceedings. Show him this letter from Colonel Hooe. Tell him of the additional murders of Caesar and Gabriel, with all the details. Please request him to come to Colonel Hooe's house in Alexandria with as much dispatch as possible. He may wish to stop here to examine the bodies of Gabriel and Caesar, but please tell him to do so as quickly as he can, and only if he must. Thank you." Mr. Fairfax ran out and was away in a few minutes. The General found his old war saber and had a servant sharpen it. We rode out of Mount Vernon with Thomas and Edward following behind, turning toward Alexandria.

Our small cavalry troop arriving at Colonel Hooe's house an hour later without incident and interrupted the Colonel at his breakfast. He arose, wiping his mouth with a napkin.

"It was pure good fortune on my part, Your Excellency," said the Colonel as we walked the two short blocks to the market square to where the gaol nestled next to the courthouse. "Williamson had gone out, and a man came to my door saying that there was a wounded man lying in an alley that needed help. I brought a couple of my servants, and the man led me to the alley down by the water. On our taking him up, he startled awake and tried to free himself, but we had a firm grip. His arm was broken by the shot, but the bleeding had stopped. He was feverish and incoherent, but he insisted on being brought to the gaol rather than to my house. Now, you may well realize that it is unusual for a man to request to be placed in gaol. Once safely ensconced in a cell, the man grabbed my arm and asked for Your Excellency, no one else would do."

"Indeed," said the General. "And his wound?"

"I brought Dr. Craik to him as quickly as possible, then left him to it and returned to my house. The doctor removed the ball from his arm, set it, and bandaged the wound. The doctor came to me after dinner and told me about it. He has every expectation that the man will recover if the wound does not fester. The prisoner insisted on having a servant in the gaol overnight—to protect him, he said. So I sent over my coachman armed with two pistols and instructions to sit up all night on the watch. Your man Fairfax arrived shortly after he left, and I gave him the note for you."

We reached the gaol and went in. The prisoner was a rather ratty, bearded individual with clothes not much better than rags. His eyes were bloodshot, and he grimaced with pain every time he moved his arm. But he was alive. Thomas placed him in a chair and carried him out into the center room.

Colonel Hooe addressed the man. "What is your name?"

"Dick Steptoe, sir." He looked at the General. "Ginr'l Washington."

"Mr. Steptoe. I believe you have something to tell me?" The General stared down at the man from his great height.

The man looked down at his feet, then up at the General."Very sorry, sir. I shouldn't a done it, shouldn't a took the money."

"Let us be clear, sir," said Colonel Hooe. "You are confessing to attacking the General with this musket on Sunday?"

"Yes, sir, very sorry I am about it too, sir. I know I'm to hang for it, sir, if I don't die from my wound first, sir."

"What is it you wish to tell me, then?" asked the General.

"I know I'm to die, sir, but I want to die right, not murdered." He closed his eyes, shifted and winced, then looked at Colonel Hooe. "Colonel Hooe, you don't know me from Adam, but I go about the waterfront doing odd work for warehouses and ship masters, sir. Well, sir, on Sunday, there me and my mate were, recovering, like, from having had a bit too much grog the night before, sitting against a wall, and your man came, asked if we had muskets, and said we could make grog money by taking care of some business on the Fredericksburg road. Even gave us a ride out there and set us up and told us what to look for."

"Wait, just a moment. You said, *my* man? *What* man?" The Colonel was apoplectic.

"Why, that man you have who does all your business along the waterfront. Don't rightly know his name, sorry sir. Small man with brown hair and eyes, good dresser, speaks low. Gave us five pound each to do the dirty work. That's a lot of money for men like us, sir."

The Colonel shut his eyes. "Williamson."

The General and I looked at each other in horror. I suddenly realized why the Sheriff and his clerk had made so little progress on the murders.

The General coldly said, "What better place for a British agent than in your household and warehouse, Colonel Hooe? The center of all mercantile activity in Alexandria, with access to the houses of all the important men there and in all Fairfax County. Including mine." He slapped the table with his gloved hand and glared at Colonel Hooe.

Colonel Hooe was speechless with horror, which quickly turned to fury. He stamped around the gaol as though he had gone mad.

"So, Mr. Steptoe," continued the General, "you insisted on gaol to avoid Williamson, is that true?"

"Yes, sir. Honest, sir, when I aimed and shot, it was the moment before I recognized you, sir. Nearly dropped my musket in shock. Then you charged us, I got hit and really did drop it, and we ran off. My mate got me back to the road, sir, but he had more work to do, so he left me to do what I could for myself and took himself down the road toward Mount Vernon. I struggled back to town somehow, I thought maybe I could get some help from a ship's mate friend o' mine. I knew I'd be done for if I tried to get help from the man that hired me, I'd be dead right there. Cool as a cucumber was that man, asking us to kill Ginr'l Washington without telling us who he was! So I hid myself to wait for my friend, but I must have fainted there in the alley. That be when you found me, sir."

"And the man with you? What was he intending to do at Mount Vernon?"

"The man that hired us wanted two slaves dead there, sir, any way possible. Told us where to find 'em. I didn't worry too much about that bit, sir, just slaves you know."

The General closed his eyes. "Yes, I know. Just slaves."

Colonel Hooe had returned to a semblance of self control and had come back to the table. "I must apologize, Your Excellency, there are no words—"

"The fewer the better, sir. Let us act. Where can we find Mr. Williamson?"

"He should be in my warehouse, Your Excellency. But if he is aware...." The Colonel rubbed his brow in an agony of suspense. "I left word for him about all this."

"Then that is where we must go, as quickly as possible, to start the search. Or, at least, Colonel Humphreys and I must go. I think you have business here. You must secure this man and guard him carefully. Mr. Cockburn should arrive at your house soon, and it would be best if you were there to prepare him for the proceedings we are likely to take. We can then discuss what to do about my other two murdered people."

The General put on and adjusted his hat, then paused, and striking the hot iron, added, "Perhaps you could also do some thinking about how to persuade the merchants of Alexandria to avoid purchasing stolen plantation produce? When we return, we can pursue that along with the rest of the course of justice." The General carefully kept any resentment or anger from his voice, but I knew him well, and his rigid back and sharp look showed the feelings that he kept close.

At that moment, two men came through the door of the gaol leading two Negroes shackled in chains.

49

The General started. "Tom and Davy!"

"Hutch!" I said at the same time; for one of the men leading the shackled slaves was indeed William Hutchison.

"You know these two, Your Excellency?" asked Hutch.

"Yes, these are coopers, run away from my mill on Monday."

"Damn, sir, fine timing! We'll just turn 'em over to you, then. If you have the reward money, that is, sir—Your Excellency." I noticed that Hutch's informality did not extend to the General. The General had that effect on people. But I noticed as well that Hutch did not shirk from asserting his claim on the General's purse.

The General responded, "I have not yet advertised for these runaways, but I will pay you the usual amount, if that is satisfactory? Ten dollars in addition to the amount allowed by law?"

"Aye, sir, that would be just fine." The General counted out the money and gave it to Hutch. "Now, sir, what should we do with these two?"

The General said, "Let's sit them down over here, against the wall on that bench. I have some immediate questions of them."

"Certainly, Your Excellency! Over there, you two."

Hutch pushed the shackled slaves over to the bench, where they sat in a tangle of legs and chains. The General stood looking down at them for a moment, his face showing no emotion. The two shackled Negroes looked up at his tall figure in the dim light of the gaol. Master and slave: it was not a vignette of the General's life that I wished to preserve in my memory, or in his biography.

He said, "Tom, Davy. I am sorry to find you here in such straits. You must have known that you would be caught and brought back to the plantation and punished. Why did you run off?"

I caught a flash of white eyes as the slaves looked away and back at their master. Tom replied, "Very sorry, massa Washington. We was scared for our lives, no mistake, sir. We heard about Massa Thompson gettin' killed down to Alexandria, we knew we was next, sir. He kill Julius for talkin', he kill Massa Thompson for talkin', he'd a kill us for just knowin' things even though we didn't talk about 'em."

"*Who* would kill you?"

"Massa Williamson, sir, that work for Massa Hooe here in Alexandria."

Colonel Hooe sat down in a chair by the table, overcome. Mr. Steptoe stared at the slaves with his mouth open, then said, "They got that right, sir! Damn bloody man ain't no better than a cornered animal. Shouldn't never have taken his money to kill you, or anyone. Pure evil, he is. Got a tongue on him could persuade the Devil himself." He shook his head as he reflected on the biggest mistake of his life—probably his final mistake, as well. I reflected that "bloody" described Mr. Williamson well.

The General said to the slaves, "Events have proved you correct, Tom. He has killed Caesar and Gabriel, in cold blood—or, at least, he ordered it done. How did you get yourselves into this frightful fiasco?"

"Mr. Williamson, he come by with Julius and wanted us to tell him things about what was goin' on at the mill, what was goin' on at the plantation. Julius promised the moon, sayin' we'd get bags of money and we'd get free if we would go along with them."

"So you two were behind the thefts at the Grist Mill, along with miller Ben?"

Tom wrapped his arms around himself and rocked back and forth.

"Were you, Tom? Davy?" The General's voice was low and calm, not threatening. Tom stopped rocking and looked up at him and finally nodded.

"Davy, you too?"

Davy nodded as well.

"And then Mr. Davenport punished you?"

"He said for us to get a load together on a cart for Alexandria. We knew that would mean goin' to Massa Williamson 'cause he the one that take our flour and sell it, and we knew he'd find a way to kill us dead, sir. We said too much to Massa Davenport 'cause we was afraid to go, and Massa Davenport, he don't like us much anyway, it was too much for him and he gave us the whip. Then we run off."

"You should have come to me."

I heard a plaintive note in the General's voice; but I could see going to the General was not possible for men in their position. The General heard the same note himself and shook off his wishful thinking.

He said, "Well, you did not. Did you find someone to help you here?"

"No, sir, we didn't know anybody, so we hid around town, around the shipyards, found some food here and there, got some food from out of the houses, but they caught us when we ran." Tom waved in the direction of Hutch and his companion.

"Ran? Why did you run?"

I saw the white flash of Tom's eyes again in the dim gaol. "We saw Alice at a window this mornin' in a house, thought it might be that she would help us. We was powerful hungry, sir. So we goes up to the window, and she disappears and Massa Williamson was there at the window, lookin' straight at us! We run off so fast we got lost. Finally got back down to the strand."

The General's eye's lit up at this revelation, and he exclaimed, "Got him! By God, Humphreys, we've got him!" I grinned at the General's excess of emotion.

Hutch put in, "I was a-lookin' for your runaway Alice near the waterfront, sir, with my friend here, right down near Franklin Street, as Lizzie Casey said she'd seen her around that area. We saw these lads running as fast as get out, sir, down Union Street on the strand, and we knew they couldn't be up to any good running like that, so we took 'em and shackled 'em. They couldn't give any account of themselves, wouldn't tell us who owned 'em. We brought 'em over here so's they could be held for their master and we could get the reward."

"Good work, Mr. Hutchison. And it appears we have found Alice and this man Williamson as well." The General said this with a return to his usual calm demeanor, but a gleam in his eye told me his excitement had not abated.

Hutch smiled and said, "I hope Your Excellency will see his way toward paying us the reward for finding her, as we brought these two in." A man dedicated to his business, was Hutch.

The General looked rather taken aback, but he recollected himself and said, "Certainly, sir; if we find her and take her, I will pay you the reward, as your quick thinking caught these two and resulted in their information." He turned back to the shackled pair. "Tom, exactly where is this house?"

"It's a couple of blocks up from the water, sir."

"You will have to show us."

"That man will kill us!" exclaimed the terrified cooper.

The General smiled and waved a hand at Thomas and Edward, who were carrying their muskets. "As you see, Tom, we are well armed; he will not kill you today. Tom, Davy: come along."

We took the shackled runaways out to the street. The two looked around helplessly. Tom said, "Don't rightly know where we is, sir."

The General replied, "Where were you before you came upon Alice in the window?"

"We just come up from the strand, sir, down toward the end, past the shipyards."

"Let us start there, then." He paused and considered, then added, "We must stop at Colonel Hooe's house on the way; perhaps Mr. Cockburn has arrived and can supply a warrant for what we must do."

50

Martin Cockburn, impatient and dyspeptic, was indeed at Colonel Hooe's house, with Mr. Fairfax. The General and I entered with Colonel Hooe while Hutch, his friend, Thomas, and Edward remained outside with the shackled slaves.

"General Washington," said Mr. Cockburn, bowing slightly. The General returned the bow.

"Mr. Fairfax has informed you of the murders at my plantation yesterday?"

"Indeed, yes. And I must inform *you* of an attempted murder at my plantation yesterday as well." The tall man overflowed with indignation, but this time not at the General.

"What!"

"Yes—apparently the man who killed your slaves intended to dispose of my overseer Cujo as part of his abominable project. He rode into my farm yesterday, asked for Cujo, and when Cujo came out, shot at him with his pistol. He missed; I believe his horse shied at the wrong moment. Three of my people dragged him from his horse and disarmed him. I came here in haste with my coach-and-four and did not stop at Mount Vernon to examine the bodies of your slaves, Your Excellency. I have put the man into the care of Colonel Hooe's servants."

"Remarkable, sir!" The General was shaking his head in wonder. "I could not fathom why the man escaped toward Fredericksburg; obviously his intent was to go to your farm, Mr. Cockburn. I daresay he would have visited Colonel Mason next." The General strode to the window to collect his thoughts. "Events here have moved quickly, Mr. Cockburn. Here is the gist: we have found that Colonel Hooe's clerk, John Williamson, is in fact a British agent and very probably also the murderer of my overseer Julius and of George Thompson, and certainly of my two slaves Caesar and Gabriel, at least by proxy. We believe he is now hiding in a house in Alexandria. We are about to locate the house with the help of witnesses who have seen Williamson there."

Mr. Cockburn showed little surprise and even more indignation at the General's revelations. "Indeed! My slave Cujo confessed to a systematic series of thefts from my plantation, orchestrated by this man Williamson. I can only assume Williamson wanted Cujo dead to prevent discovery of the plot. I have Cujo in shackles on my plantation, and he has spoken freely after a little persuasion. But you say Williamson is a spy as well?"

"Indeed. I believe Williamson meant the larcenies to disrupt our economy and politics, and that he has taken every opportunity to prevent my accepting the Presidency, all in the service of his masters in England."

The General's voice turned persuasive. "Mr. Cockburn, given my position—being about to assume a very high office—I wish to leave as little to chance as possible. Justice must be paramount in this case, and there must be no hint of partiality or arbitrariness on my part. Or, indeed, of tyranny, as under the British colonial system. The new nation cannot afford to have a leader under such a taint. Therefore, I would very much appreciate your swearing out a warrant to search this house and to arrest John Williamson for the crimes of murder, conspiracy, and grand larceny, all of which have taken place in Fairfax County."

"Very well, sir." After writing busily at Colonel Hooe's desk for a few minutes, Mr. Cockburn arose and said, "General Washington, do you swear on oath that you have reasonable grounds to suspect John Williamson of the crimes of which you accuse him?"

"I do so swear, sir."

Mr. Cockburn signed and sanded and dried the document, then handed it to the General. He smiled for the first time that day, his indignation lost in his satisfaction at bringing so many miscreants to justice—or possibly just at getting revenge for the indignities he had suffered.

"Thank you, Mr. Cockburn," said the General, with equal satisfaction. He held up the warrant as though it were a battle standard. "Let us execute this warrant as expeditiously as possible."

The General folded up the warrant and put it away in his pocketbook. He bowed to Mr. Cockburn and we hurried out to rejoin the little group waiting outside. At the General's urging, Colonel Hooe swore us all in as members of his posse.

We proceeded down to the strand along Prince Street, then walked down Union Street past the Fitzgerald and Hooe Warehouses and the shipyards all the way to the end of the strand. We moved slowly, as the shackles inhibited the walking of the two coopers.

Davy pointed at Franklin Street. "That's the street, Massa Washington. We went up to see if we could find some food."

We turned up Franklin Street and walked about three blocks.

"Down there, sir," said Tom, pointing to the left down Royal Street.

"And that," I said, pointing up Franklin, "is the Spring Gardens Tavern, Your Excellency, where Miss Lizzy Casey works as a barmaid." Hutch grinned at me.

'Indeed. Very well. Tom, which house is it?"

"It's that one, sir," said Tom, pointing at a small house about halfway down the block.

The General smiled; it was again time for action. He turned to

Hutch.

"Mr. Hutchison. If you please, would you take our two runaways here back to Colonel Hooe's and turn them over to Mr. Fairfax. They will only encumber us in our current work."

"Aye, sir." Hutch hesitated, then continued, "But Your Excellency, if you do not mind it, I would prefer to accompany you. My mate here can take the slaves back. Guess if I'm to be paid for this Alice, I should be there when you take her."

The General's smile disappeared, but he acquiesced in Hutch's request. "Very well, Mr. Hutchison." Hutch's friend took the coopers by their arms and led them off. We turned back to our task, and the General led the little troop down Royal Street to the house which we were to storm.

51

WEDNESDAY, APRIL 1, 1789, AFTERNOON

The General sent our two servants with their muskets around to the back of the house at 720 Royal Street to prevent Mr. Williamson from escaping out the back, as Mr. Thompson had done. The General stepped up to the front door and knocked loudly. There was silence for a minute, then the door opened slightly. The General pushed at it with his hand, and it opened wide.

I drew out and half-cocked my pistol. The General entered, and I went in right behind, followed by Colonel Hooe and Hutch. We found Mr. Williamson standing in the passage, hands empty and slightly raised in front of him.

"I am not armed, gentlemen." The voice was subtly different from the one with which we were familiar; it had more of a British inflection, a kind of drawl I associated with the upper reaches of the British schools system. And certainly his impudent manner differed greatly from the meek clerk we had known.

The General said, "Mr. Williamson. I have a warrant for your arrest for murder."

"Indeed. And may I ask, whom am I supposed to have murdered?"

"Mr. George Thompson; my overseer Julius; and my slaves Gabriel and Caesar. There is also the attempted murder of Mr. Cockburn's slave Cujo."

The man tutted; there is no other word for it. "Mr. Washington, I am surprised at you. Are your intelligence sources that limited?"

I comprehended that he was boasting of additional murders of which we were unaware. The General's austere look settled into a frown.

"You had best mend your manners, sir, and limit your boasting. You will hang for the murder of a single slave, and you cannot hang more than once."

"True, true, I forget myself."

"Where is my slave Alice?"

"Ah yes, the American obsession with property. She is in that room," he said, pointing to a side door. I strode across and threw open the door to a small parlor. There in a chair sat Alice, shackled hands and legs, and chained to the wall with a locked chain from her waist. I turned back to the passage.

"She is here, Your Excellency, shackled and confined."

"I did not want to lose such valuable property, Mr. Washington." Williamson grinned. "Perhaps I may claim the generous reward you offered for her return? It would pay my legal fees, I should think."

Hutch stirred restlessly behind the General.

"Do not worry yourself, Mr. Hutchison, your fee is in no real danger. I am merely joking with the General, who looks very much as though he needs cheering up. And do put that ridiculous pistol away, Mr. Humphreys. You will not need it."

"I will be the best judge of that, Mr. Williamson. Is that your true name?" I kept my pistol in hand, but pointed it downwards, as I did not wish any accident to deprive the world of the spectacle of Mr. Williamson's hanging.

Williamson just smiled and said, "Mr. Washington, before we free the fair Alice and make the journey to gaol, perhaps we may sit for a few minutes so that I may negotiate some terms with you."

"I am not inclined to grant you anything whatever, Mr. Williamson." The General's voice was firm.

"I am at your mercy, of course; but I think I may trade some valuable information for some consideration in treatment. So let us speak together for a time, Your Excellency."

The General shook his head. "I think you do not deserve even a second of my time, sir."

"You will find it greatly to your advantage, sir, when you assume the Presidency."

The General glanced at me and I raised my eyebrows. I said, "A few minutes will not harm anything, Your Excellency."

"Very well. Let us go into this parlor and sit, then we will see what you have to offer. Colonel Humphreys, do you stay ready to prevent any attempt at escape. And, sir: in addition to the Colonel and Mr. Hutchison," said the General, "I have two servants in the back of the house with muskets, so do not think you can somehow escape your fate."

"Confronted by the great General Washington, how could a nonentity such as myself ever think of escape? I wouldn't consider it, Mr. Washington."

The man's insolence was becoming unbearable to me, but the General remained calm and indicated the door with a hand, and we all entered the parlor. Alice sat chained to the wall, her face a mask of terror. I pulled around the other four chairs in the room, and the General, Colonel Hooe, and I sat across from Williamson. I laid my pistol on a small table, near at hand in case it was needed. Hutch stood at the door. Before Williamson sat down, he had the effrontery to consult his watch. He saw my frown.

"I am sorry, sir. I have played the clerk for too long: old habits die hard. I will be late for an appointment at Colonel Hooe's warehouse if this goes on too long, but I suppose there is nothing to be done about it under the circumstances. I am sorry for this delay, Colonel Hooe."

Colonel Hooe stared at his former clerk with a black look on his face.

The General cleared his throat. "I take it you are a British agent, Mr.

Williamson."

"Take whatever you like, Mr. Washington."

"My country and yours are at peace. Why have your masters abused our trust by inflicting you upon us?"

"I am sure I do not know; I know only my instructions."

"And those are?"

"For me to know and you to guess, Mr. Washington."

"I find your impudence tiring, sir."

"I am sorry for that; but I cannot help it."

"It is clear from our investigation that you have tried to gather information about our politics and business affairs: to what end?"

"Again, that is something my masters did not confide to me."

"And you are behind the series of thefts and other disruptions visited upon my county and my plantation."

"As you say, sir. Especially once I knew you might decline the Presidency, I did everything in my power to promote that choice."

"So we must add interference with our politics to intelligence gathering and theft."

"All in the aid of promoting a more balanced assessment of the country's situation, Mr. Washington, among your fellows. Disruptions make people think and consider things differently."

The General replied, "Again: our countries are at peace." The General's voice was grim.

Williamson smiled again. "Ah well. Spies often see more of the world than they expect, and think less of it. Peace is a relative thing, General. Given your experience, do you not see most men as fools?"

The General leaned forward. "I see men who want to make things better for themselves and their families, Mr. Williamson. I see slaves who would be freemen. I see a Kentucky that wants to make the most of itself in a new America. I see a new America that wants Britain gone. I see a Britain that cares little for such things. I see an agent for Britain who cares for and sees very little indeed. That is *my* definition of a fool, sir." The General's voice was low but firm.

On the mention of Kentucky, Williamson's eyes narrowed. "A rather nice speech, Mr. Washington. You may have a future in public office. I trust it will be a short one." The man grinned again.

The General asked, "Who else is working with you?"

"I believe, at this time, that everyone I have employed in illicit activities is either dead or in your custody, Mr. Washington. Really, it has been quite enterprising of you and Mr. Humphreys."

The General pursued a different tack. "Do you report your findings locally to someone? We have information that you have been seen with a British ship's officer. Is there anyone else?"

"I am afraid I report directly to my masters in Quebec and London, Mr. Washington, no intermediaries. Not that I would reveal them— their work could go on even should I hang, after all."

Colonel Hooe exclaimed, "We will find them all out, by God, and we will hang them too!"

The General moved from spying to murder. "Why did you kill my overseer?"

"Julius? A fool. I offered him freedom, he wanted money as well. A great deal of money. He threatened to reveal the whole scheme to you, sir, unless he got it."

"So you killed him. How?"

"His death is completely unimportant, Mr. Washington. He was simply a tool to use and throw away when no longer useful."

"Your evasiveness does not gain you any credit, Mr. Williamson."

"I will try to do better, then."

"What about Mr. Thompson?"

"Ah yes, poor George." The spy grinned. "You Americans are so transparent. All he wanted was money. All he got was an early grave, due entirely to his own stupidity, sir."

"What stupidity?"

"Why, running off the way he did. What better way to implicate yourself in a crime than fleeing from questioners? I let him get away on Mason's Neck; but he came to Alexandria asking for aid, so I hid him in our vacant warehouse. After a day or two of his impatience, I realized he was just a fool and a liability. He seemed to have an abnormal fear of you for some reason, I cannot imagine why." He stopped to consider, then smiled. "He also had an abnormal taste for liquor, which I felt might result in an unfortunate revelation. When, in addition, he demanded a berth on a ship to France and cash to support him there indefinitely, it was too much."

"And so you killed him."

"I must have, if Your Excellency says it."

"More evasion. You hired the men to ambush Colonel Humphreys and myself and to assassinate the slaves you had suborned. Why?" The General's voice exhibited increasing impatience.

"I detest loose ends, sir. I am perhaps too nice in that regard, as I find that it costs me more than I can afford at times." He paused, then smiled. "I will admit that there, I panicked. I do not regret the action itself, however, only the misplaced worry about my mission that led me to undertake it. All is well that ends well: all is fair in war. I do wish that the gentlemen had been better shots, but, sadly, one cannot control events as much as one might like."

The General ignored this impudence. "Why is Alice still alive? Why is she here? What is this place?"

"This house is another acquisition of Colonel Hooe's. He is probably unaware of half of his property in Alexandria, and of much else that goes on around him. I hid Alice because she had seen me with her husband and knew everything. She is too valuable to kill, I could get good money for her in the West Indies, and I have been awaiting a ship I knew to which I might consign her."

"You have held her here since she absconded from my plantation?"

"Yes. I have kept her closely confined, as she tried everything she could to escape. She came to me for aid in her escape; I had to drag her here by force once she understood that I was not going to provide such help. And then, after you had discovered the presence of a British agent here in Alexandria and I took my measures to remove you from the field, Colonel Hooe stumbled over the man who revealed my identity and I was forced to use this house as a bolt-hole."

"Then, this morning, my coopers saw Alice at that window."

"Yes. I had released her from confinement for exercise, and she suddenly pressed herself against the window. I pulled her back and looked out, only to see two slaves from your plantation. I nearly went after them but reconsidered after they made a speedy escape."

The General stared thoughtfully at Williamson. He said abruptly, "I am persuaded, sir, that you will tell us very little. You proposed to give us valuable information for consideration, but have provided none. I know little more than when I walked into this house."

"I am sorry that my efforts have not been more informative, Mr. Washington." The man again consulted his pocket-watch. "But I think we are indeed ready now, sir. A few minutes either way will not matter. I will be in good time."

The General commanded, "Give Colonel Humphreys the key for Alice's chain."

"Yes, here it is." He took an iron key from his coat pocket and handed it to me. I went over to Alice and unlocked the chain from her waist, then assisted her to stand. She wobbled a bit, and I held her arm to steady her. Suddenly Williamson shot out of his chair, barreled into me, knocking me over, and grabbed Alice. He whipped out a large knife from under his coat; he had concealed it behind himself. He held the knife across her throat from behind.

I scrambled up and took up my pistol from the table.

"Steady, Colonel. You would not care to have Mr. Washington lose more of his property, now, would you?" He moved the knife slightly, and a thin trickle of blood started down Alice's neck. She moaned. The General, who had jumped from his chair at the fracas, had his hand on the hilt of his saber.

"What do you intend, sir?" he asked.

"I intend, Mr. Washington, to take this lady down to the port, and then we will see. Ah, ah—do not move, Mr. Hutchison. You will certainly lose your fee if you do, and you may still gain it if you do not."

The General said, "Mr Hutchison, would you please fetch my servants from the back? We will all leave together." I could see that the General felt that Hutch's desire for his fee might outweigh his common sense.

Hutch left the room before Williamson could object. He pushed Alice forward toward the door and into the hall.

Hutch was shortly back, followed by our servants, but his face was white with shock.

"General Washington, sir...."

"What is it, man? We have no time."

"In the back room, sir. It's a man with his throat cut, ear to ear. There is blood everywhere."

"Ah, yes," said the spy, "Mr. Johnson. You may remember him, Mr. Washington: the seaman who heard the shot that killed Mr. Thompson. I fear he saw more than he said, and he too wanted money. I bade him stay here until I could arrange something, but I found him attempting sexual congress with Miss Alice, here, chains and all." He squeezed Alice more tightly. "I had to persuade him to leave her, tricked him into the back room, and did what was necessary. A frightfully messy business this morning. I had to bathe after."

Alice was moaning harder; she had much to moan about, I thought.

Williamson pushed her forward. "Come along, then. I will back out to the street and move down toward the port. Any untoward movement and you will lose this fine example of womanhood, sir." He suited his actions to his words, and we silently followed him as he backed out to the street. I held my pistol ready but found no opportunity to make use of it.

I have the image in my mind still, many years later. I have never seen anything more wicked than that grinning devil with his knife, not even when facing thirty British cannon. I had not, before this event, seen true evil, nowhere in my time with the General. I had been spared. No longer.

52

WEDNESDAY, APRIL 1, 1789, AFTERNOON

Williamson kept his hold on the shackled Alice. She had ceased her moaning and stumbled along backwards, held up by the ever-vigilant spy. The two backed down Royal Street to Franklin, then down to the strand. Williamson no longer held the knife to her throat, as a misadventure might rob him of his shield, but he had it ready.

I kept my pistol cocked and ready for any opportunity, but at the distance Williamson forced between himself and his pursuers, I knew I risked killing Alice through the inaccuracy of the gun. The muskets were worse, of course.

That walk took forever. As we moved slowly down the strand, we collected a few townspeople, attracted as much by the sight of the General in action as by the enthralling spectacle of the man with the knife and his slave hostage. The General sent our servants and Hutch to keep the crowd at bay. By the time we reached the wharves, word was out, and more people started appearing from the streets that came down to the waterfront. Williamson ignored them, concentrating on his footsteps, and we managed to keep the crowd back enough to allow his movement.

The port was full of ships, some tied up to the wharves, others anchored out in the harbor. As the crowd grew on the strand, seamen appeared on deck on all the ships, crowding the rails in their attempt to find out what was going on. As we approached Colonel Hooe's warehouse and wharf, Williamson suddenly stopped and gave a shout.

"Mr. Brown! Mr. Brown!" A man appeared on the wharf right across from where Williamson had stopped, clambering out of a longboat onto the wharf.

"Aye, sir? Oh, Mr. Williamson, is it?" An Englishman, mid-forties, tall and vigorous, very much in charge: an officer. The man looked at us, swiveling his head back and forth. "And guests. Our bargain was for yourself only, Mr. Williamson."

Williamson started backing up the wharf.

"That's all right, Mr. Brown. The others are just seeing me off. Except for the lovely Alice, here, who insists on accompanying me. I trust you can accommodate her, Mr. Brown?" Williamson waved his knife, which was covered with Johnson's blood, and I daresay some of Alice's, in a grotesque goodbye salute to us all. Brown grinned and nodded.

The General said in a loud voice, "Mr. Williamson! I demand that you release that woman. She will be of little use to you, nothing more than an encumbrance once you are aboard that brig!"

Williamson considered, then refused. "No, sir; I must preserve my hostage until I am on board, as I do not wish to incur any risk of rash action on your part. Sorry, Mr. Hutchison; your fee is to be lost after all."

"Mr. Brown!" The General addressed the British officer directly. "That woman is my property; taking her is an illegal act of negro-stealing that will have repercussions on you and on your ship!"

Williamson stayed the officer's response by saying, "I will release her in Quebec, Mr. Washington; she may then decide how best to proceed. I have no doubt she will have the good will and personal responsibility to come back to your kind and excellent care as slave-master. But it will be her choice, of course. For now, I will keep this knife to her throat; she, and you, have no choice at all." He suited his actions to his word, again putting the knife to Alice's throat.

Alice looked very much in that moment as though she would be perfectly willing to return herself to servitude. How she would feel in Quebec would be a different matter—if Williamson should actually free her instead of selling her off to the West Indies.

Colonel Hooe strode forward to try his hand. "Sir, I am the Sheriff of this county! That man is a spy, a thief, and a murderer, and I command you to stop and hold him!"

Brown, grinning, said, "I don't take my orders from you, sir. I take orders from the Master of the *Harriet*—and he has been well paid to ignore the small indiscretions of this gentleman." The officer openly laughed at the Colonel, who turned an unpleasant shade of purple. "If he wants a woman on his voyage, what is it to me as long as he pays enough to feed her! At that, she looks as though she eats like a bird."

"A bloody pox on you and on your bloody Master!" Colonel Hooe strode forward onto the wharf but stopped when Williamson waved his knife. "Mr. Brown! If that is your real name. You must know that if you leave with that man you cannot return here again. Damn you, this is my own wharf! You are trespassing, sir. I am arresting you!"

"A fish is caught only when you get the gaff into him, Mr. Bloody Sheriff," chortled Brown. He turned to Williamson, who had backed up the wharf until he was near the officer. "Well sir, from the look of you, I suspect you'd like to get under weigh to Quebec. And I would prefer not to surrender to this wharf-owning yokel, sir."

"I am perfectly ready, sir," said Williamson. "Is the ship as ready?"

"Yes indeed, sir, fully loaded and provisioned and shipshape for sailing, and the wind and tide are right."

Williamson had been waiting for the tide! Now it was clear why he delayed himself by answering the General's questions. Mr. Brown made to loose the longboat dock line.

Suddenly a man rushed by me. Hutch, no longer able to contain himself, rushed the two men on the wharf. He shouted, "That woman's my fee, damn you all!" Mr. Brown was better ready for action than he appeared, as he quickly drew a pistol from his belt and fired. The shot hit Hutch in the leg, and he went down, tumbling into a heap on the wharf.

Williamson had reached the ladder down to the longboat. He handed over the stumbling, shackled slave to a seaman in the boat by the simple means of tossing her down. He then clambered down himself, followed quickly by Mr. Brown, sure-footed as a monkey, who had loosed the dock line. I raised my pistol, but the General flung out his hand and pressed my arm down.

"Down your weapon, Colonel! We will pursue him by other means."

The longboat crew were pulling for their lives out into the river, aiming for a likely looking brig standing offshore flying British colors. The *Harriet,* presumably. Mr. Brown stood in the bow as cockswain, calling them on. A huge chorus of catcalls arose from the seamen leaning over the rails of their ships.

"Mr. Williamson!" called the General in his commanding tones. "We will see justice! The British government will be held to account, sir!" A huge cheer went up from the ships.

Williamson turned his head toward us, a grin on his face. "I really have half a mind to set her free, dress her, and parade her through the streets of London as a trophy, Mr. Washington! Ha! Call her the General's mistress! That will get cheers. But fear not, she will be well and safe once we get to Quebec and out of this damned country of yours! I will give Lord Dorchester your regards, and I will advise him of your complaint. It will amuse him." He gave a rude salute to the sailors in the surrounding ships, who again screamed catcalls at the longboat.

Alice, lying curled up in her shackles in the bow of the boat, did not move. I half-raised my pistol again from sheer frustration, willing to take my chances, but the boat had already moved out of range.

The man's triumphant gloating was maddening. "Sir! Can we not get a boat and pursue them?"

"Let them go, Colonel, let them go." The General shook his head, looking out to the river. "We may not have formal justice, but at least we know enough now to declare the crime solved. It is enough. Perhaps it is all for the best."

I could not understand his resignation to the injustice of letting a murderer escape. I was about to remonstrate with him when I felt someone run past, and I watched as Lizzie Casey ran to the side of the wounded Hutch. I abandoned my attempt to censure the General and ran over to them and stood beside her as she kneeled in his blood and bound up his wound with her shawl.

"Bloody stupid thing to do, you dying donkey!" While thus excoriating her friend, she took his hand and rubbed it. Hutch groaned and smiled at her.

"Never you mind, Lizzie. I've had worse. Damned fee just sailed off though."

"You're a brave man, Hutch, and a complete, fucking idiot for doing what you do!" Lizzie was loud enough to be heard over the crowd. "Sure and you need a new profession. You don't seem to have the knack for this one." She looked up at me. "Tell the man he's an idiot, Colonel."

"Anything to oblige a lady. You're a bloody idiot, man. Stop chasing slaves and catch a woman."

"Bloody hell." Hutch closed his eyes, and Lizzy continued to rub his hand.

I felt a hand on my arm and looked around. Dr. Craik had appeared beside me.

"Excuse me, Colonel. If you could just step aside?" I did so. Between Miss Casey and the good Doctor, Hutch was well aided, so I found the General and Colonel Hooe standing at the end of the wharf. I uncocked the useless pistol I still held in my hand, put it in my belt, and walked over to them.

The General was morose, and Colonel Hooe was apoplectic. They stared out at the longboat, which had reached the *Harriet*. The ship was already setting sails and getting under weigh with the tide.

"Is Mr. Hutchison all right? I sent Dr. Craik over to him." The General kept his gaze on the river.

"Yes, sir, he is in good hands. Your Excellency, I am very sorry for letting the man get the better of me," I said. "I should have been more watchful."

"I think there is enough blame there to go around, Colonel Humphreys," replied the General in a quiet voice. "The man took me in completely with his attempt to negotiate his surrender to us. Our concern for Alice addled our wits, I believe. We will have to see what may be done." He smiled. "What *shall* I tell Mr. Cockburn? Yet another body. He will not be pleased."

53

THURSDAY, APRIL 2, 1789, AFTERNOON

The whole family appeared at dinner on Thursday: Mrs. Washington, Major Washington and his wife, and Mr. Lear and myself, along with a guest who had come during the day, a Captain Winterbottom, a New Haven acquaintance of mine who served with me in the War. The General received him graciously, asking about events and feelings in New England.

We ate our roast pork and poached fish with pleasure, and Captain Winterbottom entertained us with stories of his adventures in the Northwest backwoods among the settlers and Indians. During dinner, with the ladies present, Winterbottom showed his good breeding by talking about relatively peaceful and harmonious exploits. Mrs. Fanny Washington was enthralled and kept the Captain's attention with her questions about the settlers and Indians. I looked forward to catching up with his more sanguinary exploits after the ladies withdrew.

As we ate our ice cream, I thought of the bodies that had occupied the ice house recently and had rather less than usual. After the ladies withdrew and Frank Lee laid out the port and madeira, I briefly summarized the events in Alexandria for Captain Winterbottom, Mr. Lear, and Major Washington, who were all agog at our adventures. From the look he gave me, it was clear that Winterbottom thought my letters to him had left some things out about my quiet life as a guest at Mount Vernon. Major Washington, who was still recovering from his latest bout of fever, said little and just sipped a small glass of madeira.

He looked very much as though he would rather talk about farming than murder.

After I had exhausted the General's patience by retailing his recent travails in Alexandria, Winterbottom undertook to tell some heroic stories about our shared adventures under General Putnam in New York, including artillery barrages, charges with fixed bayonets, and the defense of hastily erected forts. The General sipped his madeira and listened calmly.

After a time, the General stirred and sighed, then said, "Gentlemen, these stories and reminisces only punctuate the demands of the present moment. I find that, with our recent experience of British interference and political chaos in Alexandria, I must proceed with my resolution."

"Is this a secret code, or may a guest join in the story?" asked Captain Winterbottom.

"I am sorry, sir," said the General. "Our little affairs here occupy us to such an extent that we often lose sight of the larger world." His tone was dry, his humor as subtle as usual.

I laughed heartily at this, and the General smiled.

I said, "Captain, His Excellency the General here has struggled for at least the past year with the decision to abandon all this poverty and retirement." I waved a hand at the elegant dining room. "He has professed such a reluctance to undertake his public duty that all his friends despaired of the country. He nearly determined to refuse the Presidency."

Captain Winterbottom looked astonished. "But was there ever any doubt of his accepting it, Colonel?"

I replied, "Aye, there was, but no longer; the General has made his decision."

The General confirmed my explanation. "Events make the decision for me. British intrigue in Kentucky and the Mississipi, treaty violations in the north, spying and sowing chaos here in Alexandria: I must accept the Presidency as all my friends require of me."

Captain Winterbottom cried, "I am overjoyed to hear it, Your Excellency! A toast to it!" He stood, the rest of us joined him, and we raised our glasses to the General. He smiled and acknowledged the compliment, then drank off his glass of madeira.

"And now," said the General, "I must join the ladies and confirm this sad decision with my wife, who will unwillingly undertake the even more onerous duties of being the foremost lady in the land. She has not been looking forward to this moment. Gentlemen—please remain and enjoy yourselves." He stood, and bowing to all of us, went out the door toward the family parlor to do his family duty.

Frank poured out more port for us all, and we drank to the General's health, then to his Presidency, then to the country. I remain uncertain as to how many other toasts we drank that evening. At some point Major Washington disappeared and Mr. Lear went for a refreshing evening walk around the farm to clear his head. The General came back and excused himself to his study. I sent Winterbottom off to his bed, then joined the General.

He eyed my overly cheerful expression and said, "Sit down, Colonel, before you fall down. Everything in moderation."

I said carefully, "Yes sir; but there is a time for immoderation, Your Excellency, and if there is such a time, this is it."

"Indeed. Are you fit for a little talk? Or should you be in bed?"

"Talk, sir. Has your good lady accepted your decision?"

"She has, Colonel, though with all the appearance of a condemned prisoner." The General smiled. "I have no doubt she will enjoy the social round in New York and Philadelphia once she is used to the idea."

I was just inebriated enough to broach an unwelcome subject. "And what of your people, Your Excellency? Do you still feel that as President you cannot free them?"

The General shook his head. "I fear not, Colonel. I explained the situation to Mrs. Washington in our latest conversation. She still does not see the force of my—and your—objections to the institution, but she accepts that I must consider what to do with the 120 slaves that I may dispose of. As she has 150 dower slaves and as we lease another 40, she does not think she will suffer any privation from whatever choice I must make. I will continue to consider the issue; perhaps we can come up with some solution that does not impact either the fraught politics of the Republic or the fraught condition of my pocketbook. Failing that, I will free them all in my will." The General eyed me narrowly. "I think that is enough of that topic, sir."

I had a mind to ask whether my friend intended to pursue the unfortunate Alice, who might or might not make her way to Quebec with Mr. Williamson. I could not do it. I felt I had inflicted enough pain upon the General already, and he was clearly finished with the subject. So I moved on.

I asked, turning my mind to the future, "And what is next for us, sir?"

"The Coroner's jury tomorrow that we will attend will clear the way for our final preparations for New York. Even Mrs. Washington is reconciled and as ready as she can be to abandon our retired life here."

I smiled. "I am looking forward to being part of your future in government for a time, sir; and then, perhaps, a diplomatic position? I did enjoy my time in Europe with Mr. Jefferson. But *your* needs must take precedence."

"Very well, Colonel. I look forward to our collaboration; and I thank you very much for your efforts over the last month—and the last few years, sir. Now—take yourself off to a well-earned rest."

I ambled off to my bed, as happy a man as there was on earth, and slept as the dead.

54

FRIDAY, APRIL 3, 1789, AFTERNOON

Mr. Martin Cockburn drummed his fingers on Colonel Hooe's excellent maple-wood desk. His face, ordinarily dyspeptic, had hardened into something very like a prune. The General and I had come to Alexandria to attend the Coroner's inquest into the murders of the General's two slaves, Caesar and Gabriel.

Mr. Cockburn said, "Very well, Your Excellency. Allow me to summarize the situation as I understand it. Three men murdered by Mr. Williamson's own hand; two more men murdered and one attempted murder by conspiracy with another man, or men; a deadly attack on you and Colonel Humphreys as part of that arrangement; a widespread conspiracy within Fairfax County and perhaps beyond to steal and sell plantation goods and supplies, aided and abetted by many of the merchants of Alexandria and perhaps Fredericksburg. Oh —and a widespread conspiracy by a British secret agent or agents to destabilize the trade economy of the United States. Have I got all that straight, sir?"

The General cleared his throat. "Erm...let us not forget poor Mr. Hutchison, wounded trying to prevent the stealing of my slave Alice, Mr. Cockburn. Or, indeed, that theft itself."

"Oh, no." Mr. Cockburn grimaced. "I would never forget Mr. Hutchison. How could I forget Mr. Hutchison? I fear he was lost in the pandemonium. And of course let us not forget the stealing of your slave, a common crime these days, but in this case committed in a quite unusual manner. Well. But in spite of all this criminal activity centered in the person of one man, the collected weight of authority present in Alexandria—excepting myself, sir, as I was quietly reading in this room at the time—I say, in spite of you all, he got away. On a British ship. To Canada."

The General, with his most bland demeanor, said, "Quebec, sir. Yes, I think that sums it up well, Mr. Cockburn."

The magistrate sat back in his chair, stared at the General in silence for a full minute, then said, "Your pardon, sir. I am simply having trouble absorbing the full implications of all this mayhem and conspiracy. And considering what to do about it."

My mind went to Shakespeare. "How all occasions do inform against me, And spur my dull revenge!" Hamlet, in this case, had it right. How difficult it is to define a clean border between the countries of Justice and Vengeance.

We walked over to the Courthouse. Its large chamber rapidly filled with townspeople anxious to hear all about the case. Rumors had already circulated that there was more than just the deaths of two slaves at stake, and the prominent citizens of Alexandria sensed that there was serious entertainment to be had.

The Coroner took a dim view of all this hubbub, threatening several times to clear the room if anyone made the slightest noise. Once the crowd had settled into an expectant silence, Mr. Cockburn rose to address the Coroner and his jury. He repeated his excellent summary of the outlines of the case. The Coroner, who had informed himself of the details the day before in close consultation with the General, was not impressed, but the crowd went wild with enthusiasm, requiring more threats by the Coroner to calm themselves. Justice was proving a rather loud business, in my opinion.

In response to Mr. Cockburn's testimony, the Coroner declared the reopening of the adjourned inquests into the deaths of Julius and

George Thompson, all to be considered together. On Mr. Cockburn's prompting, he added the death of the seaman Johnson to the list.

Mr. Steptoe had recovered enough from the wound I had inflicted upon him to walk under his own power, though in a limited way due to his shackles. His companion, whose name turned out to be Jack Baker, was nursing a broken nose and a blackened eye, presumably from the effort to restrain him at Springfield Farm after his abortive attempt to kill the slave Cujo. He proved disgruntled enough to require some manhandling by Colonel Hooe's men to get him into the courtroom.

Colonel Hooe testified first to the activities of Mr. Williamson and his own activities as Sheriff, his inspection of the body of Julius and that of Mr. Thompson. He testified to Williamson's confession of the murders, including the murder of the seaman Johnson. Finally, he summarized the information he had received from the man wounded in the ambush upon the General and myself, Dick Steptoe.

The General and I then testified to our own actions in our investigations. We corroborated Colonel Hooe's testimony about Mr. Williamson's confession.

Mr. Steptoe testified to his part in the conspiracy, relating the tasks Mr. Williamson had given and his own actions and those of Mr. Baker in the ambush. On attempting to get Jack Baker to testify, however, the Coroner got nothing but abuse, and he did not take it kindly. Mr. Baker, who had a very colorful vocabulary, proved too entertaining for the Coroner's taste; he had Mr. Baker restrained and gagged for the remainder of the inquest, to the disappointment of the crowd.

The Coroner then took the testimony of the two Mount Vernon overseers, one a witness to the murder of Caesar by Mr. Baker, the other to the finding of the body of Gabriel. Although the latter could not directly identify Mr. Baker as the murderer, Mr. Steptoe had already described the tasks given to the pair by Mr. Williamson as including the killing of Caesar and Gabriel, which was enough for the

Coroner.

The Coroner then added that, as the events surrounding Mr. Thompson's death did not involve slaves, no slave could testify about it, and therefore he had not called Ben, Jack, Davy, or Nace to the court. As Mr. Williamson had directly confessed to the crime before Colonel Hooe, the General, and myself, he felt nothing more was needed for the jury to render their verdicts on the deaths.

The Coroner's jury deliberated for a few minutes, no more, and returned verdicts in the five deaths: willful murder of Julius by Mr. Williamson; willful murder of Mr. Thompson by Mr. Williamson; willful murder of Mr. Johnson by Mr. Williamson; and willful murder of Caesar and Gabriel by Mr. Baker in conspiracy with Mr. Williamson. The jury found that the murders were part of a conspiracy to murder involving Williamson, Steptoe, and Baker. The jury noted the arrest of Steptoe and Baker and ordered them held for indictment by the grand jury and trial at the next district court meeting in late April, but then noted that John Williamson had escaped justice to a foreign country, namely Canada, and required his pursuit and arrest. The Coroner declared the inquest closed, and the courtroom gradually cleared.

The General approached the Coroner and said, "Sir, given the jury's finding about Mr. Williamson's pursuit, and given the international character of that pursuit, I find myself in a position to assist."

The Coroner smiled. "I will transmit the findings to the Governor, of course; but Your Excellency could expedite matters greatly at the Federal level."

"I am not yet President, but I will be soon. Please send a copy of the inquest verdict to me, and I will pursue it with the British government to the best of my ability. At the moment, I believe that entails approaching the Consul General of the United Kingdom, currently residing in New York; he is our only diplomatic contact with Britain. We have no appointed Minister from Britain yet and no treaty covering extradition of criminals. We will see what we can do."

"That will be satisfactory, Your Excellency, thank you." The Coroner nodded gravely. The Coroner and the General bowed to each other, and the General and I walked back to Colonel Hooe's house with Colonel Hooe and Mr. Cockburn.

Mr. Cockburn said as we walked, "Your Excellency, I am gathering together the threads of the case not directly involving the murders and will submit those cases as required to the examining court. The grand larceny and negro-stealing charges against Mr. Williamson must await his capture, as must the conspiracy charges against the man Brown and the master of the *Harriet;* but the larceny charges against your slaves and my own slave Cujo will be quickly dealt with, I think, by the district court here in Alexandria. Given the nature of the grand larceny, they will be condemned to death with benefit of clergy. Do they read? My Cujo does not." The "benefit of clergy" was an old common-law tradition that allowed offenders to have their death sentence commuted by reading a text from the Bible, as a kind of privilege given to priests and other clergy in olden times that now provided a way to avoid a death sentence—if you could read.

The General clasped his hands behind his back as we walked. He said, "Given that these men were swept up in the conspiracy by the very persuasive Mr. Williamson, I am confident that my appeal to the Governor will result in pardons. Will you join me in that request?"

Mr. Cockburn nodded and replied, "Yes, although I am very disappointed in Cujo. But a first offense, and one deriving from such a source—yes, I think I can join your appeal, Your Excellency. But they must still suffer corporal punishment, I think—will 10 lashes be sufficient?"

"I suppose so, sir."

"I will so inform the court, Your Excellency. Colonel Mason has decided not to pursue any charges against anyone on his plantation. I fear that Mr. Steptoe and Mr. Baker will not be so lucky; they will of course be condemned without benefit of clergy or pardon."

The General replied, "I am sorry for Mr. Steptoe, who seems to have regretted his actions; but justice must be done."

Mr. Cockburn went on. "As far as the British conspiracy is concerned, I suppose treason charges might be brought as well against Mr. Williamson, but the broader conspiracy is really not in my jurisdiction."

"I agree, sir; I will engage to deal with the broader conspiracy once I am President. Leave that to me." The General paused, then continued with a frown. "One thing, Mr. Cockburn, in regard to justice. I have mentioned several times the willful participation of many merchants in Alexandria in this scheme of grand larceny as receivers of the stolen goods. They profess to be ignorant of the source of the goods, but really, I cannot imagine they are that credulous. I do not wish to upset any apple carts or tobacco casks, but I do think, as a plantation owner, something must be done about it."

"Ah, yes," said Mr. Cockburn. He thought for a moment. "I have such an interest as well, as a farmer. As this conspiracy seems to have been quite widespread, and because it involves several of the merchants here in Alexandria, I think Colonel Hooe should take charge of conducting a full investigation of the involvement in the larceny and the receiving of stolen goods." He looked at Colonel Hooe, who nodded his acquiescence to the request but looked as though his teeth were hurting him. I considered his position as a leading merchant of Alexandria and had little sympathy for him.

Colonel Hooe said, "I would hope that a severe warning will be enough to put a stop to the practice. We will see."

A very dull revenge, indeed.

55

Colonel Thomson arrived two weeks later on a sunny Spring day in the middle of April. Dr. Craik and Colonel Hooe had come from Alexandria for a social visit with the General. About noon, we heard a clatter approaching the house. Going out to the sweep, we saw a mud-splattered coach with a weary-looking driver reigning in some very tired horses.

A lean, lugubrious man with a firm chin and mouth, a large nose, and sharp piercing eyes under his old-fashioned white wig stepped down from the coach. He stretched himself and appeared very happy to find his feet on solid ground once more, his face showing him to be as tired as the coachman.

The General stepped up to him and bowed. "Colonel Thomson, it is good to see you again." Turning to us, he added, "Gentlemen, may I present to you Colonel Charles Thomson of Philadelphia, the Secretary of the Continental Congress."

Turning back to our new visitor, he continued, "I am aware of your mission, Colonel, as General Knox has communicated the decision to give you the task of informing me of the results of the election."

"A very pleasing mission indeed, Your Excellency." Colonel Thomson bowed in his turn.

The General directed us to the door into the New Room and exercised his role as host. "Do you wish to refresh yourself, Mr. Thomson, before we proceed?"

Mr. Thomson replied, "If you please, sir, and if you do not mind, I would prefer to get the business done. It is of foremost importance to the country and would remove a great weight from my soul. My trip was foul, my humor is foul, and only my mission is fair."

"Very well; please proceed."

The New Room, with its elegant appointments, was a very suitable and formal place for this business. Colonel Thomson noticed nothing in his desire to finish his business. He moved to the center of the room and turned, taking out a paper from his pocket-book. The General moved to face him, taking out a similar piece of paper that we had prepared over the course of several mornings. I stood behind him, as I had in Annapolis when he resigned his commission, and Mr. Lear and the two gentlemen from Alexandria stood behind us. The others in the household, aware of the momentous event, gathered in a little cluster near the door, and I could see Frank and Will and the other servants gathered there as well. A little stir there drew our attention, and Mrs. Washington pushed her way through.

"You surely were not going to begin without my presence, Mr. Washington!"

"Very sorry, my dear; thoughtless indeed. Colonel Thomson, my wife, Mrs. Washington."

"How-do-you-do, Colonel Thomson." Mrs. Washington offered her hand, and Colonel Thomson bowed and kissed it.

"Very well, madam. It is a great honor to be in your house, and I am charmed by your welcome."

Mrs. Washington smiled. "All right, you may begin, gentlemen." Mrs. Washington tossed her head, then smiled that brilliant smile that made everything well. Colonel Thomson cleared his throat a little nervously and obeyed her. His short statement of fact was direct and to the point.

There it was: the long-awaited certification from Congress. The country had finally delivered up their opinion, and the General must accede to his public duty. The General put on his spectacles and read from the sheet of paper he held.

"I have been long accustomed to entertain so great a respect for the opinion of my fellow citizens that the knowledge of their unanimous suffrages having been given in my favor scarcely leaves me the alternative for an option. Whatever may have been my private feelings and sentiments, I believe I cannot give a greater evidence of my sensibility for the honor they have done me than by accepting the appointment."

A small round of applause greeted this final acceptance of his duty to the country, and we all wore happy smiles. The General removed his spectacles and finished the speech, acknowledging the urgency of the situation and his intention to leave within two days to join the new Congress in moving forward the business of the new Nation. He thanked Colonel Thomson warmly for his service to the country. He then put his paper away and carefully folded up his spectacles. Mrs. Washington stepped forward and took the General's hand and pressed it.

The General smiled. "Good, now that is done. Colonel Thomson: would you prefer tea or madeira?"

"Madeira, Your Excellency, if you please; and a chair."

The General smiled and signaled for a chair. Frank hurried into the room and moved up chairs for us all from their places along the wall. Colonel Thomson thankfully sank into his chair with a broad smile.

I think we were all aware of the movement of history. I shall always remember the expression on the General's face, however: a sadness, sitting in his comfortable and elegant room as though it were the last time. Comfort was not for kings or presidents; power was not a soft feather bed or an exhilarating ride through the countryside. All that was done.

The President-elect smiled, and the first lady of the land asked Mr. Thomson about his journey. Frank Lee brought the madeira.

56

WEDNESDAY, APRIL 15, TO THURSDAY, APRIL 16, 1789

Wednesday dawned grey and gloomy, with a sharp downturn in the temperature. A cold wind picked up shortly after breakfast. After trying to read on the piazza, I decided to take a constitutional walk down to the Landing to get my blood circulating. I wanted to take a last look at the river and the Maryland shore from the wharf before I left for New York.

As I came down the path to the Landing, I saw I was not alone: Major Washington was standing on the wharf looking out at the river, both hands supporting himself on his beautiful walking stick. I hailed him, and he looked around and nodded, then turned back to the river.

"Good morning, Major."

"Colonel. Not a very nice one." He looked away, out to the river. The Major seemed disinclined for conversation, but he shortly turned to me with a look of resolution.

"Colonel Humphreys, I must tell someone. You are a great friend to my uncle. I really must tell someone."

Was I about to hear a disaster with the farm? Another slave absconded? No—the Major had something else on his mind. I examined him closely; he was not feverish this time, but coldly resolute.

He continued, "Mr. Williamson—he was—he lied, Colonel."

Surprised, I replied, "Lied about what, Major?"

In a rush, it came out: "My uncle has told me what he confessed that day in Alexandria, Colonel, and that the inquest has decided he murdered Julius. But he did not. He was not here that day."

Suddenly the day was colder than it had been. "How do you know this?"

"Because I was here. I killed Julius. With my old stick, it had a weighted head. I threw the bloody thing into the river and had this new one made."

Stunned, I could say nothing. I looked at his face, which had gone pale.

"That Friday, I came down here to check on whether the men had disposed of some barrels delivered the day before. I found Julius on the wharf and taxed him with being away from his farm without leave. He laughed at me, sir. He said he had come to find things to sell, by which I understood him to mean steal. Then he laughed at my uncle, most disrespectfully, saying he was to be free and he did not care anything about us, the British would free him and give him untold riches. I thought he was mad, sir; I told him to be quiet and get back to his farm unless he wished to be whipped. He laughed again and turned his back to me. He was in the water, sinking, and my stick was bloody before I knew it. I have never known such rage, Colonel. I find I can hardly bear the thought of it all now. I threw the stick into the river and fled."

If I had been stunned before, I was now bereft of speech entirely. Once my poor brain had stilled and my thoughts focused, I realized that the Major could claim the privilege of an overseer dealing with a disobedient slave. There was no legal worry for the Major here, solely a moral one.

"Major...why did you not speak up? You must know you cannot be charged with murder."

"I lacked the courage, Colonel, and I found I could not tell my uncle what had transpired. And by the time Mr. Fairfax found the body, I felt I could not reveal what had happened." He looked down. "You may remember how ill I was that day at dinner, Colonel. I felt guilty, sir; Julius threatened my control of the plantation as much as he was disrespectful toward my uncle, and I was not sure which feeling had contributed most to my actions. It has all become too much to bear alone."

I thought back to that day in Alexandria. Had Williamson actually confessed to Julius's murder?

I said, "I have just realized, Major, that Williamson did not confess to that murder. When the General asked him directly, he deflected the question with a dismissal of Julius's character, but he never actually admitted to killing him." I paused and thought. "Do you think he knew that you were responsible for the death of Julius?"

"He knew. Do you remember when I went to Alexandria, despite being ill?"

"Yes, sir."

"It was in response to a note from the man. He revealed he knew I had killed Julius; one of the slaves he questioned told him. He thought he could control me and use me to further his despicable ends. I suppose he did not reveal that to my uncle to preserve his investment in me, to keep me in place as a spy in my uncle's house."

"I see." I pondered. "And what do you intend to do, sir?"

"To die, Colonel. Soon, without doubt; my illness is far advanced. And to serve my uncle loyally and well up until that melancholy event." He stared again at the river. "I would ask that you maintain a silence about it. I do not wish my wife to know, nor my uncle and aunt."

I found myself in sympathy with his desire, if not his action. He certainly felt the regret, it was obvious in his voice and his manner; and his mortal illness was obvious in his face and carriage. I thought about the General and his feelings about Major Washington, and Major Washington's wife. I thought about the burdens the General must now bear as the leader of our new Republic. How could I burden him with this tragedy as well? Even should Williamson be caught and tried, his guilt would hang him for his other crimes. But the killing had to stop.

The silence between us grew into minutes. Finally, I said, "All right, Major. I will keep your secret, even after your death, unless some rare justice requires me to reveal it. But there must be no more violence toward the people of Mount Vernon while you atone, sir. None at all. Do I make myself clear?"

The Major, with a sad look, said, "Yes, Colonel; and it is no more than what I intend. Thank you from my heart." He shook my hand, then slowly walked off using his slave-made stick.

"Full soon the gloom was spread—" My own poetry perfectly expressed the oppression that overtook me as I watched him walk slowly up the hill to the Mansion House.

Mr. Lear and Will Lee left later that day on horseback for New York, where they were to prepare lodgings for the General. The General had allowed Will to come despite the injuries to both of his knees that had him nearly incapable of service as valet. Will's pleas to come, combined with the General's professed inability to do without Will, resulted in Will's going with Mr. Lear. The General included the young Christopher Sheels in our party to replace Will should he prove unable to serve in the rarified atmosphere of the Presidency.

The General spent most of his time either riding out on the plantation or closeted with Major Washington and Mr. Fairfax; he divided his time equally between business with those gentlemen and his more personal duty with Mrs. Washington. The General's efforts with Mr. Lear over the past month had prepared him for leaving for New York by settling his debts and other affairs. Mrs Washington was to join us in New York with her servants once the General had established a home for her there.

Mr. Lear had spent a great deal of time on Tuesday night with Mrs.

Fanny Washington. Mrs. Martha Washington was present throughout; I suspected she was intent on keeping her niece clear of any entanglements, though I may have got that wrong. I hoped that neither Mrs. Washington would ever know about Major Washington's violent act. I took my own farewell with Mrs. Fanny Washington on Thursday evening, after dinner.

Later that evening, I joined the General in his study, and he picked up a package wrapped in paper. Turning to me, he asked, "Now, Colonel, one last favor to ask of you. Are you willing to do me a small service that may extend to the rest of your life?"

"Of course, sir."

"Then take these." He handed the package to me. "These are my diaries for the last month. I have journaled most of the events surrounding Julius and the British in them for posterity; but I wish that posterity to be far removed from the present day. I do not wish to destroy them, but I cannot let them see the light of day while I live and for a good time thereafter, the events and decisions are too sensitive. Will you take these and keep them, and pass them down in your family as closely guarded secrets?"

"I will be happy to undertake this task, sir, as historian, friend, and servant." And that is what I have done these many years. I will keep this present account secret with the diaries and will pass all of it to my heirs with strict instructions to keep them close and safe for 100 years. And I have kept Major Washington's secret as well, and I will keep it to my death.

Finally, all the goodbyes said, the luggage loaded, and our servants mounted, the three of us climbed up into the coach. I sat next to the General, and Mr. Thomson sat opposite us. The coachman shook up the horses. We waved to the little group standing in the sweep and rumbled away up the drive toward Alexandria to start our new lives.

We were met in Alexandria by the leading men of the town—word had spread ahead of us, probably by Mr. Lear the day before. Whatever reservations the merchants and citizens of Alexandria may have had, they were not in evidence that day. They dragged us all to Wise's Tavern and feted us with dinner and 13 separate toasts!

The journey to New York was in turn agonizing, exhilarating, and informing, but that is another story, one that must be told another time. We arrived; and that story is known to all.

Macbeth said, "Let every man be master of his time." I wish that were true; but time, and history, are the master of all.

Epilog

The General's reputation saw him through most of his first term as President but became a little tattered in his second term, as factions and parties coalesced around Mr. Jefferson and Colonel Hamilton and their friends and foes. Most scholars rate the General one of America's best and most effective Presidents. The General handed over the reins to John Adams in 1796 and retired to Mount Vernon for good, though there was a war scare with France in 1798 that had him finding his old saber once again, but fortunately it came to nothing. On leaving the Presidency, the General's Farewell Address pleaded for America to stay out of the affairs of Europe and for politicians to avoid partisan politics, which he felt would break apart the Union. Looking back from our united nation of today, he was clearly wrong. Or perhaps not. The General died in his bed at Mount Vernon of a throat infection in December 1799. Dr. Craik attended him and bled him several times, to no avail. His widow buried him in the family tomb at Mount Vernon and followed him there two years later. His last words, to Tobias Lear, were "'Tis well."

The General's diaries from early 1789 have never been found.

Martha Washington continued to live at Mount Vernon until her own death in May, 1802. She never discussed family matters outside the family, and she burned the General's letters to her before she died, a great loss to historians.

Major George Augustine Washington, the General's nephew, died in February 1793, having left Mount Vernon in October 1792 because of his ill health. No hint of scandal ever blackened his name. After her husband's death and a suitable mourning period, Mrs. Fanny Washington married Tobias Lear in 1795; Lear had married his fiancée in 1790, but she died in the Philadelphia yellow fever epidemic in July, 1793. Mrs. Fanny Lear then died in 1796 of consumption.

David Humphreys continued as private secretary to the General until 1791, when the General appointed him Minister to Portugal and, later, Minister to Spain. He was able to work closely with Tobias Lear both as private secretary and as diplomat, calling him his friend. Colonel Humphreys's relations with the General remained warm and strong. After a reasonably distinguished career as a diplomat under the General and his successor, John Adams, his mentor Jefferson dismissed him from the service in 1801 as payback for supporting the federalists. He married an English woman he had met in Spain and returned to Boston and Derby, Connecticut, his home town, where he became the first American farmer to raise Merino sheep. He died at the age of 66 in 1818.

Tobias Lear was private secretary to the General until 1793. After marrying Martha Washington's niece Fanny in 1795, he was a frequent visitor to Mount Vernon. He went on to a diplomatic career under Jefferson and committed suicide in 1816 under somewhat mysterious circumstances.

John Fairfax managed Mount Vernon much to the General's satisfaction until December, 1790, when he left to marry and to set himself up as a farmer. He was very successful and became a member of the Virginia legislature in 1809.

Joseph Davenport served as miller until his death in January 1796. The General found him quite slothful as time went on; he never produced the amount of flour that the General expected. The General gave his widow $5 to allow her to travel back to her relatives.

Robert Hooe did take advantage of the increasing trade in Alexandria, but Georgetown grew faster as part of the District of Columbia's growth. Both John Fitzgerald and Robert Hooe are counted as the major figures of old Alexandria, and their houses still stand today in Alexandria's Old Town.

There is no evidence that the authorities took any action against the rapacity of the merchants of Alexandria. Alexandria did become part of the new District of Columbia in 1791. However, in 1840, at the request of the residents, who didn't appreciate not having a vote in the Congress and were startled by proposals to abolish slavery in the nation's capital, the Congress retroceded the territory to Virginia.

George Mason supported the new Federal government, especially after Madison shepherded the new Bill of Rights through the Congress. Mason's relationship with the General did not change, though they corresponded on political issues of interest to Mason. Mason died in October 1792.

Martin Cockburn disappeared from history.

William Hutchison gave up slave catching shortly after the events in this story. He married Lizzy Casey, and they moved west to Kentucky. After Jefferson completed the Louisiana purchase, they moved further west as frontier pioneers. It is thought that one of their sons died with Davy Crockett at the Alamo in 1836, but there is no documentary evidence of that.

The General quietly complained of the Williamson affair to Sir John Temple, the British Consul in New York, leaving no notes or diary entries to indicate that he had done so. Nothing more was heard of the affair, and Williamson disappeared from history—at least, under that name. The *Harriet* was sold off by the British navy, and nothing more was heard of its captain and crew.

Dick Steptoe and Jack Baker were convicted by the district court and hanged.

The General came up with several schemes to free his slaves but they all proved impractical. For example, he proposed to rent out the Mount Vernon farms to give his people a means to support themselves, but he had no takers who could actually afford to run the farms and pay the people. He eventually freed his slaves in his will, specifying it to occur after his wife's death, and willed that they have pensions and funds to support them at Mount Vernon for as long as necessary. Martha Washington freed the General's slaves almost immediately after his death rather than after her own. It seems that she was afraid they would do her harm, knowing they were to be freed upon her death. Many of the General's freed slaves stayed on the Mount Vernon plantation, the accounts of which showed $10,000 expended on their care through the year 1833. On Martha Washington's death, all her dower slaves passed to heirs in the Custis family, mainly to Wash (George Washington Parke Custis), who eventually founded a plantation called Arlington (now the Arlington National Cemetery).

Most of the Mount Vernon slaves disappeared from history after being freed, including Mary Ball Washington's slave George inherited by the General. Frank Lee, the General's butler, was freed with the General's other slaves; his wife Lucy was a dower slave and passed to the Custis heirs with their children and remained enslaved. Frank Lee lived in the vicinity of Mount Vernon until he died in 1821. Hercules, the Mount Vernon cook, ran away in 1797 and was last seen living well in New York. Ben the miller was a dower slave, as was Doll, the matriarch of the slaves of Mount Vernon; they passed to the Custis heirs at Martha Washington's death. Ben, Tom, and Davy, the Grist Mill slaves, along with Martin Cockburn's slave overseer Cujo, were tried and convicted of grand larceny and sentenced to death; the Governor, Beverly Randolph, pardoned them all at the request of the General and Mr. Cockburn. Alice appeared in Quebec, delivered a female child in December 1789, and became a free woman. She left for the Canadian West and disappeared from history with her child.

Will Lee returned to Mount Vernon after a year in New York, unable to serve as valet because of his injuries, and became a shoemaker. Christopher Sheels took his place as the General's new valet. Will was freed on his master's death in 1799 and continued to live at Mount Vernon with a pension until he died in either 1810 or 1828, reports vary. He was buried in an unmarked grave at Mount Vernon.

Nace and Chancey married and had children; all remained slaves on the Mason plantation, where Nace remained overseer at Occoquan and James remained butler. Neither Mason nor any of the other founding fathers freed their slaves; Hamilton was an abolitionist who did not own slaves; Adams did not own slaves but did not support abolition.

The importing of slaves to the United States was prohibited by the federal government in 1807, though there were many evasions of this law. Slavery itself and the internal slave trade persisted until the Emancipation Proclamation in 1863, followed by the 13th Amendment to the Constitution in 1865. The compromises in the original Constitution, which the General supported, led directly to the Civil War, to the near breakup of the Union, and to more than two hundred years of human suffering. Social, political, economic, and psychological issues related to slavery in America persist to the present day.

The General's farms continued to be troubled by trade, larceny, and management issues over time. A series of poor managers had the General constantly writing to Mount Vernon from his Presidential desk and generally tearing his hair out whenever he returned to Mount Vernon for a visit. The General realized during his Presidency that Mount Vernon would never return a profit; but he took the moral high ground with his managers and insisted on efficiency, to little avail.

The General did confront another rebellion during his Presidency: the 1794 Whiskey Rebellion, which was another tax revolt. The rebels backed down when the General and Colonel Hamilton took an army to Western Pennsylvania. This success produced such a great demonstration of Federal power in the West that it encouraged the British to resolve their issues with America through the Jay Treaty. The French Revolution of 1789 and subsequent coup by Napoleon in 1799 also made America largely irrelevant to Britain.

Lord Dorchester never acknowledged any espionage activity in America. The Jay Treaty settled various issues with Britain in 1795, reducing the impact of British activities in America, but was very unpopular with the Jeffersonians due to the closer ties with Britain the treaty enabled. Nothing ever came to light to indicate that there were more British conspiracies in the new country. Secretary of War Knox took no actions related to Britain. The British continued to treat America as an enemy and eventually burned down the Presidential Mansion (now called the White House) during the presidency of James Madison in 1812. Relations have improved a little since.

British and Spanish efforts to get Kentucky to secede failed, and Kentucky became the 15th state of the Union in 1792.

Author's note: I have taken historical liberties with only two characters: David Humphreys, who was perhaps not quite as much of an abolitionist as I make him out to be, and George Augustine Washington, of whom I know no harm—but he was such a good fit for the murderer that I could do nothing else. Colonel Humphreys was always a model of propriety and never expressed any special regard for Major Washington's wife, nor any issues with Tobias Lear. The Kentucky conspiracy was as I report it; but as far as I know, the British did not create a larger secret conspiracy of any kind; their strategy was complete intransigence on trade and treaties. Britain did not establish an effective intelligence service until later in the 1790s, and even then focused mainly on enemies in France and Ireland. I suspect the same may be true today.

Acknowledgments

Founders Online (accessed 2018 at https://founders.archives.gov/content/volumes#Washington) and the George Washington Papers project (accessed 2018 at https://www.mountvernon.org/library/research-library/washington-papers/) provided all the details from Washington's actual writings. Many thanks to the Mount Vernon Ladies' Association, the University of Virginia, and the National Archives for making these papers available to all online. Founders Online in particular provides many invaluable annotations to the writings. If you want to learn about the Founders in their own words, these sites are the place to start.

The Prolog story about Billy Lee at Monmouth is almost certainly apocryphal; it comes from the recollections of George Washington Parke Custis, Washington's grandson, many years later. I have taken the liberty of fitting it into the battle of Monmouth to illustrate the war-based transition in Washington's thinking about slaves. The excellent history of that battle, *Fatal Sunday*, by Mark Edward Lender and Garry Wheeler Stone, provides full details.

The books *George Washington and Slavery: A Documentary Portrayal*, by Fritz Hirschfeld, and *Never Caught: The Washingtons' Relentless Pursuit of Their Runaway Slave, Ona Judge*, by Erica Armstrong Dunbar, provide excellent insight into Washington's slaves and his attitudes toward slavery, as does the excellent article by Dorothy Twohig, "'That Species of Property': Washington's Role in the Controversy over Slavery," in the collection *George Washington Reconsidered* edited by Don Higgenbotham. The book *Slavery at the Home of George Washington*, edited by Philip J. Schwarz, contains a wealth of detail about the Mount Vernon slaves. Many thanks to interpreter Kathleen Ford at Mount Vernon for additional insights into slavery on the plantation.

Many thanks also to the interpreters at Mount Vernon, whose tours bring you down to earth at the wonderfully maintained Mansion House and grounds, all meticulously restored and maintained by the Mount Vernon Ladies Association. You can find their web site at https://www.mountvernon.org (accessed 2018). Special thanks in particular to John Zimmerman, Carole Tranovich, and Kathleen Ford for their tours in March 2018. The Mount Vernon Reynolds Museum and its special exhibit on slavery was very helpful. Much appreciation as well to Samantha Snyder, Access Services Librarian, and Angelica, at the Fred W. Smith National Library at Mount Vernon for their help in researching details of Washington's life.

I would like to thank the members of my writer's group at the Mechanics' Institute in San Francisco, who provided vital perspective on the writing.

Finally, but not least, I would like to thank my wife, Mary Swanson, for her support during this long project, and for her patience in enduring hours of wandering around Mount Vernon, Fort Belvoir, and the Grist Mill. A duty indeed!

Thanks for reading *Murder at Mount Vernon*. If you liked the book, please leave a review on Amazon.com or any other web site through which you bought it.

Sign up to our mailing list for notifications and get a free short story from Robert J. Muller's work in progress, The I Ching Stories!

http://www.poesys.com